A Deadly Truth

LM Milford

ISBN 978-1-913778-06-4

Cover art by Jessica Bell
Formatting by Polgarus Studio

For my Mam, the best that a girl could ask for
1947-2020
RIP

Acknowledgements

Creating a book isn't a one woman job. While I may have written the words, it's taken a team of people to help me get the book this far.

In order of appearance, thank you to Donna Hillyer for her excellent editing skills; to Helen Baggott for her proofreading support; and to Jessica Bell for a fantastic cover.

A credit to the lovely Mary Cusack for her eagle-eyed reading skills.

The usual thanks to all my fellow writers who have provided support over the years. Writing may happen behind closed doors, but you gotta come out some time! Special thanks go to Jane Isaac, Susi Holliday, Jeanette Hewitt and Ian Patrick.

To all those who read and enjoyed *A Deadly Rejection*, thank you and sorry it's taken so long for the second instalment. I hope it doesn't disappoint.

For Mam and Dad, who are the most enthusiastic marketers of my first novel and who kept me under scrutiny to make sure the second one actually arrived.

And last but not least, a huge thank you to my lovely new husband, Paul, for putting up with my craziness, my random questions regarding plots and making an excellent cup of tea. The next round of Friday beers are on me!

Prologue

George Peters' face was white as his fingers gripped the narrow windowsill in the viewing room, desperately trying not to utter a sound. He knew the people in the stark white room on the other side of the one-way glass couldn't possibly see him, but they would probably hear him if he made a noise. And no one must know he'd witnessed what was happening.

An Asian man was shackled to a dentist's chair in the middle of the room, one shirt sleeve rolled up to expose the smooth skin of his arm, which was fastened tightly to the armrest. He pressed his scrawny body back into the chair in a vain attempt to evade the questions of the three men who stood in a close semicircle around him. The prisoner's head twisted from side to side, eyes tightly shut as he tried to avoid looking at any of them. His body heaved against the shackles that bound him to the chair, but escape was impossible. Again and again they demanded information, which George was sure the man did not have. They never did. But this would be part of the test.

Suddenly the shouting stopped and the room seemed to ring for a moment. The prisoner's body relaxed and he looked around with a mixture of relief and fear. George held his breath too, but then one of the men turned to a small table on which there was a tray. It held a syringe and a small medicine bottle. George felt his chest contract. He knew exactly what that was and what would happen next. The prisoner screamed and fought harder against the tape that bound his arm to the chair, but he couldn't move. The syringe was filled, inserted and emptied into his arm. George stared in horror. It wasn't ready yet, they knew that. It wouldn't do what they wanted it to do.

The men stood back, arms folded, and waited. After a minute had elapsed, the questions began again. But rather than responding to them, the prisoner's eyes rolled back in his head. His body went rigid and he began to convulse. The men moved forward to release him from the chair but their movements weren't those of people dealing with an emergency. They knew there was nothing they could do now. George rubbed a hand across his eyes. The man's face was red and swollen and he was struggling for air. This was the reaction George knew would happen but it was shocking to witness it.

As he watched, a door opened and a grey-haired man entered the white room. He took in the scene in front of him and raised an eyebrow.

'It didn't work,' said one of the men unnecessarily.

'So I see.' The grey-haired man frowned. Then he looked up at the one-way glass, straight at George even though he couldn't possibly see him. But it was enough of a risk.

George turned and charged out into the corridor. The observation room door slammed shut behind him. His shoes squeaked on the floor as he ran and he heard a door open and close behind him. Running footsteps were already following him and he knew they were quicker. He yanked open the door to the stairwell and almost threw himself down the stairs. His pursuers were gaining on him. He ran across the lobby of the building, stabbed at the security lock and rushed out into the car park.

As he ran, he felt in his pocket for his car keys but the footsteps were gaining on him and an engine was starting up. If only he could get to his car, but he'd foolishly left it at the far end of the car park. On the opposite side of the road a man was jogging. He was staring at George. For a moment, George considered shouting to him but hands were already seizing him. A van screeched to a halt behind him. The side door slid open and he was thrown inside. The last thing he saw before the door slammed was the jogger stopping and tapping at the screen of his smartphone.

*

From the pavement across the road, Dan Sullivan stared at the van as it turned sharply out of the car park, leaving a good deal of its tyre rubber on the road surface. He'd seen any amount of abductions in films, but never one in real life. He quickly swiped the screen of his phone and dialled three nines.

Chapter one

Two days later, in the newsroom, Dan's routine call to the police press office was still frustrating him. He was standing in while the usual crime reporter Emma Fletcher, his girlfriend, was on holiday, and had spent a lot of time in recent days calling the emergency services to keep tabs on what stories they might have for him. This time the story was personal and, having been the person who reported the crime, he really wanted to know how far the police had got.

'What do you mean there's no evidence of an abduction? I'm telling you I saw it. I reported it,' he told Suzy, the police press officer. 'What more do you want?'

'Our officers looked around at the scene,' Suzy told him. 'You saw them yourself. There was no evidence of an abduction.'

'What about the tyre marks on the road?' Dan demanded.

'Dan, they could have happened any time.'

'What about CCTV? Allensbury Science Park is almost brand-new. They must have state-of-the-art cameras there. They'll tell you which building he came from as well.'

Suzy sighed. 'We're speaking to the management and requesting the CCTV from that night, but there's nothing else to say at present. And Dan, I'm telling you this off-the-record, because you were the person who reported it. None of this can go in the paper.'

'You're not even doing an appeal for information?'

'We need a bit more to go on before we do that,' Suzy said, sounding irritated. 'You couldn't give a good description of the vehicle, or the registration plate, or more than a vague idea of where it went. When we ask the public for help we're usually looking to fill in the gaps. Right now, we've got nothing to go on. We'll know more once we've got hold of CCTV, if there is any. Until then, it's strictly between you and me and no further.'

Dan took a breath and puffed out his cheeks. 'OK. Well, you call me the minute you hear anything.'

Suzy snorted. 'You're not Emma, you know. You don't get any special treatment. When's she back, by the way?'

Dan laughed. 'Not till next weekend. You mean my crime reporter skills aren't up to her standard?'

'No,' came the short reply, but he could hear the smile in Suzy's voice.

Dan said goodbye and hung up the phone. He'd barely put the receiver down when his mobile began to ring.

'Hi Em,' he said, pleased to hear his girlfriend's voice. She'd already been away for a week, and while he was loving taking over the crime beat in her absence, he was really missing her.

'Hi yourself. How's it going?' Dan brought her up to speed on the incident he'd witnessed. Emma was silent for a moment. 'Abducted?' she said. 'Are you sure?'

'He was running away across the car park and there were some men chasing him. A van pulled up behind him, he was dragged inside and then it drove away. What else would you call it?'

'Typical,' she said. 'I turn my back for five minutes and it all kicks off.'

'You believe me, then?' Dan felt relieved.

'Why wouldn't I?'

Dan sighed. 'The police don't.'

'Why not?' Emma asked.

'No evidence as yet.'

'No evidence? Nothing?' Emma sounded surprised.

Dan shook his head even though Emma couldn't see him. 'No other witnesses,' he said. 'They've requested CCTV footage, so hopefully there will be something on that.'

'Give them time. I'm sure they'll dig something up.'

Dan scowled. 'It's frustrating, y'know. I saw it happen with my own eyes but I couldn't give them anything useful. It all happened so fast. I'm a crap witness.'

'Don't beat yourself up,' Emma said. 'It's much harder than it looks to remember everything in the heat of the moment. I'm sure there'll be something on CCTV.'

Dan sighed. 'You're probably right. Anyway, how're things with you?'

'Yeah, good actually. No family fights as yet. It got a bit close over the Monopoly board last night, but the crisis was averted.'

Dan grinned. He'd been present when Emma's younger sister lost at Scrabble and flipped the board over onto the floor. At twenty-five, he thought, she should have learned to be a better loser. But he couldn't keep his mind from straying back to Allensbury Science Park. There were ten office blocks there but surely by eight o'clock in the evening, the buildings should be locked up. Why had the man been there so late? Where had he come from and, more importantly, where was he now?

Chapter two

Once Dan had finished his crime reporter duties and filed some stories on a spate of break-ins in the east end of Allensbury, he was back to his usual day-to-day workload for the next couple of hours. This meant mucking in with the team and heading out to interview a University of Allensbury professor about his new book. Having arrived early, he was killing some time reading the posters on the noticeboard in the university library's foyer. The campus was a familiar place for him, having studied there for three years as an undergraduate. As he turned from the board, he saw a familiar figure striding towards him. He stepped forward and called, 'Harry?'

Dr Harry Evans looked up from his smartphone and a smile broke out across his face.

'Dan,' he said, shoving his phone into his trouser pocket as he approached. He switched the hard-backed A4 notebook he was carrying to his other hand so he could shake Dan's. 'How are you? Long time no see.'

'Yes, we've not needed any political expert quotes for a while,' Dan said with a grin. Dr Harry Evans was a specialist in Cold War and Middle-Eastern politics, and recent political events had suggested a potential return to a Cold War situation. Harry's expertise had made him popular with the media, and not just the

Allensbury Post. He'd appeared on the local TV news and also in at least one national newspaper that Dan was aware of.

'How's things?' Harry asked.

Dan grinned. 'Good, thanks. Working hard.'

Harry smiled back and nodded. 'Yes, I saw your exploits in the paper last year. You're not on the trail of another hot story, are you?' The previous year Dan had hit the headlines with an investigation that had almost cost him his life.

Dan grinned. 'Sadly no; I'm here to interview one of the history professors about a book he's written and I was early so I thought I'd kill some time.'

Harry raised an eyebrow. 'I wouldn't have thought the library was the obvious place for you to loiter.'

Dan moved to one side to allow a group of students to pass and laughed. 'Hey, that's not fair. I did spend some time in here during my degree.'

'Probably not as much as you should have.' Harry wagged a mock-scolding finger.

'I passed, though, that was the main thing.'

Harry frowned. 'A 2:2 is a decent grade to get, but you could have done better if you'd put more effort in,' he said.

Dan shrugged. 'Possibly, but it was what I needed for journalism college, so that was good enough for me.'

'And how is life as a journalist?' Harry asked.

'Yeah, it's good.' Dan glanced at his watch. 'Sorry, I'm going to have to go. There's a history professor waiting for me.'

Harry shifted his notebook to the other hand. 'Hmm, good luck,' He indicated the wide spiral staircase that wound upwards through the middle of the library building. 'I'm off upstairs to find some peace and quiet to work.'

Dan smiled. 'Good luck to you too.' He'd seen several students staring at Harry as they passed. Harry was a good-looking man and tended to attract a lot of female student attention. Some men too, if Dan's memory served correctly. 'Catch up properly another time?' he asked.

'Yeah, give me a call and we can set something up,' Harry said, turning away with a wave.

Dan waved back and began to walk towards the library's automatic doors. His mobile phone rang and he pulled it out of his pocket. The word 'News desk' appeared on the screen. He answered.

'Dan, change of plan on your interview.' It was Daisy King, the news editor.

'What? Why?'

'We've just had a call to say the police have found a body in a house in Castle Street. I need you to get over there.'

'OK. What about the history book?'

'One of the juniors is already on the way to take over. I thought you'd prefer this one.'

Dan grinned. 'Thanks. I'm on my way.'

Dan parallel parked the Peugeot pool car, which he'd been assigned that morning, as best he could into a space he knew was probably way too small; he'd work out how to get it back out again later. He climbed out of the car and walked down the street to where the fluttering blue and white police tape was strung across the pavement between a gatepost and nearby tree. He joined three gossiping women, who eyed him suspiciously.

'Did you see what happened?' he asked.

One woman looked him up and down. 'Who are you?' she asked.

'Why do you want to know?' asked another.

Dan explained and the women inched away from him. 'Did you see what happened?' he asked again.

'Guy in number twelve,' the woman said, nodding towards the house. 'Gone and died, hasn't he?'

'How did he die?'

The woman frowned. 'How should I know? You'll have to talk to her. Miserable cow.' She indicated a woman in a suit standing in the doorway of the house talking urgently into her mobile. 'Told us to get back indoors and stop snooping.'

Dan looked up and grinned. It was highly likely that Detective Inspector Jude Burton would have been so abrupt. It was her default setting. Burton looked up and Dan waved at her. She ended her call, flipped her long blonde pony-tail over her shoulder and walked down the garden path towards him, scowling slightly.

'I might have known you'd turn up.' Burton's tone had a touch of resignation as if a visit from the Allensbury Post was an inevitable irritation. 'Anonymous tip-off to the newsroom again?'

'It always is,' Dan replied with a grin.

Burton snorted. 'Well, there's nothing to tell you.' She glared at the three women who were whispering among themselves. 'You can go back indoors, ladies, there's nothing to see,' she called to them. They stared at her reproachfully, before walking away, arms folded tightly across their chests and looking mutinous. 'God save us from neighbours who didn't see anything and don't know anything but just want to stick their noses in,' Burton said.

Dan grinned. 'What can you tell me?'

Burton frowned. 'At the moment, nothing,' she said.

'You've found a body though, haven't you?'

Burton sighed. 'Off the record—' she raised a hand like a traffic warden to stop Dan's protests '—off the record, yes, we have found a body. That's all I've got and I don't want to see it reported. I'll update the press office when I've got something, so keep in touch with them.'

She turned and went back into the house, leaving Dan standing alone. He heard mocking laughter and saw the three women watching him from a short distance. He waved to them and headed back to his car. But when he looked at the house opposite, he saw a pair of bright eyes peering out at him from behind net curtains. Abandoning his plans to leave, he crossed the road and walked up the front path of the house. The door opened as he got to it.

'You'd better come in,' said the elderly woman inside.

Chapter three

Daisy King rolled her eyes.

'Dan, are you sure this is right?'

'Yes, she's for real.' Dan's stomach was flickering, a sure sign he was onto something. 'She said he was a nice guy, always said hello. She usually saw him once in the morning and once in the evening, to and from work, she reckoned. Although she said he seemed to be coming home much later now than before.'

'My neighbours could say the same thing about me,' Daisy replied, tapping her pen against her hand.

Dan ignored her. 'But she said two days ago he had some friends over.'

Daisy raised an eyebrow. 'Him having friends over was that unusual?'

'So the nosy neighbour said. She said there were three or four of them. They might have had keys because they didn't wait on the doorstep or anything. They seemed to go straight in,' Dan told her.

'She didn't see them come back out?'

Dan shook his head. 'No, but she was watching TV. She said she only noticed those guys because the headlights of their van lit up her windows when they were parking up.'

'And you deduce what from him having friends over?'

Dan shrugged. 'Nothing from that, per se. But, she also said he was a scientist.'

'Meaning?'

'That guy I saw being abducted, he was at Allensbury Science Park.'

'Oh Dan.' Daisy threw up her hands. 'That's a huge leap even for you.'

'No, it could be that—'

'Dan, I can't let you go off chasing what could be nothing. We've got a paper to put together.' She sighed. 'Back to your desk, please, and write up what you've got on the body in the house and then there's a lot more to do. I need everything you got today.'

Dan turned away and walked back to his desk. But his stomach was still flickering. He had to know who the scientist was and what had happened to him.

Chapter four

The best bit of being on the crime beat, Dan reckoned, was getting out of meetings in the evening. While Emma was away he was saved from the tedium of town councils, and got to eat proper meals rather than bars of chocolate and crisps grabbed while driving around the countryside to the surrounding villages.

He and his flatmate Ed Walker had just finished dinner when the crime phone burst into life, playing an inappropriately bouncy tune. Dan answered.

'Hi Dan. It's Suzy, from the police press office,' came the cheery voice on the other end.

'Hi. How're you?'

Suzy sighed. 'Very glad to be going home soon. This is my last act of the day and I'm only doing it as a favour to Burton.'

Dan raised an eyebrow. 'Must be important.'

Suzy laughed. 'She asked if I could let you know that they've identified the body they found in Castle Street earlier. They're still not treating it as suspicious because it looks like a heart attack. Anyway, I've just emailed you the details, with a statement from Burton and a photo of the victim. The family has been told and they've asked for privacy.'

'Hang on, let me check the email's arrived.' Dan clicked Suzy onto the crime phone's speaker and grabbed his personal phone, flicking through to his work email account. 'Yup, it's here.' He opened the email, clicked on the picture of the victim and gave a sharp intake of breath.

'What is it?' Suzy's tinny voice asked through the phone's speaker.

'I know him.'

Dan looked up to see Ed standing in the kitchen doorway, dirty plates in hand, eyes widening. As the newspaper's court reporter, Ed understood the disturbance of calls in the evening, but Dan's tone had grabbed his attention.

Ten minutes later, Burton called.

'Suzy says you know the victim,' she said without preamble.

'Not know him as such, but I've seen him recently,' Dan said.

'Where?'

'You know I reported that abduction earlier this week?'

There was a short silence. 'Yes,' Burton said, slightly cautiously.

'That's the guy I saw, the one that got grabbed,' Dan said.

The next morning Dan found himself in a police interview room, facing Burton and Detective Sergeant Mark Shepherd across a table. The room was painted a bland cream and, seeing Dan pull at the collar of his shirt, Burton apologised for the stuffiness.

'The air con is broken,' she explained. Then she flipped open the file in front of her. 'Tell me again about the abduction,' she said. Shepherd sat poised with a notebook and pen ready to take down Dan's statement.

'I was out jogging,' Dan said and Shepherd began to scribble. 'I was passing Allensbury Science Park. I was looking around and saw this guy–' he tapped on the photograph which lay in the folder '– running across the car park. Two men came running after him and a van drove up behind him. The side door opened and he was dragged inside. The two men jumped in and the van roared away.'

'Did you notice anything about the van?'

'Only that it was black or very dark blue. It was a bit dirty too.'

'Get a registration number?' Burton asked. 'Direction of travel?'

Dan paused to allow Shepherd to catch up. When he came to the end of a line, Shepherd looked up expectantly.

'No, it was too far away and going too fast. The number plate was dirty so I couldn't see it properly,' Dan said, frowning as he tried to remember the details. 'Heading towards the bypass I think.'

'You didn't see which building he came from?' Burton asked.

'No, he was halfway across the car park when I saw him. He didn't look like he was used to running though.'

Burton frowned and Shepherd finished writing. Dan looked from one to the other.

'Which building did he come from?' he asked.

Burton paused. 'He worked at GITech Pharmaceuticals,' she said. 'As we put in the press release, he was a chemist.'

Dan nodded. 'And now do you believe me when I say that I saw him abducted? That I didn't make it up?'

'I never thought you'd made it up,' Burton said patiently. 'You had no reason to do that.' She leaned forward and rested her forearms on the table. 'We just didn't find any evidence.'

'None? No CCTV or anything?' Dan sat back in surprise as Burton nodded.

'The cameras were out of action and the maintenance crew only noticed the next morning,' she said, pulling a disbelieving face.

Dan puffed out his cheeks. 'That can't be a coincidence, can it? For someone to be abducted on the one day the cameras weren't working?'

Burton was silent, staring into space.

'And there's nothing else you remember or need to tell us?' Shepherd asked.

Dan shook his head and Shepherd made a note to show the end of the statement.

'I'll get this typed up and then you'll need to come back in and sign it,' he said. Dan nodded and they both stood up. Burton looked startled for a moment and then got up too.

'Thanks for coming in,' she said as they showed Dan out into the reception area.

As he walked away Dan's stomach was flickering on overtime. Never mind what Daisy had said, he was definitely onto something now.

Chapter five

As the students began to trickle back onto campus after the Easter break, Harry Evans was keen to finish the article he was working on. He needed it to be good, to get into a journal at long last. He loved teaching, but the article had to come first. He was in his office tapping rapidly at his laptop, stopping every now and then to check his notes. There was a knock at the door and Harry sighed. The last thing he'd needed was a break in concentration but now he'd have to deal with whatever this was.

'Come in,' he called, saving the document he was working on and closing the lid of his laptop.

The door opened and Olly Murton's greasy-haired head appeared around the door. His method of sliding gradually into a room, like the appearing Cheshire cat but without the grin, irritated Harry and he waved for the student to hurry up.

'I'm glad you've popped in,' Harry said. 'Shut the door.' He gestured for Olly to sit down. The student folded his lanky frame into the chair opposite Harry's desk and put his backpack carefully onto the floor. He smiled a little nervously.

Harry looked at him for a moment and then reached into his desk drawer for a folder.

'I've some feedback on your latest dissertation chapter, and quite frankly I'm impressed. It's very good, Olly.' Olly smiled a little smugly but Harry knew he was about to wipe that look off his face. 'So much better than usual that I have to ask why,' he continued.

Olly stopped smiling. 'I'm finally getting hold of the topic, I think,' he said quickly.

'Yes, but there's a difference between getting under the skin of the topic and the dramatic improvement in your work, so dramatic that I have to ask whether you did it yourself,' Harry said, flipping open the file and looking down at the first page.

Olly sat forward in his chair. 'Are you accusing me of cheating? Saying that I copied it?'

Harry shook his head. 'No, I checked it against the sources you've used and it's not copied. It's the fluidity and the interpretation that I'm wondering about. You work hard, Olly, and that's why I'm going to give you the benefit of the doubt.'

Olly stared at him, eyes wide. 'What do you mean?'

'I'm not going to report you for cheating this time,' Harry said, holding up the document. 'But I want you to go away and rewrite this yourself. Remember that I'll know if you have had help. If it happens again then I'll have to tell someone.'

Olly leapt to his feet and snatched the printed pages from Harry's hand. Without another word the student swung his backpack onto his bony shoulder and marched out, allowing the door to slam behind him.

Harry sighed. He felt sorry for Olly but the student had to learn the dangers of being caught cheating. He'd learned that lesson the hard way.

Chapter six

The White Lion was an old-man's pub in the traditional style. The lounge was dimly lit and that meant that Professor Keith Williams hadn't seen Olly Murton until the student pulled up a stool and sat across from him at the low wooden table.

'You said he wouldn't know,' Olly almost snarled, leaning forward and waving some printed pages in Williams' face.

Williams took a sip of the single malt and water in front of him. 'How did you find me?' He'd hoped for some quiet time to think away from campus.

Olly shrugged. 'You weren't in your office or the coffee bar so I thought of here next.'

Williams smiled, but it wasn't a very nice smile. 'You must have wanted to see me quite urgently to go to all that trouble?' His tone was lazy and Olly glared at him.

'You said that he'd never know,' he repeated.

'Who? Know what?' Williams took another sip of his whisky.

'Harry. He knew I'd had help with the dissertation chapter. Said it was too fluid to be mine.'

Williams laughed. 'I should think so too. After all, you had help from the best.' He laid a hand on his chest, fingers splayed. 'There's an irony in him pulling someone else up for cheating though,'

Williams continued, 'considering his history.'

Olly rolled his eyes. 'The old plagiarism allegation? Come on, Keith. No one really believed that.'

'But it was fun to watch him squirm through an investigation.' Williams paused and gestured towards Olly with his glass. 'Not drinking?'

'I'm not in the mood,' Olly muttered, eyes cast down at the table surface.

Williams sighed and sipped. 'Is he going to report you for it?'

Olly shook his head. 'He said he wouldn't if I go and rewrite the chapter myself.'

'So, what's the problem?' Williams sipped his drink again.

Olly picked at a beer mat on the table. 'It won't be as good.' He shook his head. 'I'm going to fail.' He looked up in an accusing manner. 'If I wasn't doing as much stuff for you—'

Williams raised his eyebrows. 'Doing what for me?' he asked.

'Finding that guy, getting him on the hook, keeping him supplied.' Olly counted off the points on his fingers, but suddenly he didn't like the way Williams was looking at him.

The older man snorted. 'You did nothing I couldn't have done myself.'

'Oh really? Then why didn't you do it?'

Williams shrugged. 'You don't buy a dog and then bark yourself, do you?'

'Is that what you think of me? That I'm your dog?' Olly's expression was one of both sadness and anger, a difficult mix to create, Williams thought. He gave Olly a dismissive smile.

'You couldn't have done the stuff that I did. You barely know how to use a computer,' Olly said, managing a scornful tone.

'I use it fine for my work, thank you.' Williams was starting to get annoyed now too.

'That's just opening documents and a bit of Internet research when you know exactly where to look. That's nothing compared to what I've done for you. You'd never have found that forum unless I'd gone looking for it. You'd never have been able to contact him without me.' He looked sly for a moment. 'He's going to publish it himself if you don't hurry up.'

Williams slammed down his glass. 'What do you mean?'

Olly gave a smug smile. 'He's got a blog post all ready to go if you don't deliver. He only needs to press publish and it's all out there.'

Williams' face flushed. 'No he hasn't. I'm paying him for his information. And he needs that money, believe me.'

'Is it enough though?' Olly asked, shrugging. 'Enough to keep him on the leash?'

Williams glared at Olly. 'He was the one that started this, who wanted to blow the whistle so it had better be enough.'

'I want my credit though.' Olly was speaking quietly and picking at the beer mat again.

'What credit?'

'On the research project. Like you said.'

Williams downed the rest of his drink and stood up. 'I said what?'

'That I could have credit on this project,' Olly said, looking at Williams and there was a worried edge to his voice. 'For the work I've done.'

'I don't remember saying that,' Williams said looking down at Olly with an unpleasant smile on his face. 'And I think you'll find that you have no proof of it either.'

'What do you mean?'

'There's nothing in writing so you can't prove I said anything.'

'But you did. You said—' Olly was glaring at Williams.

'I don't need you anymore. I've got him, I've got everything I need.'

Olly leapt to his feet, knocking the table and sending Williams' empty glass skidding across the wooden surface. Williams laughed, grabbing the glass before it fell to the floor. 'What are you going to do about it?' he asked.

When Olly said nothing, Williams turned on his heel and strode out of the pub.

Olly flopped down onto the seat that the lecturer had just vacated. In the space of a morning he'd been caught cheating and lost his chance at a research credit that could be vital to his future career. Well, he thought, at least one of those he could do something about.

As he headed back to his office to collect what he needed, Keith Williams saw that Harry Evans' door wasn't quite closed. He stopped beside it, his ear close to the crack in the door. He could hear two voices but one had a tinny sound to it. Clearly Evans wasn't expecting anyone else to be around and the caller was on speakerphone.

The voice on the phone was saying, 'It was great that you could attend the interview earlier this week.'

'Thanks, Kim,' came Harry Evans' voice. 'It was good to meet you. As I said, I've been a fan of your work for a long time.'

Williams leaned closer to the door. He recognised the voice of Kim Trevelyan, head of the politics department at Trenton University. He frowned. What was Evans up to?

'I can't understand why you want to leave Allensbury,' Kim was saying. 'But I'm glad you're thinking of us.'

Evans was trying to leave Allensbury?

'It's time for a change of scene,' Evans was saying. 'I've been here a while and I feel like I've achieved all I can.'

'Great news. Like I said, we've got some final deliberations, but you're first on my list,' Kim Trevelyan said. 'I should hopefully have an answer for you in the next week or so.'

'Thanks, Kim. Speak soon.'

Williams heard a beep as Evans hung up the speakerphone. He shoved open the door.

'Job interview?' he asked, enjoying the fact that Evans jumped and looked guilty.

'Were you listening at the door?' Evans asked, a look of dislike on his face.

Williams nodded. 'Don't they usually say that eavesdroppers never hear anything to their advantage? Not true today.'

Evans sighed and dropped into his chair. 'Go away, Keith. I'm not in the mood for your shit-stirring today.'

'Oh really?' Williams smirked and leaned against the door frame. 'I have no idea what you mean. By the way, does Desmond know what you're up to?'

Evans glared. 'No he doesn't. Nor does he need to know.'

Williams rubbed his chin, his stubble making a rasping noise. 'You're under pressure to publish more, aren't you? Is that why you're running away?'

'I am not running away.' Evans leapt to his feet. 'My publication rate is fine.'

'That's not what I heard. You've been struggling for the last year at least. You've not published anything since your wife had that miscarriage.' Evans flinched as if Williams had slapped him in the face.

'Desmond understands that.'

Williams sniggered. 'He might but I doubt the University Council will.'

'Shut up, Keith.' Evans leaned forward on his desk, his hands supporting his weight. 'I'm not going to play this game with you. Besides, your publication rate is lower than mine.'

'But my job isn't at risk. I have friends in high places.' Williams paused for a moment. 'I know Kim Trevelyan. I met her at a conference a few years ago.'

Evans snorted. 'You reckon you're so respected and well known that she'll remember you years later, after meeting you once at a conference? You should be so lucky.'

Williams glared at him. 'Maybe I should remind her, give her a call and tell her what a great addition you'd make to her team.' Then he smiled nastily. 'Or maybe I should tell her that you have a track record for stealing other people's work.'

Harry closed his eyes, sighed heavily and hung his head for a moment. 'For God's sake, Keith, that wasn't true; you know it wasn't. It was disproved by the university board. Why can't you just let it go?'

'There's no smoke without fire,' Williams said, grinning smugly, 'and I'm sure a nice little rumour will block that job offer.'

He was just in time to dodge the magazine that Evans had picked up and hurled across the room at him. It crashed against the wall and fell to the ground with a rustle of pages. Williams looked at Evans who was red in the face and breathing hard.

'Tut-tut, Harry. You don't want to be known as the man who throws things at colleagues when he doesn't get his own way.'

As Evans charged out from behind his desk, Williams stepped smartly out of the door and away towards his office. Evans burst into the corridor behind him.

'Keith, I swear to God that if you don't leave me alone, I'll make you pay.'

Evans stormed back into his office and slammed the door so hard a poster on a nearby noticeboard was dislodged and fluttered to the ground. Neither man had noticed Olly Murton standing around the corner, watching.

Chapter seven

Two hours later Keith Williams sat in the driver's seat of his Vauxhall Mokka, looking around the car park. He checked the dashboard clock. The man was ten minutes late and Keith didn't like being kept waiting. But this would be worth it.

When he was still waiting another ten minutes later, he was beginning to lose patience. He checked his smartphone. There were no missed calls or messages. So where was he? Keith tapped at his phone's screen and brought up the man's number. He dialled and listened while the automated voice asked him to please leave a message after the beep.

'It's me. Where the hell are you? We were supposed to meet nearly half an hour ago. I'm not waiting any longer. If you don't call me back then I'm going ahead without you. You were the one who started this, but I'm more than willing to finish it myself.'

He hung up the phone and dumped it on the passenger seat. He fired up the engine and drove out of the car park. He wasn't going to waste any more time. This was the big thing he'd been waiting for.

Chapter eight

The following day Harry was standing in the corridor of the politics department. The student whose tutorial was due to start five minutes ago still hadn't arrived. Then a voice called his name. He turned to see Dan Sullivan walking down the corridor towards him.

Harry was surprised. 'What brings you out this way?' He looked at the folded-up copy of the Allensbury Post tucked under Dan's arm. 'Have they got you on delivery now as well as writing?'

Dan laughed. 'No, that history academic we interviewed about his book asked for a copy of the story. I was passing so I said I'd drop it in for him.' He held up the newspaper to display the front page. 'This is my handiwork.'

Harry started to read the story. '"A body found in Castle Street." I thought you were supposed to be interviewing that academic,' he said with a smile.

'Nah, I got pulled off that job and sent to this one. This scientist guy, George Peters, died at home. The police say it was a heart attack but—'

Suddenly Keith Williams elbowed between them and snatched the newspaper from Harry's hands. Harry turned on him, but was shocked by the look of fear on Keith's podgy face. His usually rosy cheeks had paled. Without a word he turned and almost ran from the building, crumpling the newspaper in his hand.

'I think I'm going to have to get another copy,' Dan said as they stared after him.

Chapter nine

Harry was in his office finishing the latest draft of his article when his mobile phone rang.

'Hi Harry. It's Kim Trevelyan from Trenton University.'

Harry raised his eyebrows. 'Hi Kim, I wasn't expecting to hear from you so soon.'

There was a pause.

'Is something wrong?' Harry asked, with a sense of foreboding.

'Look, Harry, there's no easy way to say this but we have a very big question mark over you at the moment.'

Harry felt a trickle of disappointment run into his stomach.

'Really?' He tried to sound casual. 'What's the problem?'

'We've been seeking background info on each of the candidates and one of the interview panel knows your colleague Keith Williams.' Harry's heart sank. 'He spoke to Keith, and I understand there's been some allegations of plagiarism in the past.'

'They were investigated and the inquiry found that I was innocent,' Harry said, his pulse racing.

'I've seen the inquiry notes,' Kim Trevelyan said, 'and it said that the enquiry was wound up because there was insufficient evidence, rather than there being no case to answer. That's by no means conclusive.'

'What are you saying?'

'It's not a definite no to the job at present, but we'll need to look into this more closely. I'm sorry, Harry, but I'm sure you understand why. We have to make sure our reputation remains at the standard to which we've built it up.' She sighed. 'I'll get back to you in a few days but I just wanted to let you know where we're at.'

Harry returned her goodbye and put down the receiver, his face flushing angrily. Keith had gone too far this time. He enjoyed bullying Harry, but why not just let him leave?

He leapt to his feet, grabbing his keys and wallet. He'd find Keith and demand an explanation. His office door slammed loudly as he charged out into the corridor.

He marched to Keith's office and hammered on the door. Keith's neighbour, a European government expert, poked her head into the corridor.

'He's not in,' she said. Then she peered at Harry. 'Are you OK? You look a bit flustered.'

'Do you know where he is?'

The woman looked surprised at Harry's tone. 'I saw him leaving about twenty minutes ago, muttering something about the library. He seemed a bit flustered as well.'

Harry nodded his thanks and marched away down the corridor. Keith was not going to get away with this.

Chapter ten

Dan was at his desk in the office, rubbing his eyes with his knuckles. The screen of his computer was beginning to blur in front of him. He typed the last line of his story and pressed send. He shouted to the deputy news editor to say it was there and was met with a grumpy 'finally'. Clearly she was as keen to get home as he was.

He peered out of the window at the darkening sky and then checked his watch. Just enough time to get home and have some dinner before the football started. As he got to his feet, his desk phone began to ring. He knew it was risky to answer the newsroom phone at this time of night as it might mean more work but he answered it anyway, praying for a call for advertising or circulation so he could palm it off on someone else. But what he heard had him grabbing a notebook and pen. He finished scribbling, slammed down the phone a little harder than he intended to and began pulling on his jacket. As he passed the news desk, he said, 'I'm off to the university. They found a body in the library.'

The deputy news editor frowned at him. 'If this is one of your jokes, Dan—'

'I'm not joking,' Dan said, pointing back towards his phone. 'That's what the call was about.'

The deputy news editor yawned widely. 'OK, send over anything you can get tonight on this body and someone will pick it up in the morning.'

As Dan pushed open the doors from the newsroom any tiredness had gone and his stomach was flickering again.

When he arrived at the university, Dan parked as close to the library as possible, which wasn't in the end very close. The library's own car park was blocked by police cars and an ambulance, their lights flashing. A police officer directed him to wait at the front of the library with all other interested bystanders.

'What's happened?' Dan asked one of the people standing in the crowd.

'Someone's died,' the woman replied. 'We haven't been told anything else.' She sounded disappointed. Dan looked up towards the top of the front steps of the library and saw Harry Evans talking to a police officer in uniform. Dan stared.

'What's Harry Evans doing there?' he asked the man standing on his other side.

'He found the body,' was the reply.

Dan turned to ask another question but instead stared at the man. He looked very familiar. Then Dan remembered.

'It's Olly, isn't it? Olly Murton.'

The man looked at him. 'Yes. Why?'

'You studied here at the same time I did, about ten years ago?' Dan asked. 'You did politics too, didn't you?'

Olly nodded, looking puzzled. Then recognition stole over his face. 'You're Dan Sullivan. What are you doing now?'

'I work for the Allensbury Post.' Dan looked back towards the library frontage. 'Harry found the body? Any idea who it is?'

Olly paused and then shook his head. 'I was here to pick up some books when we were told to leave because there was an emergency.'

He shook his head. 'I only heard what had happened after I got outside.'

'I see. How well do you know Harry?'

'He's my supervisor for my dissertation. Did he teach you as well?'

'Yeah, I did a couple of his courses,' Dan said. 'He helped me a lot. Good bloke.'

Olly grunted. Dan raised an eyebrow. 'You don't agree?'

'He's usually alright but recently he's been different, really aggressive, y'know?' Olly said.

Dan was surprised as he looked towards the man standing meekly talking to the police officer who was scribbling in a notebook. He'd never found Harry to be aggressive. Challenging, yes, but not aggressive. As he watched, Burton approached Harry. She spoke briefly to him, shook hands and then went back into the library. Dan watched as Harry was led away to a police car and helped into the back.

'Are they arresting him?' Olly asked, following Dan's line of sight.

'I don't know, but I'm going to find out.'

Dan gave Olly a quick wave and began to thread his way through the crowd. When he reached the police cordon, an officer moved to push him back but Dan waved at Shepherd, who stood in the library doorway. Shepherd walked over to him.

'Another tip-off?' he asked, raising an eyebrow.

Dan grinned. 'Always,' he said. 'Anything to tell me?'

Shepherd frowned. 'This is strictly off the record at the moment because we've not told the family yet but we believe the victim is Professor Keith Williams.'

Chapter eleven

Dan stared at him. 'Professor Keith Williams?' he asked. 'He's the victim?'

Shepherd raised an eyebrow. 'You know him?' he asked.

'Yes, I did a course of his when I studied here.'

'What was he like?' Shepherd asked.

Dan wrinkled his nose. 'Let's just say he wasn't popular. He was really arrogant and rather unpleasant. What happened to him?' Dan's pen was poised.

Shepherd put a finger on the notebook page before Dan could put his pen to it. 'The ID is strictly unofficial because the family hasn't been informed. All you can say is that a police spokesperson said that a man was found dead in the university library at about quarter to six this evening crushed between two bookcases,' Shepherd said. 'You can also say that police are in the process of contacting the next of kin but there's nothing else we can say at the moment.'

'Are you treating it as suspicious?' Dan asked.

'It's always suspicious until we prove otherwise,' Shepherd replied.

Dan's stomach was flickering. Two potentially suspicious deaths in almost as many days.

'Why are you talking to Harry Evans?' Dan asked when he'd

finished scribbling down what he could of Shepherd's words.

'Did he teach you as well?' Shepherd asked, head tilted to one side.

Dan nodded. 'He taught a few of my courses.'

'What do you know about him?' Shepherd asked.

'He's a good bloke. Actually I only saw him again for the first time in ages a couple of days ago, around the time you found the body in Castle Street.'

'Good teacher?' Shepherd asked.

Dan shrugged. 'I always thought so.'

Shepherd raised his eyebrows. 'Others didn't?'

'He can be a bit abrasive at times. A bit grumpy when he's doing his own writing but aren't we all? My news editor is no worse.' Dan grinned.

Shepherd smiled. 'How did he get on with other staff?'

'I think Harry got on with most people, although I never saw the secrets behind the office doors.' Dan frowned. 'Actually, now you mention it.' Dan pointed towards the doors of the library. 'I think Keith Williams may have had a problem with Harry.'

'How do you mean?'

Dan's brow remained furrowed with the effort of recalling the incident. 'I remember Keith criticising a lad in my tutorial group because he used one of Harry's books when he was writing an essay. I can't remember exactly what Keith said but he was pretty scathing about it. Said he would mark the guy down if he ever did it again.'

Shepherd's eyebrows almost went up to his hairline. 'I bet Dr Evans didn't like that.'

Dan shook his head. 'I don't know that anyone ever told him. I certainly don't remember it getting mentioned again. Although we all avoided Harry's books after that when we were doing essays for Keith.' Dan glanced at his watch. 'If there's nothing else, I'd better go and file some copy,' he said.

'No names,' Shepherd said, in a warning tone.

Dan nodded. Then he said 'I was just talking to a guy I studied with here before. Harry's his dissertation supervisor for his master's. He said Harry's been a bit different recently.'

'Did he say how?'

'Have a word with him. He's over there.' Dan turned to point to Olly Murton but the student had gone. 'Oh, he's not there now. Well, his name's Olly Murton anyway. I imagine the politics department can help you find him.'

'Thanks.'

'Right, I've got to go.' Dan gave Shepherd a wave and disappeared into the crowd. His brain was racing as he walked back to his car. Had Keith been slagging Harry off to someone else and Harry had got wind of it? Whatever happened, he needed to get the full story from Harry first thing tomorrow.

Chapter twelve

Pathologist Eleanor Brody was already wearing her white crime scene coverall, curly hair tucked inside the hood, and was snapping on a pair of latex gloves when Burton and Shepherd arrived. She smiled and nodded to them before pulling on her face mask.

'What're we looking at?' Burton asked. Brody's wire-rimmed glasses flashed in the overhead lights as she turned to glare at her.

'Give me a chance to get started,' she said, her voice slightly muffled by the mask. Burton smiled an apology. Brody frowned down at Keith Williams as if he were at fault for being dead. 'First impressions,' she began, hands on hips. 'He walked between these wheeled bookcases and they somehow closed on him.'

'Wheeled bookcases?' Burton asked, looking at the shelving units.

'Yes, they're on runners and you can slide them back and forth,' Brody said.

Burton looked mystified. 'Why would you want wheeled bookcases?'

'It saves space,' Brody replied as if it was obvious.

'But on this occasion the safety feature of "shove a wooden block in the way of the wheels" doesn't seem to have been all that effective,' said Shepherd, consulting his notebook and pointing to the wooden doorstop in a plastic bag on a nearby table.

Brody had ducked under the blue and white police tape that cordoned off the area and was on her hands and knees beside the body. 'Get a picture of this please,' she ordered, pointing to Williams' head. A white-suited CSI stepped forward with a camera.

'What? What have you got?' Burton asked.

'I'll know more when I do the post-mortem but does that look like a crush-related injury to you?' She indicated Williams' head. Burton and Shepherd bent down and peered at it.

They both looked at Brody. She said, 'I'd say he was hit on the head with something heavy. He was probably dead before the bookcases were shut on him.'

Meanwhile, Sam Kingman, Brody's assistant, was collecting evidence bags, checking the information on them and entering the details on to the crime scene record. Once the first batch was done, he rustled in his crime scene suit along the corridor created by the bookshelves and put them onto a large wooden table. He turned and walked back the way he'd come, eyes looking down at the floor. Then he saw something flash under the fluorescent overhead strip lights. He stopped immediately and a CSI who had followed him collided with his back, almost knocking him over.

'What are you doing?' she demanded loudly, having had to grab at Sam with one hand and a bookcase with the other to stop herself falling over. Sam held out an arm to stop her pushing past him. Instead he edged her back a few steps.

'Wait there,' he said, kneeling down. He carefully examined the carpet in front of him, poking at something with a gloved finger.

'What is it?' the colleague asked, stepping closer and peering over Sam's shoulder.

Sam frowned. 'I'm not sure. I just saw the light glint against it.' Still on his knees, he continued to peer at the carpet. 'It's glass,' he said.

'What's it doing all the way over here?' the woman replied. 'The taped area ends at these bookcases.'

Sam was still staring at the glass on the floor. 'It's not glass like a drinking glass, or anything like that,' he said. 'It seems much lighter.'

'What is it?' a voice called. They turned to see Brody walking towards them between the bookcases.

Sam looked up as she approached. 'There's some glass on the floor,' he said. 'I can't see exactly what it is.'

Brody stepped forward and handed him an evidence bag. Sam took a pair of tweezers out of his pocket and carefully picked up the pieces of glass and put them into the bag.

'What made you look there?' Brody asked.

Sam got to his feet. 'I wasn't looking. I just walked along this way and it caught the light.' He held up the plastic bag to look at the fragments. 'Is it just me or does that look like it came from a test tube?' he asked, frowning.

Brody peered at it too and puffed out her cheeks. 'It could be. Let's get it back to the lab and find out,' she said, handing him a pen. Sam wrote 'unidentified glass fragments' on the bag, along with the date and location.

He handed it to Brody who checked the label and noted it onto the crime scene record on her clipboard. She gave a short nod and turned away. Sam smiled to himself. Coming from Brody, that was tantamount to a pat on the back.

Chapter thirteen

The following morning Olly Murton raised a hand and knocked on Harry Evans' door. A voice ordered him to come in. He was surprised to see that Harry looked a bit flustered.

'I'm glad you could come.' Harry stood up, walked around his desk and cleared some journal articles from his visitor's chair. Then he looked around, as if uncertain where to put them. He shoved them into the already crowded bookcase and gestured for Olly to sit down. Olly put his backpack on the floor and perched on the chair.

'Why did you want to see me?' he asked.

Harry tried a smile and failed. 'Olly, I've got some bad news and I wanted to be the one to tell you.' Olly looked at him and waited. 'I'm afraid that Keith Williams is dead,' Harry said. 'He was found in the library last night.'

'I heard the rumour.' Olly tried to keep his voice even. 'And you found him.' He knew it sounded like an accusation; did he really think Harry would kill Keith?

'You were there?' Harry asked. 'In the library?' His tone sounded worried and Olly wasn't sure how to proceed.

'No,' he lied. 'I was on my way there when I found out. I saw you being led away by the police.'

Harry sighed. 'I wasn't led away. I was interviewed as a formality at the scene, y'know, the usual stuff. Did I see anyone? What time was it? Did I touch anything? That kind of thing. Then they took me home.'

'And did you?' Olly's tone was sharp.

'Did I what?'

'See anyone else?' Olly asked.

'Well, no, I didn't. The library was busy but there was no one else in that section. I—' he paused. 'Are you accusing me of something?'

Olly gave a small shrug. 'I don't know, am I? I mean you had a blazing row with Keith and then suddenly he turns up dead and you were there.'

Harry leaned forward on his desk. 'How did you know we had a row?'

'I was in the corridor. I couldn't miss it. You were shouting.'

Harry sighed. 'Keith's death was an accident, Olly. He got trapped in the wheeled bookcases. Or at least that's what it looks like.'

'What did you do when you found him?' Olly asked, also leaning forwards.

Harry shifted awkwardly in his seat. 'I went for help. That's all I could do.'

'You didn't check to see if he was still alive? He could have been just unconscious and you left him to die.' Harry sat back in his chair looking shocked. 'I bet you're pleased he's dead.' Olly was almost snarling. He needed to get out of this room.

Harry looked stunned. 'No, I—'

But Olly was already on his feet. 'You've ruined everything.' He could feel tears welling into his eyes. But it wasn't for the loss of Keith. It was for the loss of other things.

'Please, sit down. We can talk about this. It's always hard to lose a friend—' Harry was saying.

But Olly shook his head. 'He wasn't my friend,' he interrupted. Getting out of the room was now imperative. He couldn't lose it in here.

Harry frowned. 'It's just that you spent a lot of time together, I assumed that—'

But Olly interrupted. 'We were working together. But you already know about that, don't you? Keith said someone had been in his office looking for something. It was you, wasn't it?' It was a long shot. Keith had been adamant that someone had rifled through his papers. Harry could have had access to spare keys. That would explain why there were no signs of a break-in.

Harry looked stunned. 'What the hell are you talking about?' He got to his feet and leaned forward, resting his palms on the desk.

'Keith said you'd stolen stuff from him before,' Olly said. 'What's to stop you doing it now?'

Harry was glaring at Olly in a way that made him very uncomfortable. Time to go. He leapt to his feet and grabbed his backpack.

'The research is mine now. You're not having it. Stay away from me, Harry. I'm warning you, stay away.'

Before Harry could say another word, Olly turned and flung open the door. He stormed out of the office and down the corridor. He was breathing hard and his hands were shaking. He was terrible at confrontation and Harry's reaction had made him nervous. He barged past a man and woman who were standing in the downstairs corridor. He needed somewhere to think.

Dan was just about to pull open the door to the politics department building when Olly Murton barrelled out. Dan only just managed to step aside and avoid getting a door in the face.

'Hey, Olly.' He grabbed the student's backpack before he could go any further, almost yanking it from his shoulder. Olly spun around, his face flushed and breathing hard. Dan stared at him. 'Are you OK?' he asked.

Olly shook his head as if he didn't know what he was doing. 'Sorry,' he said. 'I nearly hit you.'

'That's no problem.' Dan released Olly's bag and peered at him. 'Are you OK?'

Olly shrugged his shoulders, but Dan could see he wasn't that cool. Olly took a deep breath. 'The body in the library,' he said. 'It was Keith Williams. Harry just talked to me about it.'

Dan nodded. 'I know. The police told me last night off the record. Did you know him?'

'Why would you say that?' Olly asked, quickly. 'Did Harry tell you?'

'Why would Harry tell me anything?' Dan asked, raising an eyebrow.

'We were working together.' Olly paused as if editing what he was going to say next. 'Me and Keith.' Then he said, 'Why are you here, anyway?'

Dan was surprised at the sudden change in direction. 'I wanted to see Harry. He found the body, so I was wondering if he might be able to give me inside information or a comment about what he saw.' Olly looked sceptical and Dan shrugged. 'Got to try for a new angle, haven't I?'

Olly gave a pale grin and turned away.

'Hey,' Dan said. 'Look, if you need to talk or something then just give me a call.' He pulled out a business card and handed it to Olly.

'Thanks.' Olly tucked the card in the back pocket of his jeans. Hopefully it wouldn't just end up in the washing machine, Dan thought.

'How is Harry after finding the body?' he asked.

'Surprisingly calm,' Olly replied. 'I'd have expected him to be more upset. It's like he doesn't care.'

'Really?' Dan was surprised. That didn't sound like the Harry he knew.

'He seemed quite interested in Keith's research that he was working on,' Olly continued. 'But I'm pretty sure he already knows what it is.'

Dan stared at him. 'He was interested in his research? The guy's just died.'

Olly shrugged and swung his backpack over his shoulder again. 'I've gotta go. Good luck with him.' He jerked his head towards the first floor of the building and turned on his heel. 'I don't think he's in a receptive mood today.'

'Thanks for the advice. Remember what I said about calling.'

But Olly was already walking away and merely waved a hand over his shoulder.

When Dan knocked on Harry's door, the 'come in' was tinged with exasperation. Harry did not look happy when Dan stepped into the room.

'What do you want, Dan?' He sounded tired.

'I just thought I'd drop by.' Dan knew this would be a difficult conversation and so was trying to keep his tone light.

'Are you here as a former student or as a reporter?' Harry asked sharply.

'A bit of both,' Dan admitted.

Harry sighed heavily. 'Well, as I doubt I can have a conversation with the former and not the latter, I'd rather not talk to either.' He looked back down at the papers on his desk, clearly expecting Dan to leave. But Dan chose to hold his ground.

'You found the body,' he said.

'I think that's common knowledge by now,' Harry replied. 'There was a big crowd outside the library.'

'I know. I was there.'

Harry looked irritated. 'As a nosy reporter?' he asked, a scowl darkening his face.

'Afraid so.' Dan tried to keep his expression impassive. 'The police always suspect the person who found the body, y'know,' he said.

'What's that supposed to mean?' Harry demanded.

'Why were you in the library?'

'Is that any of your business?'

Dan shrugged. 'Only you didn't seem to have a bag with you, so I doubt you were there for work.'

'I took notes on my phone.' Harry gestured to the smartphone on his desk. 'I'm sure you do the same.'

'Can I see them?'

Harry glared at him. 'What?'

'The notes you made.' Now Dan pointed to the phone.

'No, you bloody well can't. You're on thin ice, Dan. Keep your nose out of what doesn't concern you.'

'I saw Olly Murton outside,' Dan said calmly. 'He said he'd been to see you and that you didn't seem fazed by finding a body.'

Harry's face darkened. 'Just because I don't show it to everyone doesn't mean I'm not upset.'

'You didn't like Keith, did you?' Dan knew he was pushing it now.

'What? Why would you say that?'

'Well, maybe it's fairer to say that he didn't like you,' Dan said, folding his arms. 'I heard him rubbish your books more than once when I studied here. Did you hear about that?' Harry didn't need to respond. Dan could see the truth on his face. 'So I have to ask,' he said 'had he gone too far this time? Said something that you really didn't like?'

Harry was glaring now and getting to his feet. Dan knew he only had one more push to make and then it would be time to get out of there.

'Did you know what he was working on at the moment?' he asked.

'What?' Harry asked, staring at Dan in disbelief.

'Olly said Keith was working on something new and that you were a bit too interested in it,' Dan said, tilting his head to one side.

He took a step back towards the door as Harry started out from behind his desk.

'Get out, Dan. I know nothing about Keith's research so just leave me alone.'

Dan quickly scooted out of the door and away down the corridor, his stomach flickering. Something was definitely going on but could his old lecturer really be involved?

Chapter fourteen

Eleanor Brody's office was almost as cold as the morgue she worked in when her assistant, Sam Kingman, showed Burton and Shepherd inside. Burton gave a theatrical shudder.

'Does it need to be so cold in here?' she asked. 'She hasn't started keeping bodies in here too, has she?'

Sam laughed. 'Nah, the heating's on the blink this morning. The engineer just arrived to fix it. Dr Brody's dealing with him at the moment.'

'Sounds painful,' Shepherd remarked.

Sam laughed again. 'Do you want a tea or coffee?' he asked.

'No, thanks. We need to get down to business,' Burton said.

Sam nodded and left the room. They heard a commanding voice in the corridor and Eleanor Brody entered, rubbing alcohol disinfectant into her hands. She was still wearing her coat and looked very stern.

'Why can't people understand simple instructions?' she asked, shrugging off her jacket.

'You haven't killed him, have you?' Burton asked. 'Because I'm sure we'd never be able to prove it.'

Brody snorted. 'You want post-mortem results on Keith Williams,' she said. It wasn't a question.

'Have you finished already?' Burton asked.

'Of course. We did it first thing this morning. Come down to the morgue and I'll show you.'

Shepherd grinned. 'That's the best offer I've had all day.'

Brody gave him a look over her shoulder and led the way down the stairs to the empty morgue. The room was even colder than her office and the easy-to-clean metal surfaces didn't add any warmth. Burton and Shepherd both automatically rubbed their hands together. Brody strode across to one of the refrigerated units and opened the door. She slid out the shelf that held Keith Williams' body.

'Not exactly a fine specimen,' she said with a frown, pointedly eyeing his domed stomach. 'I'll never understand why some people treat their body so badly. You only get one, you should look after it.' Williams' hair was completely grey, which gave the impression of him being a lot older than his early-fifty-something years, and a long-term smoking habit had taken its toll on his lined, grey-looking face.

'I doubt he was getting his five-a-day,' said Shepherd, taking out his notebook.

'What can you tell us?' Burton asked, trying to steer the discussion away from diets. Shepherd always lectured her about her love of a full English breakfast.

'Despite a lot of bruising here—' Brody indicated Williams' large abdomen and rib cage '—it's mostly superficial and inflicted post-mortem when the killer slammed the bookcases together on him.'

'He was definitely already dead, then?' Shepherd asked.

Brody nodded.

'What killed him?' Shepherd continued, scribbling in his notebook.

'As I showed you yesterday, it was a blow to the base of the skull with something heavy. Give me a hand here,' Brody called to Sam, who had followed them down to the morgue. He helped her to turn the body slightly. Burton and Shepherd peered distastefully at the wound, which was a short distance away from Williams' ear.

'What do you think did that?' Burton asked.

Brody shrugged. 'Not sure. I've not really seen a wound like that before. I think it's something relatively heavy but possibly with a corner that's quite sharp. Or a corner that was sharp but that's been worn away slightly,' she said.

'That's the oddest description of a murder weapon I've ever heard,' Burton said frowning.

'It was sharp but now it's blunt?' Shepherd asked. 'Like this?' He held out his notebook. He'd drawn a sharp ninety-degree angle and then scribbled with his pen to soften the edges. Brody looked at the notebook and nodded. Shepherd looked down at his own drawing. 'What on earth looks like that?' he asked.

'He was hit with it a couple of times as well,' Brody said.

'And that was enough to kill him?' Burton asked.

Brody nodded. 'Like I said, the object was heavy. The blows were also hard, and the remaining corner just sharp enough to cause internal bleeding. That's what killed him. I think he was hit three times in total.'

Shepherd looked up from his notebook. 'You're not sure?'

'Whoever did it has managed to deliver all three blows more or less on exactly the same spot so it's difficult to tell.'

Burton and Shepherd looked at each other.

'Unusual weapon,' said Shepherd.

'Unusual murder scene,' said Brody. 'I've never had a murder in a library before.'

'Was there anything else from the post-mortem?' Burton asked.

'He was a heavy smoker who liked cigars.' Brody wrinkled her nose. 'His lungs are a mess. He liked a drink too so his liver isn't in very good shape either.'

'Any clues about the killer?'

'Nothing on the body, but I think the killer was probably right-handed.'

Burton raised an eyebrow. 'How so?'

'The way the blows were struck could only have been by a right-handed person,' Brody said, demonstrating the movement the killer would have made. 'There aren't any defensive wounds but he does have some hefty fresh bruises on his knees.'

Shepherd frowned at her. 'He fell over just before he died?'

Brody nodded. 'That would explain why he didn't fight back,' she said. 'If he was on the floor immobilised, he wouldn't be able to do anything.'

'That might be how the killer could also hit him in the same place three times. They were pinning him to the ground,' Shepherd said looking at Burton.

'Anything else?' Burton asked.

'No. No traces of any fibres that shouldn't be there, although I'm waiting for carpet samples to come back from the scene,' Brody said, consulting her clipboard. 'The guys are still working over there so you'll have to wait until they're done to find out any more.'

'Why would someone want to kill a university professor?' Burton wondered as they left the morgue building and walked to the car.

'Maybe they didn't like the grade he gave them,' Shepherd said, grinning.

'You think this could be a student?' Burton asked, turning to look at him.

Shepherd shrugged. 'I don't think we can rule anyone out.'

Burton sighed. 'We need to see how forensics are getting on up at the library, but first I want to talk to Harry Evans and find out if there's any truth in what Dan Sullivan told you about a disagreement.'

Chapter fifteen

At first the office secretary seemed disinclined to be helpful in finding Harry Evans. It took all the persuasive skills of Shepherd's brown eyes and charming manner to get her to relent.

'OK, Detective Sergeant Shepherd,' she said. 'If you wait here, I'll see if he's in.' She tapped out an extension number on her phone. Somewhere on the floor above they heard a telephone ringing. Burton and Shepherd looked at each other as the sound continued. The secretary frowned.

'Is he expecting you?' she asked.

Shepherd shook his head. 'No. We just thought we'd pop in.'

'Is it about poor Keith Williams' accident?' the woman asked. 'Such an awful thing to happen.'

Burton raised an eyebrow. 'Accident?' she asked.

'Yes, Harry Evans told me this morning that the wheeled bookcases had crushed Keith. Is that why you want to speak to him?'

'Yes, that's right,' Burton said, glancing at Shepherd.

The secretary began to tap out another number. 'One thing you'll soon learn if you spend any time round here is to always make an appointment with an academic. Although that's no guarantee they'll remember, so it's also a good idea to ring ten minutes before your meeting to remind them.' She smiled and Burton and Shepherd felt they ought to smile too. She waited as the phone rang and then said, 'Harry? The police are here to see you. Yes, I know they didn't make an appointment. Oh good.' She covered the mouthpiece and said, 'He's just finished a tutorial and he's on his way back here now.' She turned back to the phone. 'What? You'll be ten minutes. Let them into your office to wait? Are you sure? Yes, I know they won't try to steal anything.' She blushed slightly as Shepherd started to smile. 'OK, yes, I will.' She put down the phone and, recovering her composure, said, 'If you'd like to come this way, I can let you into Dr Evans' office.' She scooped up a bunch of keys and ushered them out of the door before locking it behind her.

'You're very security conscious,' Shepherd remarked.

The secretary started to walk along the corridor. 'We don't keep much cash around but it has gone missing on more than one occasion,' she said. 'Plus one of the other women had a mobile phone stolen from her handbag.' She caught the look on Shepherd's face and continued, 'This campus is very open and you often get people wandering around.' She led the way to the first floor and they passed an office with Keith Williams' name on it.

'We'll need to see inside there as well,' Burton said, pointing to it.

'You'll need to speak to the head of department because he's deemed it out of bounds,' the secretary told them. 'I'll let him know you want to have a look and I'm sure he'll oblige.'

They reached the door and the secretary unlocked it. 'I'll leave you to it. If you need anything I'll just be downstairs.' She smiled and left them outside the door.

Stepping into the office, Burton looked at Shepherd and then glanced around the room. Every available surface in Harry Evans' office was covered with piles of paper, magazines and notebooks. The light from the window, which looked over the university lake, showed up several centimetres of dust. Burton looked at the nearest pile and found they were student essays, covered in red pen marks and notes. She flicked to the back page where Evans had not only graded it but also spent time writing a full page of comments in sharp spiky handwriting. Burton's eyes roved across the bookshelves, which covered the walls on both sides of the room, stuffed to bursting. It made the room feel very small. A photograph frame lay face down on one shelf and Burton moved to stand it up, leaving a rectangular space in the dust. It showed a couple with their arms around each other. The man was Harry Evans and the woman was a beautiful blonde. Burton returned the photograph to its original position. Then she glanced at the clock.

'Dr Evans' ten minutes are clearly a lot longer than mine,' she said to Shepherd.

'Actually, sir, the clock is about fifteen minutes fast,' said the sergeant looking at his own watch.

Everything in the room seemed to be covered in a thin layer of dust, even a suffocating pot plant. Burton tested the soil in the pot and found it was bone dry. Did no one ever clean this place, she wondered.

'I keep meaning to water that plant,' said a voice in the doorway. They turned to see Harry Evans shrugging out of his brown leather jacket.

'I think it might be past help,' Burton said.

'Really? Oh dear.' Harry seized a glass of water, the only thing in the office not covered in dust, from his overflowing desk and poured a little speculatively onto the plant. 'I think you might be right.' He smiled. 'Apologies for keeping you waiting.' He swept another pile of magazines off the visitor's chair and dusted it with his palm. He set it in front of his desk and then looked around. 'Ah, I've only got one chair.'

'No problem, I'll stand,' Shepherd said.

'Sorry, I only have one-to-one meetings with students in here or it would get a bit crowded.' Harry laughed awkwardly and sat behind his desk. 'I assume you want to talk about what happened to Keith?'

'Yes,' said Burton. 'How long have you known him?'

Harry puffed out his cheeks. 'I think it's about twelve years, basically since I came to work here.'

'How did you two get along?' Burton asked.

Harry glanced at Shepherd who was scribbling notes. 'We weren't friends but I respected him as an academic. Or at least I used to.'

'Used to?' Burton enquired.

'In his earlier years he was genuinely brilliant, developed some great theories, but in recent years he hadn't really published anything,' Harry said, leaning back in his chair.

'Is that important?' Shepherd asked.

'For an academic, yes. Research is a big part of what we do. You can only progress in your career if you're publishing and moving yourself forward.'

'And Professor Williams wasn't doing that?' Shepherd asked.

'He'd done bits and pieces but nothing of any significance,' Harry said, fiddling with his watch strap. 'Just enough to keep his head above water, if you know what I mean. I think it was frustrating for him that he couldn't come up with anything new. It was a shame because I'd always liked reading his work.'

'Did he have any particular friends?' Burton asked.

Harry frowned. 'He got along with Des quite well. Desmond Danby. He's the head of department. Keith was always bending his ear about something.' The last sentence came out quite bitterly.

Shepherd looked up from his notebook. 'Is he around today? We'll need to speak to him.'

'I saw him earlier. Ask in the office. They'll be able to tell you.'

'Can we go back to last night?' Burton asked, looking at Harry. 'What were you doing before you found Professor Williams' body?'

Harry paused and Burton wondered if he was trying to concoct a story.

'I was here preparing a seminar for today when I realised I needed a specific periodical article,' Harry eventually said. 'So I went to the library.'

'Did anyone know that you were planning to do that?' Burton asked.

'No. I'd only just realised I needed the article.' Harry's fingers were still playing with his leather watch strap.

'Did anyone see you around the department?' Shepherd asked, gesturing over his shoulder towards the door.

Harry frowned. 'I was working in here on my own, but I saw Natalya when I left. She works a couple of doors down.'

Shepherd made a note in his book. 'Then what happened?' he asked.

Harry gave a small shrug. 'Like I said last night, I knew where the article would be so I went straight to the periodical section.'

'Did you see anyone else around?' Shepherd asked.

'Not in that section. There were some students sitting at the tables in the middle of the floor but they were all working and looked like they'd been there for a good while,' Harry said.

'What happened after that?'

'I got to the end of the shelves and reached for the handle to open them when I realised one section hadn't closed properly. When I looked inside I could see Keith stuck there.' Harry shuddered.

'I realise this is upsetting,' Burton said, 'but we need to get the facts straight. Did you touch anything?'

'No, no, I didn't. Well, you're not supposed to, are you?'

'You didn't check for a pulse or to see if he was breathing?'

Shepherd asked, his eyebrows raised.

'Sorry, I guess I got such a shock that I didn't think.'

'Then what happened?' Burton asked.

'I just ran downstairs to get the staff to call an ambulance.'

'You didn't just call from your mobile?' Burton asked pointing at the smartphone lying on the desk. Harry picked it up and stroked it with his hand as if to protect it.

'You can't get a very good signal in that section of the library,' he said. Then he frowned.

'What is it?' Burton asked.

'The library isn't a noisy place and, at that time of the evening, the students are there for peace and quiet. But if Keith had called for help, they would have heard him.'

Shepherd paused and looked at Burton. Seeing the look Harry continued, 'That's what I'd have done. If he'd shouted, someone would have definitely heard him.'

'What would you say if I told you Professor Williams couldn't call for help?' Burton asked.

Harry frowned. 'How do you mean? I don't understand.'

'Professor Williams was already dead when the bookcases were closed on him. Prior to that he'd been hit on the head with something heavy. He was murdered.' Burton's eyes were fixed on Harry, waiting to judge his reaction.

Harry stared.

'Murdered?' He shifted awkwardly in his seat. 'By whom? There were lots of people in the library. Someone must have seen something.' The second part of his statement came out almost in a whisper.

'We have people searching the library and the surrounding area for the murder weapon. We're also speaking to everyone who was in or around the library at the time,' Shepherd said.

Harry nodded silently. 'But who would want to kill Keith? He was just an academic. Why would someone want to kill him?'

Burton fixed him with a stony glare. 'That's what we're going to find out.'

Chapter sixteen

Dan looked down at the scribbled notes in his book. People were always impressed by the lines, whirls and dots when he used shorthand, but right now he was struggling to read them himself. He'd been in and around the university library for over an hour and everywhere he turned he met blank faces.

'Sorry, but I was studying,' one student sitting at a nearby table had hissed, trying not to disturb others. 'I don't have time for gazing around.' Dan had apologised and left him to get on with his work. It looked like incredibly complicated mathematical equations and the student was welcome to them.

As he wandered between the bookshelves, Dan spoke to a few other people but had no luck. He sighed in frustration. Someone must have seen something.

Then he struck gold. A student who was gathering a pile of books from the shelves nodded when Dan asked if he'd seen anything.

'Aye, mate,' he said in a thick Geordie accent. 'I was just gettin' some books together that I needed, like, when I saw that professor, the one that got killed. Here, can you hold these for me?' He handed Dan a couple of books. Dan managed to quickly stuff them under his arm and continued scribbling.

'What was he doing?' he asked.

'He was going up in the lift. It's glass, y'see, so you can see the people in there.'

'Did you see what floor he got off on?'

'Aye, it was the second floor, where all the politics books are. Not surprising really.' The lad laughed.

'Was he with anyone?'

The lad shook his head. 'No, but he seemed to be looking for someone though cos he kept peering out of the lift window.'

'Did you see anything else?'

'Another one of the politics lecturers. I don't know his name, but everyone thinks he's hot,' he said with a wink. 'There was a skinny lad with dark hair as well. I think he's a politics postgrad but I don't know 'is name either, like.'

'Thanks, that's really useful.' Dan followed the lad back to his table, figuring carrying some books was the least he could do.

Just ahead of him, walking towards the lift, carrying his own pile of books, was Olly Murton. Dan hurried to catch up with him and got into the lift at the same time.

'Hi,' he said. 'Here, let me help with those.' He seized a couple of books before Olly could stop him. The lift doors closed and it began to descend. 'How are you?' Dan continued.

Olly shrugged. 'I'm not sure, to be honest.'

Dan nodded. 'It's got to be strange to lose a lecturer like that.'

The doors of the lift swished open on the ground floor and they pushed their way through the students waiting to get in.

Olly led the way to the self-service machines to check out his books. 'It is a bit weird,' he continued, swiping his library card through the machine and then beginning to scan the barcode in each of the books. 'I saw him earlier in the day and then–' Olly clicked his fingers '–he's gone.' Dan nodded and picked up a couple of the books as Olly tore off the receipt from the machine.

'You look like you could do with a coffee,' Dan said, turning and starting to walk towards the library's ground floor café, still holding some of Olly's books. He could see Olly glance at his watch as if he was trying to invent somewhere else he had to be but eventually he gave in and followed.

Dan kept up a flow of chatter about nothing as they walked, desperately trying to cut through Olly's emotional armour. He reckoned with another couple of minutes he'd have managed it. Olly insisted on buying the drinks and Dan was surprised to see so many twenty pound notes in Olly's wallet. That seemed quite flash compared to my time at uni, Dan thought. It was also incongruous with Olly's slightly frayed clothes and worn-down shoes. Once they were sitting opposite each other at a table, Olly looked at Dan.

'I assume this isn't a social call,' he said.

Dan blew at the froth on his cappuccino. 'What do you mean?' he asked.

Olly raised an eyebrow. 'You're here for the story, right?'

Dan shrugged. 'In the sense of I've been trying and failing to interview some people for a bit of colour, yes.'

'And you want my comment?' Olly regarded Dan very directly.

'No,' Dan lied. 'I just wanted to see how you are.'

Olly was eyeing him suspiciously. 'I don't have anything to say.'

Dan smiled. 'You're off the record and I'm not the police,' he said, putting away his notebook and pen. He pressed a few buttons on his phone to check the time. 'You seemed upset last time I saw you so I thought I'd come and see you,' he said, flipping the phone's leather cover closed and sliding it onto the table. 'In case you needed a sounding board or something.'

Olly stared into his cup of Earl Grey tea. 'I don't know how I feel to be honest.' Dan followed his instinct and stayed quiet. It often prompted people to say more. And it paid off.

'He was more than just a teacher really.' Olly looked up to see Dan, wide-eyed and frozen with his cappuccino halfway to his lips. 'Nothing like that,' he continued, shaking his head. Dan let out his breath and sipped. That would have been a turn-up for the books, he thought.

'I told you that we've been working together on a project,' Olly said.

'What about?' Dan asked.

'I can't really say. It's a bit hush-hush really.' Dan tried not to raise a sceptical eyebrow. Olly sounded like he was being a bit too cloak-and-dagger.

'It relates to something that happened during the Cold War,' Olly continued. 'Keith had found something that no one else knew about.'

Dan snorted and put his coffee cup down on to its saucer with a click. 'He should have asked Harry for help. I doubt there's much about the Cold War that he doesn't know about.'

Olly shook his head. 'No, Keith was adamant that no one else knew about it. I think he was looking forward to getting one up on Harry.'

Dan paused and decided to test the water. 'Maybe Harry could help you, now that Keith's not around. I'm sure if you asked him—'

But Olly choked on a mouthful of tea. 'No, I can't tell Harry anything. You mustn't tell him that you've talked to me about it. I told you, it's something completely new.'

'But you've not told me anything,' Dan said, shaking his head.

'I have to keep it that way,' Olly said, sounding desperate. 'I don't know what Keith did with the research. He wouldn't tell me where he hid his notes, but I can probably take a good guess.'

Olly paused and Dan took a sip of coffee, waiting for him to speak again. But Olly was getting to his feet and downing the last of his tea.

'Where are you going?' Dan asked, sitting back in surprise and putting his cup back in its saucer with a crash.

'Sorry, I've got to go. Stuff to do,' Olly said.

Dan pulled out his notebook and opened it to a clean page. He pushed it and his pen across the table. 'Can I have your number in case we need to get in touch again?' he asked.

Olly looked like he was going to refuse but then gave in to his internal struggle and grabbed the pen. He scribbled his name and a mobile number. Then, without another word, he gathered up the books and his backpack and was gone before Dan could say anything. There was no point in following him as Olly disappeared through the café door at speed, almost flattening two women coming in. Dan turned back to his coffee and took another sip. Then he picked up his phone, opened the screen and stopped the recording app. He wouldn't be able to use any of that officially, but Olly's reaction to the idea of asking Harry for help was interesting. The fact Keith seemed to have picked a topic that would give him one up on Harry was also food for thought. It also begged the question of whether Harry knew about the research.

He finished his coffee and was moving towards the exit of the library when someone tapped him on the shoulder. It was the Geordie student from earlier.

'Yer might want to head over where the police are, like, cos I think they've found something else,' he said.

Dan felt his stomach flicker. 'What do you mean?' he asked.

'I heard a bit of commotion while I was upstairs and saw a blonde lass with the police crying. They were down in that politics section.'

Dan thanked him again and started up the stairs towards the police-taped area. When he arrived, he heard Burton's voice and peered around the corner, not wanting her to know he was there. But she and Shepherd had their backs turned and were staring at a heavy-looking book in a transparent plastic evidence bag.

'And this is definitely the murder weapon?' she was saying.

'Must have just grabbed the nearest thing to hand,' Shepherd replied.

Dan turned and walked away, his brain whirring. If that was the murder weapon, then there were going to be a lot of people in the frame.

Chapter seventeen

Shepherd leaned over the table, examining the leather-bound book in the plastic bag and then looked up at the woman with short blonde hair sniffing and dabbing at her eyes with a tissue.

'What can you tell us?' he asked.

'I'm really sorry,' she began. 'I shouldn't have gone into the crime scene—'

'No, you shouldn't,' Burton interrupted.

Shepherd gave Burton a look and she stepped away, sighing heavily.

'What happened?' Shepherd asked the blonde.

'I knew the forensic guys were down at that end of the shelves,' she indicated with a shaking hand. 'I thought I could just sneak through this end and grab the book I wanted without them seeing.'

'And you went for this one?' Shepherd pointed to the book.

The woman shook her head. 'No, I wanted the one next to it. Someone had overfilled the shelves and they were stuck together when I tried to pull it out.'

'Then what happened?'

'I pulled the books apart and saw there was some red stuff on the corner of that one.' She pointed to the book in the plastic bag. 'It was a bit damp on the cover where the books had been stuck together. I touched it and then I thought it might be blood and I screamed and dropped it.'

Shepherd looked up at the two CSIs who were hovering nearby with clipboards in hand. 'Have you fingerprinted her?' he asked.

They both nodded. 'First thing we did,' said one. They looked a bit shifty, clearly worrying that they were in for a bollocking for allowing a civilian to get into the crime scene.

'OK, you can go, then,' Shepherd told the woman. 'But give me your contact details in case we need to speak to you again.'

The woman recited her name, phone number and address and then escaped the crime scene, where a waiting friend put an arm around her shoulders and led her away, still sniffing back tears.

Burton returned to the table and looked at the two CSIs. Both shuffled awkwardly.

'And she just walked into the crime scene?' Burton asked, hands on hips.

'We were down there.' One pointed to the end of the bookcases. 'She must have come in the other way. First thing I knew was when she screamed.'

'Has anyone else been by that you've seen? Anyone paying unusual attention to the area?' Shepherd asked.

One CSI nodded. 'The world and his wife have been by. They've only ever seen this on the telly so they're all trying to get a look while pretending they're not.'

'But no one else who looked like they were trying to access the crime scene?' Burton asked.

The second CSI shook his head. 'No, just people passing by and trying to get a glimpse of what we were doing.'

'OK, fine. You can get on,' Burton said and the two men moved away willingly.

Shepherd straightened up from where he was leaning on the table.

'What are you thinking? Returning to the scene of the crime to try and remove the murder weapon?'

Burton snorted. 'I doubt she's strong enough to kill anyone with a whack on the head, even with such a heavy book, but it wouldn't surprise me if the killer had the same idea of popping by to retrieve it.' She frowned. 'It would be risky to do that though with CSIs crawling all over the place. Plus since we didn't know what the murder weapon was, we would never have searched all the shelves looking for it.'

Shepherd looked down at the plastic bag on the table. 'There is a certain irony in an academic being murdered with a book,' he said with a grin.

Burton wasn't smiling. 'So it looks like the murder wasn't premeditated. It was just done with whatever came to hand.'

'A crime of passion, you mean?' Shepherd asked.

'Exactly. So we're looking for someone who was so angry with Keith Williams that they followed him here and killed him with whatever there was to hand.'

'But if there'd been an argument, surely someone would have heard. It is pretty quiet around here, especially in this area,' Shepherd said, glancing around.

'The argument needn't necessarily have happened here. Maybe this fit of temper followed on from an argument or something earlier in the day. The killer knows Williams is coming here, follows him and that's that.'

'But they could have been seen here. There must be hundreds of places on campus that are less public than this.'

'Maybe Williams wouldn't go somewhere private on campus,' Burton said, rubbing her chin.

'You mean Williams knew the person was after him and went somewhere public, thinking he'd be safe?'

'Exactly. Which means he knew who he'd pissed off and what they were capable of.'

'Shame he didn't leave us a note,' Shepherd said.

'Let's hope the killer has been more obliging,' Burton said, 'and left us a set of fingerprints.'

Chapter eighteen

Olly was sitting on a bench by the university lake. His books and backpack were on the seat beside him. Sunlight reflected off the surface of the water like thousands of flickering lights, but he was too deep in thought to appreciate the beauty. Keith Williams was dead. He wouldn't need the research now. Olly reasoned that he'd done most of the work to start with so it was his by rights. Searching Keith's body for his office keys had been distasteful and he'd tried to avoid looking at the man's staring, accusing eyes. But he had to find Keith's laptop and, as Keith never took it out of his office, he needed the keys.

Suddenly a voice right behind him shouted, 'Olly!' and a hand clapped on his shoulder. Olly jumped and, as he tried to get his breath back, his backpack was moved onto the ground and replaced by his housemate. Tom seemed incapable of speaking quietly but Olly supposed that was because he was used to roaring instructions on the rugby pitch. When Tom came home from a nightclub at two o'clock in the morning, the whole house knew about it.

'Are you OK?' Tom asked, peering at Olly. 'You look a bit funny.'

'I'm fine, I'm just tired,' Olly replied.

Tom gazed at the lake for a moment and said, 'You know that professor who was killed in the library?'

'Yes,' Olly said warily.

'Well, apparently he was killed with a book. A mate of Julie's found it on the shelf with blood on it. She said it was still wet.' Tom's eyes gleamed with ghoulish glee. 'Makes me think I'm better off staying away from the library. Too dangerous,' he said, shaking his head.

'Do you even know where the library is?' Olly asked, with a mock frown.

Tom grinned. 'I think I've been there once or twice.' He was a second year geography student who never seemed to do any work, appearing to divide his time between the rugby field and the pub.

Then Tom stared at Olly. 'You're not working,' he stated. 'And you're outside.' He seemed surprised.

'I needed some air,' Olly said, giving a pale smile.

Tom laughed. 'I would too if I spent all my time with my nose in a book.'

'At some point you are going to have to do some study, or you'll fail your end-of-year exams,' Olly told him, wagging a finger, but smiling at the same time.

Tom waved a hand airily. 'Loads of time to prepare for that,' he said. 'Anyway, I'm going to the pub with the lads. Want to come?'

Olly shook his head, remembering how ill he'd felt after his last daytime trip to the pub with The Lads. The hangover had been the worst thing he'd ever experienced. He stared at the lake, now feeling sicker than that occasion, and knew without a doubt that this was the worst experience of his life. He knew he'd never be able to get rid of the image of Keith's body lying on the floor. He hadn't expected a dead body to look as though it could get up off the floor and walk.

Tom stood up, making him jump. 'I've got to go. So, are you coming along?'

'I might come later,' Olly said, glancing at his watch. 'I've got some stuff to do.'

Tom nodded. 'OK, text me when you're done and I'll let you know where we are.'

Olly watched Tom walk away, all broad shoulders and swagger, attracting female attention with ease. Then he stood up, jingling the keys in his pocket. The sooner he got this over with, the better.

Chapter nineteen

Professor Desmond Danby, the head of the politics department, looked at Burton and Shepherd, pale with shock.

'This is just terrible. I've never had a colleague die before. Well, not while I was working with them. And now you say he was murdered?' He almost whispered the last word and then sighed heavily. 'Just at the start of term. This couldn't have happened at a worse time.'

Burton raised an eyebrow. 'Is there a good time for one of your academic staff to be murdered?' she asked.

Danby shook his head. 'Sorry, that came out wrong. Of course I'm sorry about Keith. He wasn't an easy man to get along with, but he's a talented academic—' he sighed '—was a talented academic. I don't even know where to start when it comes to replacing him. Well, not replacing him, but finding someone to cover his lectures and tutorials.'

Burton looked at Shepherd. The sergeant's face was impassive. Burton shook her head slightly and continued.

'Professor Danby, we've been trying to track down Professor Williams' next of kin.'

Danby snorted. 'Good luck with that.'

'How do you mean?' Burton asked, tilting her head to one side.

'He doesn't have any. Or at least none that I've heard of for a long time. There's an ex-wife somewhere and at least one grown-up son, but I don't think Keith was in touch with either of them. I've no idea where you would find them. I don't think we've even got any details in his human resources record but I'll have someone pull that for you.' He made a note on a jotter tucked beneath his computer keyboard.

'He had no one?' Shepherd asked, sounding almost sympathetic.

Danby smiled. 'Don't feel too sorry for him. Keith brought it all on himself. Like I said, he could be a very arrogant and unpleasant man. He wasn't what you'd call a people person.'

Shepherd frowned. 'How do you mean?' he asked.

'Keith had a brilliant mind,' Danby said. 'He was a clever chap but he lacked certain social skills.'

'He was rude, you mean?' Shepherd asked, looking up from his notes.

'He could be. I've always got the impression his students don't like him. I've had a few complaints from people, but it was mostly for being over-critical. Students seem to consider that rude these days. If you were lucky and he liked you, he would usually be OK. If he didn't like you, he could make life almost impossible.'

'Was there anyone whose life he was making impossible at the moment?' Burton asked.

Danby took a deep breath. 'He and Harry Evans have an ongoing problem,' he said, choosing his words carefully.

Burton narrowed her eyes. 'Problem?'

Danby sighed. 'This is a university. It's full of very clever people who are often in competition for grant funding. It can be awkward if more than one person is bidding for the same funding pot.'

'Meaning?'

'Keith was top dog for a long time until Harry came on the scene.

I chose to employ Harry after reading a paper he'd written and hearing him lecture. He's so passionate, so brilliant. I'd almost say he was like a young Keith, but he had more personality.'

'Did you ever tell Professor Williams that?' Shepherd asked.

Danby laughed. 'God, no. I would never be that cruel, even to someone as difficult as Keith. It would just have made the situation worse.'

Shepherd looked at him. 'There was a situation?'

'You've met Harry. He's a very good-looking chap and the students hang on his every word,' Danby said. 'He can make even the dullest subjects sound interesting and it really inspires the students. I think Keith was jealous of that.'

'Students didn't hang off Professor Williams' every word?' Burton asked.

Danby shook his head. 'Like I said, Keith wasn't a people person. Especially in later years because I think he'd become frustrated, mostly because he wasn't publishing very much and his "expert opinion" wasn't being sought.' Danby sketched the quote marks in the air. 'Then Harry arrived and soon developed a reputation as a superb teacher, as well as a talented researcher and writer. It doesn't help that the students refer to him as the "hottie" of the department.' Burton raised an eyebrow and Danby smiled. 'They think we don't hear that kind of thing, but we do.'

'You said they had problems. What form did their animosity take?' Shepherd asked. 'Did they argue a lot?'

Danby paused and then said, 'I've never really heard them argue to be honest, but Harry is under a lot of pressure.' He sighed. 'Harry is struggling to get anything published. It's been a while since he even had an article in a magazine and when you add marital strife to that—' Danby stopped speaking as if fearing he'd gone too far.

Burton frowned. 'Marital strife?' she asked.

Danby sighed heavily. 'Harry's wife miscarried a child last year. It was a child that was very much wanted and the grief has pushed them apart,' he said. 'He's working more and more hours to keep away from home but it's not helping his publication rate. At the moment it's all I can do to help him keep his job.' He looked at the detectives. 'You won't tell him about the threat to his job, will you? I don't think he knows how far it's got and he doesn't need any more stress.'

Shepherd raised an eyebrow. 'You can lose your job for not publishing articles?'

Danby nodded. 'A university is judged by the quality of its research, as well as teaching,' he said. 'We need our academics to be publishing quality books and papers to maintain that standard.'

'Did Professor Williams know about Dr Evans' publishing problem?' Burton asked.

Danby nodded. 'I imagine so. He'd never have been told specifically but this is a very close environment, so it's difficult to keep anything secret for long.'

'You said that Professor Williams had problems too?' Shepherd asked.

'He was in a similar publishing situation to Harry except his "dry spell" has been much longer,' Danby said, again sketching quote marks in the air. When Burton raised an eyebrow, Danby said, 'That's how Keith used to describe it if anyone queried him.'

'Had he been threatened with the sack too?' Shepherd asked.

'Not yet,' Danby said, looking down at his hands. 'He has friends on the university board and they seemed to be giving him the benefit of the doubt. He's been using it as a stick to poke Harry with. Keith got pleasure from needling people and because Harry is under pressure, I think it was getting to him.'

'Did you not think to lessen the pressure?' Shepherd demanded, earning a glare from Burton, but Desmond Danby was unperturbed.

'I can only deal with it if it's reported to me and Harry never reported it,' he said.

Shepherd exhaled heavily and Burton stepped in.

'Were there other problems?' she asked.

Danby sighed. 'It's an age-old story but Keith did accuse Harry of plagiarising his work. They research in a similar field, and in Harry's doctoral dissertation he'd used some of Keith's work,' Danby explained. 'Keith said Harry had copied it and not given him credit. We investigated and there wasn't enough evidence.'

Burton frowned. 'Not enough evidence?' she asked. 'That's not the same as being innocent of the crime, is it?'

Danby shook his head. 'Sorry, I put that badly. What I mean was that there wasn't enough evidence that Harry hadn't referenced the parts of Keith's book that he'd used.'

'So he had used it?' Burton asked.

Danby nodded. 'That's standard practice. All academics use each other's work, but it's making sure that you reference everything that's important.'

Burton frowned. 'And Dr Evans hadn't done that?'

'Of course he had,' Danby said impatiently.

'But Professor Williams wouldn't let it go?' Shepherd asked.

Danby sighed. 'Sadly not. He used the same interpretation as you did.' He indicated to Burton. 'It reared its ugly head several times over the years and I warned Keith each time. I had the impression that he was just stirring and didn't really believe it himself.'

'How would Dr Evans have felt if he found out that Professor Williams kept telling people about it?' Shepherd asked.

'I assume he didn't know because he never said anything to me. Keith was very good at talking behind people's backs, but not using a frontal attack, for want of a better phrase. Whether any of the people he spoke to said anything to Harry I don't know. As to how

Harry would react, you'd have to ask him.' He glanced at the clock. 'Is there anything else? I have a meeting to prepare for.'

'Not for now,' Burton said, getting to her feet. Shepherd clicked the nib of his pen away and put it and his notebook in his suit jacket pocket before standing up too.

Desmond Danby slapped his hands on the arms of his chair and stood up. 'You wanted to see Keith's office. Let me lead the way.' He seized a large bunch of keys from his desk drawer and led the way out of his room.

As they turned the corner into the next corridor, a loud slam made them all jump. A student had come out of an office just ahead of them, closing the door loudly.

Danby stared. 'Olly? What are you doing? That's Keith's office. How did you get in there?'

The student jumped at Danby's voice and turned to face them. 'The door wasn't locked,' he said quickly.

'It was. I locked it myself,' Danby insisted, hands on hips.

'It was open when I got here,' said Olly, but Burton could have sworn she heard a jingle of keys in his pocket.

Danby scowled. 'It shouldn't have been,' he said. 'What were you doing in there?'

Olly looked at him, wide-eyed. 'Keith borrowed a library book from me and I wanted to get it back,' he said, clearly trying to resist the urge to push his hands into his pockets. 'I thought it might be in his office, but it's not.'

Danby walked forward and shooed Olly away from the door. 'Keep out of there in future or the police will have something to say to you.' He indicated Burton and Shepherd.

Olly stared at them and began to edge away down the corridor.

'Who was that?' Burton asked.

'Olly Murton, one of our postgraduate students.'

Shepherd raised an eyebrow. 'Olly Murton?' he asked. Burton looked at him, puzzled.

Danby nodded. 'Sometimes I think we give them too much leeway, thinking they can just walk into people's offices. Keith wasn't even his supervisor.'

'Who is?' Burton asked.

'Harry Evans.' Danby shrugged and turned back to the office door. He tried the handle and the door didn't move. 'See, locked,' he said. He selected a key from the bunch and unlocked it, muttering under his breath.

Keith Williams' office was the opposite of Harry Evans'. The desk was perfectly tidy with everything set at right angles. A whole dust-free shelf was filled with books written by Williams himself. There were no family photos, personal touches or knick-knacks. Burton stood in the middle of the room looking around, while Shepherd took a closer look at the desk, snapping on a pair of latex gloves.

'Does anything look different?' Burton asked Danby, who had remained in the doorway.

'Different?' Danby asked. 'How do you mean?'

'Is anything missing or out of place?' Burton gestured around the room. 'It looks very clean and tidy. Was it always like this?'

'Keith was always a very tidy person, but yes, I suppose it does look tidier than when he was working.' Danby paused and then frowned. 'His laptop is missing.'

Shepherd looked at him. 'What do you mean?'

Danby pointed. 'It's always on his desk. He never moves it.'

'Never?' Shepherd asked, frowning.

'It's a standing joke – not to his face obviously,' Danby said, 'that he hasn't realised it's portable.'

Shepherd gave a slight smile and began to pull at the desk drawers. 'Maybe he put it away in here.'

Danby frowned. 'It looks the way it does when he's preparing to go on holiday.'

'Was he due to have time off?' Burton asked.

'No.' Danby shook his head. 'At least, he hadn't told me about any or filled in the necessary paperwork. I'd have to sign it off.'

Shepherd looked up at Burton and made a tiny movement of his head. Understanding, Burton turned to Danby and said, 'I think we can take it from here. If you leave the keys, we'll lock up and drop them back to you when we're finished.' Danby recognised the dismissal and left. Burton closed the door and turned to Shepherd.

'Do you know that student?' she asked.

Shepherd nodded. 'I know the name. Dan Sullivan mentioned him outside the library last night. He said Olly knows Keith Williams well.'

Burton raised an eyebrow and then pointed to Williams' desk. 'What have you found?' she asked.

'Did you notice that student was rattling when he left?' Shepherd asked.

'Yes, it sounded like he had a set of keys.'

Shepherd nodded. 'He used them to get into the room and also into this drawer.' He beckoned her to join him on the far side of the desk. 'Look.' He tugged the drawer on one side. 'Locked. But on the other side—' He demonstrated by pulling the drawer open.

'Hmmm, why would you lock one side of the desk and not the other?' Burton asked, hands on her hips.

'And a locked drawer is a funny place to keep a library book,' Shepherd added.

Burton raised an eyebrow. 'You think our student was looking for something else?'

'Clearly,' Shepherd said. 'Although I have no idea what it is.'

'Why did he have keys?' Burton asked.

'They clearly didn't share the office.' Shepherd gestured around. 'There's no room for a second desk or any space to work.'

Burton frowned. 'Do you remember seeing any keys on the inventory from the crime scene? From Williams' personal effects?'

Shepherd screwed up his forehead. 'Not off the top of my head. But they would have gone with the body surely?'

'Brody turned his pockets out at the scene and showed me his wallet,' Burton said. 'But I don't remember seeing any keys.'

'What are you thinking?'

'I may be barking up entirely the wrong tree here, but what if the keys that student has are Williams' own set?'

Shepherd frowned. 'Taken with or without permission?' he asked.

'That's what we need to find out.' Burton glanced around the room. 'Right, get forensics down here and then we'll find Mr Murton.'

Chapter twenty

They found Olly Murton, as to be expected, in the library. Shepherd approached the desk where he was studying and politely but firmly invited him for a coffee. Burton stood by the stairs and they walked Olly down to the ground floor café. The student looked uncomfortable as Burton kept her steely eye on him until Shepherd returned with coffee for himself and Burton, and an Earl Grey tea for Olly. Once they were all settled, Burton began.

'You knew Keith Williams, yes?' she asked.

Olly nodded. 'He was one of my lecturers. I took a course of his last year.'

'Did you like him?'

'He was all right, I suppose?' Olly gave a shrug. 'I didn't know him that well.'

'We've heard differently,' Burton said, leaning forward on the table and clasping her hands. 'We've heard that you spent a lot of time together.'

Olly looked down at the surface of the table and said nothing.

'Oh, come on, Olly,' Shepherd said, eyes locked on to Olly's face. 'You must have been friends. Why else would he have given you keys to his office?'

'He didn't give—' Olly stopped speaking and closed his eyes.

Then he rested his face in one hand, elbow balanced on the edge of the table.

'If he didn't give you the keys, where did you get them?' Shepherd asked, staring intently at Olly. The student was silent but Shepherd continued to stare at him. Olly didn't feel good about what he'd done. But if he admitted it, the police would suspect him. Or was it too late and they already thought he was involved? What was the worst they could do to him? He hadn't really broken the law, had he? It would certainly change how the police viewed him, but what did that matter now? Keith was dead.

Eyes fixed on the surface of the table, he took a deep breath and said quickly, 'I took them from him.'

'From him?' Shepherd was puzzled. 'From his office, do you mean?'

Olly shook his head as if he wanted the chair he was sitting on to swallow him whole.

'So where?' asked Shepherd leaning forward. Burton sat with her arms folded and eyes fixed on Olly.

'I got them from him in the library. When he was—'

Shepherd's face twisted as if he had a bad smell under his nose. Burton sat forward, leaning her forearms on the table.

'Let me see if I've got this right,' she said, her face mirroring Shepherd's. 'You took the keys from your friend's body, when he was dead or dying on the floor.'

Olly nodded, unable to speak.

Shepherd sat back in his chair, shaking his head. 'So, instead of getting help, you pick his pocket. Why stop at his keys? Why not grab his wallet while you were there? His mobile phone?'

'No, I—'

'Because, to be honest, Olly, it wouldn't surprise me if you did. Once you stooped to the depths of corpse-robbing—'

'It wasn't like that,' Olly burst out. 'I found him, yes, but he was already dead. He owed me, so I took his keys.'

'You just left him there? You didn't even stop to report it?' Shepherd was staring at Olly, a look of shock on his face.

Olly nodded miserably. 'I heard someone coming and I knew how it would look so I just got out of there.'

'What were you doing in the library?' Burton asked.

'I was studying.'

Burton raised an eyebrow. 'Bit late, wasn't it?'

Olly shrugged. 'I study all the time. Postgrad courses are tough.'

'And how did you come across Professor Williams' body?' Burton asked still leaning over the table towards him.

'I was looking for a book. I heard a thump so I went to see what had happened.'

'And you saw Professor Williams?' Shepherd asked.

Olly shook his head. 'I didn't see him at first because he was in between the bookcases.'

'And when you did see him, all you did was steal his keys?' Shepherd was still disgusted.

Olly avoided looking at him. 'When I got to him, I could see that he was already dead. He wasn't moving. I decided to grab his keys and then get help but I heard someone coming so I ran.'

'You didn't see who it was?'

'No. I assume it was Harry.'

Burton was silent for a moment. 'Did you see anyone else? Hear anything?'

'No I didn't.'

'Where did you go after you took his keys?' Shepherd asked. He couldn't get the disgusted look off his face.

'I went back to my table and—'

'You went back to studying?' Shepherd leaned forward on the

table, suddenly closing the space between himself and Olly. 'You found someone dead and just left it at that?'

'I didn't know what to do,' Olly protested, sitting back away from Shepherd. 'I'd barely been there a couple of minutes when the fire alarm went off and we were told to go outside.'

Burton took a deep breath and puffed out her cheeks. 'What do you know about Harry Evans?' she asked.

Olly looked surprised at the change of topic. 'Harry's OK. He can be a bit aggressive though. Especially recently.'

Burton raised an eyebrow. 'Aggressive?'

Olly nodded. 'He shouted at me last week because I disturbed him in his office while he was working.'

'Is that normal behaviour for lecturers?' Shepherd asked.

Olly shrugged. 'No, but Harry could be like that if you broke his concentration. Actually, he's been worse recently.'

'He'd expected to have peace and quiet in his office?' Shepherd asked.

Olly nodded. 'I guess so. His office is probably the only place he can avoid people.' He smiled. 'Where Harry goes, the entire female student population, and some of the male, go too.'

Burton was frowning. 'Was he aggressive with anyone else?'

Olly looked awkward for a moment. 'I heard him having a shouting match with Keith a day or so ago.'

'Really?' Burton asked. 'What was it about?'

'I'm not quite sure.' Olly squirmed in his chair. 'It started out with Keith talking about a job interview.'

'Professor Williams had been for a job interview?' Burton asked.

'No, I think Harry had. Keith was talking about knowing the woman who had interviewed him and saying that he would tell her about Harry plagiarising his work.'

Burton and Shepherd exchanged a look.

'You knew about that?' Shepherd asked.

'I think there's probably a lot of people who know the story,' Olly said.

'Did you believe it?' Shepherd asked.

Olly frowned. 'I can't see Harry being stupid enough to copy someone else's work. It's too much of a risk.'

Shepherd looked up from his notebook. 'What would happen if he got caught?' he asked.

Olly looked at him in surprise. 'Well, it would ruin him,' he said as if Shepherd should already know that. 'He'd lose his job and his reputation would be destroyed. He'd never risk it.'

'Did you overhear anything else?' There was a note in Shepherd's voice that told Olly what he thought of eavesdroppers.

Olly paused. 'Harry threw something at him.'

Shepherd sat up straight. 'Dr Evans threw something?'

'Yes. I don't think it hit Keith but then—'

'What?' asked Burton.

'When Keith left, Harry followed him into the corridor and said if Keith didn't leave him alone he'd make him pay.'

Burton and Shepherd exchanged a look.

'What did you think he meant?' Burton asked.

Olly shrugged. 'I suppose I thought he meant he'd report him to Desmond or something. I didn't think he'd kill him.'

Burton leaned forward on the table again. 'You think Dr Evans would kill Professor Williams over that?'

'I don't know,' Olly said earnestly. 'All I know is that Harry's been really wound up for weeks and he threw something at Keith. I've never heard of him being violent before.' He paused and sipped his cup of tea, then looked at the two detectives expectantly. They both looked back at him.

'Any other problems?' Burton asked.

Olly frowned. 'There was sort of something else. I'm not sure.'

'Like what?' Burton was feeling the first pangs of frustration.

'Well, Keith was working on some new research, which I reckon Harry would love to get his hands on.'

'Does he know about it?'

'I'm not sure. I thought Keith had kept it all secret but Harry was kind of asking me about it after Keith died. If Keith had any notes or anything, it would have been on his laptop.'

'Is that why you went into his office earlier today? Looking for his laptop?' Burton asked.

'No, I told you I was looking for a book.'

'Oh, come on, Mr Murton, we weren't born yesterday. We both know that you had his keys to let yourself into his office. You must think we're stupid if you think we're going to believe you went there to get a book. One of the desk drawers had been unlocked. You searched his office, didn't you? Why?'

When Olly said nothing, Burton slapped the table with the palm of her hand. The couple on the next table looked around in surprise. 'You weren't looking for a book, you know that and I know that. You wanted his laptop, didn't you? But it wasn't in the office?'

Olly shook his head. 'No, it wasn't. But I wasn't really going to steal it, just make sure it was safe.'

Burton snorted. 'You must think we came down in the last shower,' she said. 'You were expecting it to be in his office?'

Olly shifted in his seat, trying to think of what to say next, but then nodded. 'But it should have been there because Keith never takes it out of his office.'

'There's nowhere else he might be keeping it?' Shepherd asked. 'Might he have taken it home?'

Olly shook his head. 'Like I said, he never takes it out of the office.'

Burton drained her coffee cup and glared at Olly. 'Mr Murton, you are not helping yourself here. Your story sounds very dodgy. I hope I'm wrong, but if I'm not, the next time we have this conversation it will be in a police interview room and you'll be under caution. Do you understand?'

Olly didn't raise his eyes from the table but he nodded. Without another word Burton got to her feet and strode out of the coffee shop with Shepherd in hot pursuit.

'There's another name to add to the list of people who might want Keith Williams dead,' Shepherd said after the door swung closed behind them.

'Yes. He knows more about that research than he's letting on. But if they were working together, why kill Williams?' Burton asked.

'Maybe Olly wanted the research for himself. He was prepared to steal Williams' keys from his body,' Shepherd said.

Burton's jaw was clenched. 'Did he find the body, or did he try to take Williams' keys while he was alive? They struggle and Olly grabs the nearest thing to hand?'

'Then he hears someone coming, takes the keys and runs,' Shepherd added, pushing open the door, letting them out into the fresh air. 'That's a good theory. If he's in the library a lot, then no one would really notice him wandering around.'

'Did the search at Williams' house not find the laptop?' Burton asked.

Shepherd shook his head. Before he could say anything else, Burton's mobile beeped. She pulled it out of her pocket and tapped at the screen several times.

'What's our next move?' Shepherd asked.

Burton held up her phone. 'We've been summoned to the morgue.'

'Oh joy.'

'Cheer up, Brody might have something definitive for us.'

Chapter twenty-one

When Dan got home that evening, he found Ed in the kitchen, wrapped in an apron and browning some mince.

'What are you doing?' he asked.

Ed waved a wooden spoon and grinned. 'If I say cooking, it sounds facetious, doesn't it?'

'It certainly does, but then I kind of asked for it,' Dan said with a grin. 'What's for dinner?'

'Spaghetti Bolognese,' Ed replied. 'Are you in?'

'Nowhere else to be.'

'I should be hurt that you're only eating my dinner cos you've got no other option,' Ed said. Dan grinned and fetched them both a beer from the fridge.

'Not with Emma away.' He pulled a bottle opener from the cutlery drawer and popped off the lids. 'Can I do anything to help?' he asked, sliding one bottle within easy reach of Ed. The head chef seized the bottle, clinked it to Dan's and took a swig.

'Ahhhhh,' he sighed. 'The first mouthful is always the best.'

Dan laughed. 'Can I do anything?'

'Actually, yes.' Ed pointed to a tin of tomatoes on the kitchen counter. 'Can you open that?'

Dan took the tin opener out of the cutlery drawer. It wasn't easy to use for a left-handed person, particularly one whose mind was not on the task in hand. All he could think about was Keith Williams. He knew the man was nasty, and liable to upset people, but enough to make someone kill him? And who would have done it? Would Harry really have killed him? Harry wasn't a big bloke, but Williams was out of condition. If Harry had attacked him, what would he have done? He turned to hand the now-opened tin to Ed and found his flatmate staring at him.

'What?' Dan asked.

'I know you find that tin opener difficult,' Ed said, taking the tomatoes. 'But you don't have to completely ignore me while you're using it.' He turned back to the cooker.

'Oh, sorry, I wasn't thinking about the tin opener,' Dan said, walking to the sink and rinsing tomato juice off it. He dried it and walked back to put it in the drawer.

'What were you thinking about?' Ed asked, over the loud hissing from the saucepan as he poured the tomatoes over the fried mince.

'This case.'

Ed looked around, wooden spoon suspended over the pan. 'What case?'

'The murder at the university. Keith Williams.'

Ed half turned his body away from the cooker so that he could stir the sauce and look at Dan at the same time. 'What about it?'

'I think Harry Evans might have done it.'

Ed's eyes widened. 'Your old lecturer? Why?'

Dan leaned against the kitchen counter and swigged his beer. 'When I saw him before all this happened, he seemed OK. Not stressed, not worried, just chatty, y'know.'

'And now?'

'Now he seems really irritable. I kinda pushed him a bit, pretended I thought he'd done it and he told me to keep my nose out of it.'

Ed raised his eyebrows. 'I'm not surprised he said that if you were accusing him of murder. What makes you think it was him?'

'The whole change of attitude. The fact he found the body.' Ed made a snorting noise and turned back to the pan. Dan ignored him and continued 'The fact that he seems less concerned about Keith dying than finding the research he was working on.'

'What?' Ed frowned. 'What do you mean by that?'

Dan rubbed his nose. 'It's something one of his postgrad students told me. Olly's been working on some research with Keith, so he says, and when he saw Harry after Keith died, Harry was asking him about the research.'

'Why's that a problem?' Ed took a spoonful of sauce and tasted it. 'Hmm, I hope you don't mind it being a bit garlicky.'

'I'll cope.'

Dan watched as Ed took a small jar out of a cupboard and shook it over the contents of the pan. Ed put the jar back and looked at Dan. 'Go on,' he said, pointing with the wooden spoon in his hand. 'Why is Harry asking about the research a problem? Maybe he thinks it's interesting and is worried it won't get published now that Keith is dead.'

Dan walked to the kitchen doorway and leaned against the frame. 'But Harry isn't supposed to know anything about it. He and Keith had a massive falling out years ago about Harry supposedly copying Keith's work in his doctoral dissertation. After that, Keith was apparently really weird about Harry knowing about his work.'

'Has this Olly said anything about what it is?' Ed asked.

'That's just it. Listen to this.' Dan pulled out his phone and played the relevant clip of his interview with Olly. Ed listened carefully and raised his eyebrows at the end.

'Wow, he really doesn't want you to tell Harry about it, does he?' Ed put a lid on the pan and turned the heat down. Then he leaned back against the kitchen cabinet opposite Dan, beer bottle in hand.

Dan nodded. 'I know. What does he think Harry's going to do if he finds out what the research is all about?'

'Search me.' Ed saw the look on Dan's face and asked, 'What's wrong?'

Dan took a sip from his beer bottle. 'I don't know. I've got a feeling that there's more to this than meets the eye.'

'How do you mean?'

Dan put the bottle down on the counter and rubbed his face with both hands. 'I was talking to a lad in the library who was there on the night Keith was killed. He said he saw Keith but then he also saw two other people who, from his descriptions, could have been Harry and Olly.'

'But it's not in dispute that they were there, is it?'

Dan shook his head. 'Well, Harry has admitted to being there, but Olly told me he hadn't been inside.'

'So,' Ed asked, 'what's the problem?'

'The lad didn't say when exactly he saw them, but what if Olly and Harry were there together?'

Ed took a breath and puffed out his cheeks. 'I don't know, Dan. I mean, are you saying that you think they killed him together?'

'I don't want to think that, but—'

'Okay,' Ed said, holding his hands up as if in surrender. 'You said Harry might have wanted Keith's research and that's fair enough. I mean, apart from the fact it's crazy to think that he'd kill someone for that research, no matter how important it is. But didn't you say that Olly was working on the project with Keith? Why would he want Keith dead? Surely that puts an end to their working together?'

'But what if Olly wanted the research for himself?'

Ed snorted. 'I'm still struggling with the idea that anyone would kill over a research project.'

Dan shrugged. 'It depends on what they're researching, doesn't it?'

'I don't know, mate,' Ed said, frowning. 'You think that could be it? That whatever they're researching is worth money or something?'

'It could be something prestigious, but I think it's more likely that you're right and it's worth money. I know academics have to keep publishing stuff or they can lose their job, but what if there was the nice little bonus of making some money on the side? Maybe that's why Harry did it.'

'And what about Olly?' Ed asked. 'He's not trying to keep his job.'

'No, but he might be trying to get one.' Dan picked up his beer bottle and pointed it at Ed. 'If he can get credit on a big piece of work, that would be a really good start to an academic career, wouldn't it?'

Shaking his head, Ed walked across to the cooker, lifted the saucepan lid and gave the contents a stir. 'What are you going to do?'

'The only thing I can do is talk to them both again, separately, and see if I can get either to open up.'

Ed frowned at him. 'Just be careful. I mean, if you're right about Harry Evans, he already knows that you're questioning whether he did it.'

'You think he'd kill me?' Dan tried, and failed, to keep the sceptical note out of his voice.

Ed glared at him. 'We've had this conversation before, Dan. The conversation where I tell you to be careful and not to put the story ahead of your own personal safety. Remember, last time that ended up with us getting shot at in the woods.'

'That's true,' Dan said. 'But it won't be like that this time.'

Ed exhaled heavily. 'Just think about what you're doing. If either or both are involved, then you don't want to end up caught between them.'

'You think I should tell the police?'

'Maybe.' Ed moved to another kitchen cupboard, opened the door and took out a packet of pasta. He looked around at Dan who stood leaning against the counter, arms folded, staring at the floor. 'There's no use sulking,' Ed remarked, opening the packet and measuring the dried shapes onto two plates placed next to the cooker.

'I'm not sulking. I just don't really have anything to tell them at the moment,' Dan said. 'I don't want to drop either Harry or Olly in it with Burton unless I've got good reason to.'

'What are you going to do?' Ed asked, raising his voice as he poured boiling water from the kettle into a second saucepan and put it onto the cooker.

'I need to speak to them both again. I take your point,' Dan said holding up a hand to stop Ed from arguing. 'I'm going to talk to them as if I don't believe anything and then see where that takes me.' He sighed.

'What?' Ed asked, looking at the pan to check that the water was boiling enough.

'Usually my gut instinct would tell me who it is and I'd be pleased about it. But for once, I'd be quite happy to be completely wrong.'

'Wonders will never cease,' Ed said, pouring the pasta into the boiling water.

Chapter twenty-two

As they pushed their way through the doors to the morgue, Burton shivered.

'Why can't we have update meetings in her office?' she complained, huddling into her suit jacket. Shepherd grinned and leaned his bulky frame against the sink in the corner of the room, hands thrust into his trouser pockets.

'Maybe she likes making you suffer?' he suggested.

'Why would she do that?'

'Because you're always hassling her for quick results,' Shepherd grinned.

Burton gave a snort. 'She loves it. She thrives on the challenge.'

'Not your kind of challenge she doesn't,' came Brody's voice from the doorway, making them jump. Burton cleared her throat and began to speak, but Brody cut across her with a smile. 'Save it. I've heard it all before.'

'What have you got for us?' Burton asked, returning the smile.

Brody picked up her clipboard. 'Do you realise you start every single conversation we have with those words?' she asked, still smiling.

Shepherd laughed. 'She's so demanding.'

'Never even offers me a coffee,' said Brody, putting down the clipboard and walking across to the refrigeration unit.

'OK, OK, I'll buy you a coffee if I can just get a straight answer,' Burton said, raising her hands in surrender.

'Oooh, I think you'll be treating me to more than that when I tell you what I know,' said Brody, sliding out Keith Williams' shelf and pulling back the sheet that covered him. Burton looked at Williams and then back at Brody.

'Well? Don't keep us in suspense.'

'The book is definitely the murder weapon.' Brody picked the book up from where it sat on a metal tray on the work surface and held it against the wound. 'He was hit two or three times relatively hard but what's interesting is that I was right. The blows were delivered on exactly the same spot.'

'Three blows? On exactly the same spot?' Shepherd frowned.

'Almost exactly. What's wrong?' Brody's face was stern.

'Is that not a bit weird? Was he immobilised in some way?'

'I was getting to that,' Brody said. 'You're right, he was immobilised.'

'Drugs?' Burton asked.

'No, the good old-fashioned way. It looks like they got him on the ground on his chest and then knelt on his back. There's a bruise on his spine that would indicate that. I almost missed it because of the other ante-mortem bruising from the bookcases. One of his spinal discs has been compressed by the pressure that was put on him.'

'Sounds painful,' said Shepherd.

Brody nodded. 'Most likely and in that position you wouldn't be able to scream at all.'

'Hence the reason no one heard anything,' Burton said, nodding.

'Yes.'

Shepherd frowned. 'Would it need to be a big person to do that?' he asked.

Brody shook her head. 'No, if you trip him up and then attack while he's winded by that, I could have done it,' she said. 'You'd need some arm strength but, with the weight of the book, gravity would do most of the work for you. The blood on the book is his.'

'Any clues about our killer?' Shepherd asked.

'No fibres or anything, but there's a nice clear set of fingerprints on the lower part of the book and they don't match Professor Williams or the girl who found it.' She looked triumphant. 'If you bring me some fingers, I can match them for you.'

*

'What's next?' Shepherd asked as they pushed through the double doors out of the morgue.

Burton frowned. 'Let's get Dr Evans in the interview room and find out more about him throwing things at colleagues.'

Chapter twenty-three

Harry stared at the blank cream wall of the police interview room. He knew he shouldn't have lied to the police, but what choice did he have? He took a deep breath to try and get his racing heart under control. What did they know? He was sure they couldn't have found a witness. He'd been certain there was no one around.

The door opened making him jump. Burton and Shepherd entered the room. They sat opposite him and the recorder was set in motion. Shepherd explained who was present and then they both looked expectantly at him.

Harry knew he was about to fall into the oldest trick in the interrogation book, but he couldn't stay silent.

'Why do you want to speak to me again? I've told you everything I know.'

Burton frowned. 'We want to speak to you again about the night that Keith Williams was killed.'

Harry spread his hands wide in a gesture of innocence. 'But we've been over this. I don't know what else I can tell you,' he said, pleading eyes looking from Burton to Shepherd and back again.

'Humour me,' said Burton. She sat back in her chair and folded her arms. 'You claim you found him dead.'

'I did find him dead,' Harry insisted.

'You also claim you were in your office until half past five that night, yes?'

'I don't claim it, it's true,' Harry said, wondering where this was going.

'Can anyone vouch for you?' Burton asked.

Harry thought for a moment and then said, 'Yes, I spoke to Natalya Ellis as I was leaving. She has the office next to Keith's and—' He closed his eyes, angry with himself for giving something away so easily.

'Why were you outside Professor Williams' office?' Shepherd asked. 'You don't need to walk that way to leave the building, do you?'

Harry looked down at the table. 'No, I don't.'

'So, why were you outside his office?' Shepherd asked again.

Harry said nothing.

Shepherd raised his eyebrows. 'Are you refusing to answer?' he asked.

Still, Harry said nothing.

Shepherd sighed. 'Dr Evans, we've heard from a witness who said that they overheard an argument between you and Professor Williams the day before he was killed. What was that about?' he asked.

Again, Harry said nothing.

'Come on, Dr Evans, this isn't going to go well for you if you don't say anything,' Burton said. 'All you're doing is making me more suspicious that you have something to hide.' She paused and stared at Harry unblinkingly. Harry refused to meet her eyes and stared down at the table surface.

'It must have been quite an argument,' Shepherd said. 'We've heard that you threw something at him. Is that normal office behaviour around here?'

Harry looked up and met Shepherd's gaze. 'Who told you that?'

'Did you throw something?' Shepherd asked, ignoring Harry's question.

Harry hung his head. 'Yes I did,' he said quietly.

'What did you throw?'

'A magazine. It didn't even hit him,' Harry said, defensively.

Shepherd's eyes were calmly looking into his face. 'You seem to have quite a temper, Dr Evans,' he said.

'No, not really,' Harry said, trying to control his irritation.

'Only with Professor Williams?' Shepherd asked.

Harry said nothing.

'Although,' Shepherd continued, 'we have also heard that you've been aggressive with other people. Did you throw things at them too?'

'What? No, I've never been aggressive towards people. Who said that?' Harry demanded.

Shepherd raised an eyebrow at Harry's tone. 'A student told us you've shouted at him a few times recently,' he said.

Harry exhaled heavily. 'Olly Murton. Bloody Olly, I might have known.'

Burton raised an eyebrow. 'It sounds like you don't much like Mr Murton.'

'It's not a case of not liking him,' Harry said. 'He always seems to be around when you least want him to be, listening at keyholes.'

Shepherd looked at Burton and she shrugged.

'When you went to Professor Williams' office on the evening he died, what did you want?' she asked. 'Was it a continuation of that row?'

'No, I just—' Harry stopped, not even sure what he'd been about to say.

'It must have been something serious to make you go charging off to the library to look for him,' Shepherd said, leaning forward with his forearms on the table.

Harry frowned. 'I didn't charge anywhere.'

'That's funny because another witness described you as "flinging open the door of the building and storming outside with a face like thunder",' Shepherd said. 'Why might that have been?'

Harry stayed quiet.

'And the next thing, you arrive at the library and go straight to the politics section,' Shepherd continued.

'I was looking for an article for a seminar the following day,' Harry said, laying his hands flat on the table. 'I realised as I left my office that I hadn't picked up a copy so I went to the library to get it.'

Shepherd frowned. 'You didn't have any articles with you when we saw you at the library?'

'No. I didn't even get to the shelf where the book is because I found Keith on the floor,' Harry protested.

'Did you kill him?' Shepherd asked.

'What? No. I told you, I found him dead,' Harry said.

'But this was a man you hated, a man who was trying to hold back your career?' Shepherd said.

'We've also heard that you were both at risk of losing your jobs because you weren't publishing, but somehow Professor Williams was managing to stay in his post because he had friends in high places,' Burton said.

Harry glared at her.

'Was that true? Were you jealous that he was safe and you weren't?' Burton continued. 'I'm sure he took every opportunity to remind you of that.'

'I know that would rile me,' Shepherd said, looking at Burton and then back to Harry. 'I mean, someone abusing their position to keep one step ahead when they really should be losing their job too—'

'I didn't kill him!' Harry banged his palm down on the table. 'He was a pain in the arse but killing him wouldn't have helped me.'

Burton and Shepherd both looked down at his hand, planted on the table. Then they looked at each other. Harry felt his heart sink.

Then Burton spoke. 'That's enough for now,' she said. 'As you're here voluntarily, you can go. But don't leave town without speaking to us, Dr Evans, because I'm sure we'll have more questions soon.'

She showed Harry out through the reception area of the station and then went back into the building. Harry sat down on the low wall outside and put his face in his hands. What was he going to do now?

Chapter twenty-four

Olly came back from campus via the corner shop with bread and milk in his backpack. He headed straight for the kitchen and opened the fridge to find an empty plastic milk bottle tucked into the door pocket. Typical, he thought. Clearly Tom had breakfast at home that morning. Olly put away the bread and flicked on the kettle. It had been stupid to let the police catch him coming out of Keith's office, but at least they hadn't caught him taking anything. They couldn't have; there hadn't been anything to take. He was so sure that Keith's research would be in his office, but there wasn't even a scrap of paper connected to it anywhere. Even the laptop was missing, which was a surprise as he'd never seen Keith with it outside his office.

He mulled over his plan as he took a mug from the cupboard and the last teabag from the box. Sighing, he crushed the box and put it into the recycling. Time for a proper trip to the supermarket, he thought. Tom could come and put his muscles to good work carrying the bags.

But right now he had a bigger problem than trying to bully Tom to the supermarket. He slumped into a chair by the kitchen table. Keith was dead and his research was missing. Why hadn't he, Olly, made a copy at some point? He snorted; as if Keith would have allowed him that opportunity. Maybe he could go straight to the man. After all he had his email address. The man might not know yet that Keith had died. He seemed to be a workaholic and may not have left his notebook long enough to read the news. Maybe he would have a copy.

'Are you making tea?'

Olly jumped at the sound of Tom's voice. Tom laughed.

'Sorry, I didn't mean to frighten you.'

Olly gave a weak chuckle. 'No, I just didn't know that anyone was home. I thought you were going to the pub.'

Tom waved his wallet. 'I realised I'd left this at home,' he said. 'Not the done thing to turn up with no money for your round.'

Olly nodded. 'I see what you mean.'

Tom pointed to the kettle, which had finished boiling. 'Are you going to make your tea or what?'

'Yeah, just doing it now.' Olly got up and put his mug down beside the kettle.

'Right,' Tom said. 'Still can't tempt you to come for a drink?'

'I'll come along later,' Olly said. 'I'll text you.'

'Good enough.' Tom headed down the hall towards the front door. Then, as Olly was pouring water into his mug, Tom clumped back down the hall with a padded envelope in his hand.

'I almost forgot,' he said holding up the envelope. 'This came for you this morning. Postman had to ring because he couldn't get it through the door.'

'Sorry, did he wake you?'

'Yeah, but it was no problem.' Tom stretched his arms above his head. 'I needed to get to uni to hand in an essay. If he'd not woken me, I'd have been late.' He checked his watch. 'I gotta go. Laters.' He disappeared down the hall and Olly heard the front door slam.

Olly smiled and shook his head. How Tom was ever going to get his degree, he never knew. He took his tea and the package and went upstairs to his room.

With his mug safely placed on his desk, he looked down at the package in his hand. He didn't remember ordering anything online. It felt very light. The address was handwritten and the writing looked familiar. He ripped the envelope open and peered inside. He shook it over his bed and a flash drive fell onto his duvet cover. He picked it up and turned it over. It said 20 GB on the side but had no other label. He looked inside the envelope again but there was no note.

Well, there was only one way to find out what it was about. He took his laptop from his backpack and switched it on. He pulled the plastic cap off the memory stick. He paused a moment, considering the risk that it could be a virus, but he had all his files and programs backed up. He pushed the memory stick into the laptop's USB port and waited while it ran. A dialogue box popped up asking him for The Specialist. Olly's eyes widened. He'd never thought he would need this. He reached over and pulled open his top desk drawer. He looked inside and unpicked the sticky tape holding a flash drive to the roof of the drawer. He took it out and plugged it into the computer's second USB port. An egg timer appeared on the screen and turned over three times. Then another box popped up on the screen with six files in it. One was a Word file called 'OLLY'. He stared for a moment and then double-clicked on it. There were only about seven lines of text but as his eyes ran down the document, he shivered as if someone had dripped cold water down the back of his neck.

This was it. Now he definitely needed to get in touch with the man. He opened his email account and began to type.

Thirty minutes later Olly was back in the kitchen staring blankly out of the window. All he could think about was what he'd read on the flash drive. He'd been surprised that Keith had sent it but not the tone of the message: 'Olly, you're the only person I can trust to keep this safe. You won't be able to understand it but no one will think that I would have left it with you. I have to go away for a while but keep this safe until I get back and don't show it to anyone. Keith.'

Of course the first thing Olly had done was to open all the additional files and review the contents. Some of it he really couldn't understand, the letter and number combinations and diagrams meant nothing to him. He could, however, understand what Keith had written so far. What bothered him most were email trails between Keith and an unnamed person about him.

With his tea made, he headed back up to his room and read the lines again.

Keith had written, 'You need people, I have a supply who will do anything if you're paying them enough and I also have someone who can arrange everything for you. Will there be much paperwork for them to fill in?'

The response said, 'Just a simple form with a disclaimer.'

Keith then replied, 'I suppose that's standard. When do you need this to start?'

'ASAP,' said the reply.

Olly checked the date. It was about a year ago, just after he and Keith had started working together. He'd only been able to get a few people to sign up. Another of the files on Keith's flash drive held a list of names. Olly scanned them and one name leapt out. Leanne Nelson. He remembered her. She'd heard that he could help her to get some money fast so he'd recommended her to Keith. He frowned. He didn't recall seeing her again but it was a big campus. He went back to Keith's email trail and the next section made him go cold. Keith had asked how the project was proceeding.

The response said, 'Slowly. There's always trial and error and some collateral damage. Plus you're providing weak specimens.' Keith had then asked if anyone was hurt. The response was dismissive.

'You don't get things right first time. This is experimental work we're doing.'

Olly sat back in his chair and put a hand over his mouth. What had he done? His computer gave a soft ping as a new email arrived. He clicked into it eagerly, hoping it was the man. Instead it was from Detective Sergeant Adams.

It said, 'We need to have another interview. Please advise where would be the best place to meet.'

It felt like a sign to him. Just as he'd found out what he'd done, what other people were doing, he had the opportunity to make amends. He quickly typed a reply asking to meet by the lake on campus in an hour. He figured if they wanted it, they'd be quick. But before he went anywhere he needed his insurance.

Seizing his mobile phone and Dan Sullivan's business card, he tapped out a text message.

'Dan, I've done something awful. It was Keith's fault but I need to end it. I'm going to the police now. No doubt they'll tell you about it later.'

As he grabbed his backpack, his mobile bleeped a message from Dan.

'Before you go to the police we need to talk. Where can I meet you?'

Olly texted back: 'I'm meeting the police on campus by the lake in an hour. See you there.'

The reply came: 'Will do.'

Olly checked that his insurance was in his bag. The envelope was safely stowed inside. He squared his shoulders and set off towards the university campus.

At three o'clock Olly parked his car behind the politics department and hurried to the bench by the lake where he was due to meet

Detective Sergeant Adams. He couldn't remember the name of the detective who had bought him tea, but he assumed that was Adams. He was surprised that Dan wasn't here yet. He'd have thought the journalist would have been fighting for the story. He was just glancing at his watch when a figure in a leather jacket approached him. Olly looked up and frowned. This was a stranger.

'Olly Murton?'

'Yes. Are you Detective Sergeant Adams? Where's the other one?'

'We need to have a little chat.' The voice was very smooth. Olly stood up, sensing that he really shouldn't have come to this meeting, but he was pushed back down onto the seat.

'Now, why don't you tell me what you know?' the stranger asked.

Chapter twenty-five

Dan stared down at the mobile phone in his hand. What on earth could Olly Murton have done that was so bad? And if he was going to hand himself in, Dan had to get there first. If Burton and Shepherd were ahead of him, he'd never find out what was going on.

He started to jam his notebook and pens into his bag. Ed, who sat at the desk opposite him, looked up.

'Where are you going?' he asked, fingers suspended over the keyboard.

'I've got to pop out.'

'Story?' Ed asked, eyebrows raised.

'Sort of.' Dan looked at Ed, slightly guiltily.

'You're off after the university story again, aren't you? Daisy's gonna flip if she finds out.' Ed whispered the second sentence.

'She's not going to find out. You're going to distract her and then I'm going to sneak out. If she asks where I've gone, tell her I nipped out for a coffee.'

Ed shook his head. 'I'm going straight to heaven for the number of times I've got you out of trouble.' He got to his feet and walked purposefully towards the news editor. He walked around her and sat at the next desk so that Daisy had to turn her back to Dan to speak to him. Dan took his chance and scooted out of the rear door of the office. He rushed to the pool car he'd parked outside the building and leapt inside. He almost over-revved the engine as he pulled out of the parking space.

Later he would say he didn't remember how he got to the university, but he was soon pulling into the politics department car park. He abandoned the car on a slant in a parking space and just about remembered to lock the door before running to the front of the building, which looked out over the lake. When he got to the lakeside, he stopped, hands on hips trying to catch his breath. His eyes scanned the grassy area that ran down to the water. Shit, no sign of Olly or Burton and Shepherd. He looked at his watch. Damn it, ten past three. He must've missed them. Dan started to walk across the grass staring at the lake. Then something in the rushes caught his eye. He took two steps forward. There was a flash of red and then a Nike brand mark. Was that a shoe? Dan took another two steps and then, realising what he was seeing, sprinted down to the edge of the lake. He tried to grab the shoe, knowing there was a foot inside.

'Help! Help me!' he yelled, trying to pull the shoe towards him. Several students rushed over when they realised what was happening and a burly rugby type managed to grab the leg. Between them, he and Dan hauled the body onto the grass.

'Call an ambulance,' said a woman, turning the body over. 'It's OK, I know CPR.'

'I think he's beyond that,' said the rugby player, pulling out his phone. 'You OK, mate?' he asked, but Dan couldn't speak as he looked down at the dead face of Olly Murton.

Chapter twenty-six

Dan was still sitting on the grass by the lake, watching Eleanor Brody examine Olly's body, when Burton and Shepherd arrived.

'How is it you get here so quickly?' Burton asked.

'He found the body, sir,' said the uniformed constable who stood nearby.

Shepherd looked down at Dan and held out a hand to pull him to his feet.

'What were you doing on campus?' he asked.

'Olly texted me,' Dan said, brushing grass off his trousers. 'He asked me to meet him here. He also said he was meeting you. Where were you?' he asked, glaring at the detectives.

Burton and Shepherd looked at each other.

'Meeting us?' Burton asked.

'Yes. He said he was going to the police, that he'd done something bad that he had to tell you about.'

Burton looked at Shepherd frowning. 'Have you had any calls?'

Shepherd shook his head. 'I'll check with control.' He stepped away, tapping some buttons on his phone and then pressing it to his ear.

'Are you OK?' Burton asked Dan, her tone more kindly than usual.

Dan looked down at his trembling hands and shook them as if that would help. 'Yeah, I'm fine. I think so anyway.'

They lapsed into silence. Then Shepherd returned, shaking his head.

'No calls to control,' he said. 'Are you sure he said he was meeting us?'

Dan pulled out his phone and opened Olly's text message. He held the phone up to Burton and Shepherd who read it. Burton frowned.

'So who did he speak to?' she asked, looking at Shepherd with her forehead creased in a frown.

Shepherd opened the camera app on his phone. 'May I?' he asked indicating Dan's screen. Dan nodded and Shepherd snapped a couple of pictures, scrolling to make sure he had the whole conversation.

Dan turned back to Burton who was staring at Olly's body.

'What happens now?' he asked.

'You need to go home or back to your office, somewhere we can easily find you to take a proper statement,' Burton said.

'But I—'

'Dan?' called a voice. All three turned round to see Harry Evans walking towards them from the direction of the politics department building. 'What's happened?' His eyes were drawn to the legs which were just visible behind Eleanor Brody and her team. 'Oh my God,' he said. 'Has someone been hurt?'

'We don't know what's—' Burton started to say.

'Harry, it's Olly,' Dan broke in. 'Olly Murton. He's dead.'

Harry stared at him. 'What? What are you talking about?' But there was a look in his eye that Dan found odd. He couldn't quite place the emotion that hid in Harry's brown eyes.

'Where were you?' he asked Harry, realising that he wasn't wearing his usual jacket or carrying a bag.

'I was in my office,' Harry said, gesturing to the politics department building.

'Your office faces the lake, doesn't it?' Shepherd asked.

'Well, yes, it does, but—'

Burton turned to Dan. 'Like I said, go back home or to your office. Someone will be along later to take a statement.'

Dan opened his mouth to protest but the look on Burton's face told him not to push his luck.

'Call me later,' he said to Harry, passing him a business card.

As he walked away, he glanced back to see Burton and Shepherd closing ranks on Harry. Again he didn't like the expression on his former lecturer's face. If he'd been in his office, as he'd claimed, he must've seen what had happened. If he hadn't, then where had he been when Olly died?

Burton and Shepherd turned to look at Harry.

'How long have you been in your office this afternoon?' Burton asked.

Harry looked uneasy. 'Since lunchtime.'

'And you didn't see anything?'

'No, I wasn't really looking out of the window.'

Burton was frowning at him. 'Did you hear anything?'

Harry shook his head. 'I went out to pick up a coffee about half an hour ago and I was on my way back when I heard the commotion out by the lake. So I walked round to see what had happened.'

Shepherd looked down at Harry's empty hands. 'You seem to have forgotten your coffee,' he said.

'I went for a stroll and drank it then,' Harry said. 'But I wasn't by the lake.'

'Did anyone see you on this stroll?' Shepherd asked.

Harry shrugged. 'They may have done. I wasn't trying to hide or anything.' He looked from one detective to the other. 'Am I being accused of something?' he asked.

'It just seems very odd that you, who have a clear view of the lake, just happened to go for a coffee at the time a student was killed,' Shepherd said.

Harry went very still. 'Killed? What do you mean killed?' he demanded. 'Did he not drown in the lake? He's all wet, I can see that.'

'We don't know yet,' Burton said. 'Olly may have fallen into the lake, but equally someone might have put him there.'

Harry looked as her, seemingly taken aback. 'Are you suggesting that I did it?'

'Did you?'

'No. I couldn't— I wouldn't do something like that.'

'Even though you and Olly didn't get on? That you'd been aggressive towards him recently?' Shepherd asked.

'I wouldn't say that we didn't get on. We sometimes had a difficult relationship because I mark work very hard. It's better in the long run,' Harry explained. 'Sometimes Olly struggled to handle criticism.'

'He wasn't a very good student?' Burton asked.

'He was OK, but he wasn't going to set the world alight.' Harry paused.

'What?' Burton asked.

Harry shook his head. 'I was just going to say that probably the person who knew Olly best was Keith. They've been spending a lot of time together recently.'

Burton raised an eyebrow. 'Do you know what that was about?' she asked.

Harry shrugged. 'Some research project, so I'm told.'

'What's it about?' Shepherd asked.

'I don't know.' Harry sniffed. 'Keith would never have told me anything about what he was working on. Apparently he thought I would steal it.'

'Plagiarise it, you mean?' Shepherd asked.

Harry frowned at him. 'What makes you say that?'

Shepherd gave a tight smile. 'We'd heard that you've done that before.'

'That was a complete lie,' Harry said, firing up immediately as Shepherd had known he would. 'It was proven to be a lie by an official inquiry. Who told you otherwise?'

But Shepherd just smiled. Burton had turned to look at where Brody was kneeling beside the body and now re-joined the conversation. 'Thank you for your time so far, Dr Evans,' she said. 'We'll need a fuller statement but that's all for now.'

Harry opened his mouth to say something and closed it again.

'Someone will be in touch,' said Burton, turning and leading Shepherd away.

The sergeant looked back over his shoulder at Harry Evans who was staring at Olly. 'Why did you stop me? We were getting somewhere,' he said.

They reached the spot where Brody was kneeling over Olly Murton's body.

'I want to find out whether he has been in his office all afternoon, what time he took his stroll and where he went, before we question him again,' Burton said. She pointed down at the body. 'This is the second person that's been found dead on campus with Dr Evans in the vicinity. I don't want there to be a third.'

Chapter twenty-seven

'You'd better come in.' Desmond Danby ushered Burton and Shepherd into his office and directed them to chairs. 'So sad, so tragic,' he said, wringing his hands. 'How do you think he died?'

'We'll know more about that after the pathologist has examined him,' Burton said.

'But surely it was an accident?' Danby asked, his brow furrowing.

'We're really not sure at the moment. It's too early to say,' Burton said.

'Oh God.' Danby's hand flew to his face. 'What am I going to tell his mother?'

Shepherd pulled out his notebook and pen. 'Where does she live?' he asked, clicking out the nib of his biro.

'Somewhere near Exeter,' said Danby. 'I pulled his file as soon as I heard what had happened. There's only her at home, no father.'

'Is he dead?'

'I don't know.'

'Can we have her contact details?' Shepherd asked. 'Someone from the local police will go round and break the news.'

'They will be gentle, won't they?'

'Sadly it's all part of the job,' said Shepherd, as Danby flicked to the relevant page in the file. He noted down the woman's details.

'We'll need his home address too and details for his friends.'

'Not a problem.' Danby flicked back to the first page in the file. 'Well, I can give you his address, but we don't keep a record of friends. His housemates might know that.'

Burton raised an eyebrow. 'You don't know who hangs out with who?'

Danby smiled. 'This is a big place and it's not like a school. The people here are adults and we treat them as such. Like I said, his housemates might be able to give you a steer on who his friends were.'

'So you wouldn't know if there was anyone who might want to hurt Olly?' Shepherd asked.

Danby shifted awkwardly in his seat, as if he was trying to decide whether he should share the knowledge he had. It seemed that his conscience got the better of him.

'Previously I'd have said no,' he said. 'But recently—' He stopped again as if wrestling with himself.

'Please, Professor Danby, we need to know everything,' Shepherd pressed him.

'Well, recently I've noticed some difficulties between Olly and Harry Evans.'

Shepherd raised an eyebrow. 'Difficulties? In what way?'

'Olly was a good enough lad, but not the most able student. Harry's been supervising his dissertation and I think the pressure may have been getting to them both. I heard raised voices in Harry's office on more than one occasion.'

'Did you speak to either of them about it?' Burton asked.

Danby shook his head. 'No, if there are differences of opinion then I let them sort it out themselves. If it goes so far as one person making a complaint, then I have to step in. Other than that, the students are adults, and they have to learn to fight their corner.'

Burton was silent, waiting for Shepherd to finish scribbling. Then she asked, 'Have you seen Harry Evans this afternoon?'

Danby shook his head. 'Sorry, I was giving a lecture from one o'clock until half past two. Then I came back here and I've been reading and making notes for a seminar till now.'

'You haven't seen or heard Harry Evans at all?'

'No. I heard a door down the hall at about two forty-five, which may have been him coming in or going out, but I couldn't say for certain.'

Burton and Shepherd thanked Danby, promised to keep him informed about the investigation and left his office. As they walked down the corridor, Shepherd peered down at his notebook.

'We still have no idea where Harry Evans was when Olly Murton was killed,' he said, tapping his pen against the open page.

Burton was frowning. 'If he was in or around the department, someone must have seen him. Let's see what the uniform team comes back with from their canvassing. But unless he's got an alibi, then he's squarely in my sights.'

Chapter twenty-eight

When Dan arrived back in the office, Daisy got to her feet, clearly preparing to deliver a dressing down. But he raised a hand like a policeman directing traffic. She closed her mouth and stared at him, eyebrows raised. Ed got to his feet too and joined them.

'What happened?' he asked. 'What did you find at the university?'

Daisy put her hands on her hips, chin jutting forward. 'You were following that story after I specifically told you not to?' she demanded.

'I found a body,' Dan said. Daisy and Ed stared at him.

'Whose?' Ed asked.

'Olly Murton, the guy I went to meet. He was floating in the lake.' Dan rubbed his face with his palms.

'What?' Daisy asked. 'You sneaked out to meet him and he was dead?'

'Yup.' Dan sighed. 'The police told me to go home or back here and I thought at least I can be useful here until someone comes to take a statement.'

'It might be best if the editor doesn't see the police coming for you again,' Daisy said. On a previous occasion Dan had been arrested on suspicion of murder in the middle of the newsroom, which had led to the editor suspending him.

Dan pulled a face. 'OK, but what if he notices I'm not here?' he asked.

'I'll cover, say you've gone home ill,' Daisy said. 'But try to keep your eye on this case and see what else the police can give you. We need to get ahead of the competition. File me a line for the website when you get home and I'll upload it.'

Dan nodded, picked up his bag and headed for the back door of the office. He was sad about Olly but he was intrigued by what the student might have been about to tell him. His stomach was flickering again.

When the flat doorbell rang, Dan opened the door to a sharply suited man who introduced himself as Detective Constable Garry Topping. Not recognising him, Dan took the man's police ID and studied it carefully before allowing him inside.

'No Burton?' he asked as Topping followed him down the hall into the living room.

'Following up leads,' came the reply.

Dan led the way into the living room and offered tea, which Topping declined. Instead he settled himself on the sofa and waited for Dan to fetch his own cup of tea and sit down.

'I know this must be difficult because you knew Olly, but I need you to tell me everything you remember,' Topping said, taking out his notebook and pen.

'I went to university with Olly – like I told Burton and Shepherd,' Dan said. 'Well, we were there at the same time but I didn't really know him. I bumped into him outside the library just after Keith Williams' body was discovered. We got chatting but then he left when I went to talk to DS Shepherd.'

'Did Olly say anything about Keith Williams?'

'He didn't really say anything then, but I saw him a few days later.

He told me that they were working together on something and he seemed really upset, but then he said Harry had only just told him who had died.'

'Upset by the death or upset with Harry Evans?' Topping asked, looking keenly at Dan, who frowned.

'Now that you mention it,' Dan said, 'I don't know. He did say that Harry was asking about Keith's research, which struck me as a bit odd when Keith had just died and he found the body.'

Topping finished the sentence he was writing and looked up. 'Then what happened?' he asked, pen poised.

'I gave Olly my card and said to call if he ever wanted a chat or whatever.' Dan took a sip of his tea and put the mug back on the table on a coaster.

'Did he call you?' Topping asked.

'Not then. I bumped into him again a day later and took him for a coffee.'

'Did he say anything?'

'Well, he insisted on buying the drinks and his wallet was pretty stuffed with twenties,' Dan said. 'More than I usually have, anyway.' Topping finished scribbling and looked up at Dan. 'I managed to get him onto the subject of the research he was doing with Keith, something new he'd found out about the Cold War apparently. That's Harry's specialist subject so I suggested that Olly should ask Harry for help now that Keith is not around.'

'How did he react?'

'It was weird. He freaked out, nearly spat his tea onto the table,' Dan said. 'He was adamant I couldn't tell Harry about it. He said that Keith had hidden the research but he probably knew where to find it.' Dan shrugged, then frowned and picked up his mobile phone. 'I recorded this while we were talking.' He found the audio file and played it. Topping listened carefully and then made a note in his book. He pointed to the mobile with his pen.

'I'm going to need a copy of that,' he said.

'No problem. I can email it.'

Topping held out a business card and waited while Dan tapped in his email address and sent the file.

'Did Olly tell you anything else?' Topping asked.

Dan shook his head. 'No, but—'

'But what?'

Dan sighed. 'I wish I'd pushed him. I knew there was something wrong, but I thought if I let him tell me, rather than asking, that he'd confide.'

Topping looked at him in silence for a moment and then said, 'Don't beat yourself up. You couldn't have known what would happen.'

Dan looked down at the floor. 'I suppose.'

'And then he sent you those text messages this afternoon?' Topping asked, pointing at Dan's mobile phone on the table.

'Yes. To be honest, I was a bit surprised,' Dan said. 'I'd given him my card but I wasn't convinced he was going to get in touch. I certainly didn't think he'd get murdered.'

Topping finished scribbling and looked up, meeting Dan's eyes without speaking. Feeling like he'd overstepped the mark, Dan said, 'Sorry, I just assumed that—'

'I'd keep your thoughts on that to yourself for now,' Topping said, preparing to stand up. 'We've not had the post-mortem or spoken to his family yet.' Dan opened his mouth to speak, but Topping got to his feet. 'You'll be able to get more from the press office later, but we're not releasing any details about him yet because the family hasn't been informed.' He snapped his notebook shut. 'That's all we've got for now. Thanks for your time. We'll be in touch.'

When Dan closed the door behind Topping, he leaned against it, staring at the wall. What had Olly planned on telling the police? Had someone silenced him? He sighed. It seemed like Harry had no alibi either. Would his old lecturer really kill someone for a research project, or was something else going on?

Chapter twenty-nine

Olly Murton's body lay on the cold slab, staring at the ceiling. His already pale face had a waxy sheen and his limp hair was drying with a slight frizz, although all traces of weeds from the lake which had clung to it were gone. Burton and Shepherd stared down at him as they waited for Brody to change out of the scrubs she'd been wearing to carry out the post-mortem. They were both still wearing masks, as though they'd forgotten to remove them. Olly looked relaxed for the first time since they'd met him.

'What was he going to tell us?' Shepherd asked, pulling away his mask and taking a deep breath. 'I feel like I'm suffocating under this.'

Burton frowned. 'It's likely that it was something to do with Keith Williams' murder, but I want to dig into his life and find out what else he had going on,' she said, her voice slightly muffled. 'We've already got a head start from Desmond Danby, that he was having problems with Harry Evans. Now we need to speak to his housemates and see if they know any more.'

Before they got any further, Brody returned, clipboard in hand and wearing clean scrubs.

'Right,' she said, looking at the notes in front of her. 'Male, early-thirties. He clearly has a sedentary lifestyle because he's got no more muscle mass than the average person who doesn't exercise.' She frowned down at Olly as if scolding him. 'No signs of any serious illnesses or previous injuries. There's no head wounds or any other wounds except this.' She indicated Olly's neck with her pen. Burton and Shepherd leaned down to examine the bruising that encircled Olly's neck.

'Strangled?' Shepherd asked. 'That might be why no one heard anything.'

'He did struggle,' Brody said, pointing to the two broken fingernails on Olly's right hand. 'But clearly it was against someone much stronger than him. However, that's not what killed him,' she said.

Burton and Shepherd stared at her.

'So what did kill him?' Burton asked.

'A heart attack,' Brody said.

Shepherd frowned. 'Someone strangled him and he had a heart attack?' he asked.

Brody nodded.

'A healthy thirtysomething-year-old had a heart attack?' Shepherd asked.

Burton folded her arms. 'As a result of being strangled?' she asked.

Brody shrugged. 'Could be,' she said.

Shepherd pursed his lips. 'He could have panicked, I suppose,' he said. 'Not surprising if he was a bit of a weakling and couldn't fight back.'

'Enough to bring on a heart attack?' asked Burton, looking sceptical. 'I'm not buying that.'

'He died on the bank and then they threw him in the lake,' Shepherd said, leaning down to peer at the strangulation marks around Olly's neck.

'Yes, he was definitely dead when he hit the water, there wasn't any in his lungs. All the water did was get rid of any useful DNA or evidence we might have been able to gather.'

'They went to a lot of effort to make sure we'd have no leads to follow,' Burton said, looking at Olly's hands to examine the broken fingernails.

Brody consulted her clipboard. 'I did find one thing when I was measuring his organs,' she said.

Shepherd wrinkled his nose. 'That sounds lovely,' he said.

Brody battled to hide a smile at his discomfort. 'I found that his heart was enlarged,' she said.

Burton looked at Brody. 'Enlarged? What does that mean?' she asked.

Brody shrugged. 'I don't know yet,' she said. 'But I'll look into it.'

Burton sighed and stood with her hands on her hips looking down at Olly. 'So right now we've got nothing,' she said gloomily.

'We're not out of the running yet,' Brody said, smiling. 'There's this.' She walked around the body and pointed. 'Olly has a puncture wound in his neck.'

Burton bent down and peered at the tiny wound. 'Drugged?' she asked, looking up at Brody.

'I'll know more when I get the toxicology results back. They held him around the neck, very tightly, and injected him with something.'

'Is that what killed him?' Shepherd asked.

Brody shrugged. 'Let's see what the toxicology report says, but it could be.'

Burton and Shepherd were silent as they walked across the morgue car park to their vehicle. Burton pulled the car keys from her bag and tossed them to Shepherd.

'You drive. I need to think.'

'Yes, boss.' Shepherd beeped the alarm and unlocked the doors.

They climbed inside and Burton settled herself in the passenger seat, handbag tucked neatly at her feet.

She was silent for a moment as Shepherd pulled out of the parking space and nosed the car to the exit of the car park. As he indicated and pulled out onto the main road, she spoke.

'Olly Murton and Keith Williams were killed by the same person. There can't be two separate murderers around, that's just unlikely.' She paused, frowning. 'But why the different methods?'

Shepherd checked over his shoulder and indicated to change lanes before he spoke again.

'You said it yourself in the library. Keith Williams' murder wasn't planned. Or if it was, it wasn't planned to happen in the library so they had to improvise with whatever came to hand.'

'Whereas Olly Murton arranged to meet them so they had time to plan,' Burton said, staring out of the car window.

Shepherd braked at a red traffic light. 'They brought something with them, something quiet that wouldn't attract attention,' he said, eyes on the car in front of him. Then he frowned. 'But would it be unobtrusive enough for someone whose office overlooks the lake not to see it?'

Burton frowned as Shepherd pulled away from the now green traffic light.

'Harry Evans,' she said grimly, 'had a major problem with Keith Williams and found him dead. Then Olly Murton, who he's been aggressive towards in the past and clearly doesn't like, is found dead in the lake in full view of his window.'

'Was Olly going to tell us something about Harry, do you think?' Shepherd asked, indicating at the roundabout that led into the police station car park.

Burton frowned. 'No. He said that he'd done something bad, didn't he? That's what he was going to tell us about.'

'Could he have killed Keith Williams?' Shepherd asked, pulling into a parking space.

'If he was lying about Williams being already dead when he stole the keys from his pocket, but I don't think he was.' She sighed. 'Anyway, drop me here and get yourself away. I want to get home for tea time at least once this week.' She opened the car door and stepped out. Then leaning down she asked, 'Any plans?'

'Dinner at my sister's,' Shepherd said, patting his stomach and grinning. 'I'll be a stone heavier by tomorrow.'

Burton smiled back. 'Well, tonight eat, drink and be merry, and we'll hit this hard again in the morning.'

Chapter thirty

The next morning, a pair of red-rimmed blue eyes scrutinised Burton and Shepherd's warrant cards. Clearly Olly Murton's housemate was expecting them, because once he'd finished his examination, he stepped back and held the door open.

'You'd better come in,' he said in a subdued voice. 'I'm Ian. Desmond Danby said that you'd be coming round.'

Burton cast a swift glance at Shepherd and then stepped into the dark, slightly dingy hallway.

'How are you bearing up?' Shepherd asked Ian, his broad shoulders filling up the space in the narrow hallway. The younger man shrugged. Shepherd looked around. 'Isn't there a family liaison officer with you?'

Ian shook his head. 'We said we don't need someone to stay here. We can support each other. The woman said she'd pop back if there was any news. I don't think it's really sunk in yet.'

'It does take time,' Shepherd said. We just need to ask you a couple of questions if that's OK?'

'We're all in the kitchen.'

'All?'

'There's five of us living here. Or at least, there were five of us living here.'

Burton pointed to a door. 'In here?'

'No, that's the living room; the kitchen is through there.' Ian indicated the door at the end of the hall. Burton followed the light and tramped down three small steps to push open the wooden panelled door. Three ashen faces seated around a rectangular oak table, which took up most of the floor space at one end of the room, looked up from mugs of tea.

'Police,' Ian said, following Burton and Shepherd into the room.

'Have you found out who hurt Olly yet?' one young man demanded, standing up. He was built in a similar style to Shepherd and looked like he belonged on a rugby pitch.

'Not yet,' Burton answered.

'Why not? Why aren't you out there catching whoever did this?'

'Tom,' interrupted Ian, 'the police are doing everything they can. Why don't you stick the kettle on? I'm sure another round of tea will do us good.'

Tom looked like he was going to argue but then his eyes filled with tears and he turned quickly away.

'I don't know if I can drink any more tea,' said a lad with a ring through his lower lip sitting at the table.

'Well, it's better than starting on anything stronger,' muttered Ian, casting his eyes in Tom's direction. Shepherd patted Tom on the shoulder as he moved past him to stand by the fridge, notebook in hand.

'When did you last see Olly?' Burton asked, looking at Ian, who was clearly the spokesman for the group.

'It was the day he was killed,' Tom answered from beside the kettle. Burton looked round at him. 'I saw him on campus in the morning and I asked if he wanted to come for a pint.'

'Did he?' asked Burton.

Tom shook his head. 'I saw him here a little while after that and he seemed a bit weird.'

'How do you mean?'

'I don't know. A bit dreamy maybe, distracted.'

'He was probably tired,' Ian said. 'He'd been putting in a lot of extra study.'

'He was always studying,' Tom said as the kettle came to the boil next to him. 'He always had his nose in a book.' He started to put bags into several slightly chipped mugs.

The blond man with the lip ring smiled. 'That's what students are meant to do, Tom.'

Tom gave a short laugh and then became serious. 'It seems wrong to be laughing when Olly's been murdered.' He looked at Burton and Shepherd. 'That's what they're saying on campus.'

Burton nodded. 'Sadly, yes, we now know that Olly was killed by someone else. Can you think of anyone who might want to hurt him?'

All the students around the table shook their heads.

'Was there anything going on with him at the moment? Any problems in his life?' Shepherd asked.

'Ol was pretty cut up after that professor guy got killed. He seemed edgy since that happened,' Tom said.

Burton raised an eyebrow. 'You knew he and Professor Williams were close?'

Ian shrugged. 'They seemed to spend a bit of time together. Olly always seemed to be popping in to see him,' he said.

'I saw them in the Students' Union bar together a few times,' the man with the lip ring put in. 'It looked like they were having a private discussion.'

'What makes you say that?' Burton asked.

'Well, they looked a bit furtive, y'know, glancing around while they were talking as if someone might be listening.'

'Were they having a relationship?' Burton's question was met with four scornful noises.

'No, Inspector,' Ian said, smiling. 'Olly may not have had much success with women but he certainly wasn't gay.'

Tom laughed openly. 'And if he was, I think he could have done better than some fifty-year-old fat guy who smoked like a chimney. Ol always stank of cigars when he'd been with that guy. I reckon his supervisor would have been more his type, eh Ian?' Ian smiled too.

'What do you mean?' Burton asked, desperately trying to get the interview back on track.

'He talked about that guy a lot,' said Tom. 'He was always trying to impress him but it never seemed to work. His essays and stuff always seemed to come back with loads of corrections and comments. It used to get Ol down a bit.'

'Did Olly have a problem with Harry Evans?' asked Shepherd, scribbling.

Tom thought for a moment. 'I don't think Olly had a problem with him. It was more like the other way round.'

'Harry Evans had a problem with Olly? What makes you say that?' Burton asked.

'I have a couple of mates in the politics department and they all say he is a stand-up guy, but then one of them heard him shouting at Olly.'

'Did your friend hear what the argument was about?'

Tom shook his head. 'She said she couldn't really hear, but it was more of a one-sided bollocking. She asked Olly about it later and he went bright red in the face and gave her some guff about how it was because he disturbed the guy when he was writing.' Tom snorted. 'That Harry needs to get his nose out of his own arse if that's how he's going to behave.'

Burton gave Shepherd a look and waited for him to finish scribbling.

'Did Olly have any particular friends other than you?' Burton asked, indicating the group. They all looked at each other and shook their heads.

'He didn't really make friends that easily,' Ian said. 'He could be quite intense and I think that put a lot of people off. I wondered whether that was why he got on well with that professor guy.'

'Actually, now you mention it,' Tom said, 'I did see Olly with someone a month or so ago.'

'Who was it?' asked Burton.

'I didn't recognise him but he was proper yelling at Ol. He was giving as good as he got, but then the bloke actually poked him in the chest. I mean, who does that?' he asked, spreading his hands wide.

'What happened next?' Shepherd asked, managing to talk and write at the same time.

'I was worried about Olly so I started walking over. I heard the guy shout, "Where is she then? What's happened to her?" Olly just shrugged and said that wasn't his problem. Then they saw me coming and the other lad scarpered,' Tom finished.

'What did Olly say?' Burton asked.

Tom shrugged. 'He just said it was some guy who had mistaken him for someone else. It didn't look like it to me but Ol wouldn't say anything else.'

Shepherd put away his notebook and pen. 'Maybe we could see Olly's bedroom,' he asked. 'Tom, could you show us?'

'Sure.' Tom pushed himself away from the wall and headed for the kitchen door. Shepherd followed but Ian stopped Burton in the doorway.

'Should I go too?' He looked worried.

'No, that's fine,' Burton said with a smile. 'I'm sure Tom can help us.'

'Just be gentle with him,' Ian said in a low voice, folding his arms across his chest. 'He may look big but he's only twenty and he's really shaken up.'

Burton nodded. 'We'll look after him,' she said, heading out of the kitchen. She followed Tom and Shepherd up the stairs to the first floor. Both were wide enough to block out any light on the staircase and she kept a close eye on her footing.

'Here it is.' Tom pushed open a door directly at the top of the stairs and stepped to one side, pushing his hands into his pockets. He seemed suddenly awkward without the support of the others. His eyes widened as Shepherd snapped on a pair of latex gloves. 'What are you doing?' he asked, edging away.

Shepherd grinned. 'It's just in case we need to check the room for forensic evidence.'

The lad laughed. 'Sorry.'

'It's very tidy,' Burton remarked, following Shepherd into the room, hands already gloved. The bed was neatly made and a laptop computer sat on the desk, whose surface was clear of any papers. Tom pointed to the laptop.

'That's weird. It's there,' he said.

'Why?' Burton asked, stepping over to take a closer look.

'He usually had it with him for when he was studying.'

Burton and Shepherd exchanged a look. 'He must be a good student if no one thinks he went to campus other than to study,' Shepherd said in an undertone.

A bookcase next to the desk was neatly stacked with textbooks and lever arch files. A photograph of a middle-aged woman with short, dark, curly hair posing in a rose garden stood on the shelf too. Burton picked it up and looked questioningly at Tom.

'That's his mum. She's really nice. She came to visit a month ago and brought us some cakes she'd baked.' His face fell. 'Oh man, has anyone told her yet? About what's happened to Olly?'

'Someone from the local police will have been to see her by now,' Shepherd said.

'Were she and Olly close?' Burton asked.

'He used to call her quite a lot,' Tom said, 'but he never seemed to visit very often.'

'Expensive to travel, I suppose,' Shepherd said, flicking through one of the files.

But Tom shook his head. 'That never seemed to be a problem for Olly.'

'What do you mean?' Burton asked, looking up from where she was poking around in the drawer of Olly's bedside table with a latex-gloved finger.

'He always had money,' Tom said with a shrug. 'The laptop is new. He bought it a couple of months ago. He got a new external hard drive too.'

'Was the money from his mum?' Shepherd asked.

'That's what I thought at first, but when we met his mum she said she'd had to bake him the cakes she brought because she couldn't afford to take him out,' Tom said. 'Plus she made a joke about her coat being second-hand. I think he bought her dinner in the end, although she wasn't happy about him spending so much money on her.'

Burton frowned. 'Did Olly have a job?'

'Not that I know of,' Tom said, shaking his head. 'He always seemed to be studying.'

Shepherd frowned. 'So where did his money come from?' he asked.

Tom shrugged. 'I never really thought about it, I suppose.' Burton and Shepherd exchanged a glance. Shepherd seized a file and, opening it, discovered it was full of bank statements. He showed the top page to Burton who nodded.

'Right, we'll take the computer and this file with us for checking,' she said. Tom opened his mouth to speak. 'We'll leave a receipt,'

Burton continued, taking a piece of paper from Olly's printer and a pen from her pocket and beginning to scribble. 'We'll make sure it all comes back.'

At her side Shepherd was poking through the bin.

'What was in this?' he asked, holding up a padded envelope.

Tom shrugged. 'I don't know. It came in the post for Ol on the day he was killed.' His mouth turned down at the corners. Then he frowned. 'It was weird because he didn't seem to be expecting anything.'

Shepherd slipped the envelope into a plastic evidence bag. Then he examined the remaining shelves of the slightly battered wooden bookcase. The bookcase had a decorative raised edge on the top and Shepherd ran a hand around it. He frowned as his gloved fingers came into contact with something. He picked it up and examined it then held it out to Burton.

'A flash drive,' he said.

She held out an evidence bag and he dropped it inside.

'Any idea what's on here?' Burton asked Tom who shrugged.

Shepherd stepped away from the bookcase dusting his fingers.

'Look, is this a crime scene?' Tom asked, looking uncomfortable.

'No,' said Burton, clicking her pen shut and handing Tom the list, 'but please stay out of the room until we tell you otherwise.'

Chapter thirty-one

Shepherd, hands full of files and laptop, shouldered his way through the office door. Burton followed, turning the plastic-bagged flash drive over and over in her hands.

'What do you suppose it is?' she asked.

'Illegal computer software? Porn?' Shepherd suggested with a grin.

Burton raised an eyebrow. 'Would you really hide that on top of a bookcase? We'll give it to tech along with his laptop.'

Shepherd put the computer and lever arch file onto his desk. 'I'll give tech a call now.'

Burton flopped onto a nearby chair and propped her feet on the desk while she waited for him to put down the phone. When he turned to face her, she pointed to the lever-arch folder on his desk. 'What's in the file?'

'It looks like Olly Murton's financial paperwork,' Shepherd said. 'His mate said he always had money but didn't have a job. So, where was his money coming from?'

'Student loan?'

'I don't know whether that would cover laptops and other expensive gadgets,' Shepherd said, frowning down at the page. 'It's always in the papers about how poor students are and how much debt they get into.'

'From what Tom said it didn't sound like there was a bank of mum and dad, or at least a bank of mum,' Burton said.

Shepherd began to flick through the pages. 'Look, in just the last two months, four cash deposits of five hundred pounds. If that goes back over a number of months, it's building into a nice little nest egg.'

'Especially for a student who doesn't have a job.'

'Exactly.'

'But what was he getting paid for? And by whom?' Burton asked, rubbing her chin with the ends of her fingers.

'That's what I can't get my head around,' Shepherd said. 'His paperwork is really organised but there's no sign of payslips or anything like that. Clearly his income isn't from a legitimate source.'

Burton frowned and rubbed her chin. 'Paid cash in hand to avoid tax?'

Shepherd exhaled heavily. 'It's possible, but his mates said he didn't have a job at all, so where did it come from?'

'Could he have been involved with drugs?'

Shepherd was shaking his head. 'In that case I would have expected the money to be more.'

Burton sighed. 'For now, all we know is that one of our murder victims was receiving a thousand pounds a month from an undisclosed source.' She looked at Shepherd's dark head bent over the file. The sergeant gave a low whistle. 'What? What have you found?'

'This payment system must have been going on for a while, and he certainly wasn't spending every penny that came in.' Shepherd walked over to Burton and pushed a piece of paper under her nose.

'It's a savings account,' Burton said, taking the piece of paper and examining the numbers on it.

'Look at the total,' Shepherd pointed with a stubby finger.

Burton inhaled sharply. 'There's twelve thousand pounds in there.'

'Yup. He must be keeping most of the money he's getting for something, but what?'

Burton sat back in her chair staring into space. 'His only real friends, who live in the same house as him, don't know where he gets his money from. How can someone keep that kind of secret?'

Shepherd perched on the edge of the desk. 'Maybe they're used to him being secretive. Some people are really private about money.'

Burton fell silent and stared into space again. Suddenly she stood up. Shepherd stood too, waiting for instructions. 'Right, you stay here. Go through those bank statements. See if there are any patterns of when the money arrives. Check his computer and see if he has a diary of where he's been. That might help.' She headed towards the door.

'Where are you going?' asked Shepherd, sitting back down.

'To update the boss on progress and hope he thinks we're making enough.'

Chapter thirty-two

Dan lay awake for hours thinking over his discussion with Garry Topping. Two people were dead and connected by a research project they'd been sharing. Unless sharing was too strong a word. From the sounds of it Keith had been in charge and Olly was trying to get his foot further in the door.

He called Daisy, lying that he was still waiting to speak to the police. Once he'd scoffed a bowl of cornflakes, he grabbed his laptop and began his own investigation.

An Internet search threw up hundreds of entries for Keith Williams. He'd written a lot of articles and books and each seemed to be as dull as the one before. Some even repeated ideas from previous articles.

'But I don't think anyone would kill you for being dull, eh Keith?' he said aloud to himself.

He was three pages into the search results when one entry caught his eye. He clicked on it and found himself on a student forum. The thread was discussing where to study politics.

One poster said, 'If you go to Allensbury, stay as far away from Keith Williams as possible.'

'Why?' asked a response. 'Is he letchy?'

'No, but one of my mates went to work for him on a project. She was desperate for money and he said he would help her.'

'What did she have to do for that?' came another reply with a sad face emoticon.

'She had to go and meet some guy and he'd put her in touch with someone.'

'OMG! Did she tell you what she had to do?' another poster asked.

There was a sad face emoticon to start the next post. 'No. She never came home and I've never seen her again.'

Dan stared at the screen. The woman had never been seen again? Who had Keith introduced her to? He carried on reading.

The next response said, 'WTF??!!'

'Shit. What did you do?' asked another.

'We reported it to the cops and they did investigate but there was very little to go on,' the original poster had written. 'It was difficult because she's an adult and, other than the issues with money, she wasn't considered vulnerable. The uni did what they could to help but they didn't know anything about what she was going through.' Dan could almost hear the disappointment in the words.

On the next line someone else asked, 'What happened when they found her?'

'She's never been found. It was about six months ago that she disappeared.'

Dan stared at the screen. Most missing people turned up or were found within forty-eight hours, safe and sound. To be missing with no information at all for that long wasn't unheard of, but it usually meant one thing. That the person was dead. What worried him most was what the woman had had to do for the money.

The next post said, 'How is he still at Allensbury? Has no one done anything about it?'

'We told the police that she'd been going to see him about getting money, but he denied everything and we had no proof in writing, he's too clever for that,' the original poster wrote. 'But I'm going to make sure he never does it again.'

There were a few more responses, but the original poster hadn't contributed again.

Dan sat back so suddenly he almost overbalanced his laptop. He stared off into the distance and then looked back at the screen. The posts were only from a month ago. The student posting may well be still at the university and was clearly still furious with Keith. He grabbed his notebook and scribbled down the nickname the poster had used on the forum, 'WillT1998'. He thought for a moment. He checked the thread again, but there was no mention of the woman's name. He thought for a moment and then grabbed his phone. There was someone he knew who might remember.

Emma answered the phone after three rings.

'I just need to take this,' he heard her say away from the mouthpiece. A door closed and the background chatter cut out. 'Hey babes,' she said.

'Babes?'

'Hmm, it doesn't really suit you, does it?' She laughed. 'So how are things?'

Dan sighed heavily. 'Where do I start? There's been another murder on campus and I found the body.'

'What? How did that happen?'

Dan told her about the texts from Olly Murton and what had happened by the lake.

'I bet Burton bloody loved that,' Emma said. 'I'm surprised she didn't just arrest you on the spot after what happened last time.'

'Me too. But that's not why I'm calling—'

'Really? You had something more important to tell me than that?'

Emma sounded surprised. 'I'd have thought that was pretty high on the list of priorities.'

'Yes, but there's something else I need your help on,' Dan said, trying to hurry the conversation on.

'Intriguing,' Emma said, and he could almost see her cocking her head to the right as she always did when she thought she was about to hear something important. 'I'll do my best.'

'Do you remember a student going missing at Allensbury University? It was about six months ago. A woman.'

There was a silence at the other end of the line. Dan waited, tapping his fingers against his knee.

'Emma?' He knew she was rifling through the filing cabinet of information in her head.

'I think I do,' she said. 'Leanne Nelson. I think that was her. We did a lot of coverage at the time, interviews with friends and family, appeals for information. But there was no sign of her so it kind of petered out.'

'Anything else?'

'Actually, one of her friends contacted me a couple of months ago to see if we could do anything to generate any interest, but there wasn't really. The police had no new leads. I did a filler about it, the usual call for help, because I felt so sorry for him. Daisy wasn't too keen on doing anything else.'

'Was it Burton and Shepherd's case?'

Emma was silent again. 'DI Chandler, I think,' she said. 'He'll be quoted in the stories I wrote. I wouldn't bother with him though.'

'Why not?'

'He's a grump and he wasn't happy when I contacted him recently looking for info.'

'Thanks for the warning.' Dan frowned. 'You don't remember the mate's name, do you?'

There was a short silence. 'Will Turner,' Emma said. 'That's him.'

Dan grinned. Just what he'd been hoping she'd say. 'Contact number?' he asked hopefully.

'It's in my diary, in my desk drawer in the office. If you look ahead about three months, it'll be in there.'

Dan grinned. 'Follow-up time?'

He could hear her grinning smugly. 'Absolutely,' she said.

'You're a marvel.'

'No problem, babycakes.'

Dan laughed. 'Keep working on the pet names, eh?'

Emma laughed, said goodbye and hung up.

Dan put his mobile phone down on the coffee table and stared at it. What might Will Turner be able to tell him about Leanne Nelson, and could it be linked to the murder of Keith Williams?

Chapter thirty-three

Burton could hear Shepherd's soft chuckle as she pushed open the office door. The burly sergeant was sitting at his desk looking at Olly Murton's laptop. It was angled towards a pretty ponytailed woman, wearing jeans and a checked shirt, who was sitting next to him. She was tapping rapidly at the keys and Shepherd was chewing the knuckle of his left index finger the way he always did when he was nervous.

'I see what you mean,' he was saying as the woman pointed at the screen. He looked up at Burton. 'Hey boss, this is Carol from the tech section.' The woman stood and offered her hand to Burton, who shook it.

'I brought back the laptop,' said Carol. 'We cracked the password really quickly.'

'I wish everyone in tech was that efficient,' said Burton with a smile.

'We are really busy, but Mark – I mean, Detective Sergeant Shepherd – said it was urgent,' Carol said, looking down at Shepherd with a smile and a slight flush to her cheeks.

Burton raised an eyebrow and smiled at Shepherd who was also now blushing. Carol sat back down and tapped at a few keys.

'There you go, that's everything I found,' she said, smiling at Shepherd. She stood up.

'What about the flash drive?' Burton asked.

Carol frowned. 'We're having a bit more trouble with that one,' she said. 'It's got a pretty good encryption and—'

'Encryption?' Burton and Shepherd said together.

'What the hell is a student doing with an encrypted flash drive?' Burton asked, hands on hips.

Carol looked frightened. 'I— I don't know,' she said, looking from Burton to Shepherd.

'It's ok, you don't need to answer that,' he said smiling at her.

She smiled back. 'There's no evidence of an encryption programme on the laptop. Did you find any other flash drives?'

Shepherd shook his head.

'Ok,' she said. 'That makes it more difficult but I'll let you know if we have any success.' She turned and headed towards the door. Then she hesitated and turned back. 'So, call me,' she said, winking at Shepherd and leaving the room. Burton laughed and shook her head.

'What?' demanded Shepherd.

'Are you going to call this one?'

Shepherd looked down at his hands clasped on the desk. 'Probably not.'

Burton sighed heavily. 'You're going to have to call one someday.'

'Why?'

'I don't understand you. Women throw themselves at you but you never do anything about it.'

Shepherd shrugged. 'I don't want to.'

Burton paused for a second. 'Stacey's gone, Mark, and I don't think she'd want you to mope around forever.'

Shepherd stared at his hands, still folded on the surface of the desk and said nothing. He still found talking about his dead wife difficult and Burton knew not to push him any further.

Burton cleared her throat. 'So, what is Olly doing with an encrypted flash drive?' she asked.

'And no way to decrypt it,' Shepherd added.

'There definitely wasn't anything else in his room?'

Shepherd shook his head. 'Forensics finished the sweep and there was nothing else.'

'Could he have left it at university?'

Shepherd shrugged. 'It's not like they have lockers and stuff so I doubt it.'

Burton growled in the back of her throat. 'Right, what have tech found on the laptop?'

'I was just about to start looking at the laptop. I've been through his bank statements and they make for interesting reading,' Shepherd said, patting a hand on top of the folder containing Olly's financial paperwork. 'The cash payments go back over at least a year. That's the statements that he's kept. I've got a call in to his bank for earlier stuff.'

'And being cash we can't trace them?' Burton asked.

Shepherd nodded. 'Sadly not. But I have found something interesting.'

Burton moved to stand behind him. 'Go ahead,' she said.

Shepherd made a few clicks with the mouse and opened up Olly's emails. 'This is his personal email, rather than his university account,' he said. 'And this is his calendar.' He clicked on a small icon at the bottom of the screen and a calendar opened. Shepherd clicked on a button to take the calendar back a week. Then he pointed a finger. 'Look, a blank appointment of an hour on that day.' Then he flicked through the statements and pointed. 'And a cash payment into the bank the following day.'

Burton leaned forward to look at the screen. 'Is there any indication of who he was meeting?'

'Not as yet. There's no name on the appointment.'

'That would have been too much to ask,' said Burton, standing up straight with her hands on her hips.

Shepherd looked up at her. 'There's something else,' he said. He turned back to the computer screen and clicked on one of the emails. Burton leaned down behind him and looked where he pointed.

She frowned. 'Olly was meeting DS Adams?' she asked, standing up straight and folding her arms.

'Yup,' said Shepherd turning in his chair to look at her.

Burton stared at him. 'Who's DS Adams?' she asked.

Shepherd shook his head. 'No idea,' he said. 'But it's a bit weird that Olly was on his way to meet this person when he was murdered.'

Burton was staring down the office. 'I don't know any Adams,' she said.

Shepherd nodded. 'Me neither. I've got some calls in though to see if I can track him or her down.'

Burton sighed. 'If Olly was involved in another investigation and no one told me then there's going to be hell to pay.'

Shepherd turned back to the computer. 'Olly's deleted loads of emails but Carol's managed to find them and has put them onto this.' He waved a computer memory stick. 'I still need to look through them.'

'What about his university account?' Burton asked.

'That's even more interesting,' said Shepherd, opening up another email account. 'Most of it is junk mail or notes from lecturers and other students.'

'I thought he didn't have any friends?' Burton asked, frowning.

'Well, these don't so much seem like friends. Again, they were deleted but Carol managed to recover them. Look.' He clicked open one of the emails.

Burton leaned down to read the screen. Then she gave a low

whistle. 'That doesn't sound very friendly, does it?'

'I can't quite work out what this guy is on about, but it seems like he's suggesting that Olly did something to one of his friends,' Shepherd said. 'Something about a woman going missing.'

'Did Olly reply?'

Shepherd shook his head. 'I can't find one. But then, would you reply to that?'

'Hmm, not if it was going to lead to me "having my legs broken or worse",' Burton quoted. 'Does it say who the friend is?'

Shepherd shook his head. 'No, it's just this one email from this guy.'

'Any others?' Burton asked, straightening up and stretching her back.

'There's a couple that seem to be asking him about a job. Olly replies and asks them to meet him. They agree and that's that.'

Burton was frowning so hard Shepherd was worried her face would get stuck like that. It wasn't a pleasant look. While she stood without speaking, he scrolled back up to the top of Olly's university account. He began to flick down the emails and one brought him up short. His sharp intake of breath made Burton's face relax.

'What?' she asked.

'There's one here from Harry Evans,' Shepherd said, his eyes scanning the email.

'About the dissertation Olly was working on?'

It was Shepherd's turn to frown. 'I'm not sure that's what it's about.'

Burton leaned down again, resting her hands on the back of Shepherd's chair and reading over his shoulder.

'"Please Olly, don't do anything stupid. There are some things that you can't take back once you've done them, so just think of the repercussions",' she read aloud. '"We need to talk. When can we meet?"' Then she stepped back. 'What on earth was Olly going to do?'

But Shepherd was still reading. 'That's in response to an email from Olly that says "I know who killed Keith and I'm going to the police. I've done something terrible and it's the only way out that I can think of."'

'Did they meet?' Burton asked.

Shepherd peered at the screen. 'There're no more emails from Harry Evans here.' He clicked on the sent items folder and read the list of emails. 'Aha, here's Olly's reply.' He read silently and then leaned back in his chair and exhaled heavily.

'What?' Burton asked.

'He tells Evans that he'll be on campus by the lake at three o'clock,' said Shepherd, pointing to the screen with a stubby finger.

Burton was silent, arms folded across her chest. Then she said, 'That sounds to me like Olly's suggesting that he knows – or suspects – that Evans killed Keith Williams and is going to tell the police.'

Shepherd nodded. 'And Olly's told him exactly where he's going to be.'

'Olly's killed and Evans happens to be in the area with no alibi.' Burton turned and grabbed her handbag. Shepherd stood up too. 'Let's go and pick up Dr Evans and see what he has to say for himself,' Burton said.

Chapter thirty-four

Harry was summing up the key points of a seminar for a group of first year students. He was pleased with their progress, but they were starting to look glassy-eyed. Although notes were being taken he wondered how much of it was sticking in their tired brains. They were just beginning to pack away notebooks and pens into bags when the door opened. Desmond Danby stood there looking awkward.

'I'm sorry, Harry, the police – they insisted.' Behind Danby, Burton and Shepherd were stony-faced.

Harry sighed. 'Can't you wait in my office? I'll be straight back.'

'I'm afraid this can't wait.' Shepherd stepped forward into the room. A couple of the female students, and one of the male, shot him admiring glances.

'Dr Evans, we need you to come down to the police station and answer some questions in connection with the murder of Professor Keith Williams,' Shepherd said. 'I need you to come with me now.'

Harry stared at him, his face flushing, as all the students' eyes turned towards him.

'Are you arresting me?'

Shepherd ignored his question. 'You need to come with us,' he said, and indicated for Harry to walk ahead of him.

Shepherd followed Harry out of the door and, as it closed behind them, excited chatter broke out in the seminar room.

Chapter thirty-five

Dan was almost waiting by the door when Ed came in from work.

'The things I do for you,' Ed said, pulling Emma's diary out of his bag. Dan took it from him and walked into the living room, flicking through the pages.

'Cheers, mate. Did you have to explain to Daisy?' Dan asked.

Ed shook his head, grinning. 'I managed to get it without her seeing. Got a few funny looks from the junior reporters but none of them argued. Hopefully they'll not mention it to Daisy either.'

'Would have looked dodgier if I appeared in the office, raided Emma's desk and then left again,' Dan said with a grin, sitting down on the sofa. Ed padded into the room, his left big toe poking out from his sock, and sat in the armchair opposite.

'So why am I stealing stuff from your girlfriend's desk?' he asked.

'Not stealing. She gave me permission,' Dan replied, holding up the diary.

'OK, why am I taking stuff from Emma's desk with her permission?' Dan quickly told Ed the whole story. Ed stared at him.

'You think this WillT1998 might be connected with two murders and you're going to see him? On your own?' Ed asked.

'Don't worry, I'll make it somewhere public. I'm not that stupid.'

Ed pulled a sceptical face. 'I don't know, mate. What are you hoping to get out of him? That he killed Keith Williams?'

Dan looked down at the diary open in his hands. 'I don't know, to be honest. I want to know what he knows about his mate's disappearance – from his own mouth, not through reports of it. I also want to know what he thinks Keith did and whether he knows who she went to meet and just hasn't said.'

'And you think Olly Murton might be involved as well?'

Dan thought for a moment. 'He said he'd done something terrible. What if it was that he'd made her run away? Or that he hurt her.'

Ed frowned. 'Is that likely?'

'He didn't seem like the type, but, to be honest, I didn't really know him,' Dan said, shaking his head. 'He was working with Keith Williams so it's likely he knew something.' He sat back on the sofa cushions and flipped idly through the diary pages. 'The thing is,' he went on, still looking at the diary, 'if he did know something, and he's been killed for it, then who else is involved? Who could have killed him?'

Ed frowned. 'It could be Harry Evans, couldn't it? I mean, he had a problem with both of them from what you've said.'

'I'm just not convinced,' Dan said.

'He has no alibi for Olly's death, does he? I mean, like you said, his office overlooks the lake and yet he claims to have seen nothing?'

Dan was silent.

'I get it,' Ed said. 'You like the guy, you don't want it to be him, but you have to consider the possibility he could be involved. Does he have an alibi for Keith Williams' murder?'

'He was in the library,' Dan said, looking up at Ed.

Ed's eyes widened. 'That looks really dodgy. He was there and just happened to find the body of a man he hated?'

Dan puffed out his cheeks and exhaled a long breath. 'I need to talk to Harry, don't I? It's not going to be a fun conversation.'

'If you're going to sort this out, then you need to get the truth out of him, Ed said.

'And I will, once I've talked to Will Turner.'

Ed slapped his hands on his knees and stood up. 'OK, but be careful. I've got to get back to the office and pretend I've been out for lunch.' He paused and then pulled an envelope from his pocket. 'I almost forgot. This came in the office post for you this morning.'

'Thanks.' Dan took it and glanced at the writing on the front. He ripped it open and pulled out a sheaf of A4 printed pages. He looked at the diagram of numbers and letters linked by straight lines.

'What is that?' Ed asked, staring at the pages.

Dan shrugged. 'No idea.' He folded the pages and shoved them back into the envelope.

'OK, well, call me if you need anything,' Ed said, heading for the door.

'Will do.' Dan's attention was fully back on the diary, flicking through the pages until he found Emma's note to herself to contact Will Turner. There was a mobile phone number copied next to his name in Emma's careful, precise handwriting. Dan picked up his phone and began to dial.

Dan was glad that Will Turner had agreed to meet somewhere other than the university library café. In fact, the student seemed pleased to meet somewhere off campus.

'It can get a bit claustrophobic there, and I'd prefer it if we weren't seen together,' he'd said.

Dan thought that was a bit weird, given that no other students were likely to know who he was, but if it got him the story then it was fine by him.

When he arrived at the café on the High Street, Will was already waiting. He'd bought himself a coffee and was sitting in a window table, staring out at the street. He looked up as Dan sat down in front of him.

'I thought the paper wasn't interested in the story?' he said without preamble. 'Your colleague only wrote a few paragraphs.'

Dan took a deep breath, trying to think of the best way to approach it. He decided to be truthful. 'I came across this forum online,' he said, pulling the printouts from his bag and laying them on the table. Will leaned forward and looked at them without touching them.

'I see,' was all he said.

'The story we were given said nothing about this.' Dan pointed at the pages. 'It said nothing about the possible involvement of Keith Williams and some shady character.'

'Well, it wouldn't, would it? They hushed it up.'

'Who did?'

'The university. They didn't want people to know that one of the staff was up to something with a student.' Will leaned forward aggressively. 'They didn't really listen to me.'

'And you're convinced that Keith Williams was involved?' Dan asked, holding up the printout of the forum.

'She told me!' Will's voice was loud enough that it rang around the café. He paused, looked around and lowered his voice again. 'She told me that he'd agreed to help out with some money. She needed money for rent and none of us could sub her. I said she should ask her parents but she didn't want to.'

'Why not?' Dan sipped his coffee. 'I'd have thought they'd be first port of call.'

Will shook his head. 'They're quite tight with money. Always going on about her learning to stand on her own two feet. So she tried to find another way to get it.'

'Did you think Keith was going to lend it to her or suggest someone else who could do it?' Dan asked.

Will paused in the act of lifting his coffee cup to his lips, shrugged and put his cup back on its saucer. 'I don't know what I thought was going to happen. All I know is that she went out saying she had to meet this guy. She texted me to say she'd left her keys behind so would I be in the house later. I said yes and I waited up till one o'clock in the morning. But she never came home.'

'Did you try calling her?' Dan asked, and then regretted stating the obvious when he saw the look of disdain on Will's face.

'Of course we did, but it only ever went to voicemail. No response to texts or emails or anything.'

Dan frowned. 'Did they try to locate her phone through GPS?' he asked.

Will nodded. 'They tried, I think, but her phone was switched off or out of battery.'

'Did she have any money with her? Did the police check bank and credit cards and stuff?' Dan was wracking his brains to think of what the usual police procedure was.

Will nodded. 'They said she used her card to buy a weekly bus ticket in the morning and then nothing after that.'

Dan sat forward. 'Bus ticket? I don't remember hearing about that.'

'Maybe they didn't release it,' Will said, sipping his coffee, 'but that's what the police told us had happened.'

'Did she usually travel by bus?' Dan asked.

Will shook his head again. 'No, she walked or took her bike. That's why we thought it was so important. It was out of character for her.'

'So she may have been going somewhere further afield,' said Dan, staring at the froth on his cappuccino, his brain whirring.

Will shrugged and took a sip from his cup.

'Was she ever seen getting on a bus? Any CCTV or anything?' Dan asked.

Will frowned. 'Not that I know of, but the police must have looked into that, mustn't they?'

'If she bought a bus ticket, then I'm sure they did.' But Dan wasn't convinced. He didn't remember Emma mentioning anything about CCTV footage or still images being used in appeals for information. Surely the police couldn't have overlooked it. He opened his mouth to speak but Will's mobile was beeping. He picked it up.

'Sorry, a text from my housemate asking where I am. I'll let him know. Since Leanne went missing he's a bit nervy.' His thumbs rapidly tapped at the screen, while Dan stared into space, trying to make sense of everything. What had Leanne been doing with Keith Williams? Could she have been responsible for his death? That was a stupid idea. Could he be responsible for her disappearance? Was she connected to Olly too?

He looked up to find Will staring at him.

'Any more questions?' the student asked.

Dan took a punt. 'Do you know Olly Murton?' he asked.

Will raised an eyebrow. 'The guy who died the other day?' he asked. 'I know him by sight but I don't think I've ever spoken to him.' He lifted his cup to his lips without sipping and seemed keen to avoid Dan's eye.

But before Dan could say anything else, the door flew open and a man stumbled into the café. He looked around and spotting Will, rushed to the table.

'Will, you're not going to believe this.' He dropped into a chair. 'Harry Evans has been arrested.'

'What?' asked Dan.

The lad turned to him as if noticing him for the first time. 'Who's this?' he asked Will, indicating Dan with his thumb.

'One of the reporters from the Post. Asking questions about Leanne.'

The lad flapped a hand. 'Never mind that. Don't you see, they've arrested Harry for murdering Keith. Harry was really mad with Keith when you told him about Leanne. What if he's actually killed him? He told you he'd sort it out, didn't he? And we saw him in the library that night.'

'Killing Keith wouldn't sort it out. Harry would know that, wouldn't he?' Will was looking nervously at Dan.

But Dan was gulping the last of his coffee. 'I've gotta go. I'll let you know if I hear anything about Leanne.' He was out of the café, door banging behind him before either student could react.

Chapter thirty-six

This time, when Burton and Shepherd entered the interview room, Harry was ready for them, with a solicitor by his side. He saw Burton and Shepherd give each other a sideways look as they sat down. Shepherd was carrying a large book in a plastic evidence bag and a brown cardboard folder. Harry noticed that the gold lettering on the book's spine said *Politics Today*. The recording machine was set in motion and introductions were made.

The solicitor spoke first. 'My client tells me he's already been interviewed at length about the death of Professor Keith Williams,' he said. 'He's told you everything he knows and I'd like to hear good reason why he's been taken so publicly from his workplace.'

Burton looked at him, stony-faced. 'Dr Evans' answers as to his location at the time of Professor Williams' death have been called into question by evidence gathered since we last spoke.'

Harry opened his mouth to speak but the solicitor raised a hand to stop him. 'What evidence? We haven't been made aware of anything.'

'Dr Evans, what time did you arrive at the library on the night you found Professor Williams?' Shepherd asked.

'I swiped in at about five-forty. I remember looking at the clock in my office before I left and thinking my wife would be angry with me for being late home again.'

'If you were running late, why stop off at the library?' Shepherd asked.

'I've told you this before. I needed an article for a seminar I was planning for the following day. I wanted to be able to finish the prep when I got home.'

'You're sure it was five-forty when you arrived?'

'Yes.'

'See, that's not what our CCTV footage says,' Shepherd said, leaning forward and sliding a photograph across the table. It was a still image taken from a CCTV recording showing Harry swiping a card to enter through the library barriers. Shepherd tapped a finger on the time stamp in the top right-hand corner. 'It has you arriving at about five-twenty-five.'

Harry stared at the photograph and then looked at his solicitor. The man was looking at the picture. 'That must be wrong because, when I left, the clock in my office said it was five-twenty-five. There's no way I got to the library any earlier than that.'

Burton raised an eyebrow and then looked back at the notes in front of her. 'What did you do when you got to the library?' she asked, without looking up.

'I went straight to the politics section. I knew what I was looking for and where it was.'

'Did you see anyone around?' Burton asked.

Harry nodded. 'I saw some of my master's degree students in their usual seats. I waved to them.'

'Who are they?' Burton asked.

'Will Turner and two of his friends.'

Burton leaned over and murmured something in Shepherd's ear. He began to tap at the screen of his phone and then showed it to her. When she finished reading what was on the screen, Burton continued

'Our officers attended the scene at the library and interviewed everyone who was there. We have no record of speaking to a Will Turner. Are you sure you saw him?'

The solicitor was glaring at Burton. 'Again, Detective Inspector, we've had no warning of this evidence, or lack thereof.'

But Burton raised a hand. 'This proves that Dr Evans can't say for certain what time he arrived at the library. No one remembers seeing you at five-forty when you say you arrived. In other words, you have no alibi for the time that Professor Williams was killed.'

Harry stared at Burton.

'Don't say a word,' the solicitor advised, putting a hand on Harry's arm. Harry obeyed.

'There's also this,' Shepherd said, pushing the book across the desk.

Harry leaned forward. '*Politics Today*? That's what I was looking for.' He saw the smile on Shepherd's face and felt his stomach drop.

'It's also the murder weapon,' Shepherd said. He leaned forward, clasping his hands on the table. Burton did the same. 'If you hadn't yet got the book, want to tell me how your fingerprints are on it?'

Chapter thirty-seven

Harry stared at him and it took a warning glance from his solicitor to keep him from speaking. Shepherd stared back at him for a long time and then spoke in the direction of the voice recorder.

'Are you refusing to answer the question, Dr Evans?' he asked.

Burton was watching Harry with a directness that made him very uncomfortable. 'Is there a good reason why your fingerprints are on it? Had you perhaps used the book recently?' she asked.

Harry shook his head. 'I don't know. I might have used it a couple of weeks ago.'

'How often do people pick it up, would you say?' Burton asked.

The solicitor interrupted. 'Don't answer that. Detective Inspector, how could my client possibly know that? It could have been handled by any number of people. How many sets of prints did you recover?'

'Just your client's.' Harry thought Burton was looking irritated. 'The rest of the book was clean.'

'Well then,' said the solicitor, 'if my client had used the book to bludgeon his colleague, wouldn't he have wiped his fingerprints away?'

A thought struck Harry and he sat forward and put his face in his hands. 'I picked it up off the floor,' he said quietly. 'I picked it up and I was about to walk away with it when I saw that someone was trapped between the bookcases. I shoved it back onto the shelf and then ran over to see what had happened.' When he looked up, Burton, Shepherd and the solicitor were all looking at him.

Burton sighed heavily. 'You told us you didn't touch anything.'

'I forgot. In the shock of finding Keith it went out of my head until now,' Harry said. 'Besides, it wasn't that near his body so I didn't think anything of it.'

Burton scowled at him for what felt like five minutes, but was probably less than one. Harry shifted awkwardly in his seat. She seemed to be trying to look into his brain to see what he was really thinking.

'Moving on,' she continued. 'We have the death of Olly Murton, a student of yours. He was found dead in the lake on campus, in full view of your office window. You claim to have been in your office all afternoon and yet heard and saw nothing.'

'I was in my office, but I stepped out to get a coffee,' Harry said. His stomach was clenching.

'How convenient,' Burton said. 'You just happened to step out of your office at exactly the time someone was being murdered.' She indicated to Shepherd and he took a sheet of paper from the cardboard folder and slid it across the table. Both Harry and the solicitor leaned forward to look at it but neither touched or picked it up.

'That's an email conversation between you and Olly Murton,' Shepherd said, pointing to it. 'In it he tells you exactly where he's going to be so you can meet.'

Harry looked down at the page and nodded. 'Yes, I saw that.'

'So why weren't you by the lake at three o clock as arranged?'

Harry stared at him. 'I was. I went to the lake at three o clock and waited for about ten minutes. Olly didn't show up so I went to get a coffee. I was going to come back. I assumed he was just running late.'

Shepherd was staring at Harry as if he'd lost his mind. 'You weren't there at three o clock waiting,' he said. 'No one reports having seen you there.'

'I was there,' Harry insisted.

'What had Olly done?' Burton interrupted.

'Sorry?' Harry was puzzled.

'In the email he says he's done something terrible, that he knows who killed Keith Williams,' Burton said. 'Was he threatening you? Did he know that you did it?'

Harry frowned. 'What are you talking about? Why would Olly think that? He wasn't in the library when Keith died.'

Shepherd nodded. 'Yes, he was. In fact he found Professor Williams before you say you did and stole his office keys so he could look for the research.'

Harry turned a bewildered glance towards his solicitor. 'Stole his keys to— I don't understand what's going on.'

The solicitor stepped in. 'This interview is becoming very jumbled,' he said. 'Surely if this student found the body before my client did then Dr Evans couldn't have killed Keith Williams.'

Burton frowned. 'Dr Evans claims that he found Professor Williams dead, but we have no proof because he was already in the library at the time we believe the murder took place,' she said.

'Exactly what are you accusing my client of?'

'We believe that Dr Evans killed Professor Williams in a fit of rage because he was going to prevent you from getting a new job,' Burton said.

'What are you talking about? How did you know about the job?' Harry demanded and then kicked himself mentally. 'I didn't think anyone else knew about that.'

Shepherd looked steadily at Harry. 'So it's true? He did block you from getting the job you wanted?' he asked.

Harry sighed heavily. 'I had heard from the person who interviewed me that Keith had bad-mouthed me to someone else on the panel and it meant they were questioning whether to employ me. Yes, I was angry and I went to the library looking for him. But he was dead when I found him.'

'Olly Murton saw you, didn't he, in the library?' Burton asked. 'Did he see you kill Professor Williams and that's why you killed him too? Am I getting close?' She was leaning forward on the table staring at Harry. 'Did you think that Olly was going to tell the police what you'd done?

'But I didn't do it. I don't know why Olly would think that I had,' Harry said. 'I was worried about him. I assumed he had killed Keith and was going to confess.'

'Surely that would have been helpful,' Burton said, still leaning across the table. 'It would have taken the heat off you.'

'Maybe, but I didn't kill Keith and I don't think Olly did either,' Harry said. 'They liked each other. Well, in so much as Keith liked anyone. In fact, I suspect that Keith recently helped Olly to cheat on an assignment.'

Burton sat back and folded her arms. 'What makes you think that?'

'I marked a chapter of Olly's dissertation and, quite frankly, it was way too good to be something he'd written. I told him to go away and rewrite it without help and I'd re-mark it. It was only afterwards that I realised whose style it reminded me of.'

Shepherd was frowning, head cocked to one side. 'You were going to stop Olly from confessing to the murder?'

'I wasn't convinced he did it. But then I didn't know about him finding the body or stealing keys,' Harry said. 'I wanted to hear his side and then decide whether I thought he had done it and should go to the police. I knew if he lied to the police he could be charged and I didn't want that on his record.'

'You and he didn't get on though, did you?' Shepherd asked.

Harry shook his head. 'It wasn't a matter of whether we got on. We only met about his dissertation so I didn't spend a lot of time with him, to be honest. It was more than enough though.' He paused and then went on. 'Olly wasn't a particularly nice person. He spent a lot of time listening at doors and passing on information to other people.'

'Would that explain the sums of money being paid into his bank account, do you think?' Shepherd asked, leaning his forearms on the table. Burton looked at him but didn't interrupt.

Harry was surprised. 'You think someone was paying him to spy on people?'

'Would Keith Williams do that?'

Harry shrugged. 'I don't know. Maybe. Keith did always seem to know a lot about what was going on.'

Burton was staring at the file on the table in front of her. Harry could almost hear the cogs of her brain whirring as she thought about the next move.

The solicitor spoke. 'Detective Inspector, my client is not under arrest and he's been questioned for over an hour without a break. I suggest we leave it there unless you've got something pressing to discuss.'

Harry expected Burton to argue but instead she agreed, looking like she was grinding her teeth.

There was a knock on the door and a uniformed constable entered clutching a piece of paper. He strode around the table to give it to Shepherd, who looked down at it. He frowned and showed it to Burton. Then he gave a jerk of his head towards the door. She raised an eyebrow and turned back to Harry.

'Okay, Dr Evans, we need to take a break and come back to you. We'll have someone bring in some coffee while you're waiting.' Burton and Shepherd got up and followed the constable out of the room.

Chapter thirty-eight

In the corridor outside the room, Burton turned to Shepherd, hands on hips.

'Are we really pausing an interview to go and speak to Dan Sullivan?' she asked.

'I thought we needed a break,' Shepherd replied, beginning to walk down the corridor to the reception area. 'Let Dr Evans stew for a bit longer. His solicitor was starting to look irritated.'

They pushed through the door and found Dan reading a poster about not leaving items on view in your car when parking.

'What kind of numpty does that?' he asked when he saw them approaching, pointing at the poster.

'You'd be surprised.' Shepherd looked at Dan. The journalist appeared excited. 'What can we do for you?'

'It's about the Keith Williams case.'

'We've told you everything we can,' Shepherd began, but Dan held up a hand.

'For once I'm not looking for information. I've got something I think will interest you.'

Burton turned to the reception desk and asked the officer on duty to open the door of the interview room on the right-hand side. The lock buzzed and she pushed open the door. Dan followed her inside.

When they were seated at the table in the middle of the room, Dan pulled a plastic wallet out of his ever-present satchel.

'I found this out about Keith Williams.' He pushed the wallet containing several sheets of paper across the table and sat back, looking pleased with himself.

Shepherd pulled out the printed pages and began to read, Burton looking over his shoulder. They'd barely reached the end of the first page when Shepherd looked up at Dan, frowning. 'Is this what I think it is?' he asked.

Dan nodded. 'I got it from a students' forum. After I gave my statement to your mate I got to thinking. Olly had said he was working on something with Keith. I did a bit of Googling to see if I could find out what it was. Instead, I came across this.' Dan pointed at the printed pages. 'What if their deaths are connected to this?'

'Connected to this woman going missing?' Shepherd asked.

'Yes. The people posting aren't using their real names, but then I remembered that we'd covered the story at the time she went missing. Well, Emma did. So I rang Emma. She remembered the name of the woman's friend who'd reported her missing, Will Turner. So I called him up—'

'You called him? Where did you get his number from?' Burton asked, intrigued in spite of herself.

'Emma had it. He'd called her recently wanting to do another appeal for information but Emma couldn't get the news desk to do much about it. I went to see him this morning. He's still pretty angry with Keith Williams.'

'He blames Williams for her disappearance,' Shepherd said, pointing to the relevant paragraph.

'What I can't work out,' Dan said, 'is what she was doing for him. She needed money, so it was obviously a way to get that, but why would she then just disappear?'

Burton and Shepherd sat quietly for a moment, staring down at the pages. Then they looked up at each other, neither knowing how to make sense of what they were seeing.

'That means,' said Dan, tapping the pages again, 'that there's someone else out there who would have been angry enough to whack Keith Williams on the head if he met him.'

'And Olly Murton?' Burton asked, wondering where Dan was going.

Dan's eyes were shining. 'When I saw Will this morning he said she'd had to go and meet a guy. What if that guy was Olly Murton?'

Burton looked at Shepherd. He was frowning in the way that suggested that he was making some connections.

Dan was sitting forward in his chair, forearms on the table, nodding as if he could hear Shepherd's thoughts. Then he said, 'So you see, now that we know there's someone other than Harry who would want Keith Williams dead, you can let him go.'

'How do you know Dr Evans is here?' Shepherd asked, raising his eyebrows.

'Will's mate turned up while we were talking and told him. It's all over campus apparently.'

'Did Dr Evans know about this?' Shepherd asked, gesturing to the pages.

'He knew that she'd gone missing obviously and Will Turner said Harry had told him he'd look into a possible connection with Keith. But whether he went looking at student forums, I don't know.'

'Would Will Turner have told Harry about his suspicions?'

Dan shrugged. 'He didn't say for sure, but I'm guessing he told them to anyone who'd listen. Will said the university had hushed it up, kept Keith Williams' involvement under wraps. I don't know whether that's true or not. Maybe they just didn't believe Will.'

Shepherd was staring into space again.

Burton shuffled the pages into a neat pile. 'Thanks for bringing this in,' she said, slipping them back into the wallet. 'It is appreciated, but please don't go digging into this any further. Stay away from these students until they've been fully investigated.'

Dan nodded, but Burton didn't look as if she really believed him. She got to her feet, nudging Shepherd as she did. He got up too.

'You'll keep me posted on it?' Dan asked, standing up and slinging his bag across his shoulders.

'As far as we can.'

'Fair enough.' Dan followed them out into the reception area. 'One other thing I've been meaning to ask,' he said as he moved towards the door. 'Have you made any more progress on the George Peters case?'

'It still looks like it was a heart attack, so we'll be wrapping things up for the coroner relatively soon,' Burton said.

'Did his parents ever change their mind about speaking to the media?'

Shepherd shook his head. 'No, so the instruction is still to leave them in peace.'

'No problem. Thanks again. I'll call for an update soon.' With a grin and a wave, Dan left, leaving Burton and Shepherd standing in the reception area looking after him.

Chapter thirty-nine

Harry felt like he and his solicitor had been drinking coffee for hours when Burton and Shepherd returned to the room. He straightened up in his chair as they sat down, and pushed his plastic coffee cup to one side. Shepherd put the printed pages on the table, as Burton switched on the voice recorder and repeated the details of who was present.

'We've just been given this,' Shepherd told Harry, pushing the papers towards him.

Harry and his solicitor peered down at them. Both raised their eyebrows and then looked up at Burton and Shepherd. Harry was about to speak when his solicitor laid a warning hand on his arm.

'What's going on, Detective Inspector Burton? You can't introduce something without prior warning. This wasn't in the initial disclosure.'

Burton sat back in her chair.

Harry was staring down at the pages. 'I don't understand. How is this relevant? What's it about?'

'Do you remember a student called Leanne Nelson?' Burton asked.

'Yes, of course. She went missing last year. I helped with the searches around campus.'

'Did you know at the time that Keith Williams was accused of being involved in her disappearance?'

Harry frowned. 'I know he was questioned about it, we all were, and that there were rumours flying around—'

'You didn't believe these rumours?' Burton interrupted.

Harry shrugged. 'I know Leanne's friends were really upset, as you'd expect. They were very vocal about what they thought had happened. Something about Leanne needing money and Keith saying that he'd help her. But there was no proof that he'd said anything of the kind.'

'No emails?' Burton asked.

Harry laughed mirthlessly. 'Keith wouldn't be stupid enough to leave a paper trail.'

'You believed that he was involved?' Burton asked.

Harry shrugged. 'I wished that he was. I think I hoped that it would be the end of him, get him away from me. It might also have helped us to find Leanne, but at the same time I didn't want to believe that he was capable of hurting a student.'

Shepherd looked down at the forum posts and then back to Harry. 'You weren't angry with Keith about that? You didn't hold him responsible?'

'I did at first. The students were so adamant about it, and I'd love to think badly of Keith, but the more I thought about it the more I thought it couldn't be possible,' Harry said. 'I mean, what would he have made her do for the money? To the best of my knowledge he wasn't taking on research assistants or anything like that.'

'You think what the students are alleging isn't true?' Shepherd asked.

Harry looked sadly down at the table. 'I really don't know. At first I was so sure she'd been involved in something with Keith but, like I said, there was no evidence.'

Burton looked at Shepherd and Harry held his breath. What was coming next?

'OK,' she said. 'I think we're done for now. But stay in town. We may need to speak to you again.'

Harry said goodbye to his solicitor outside the police station having turned down a lift back to campus. He needed time to think. He hadn't gone five steps when a voice called, 'Harry!'

He turned to see Dan Sullivan sitting on a wall near the police station door. He was getting to his feet and shoving his mobile phone into his pocket. Harry turned away.

'Hey, wait up.' Dan jogged a few paces and appeared at his elbow. Harry thrust his hands into his jacket pockets and carried on walking. 'Hey, come on, Harry.' Dan moved forward and stood in Harry's path, stopping him from going any further. 'Come on, Harry, talk to me.'

'As a journalist or a former student?' Harry tried to push past but Dan stood his ground. 'How did you know I was here?'

'A little bird told me,' Dan said. Harry raised his eyebrows. 'Alright, it was one of your students. He said you'd been arrested.'

'Not arrested,' said Harry, kicking the toe of his shoe against a wonky paving stone. 'Just in for questioning. But I guess that's not the story that's now flying around campus.' He started to walk and Dan fell into step.

'I knew they'd have to let you go once I'd given them that stuff,' he began conversationally.

Harry stopped dead and Dan had walked a few paces before realising he was alone. He turned back.

'Gave them what stuff?' Harry asked.

'I found some stuff on a student forum, accusing Keith of having something to do with the disappearance of a student last year. I printed it out and gave it to Burton and Shepherd.'

Harry was staring at him. 'You gave them that stuff? Why?'

'Because I don't think you killed Keith. But Will Turner, who I was having coffee with earlier said—'

'You were having coffee with Will? Why?'

'He's behind those forum comments,' Dan said patiently. 'He spoke to Emma, our crime reporter, a little while ago about doing another appeal for information about his friend, but there wasn't much we could do. Emma kept his number though.'

'What did he say?' Harry asked. They'd reached the main road and were waiting at the traffic lights.

'He said you were angry when you found out about Keith being involved,' Dan said as the pedestrian crossing lit up green and they stepped into the road. 'He said you'd told him you'd sort it out.'

Harry sighed. 'I didn't mean I'd kill him. I meant that I'd push the police and the university to investigate him properly.'

'And did they?'

Harry shrugged. 'I wasn't completely satisfied, but then I thought why would Keith hurt a student? It just seemed ridiculous.' He stopped walking when they reached the pavement and looked around. Dan stopped too.

'Where are you going?' he asked.

'Back to campus. I suppose I'll have to get the bus as I arrived by police car.'

'I'll give you a lift,' Dan said. 'We can pick up my car from the flat. It's not far.'

'Why? What are you going to do?' Harry asked, starting to walk again.

'We are going to be working out who could have killed Keith and Olly, and why.'

Chapter forty

Dan and Harry were walking up the stairs towards Harry's office when they heard a door slamming. They walked quickly up the next couple of stairs and saw Desmond Danby walking towards them with a laptop case tucked under his arm. Dan thought that as soon as Desmond saw them he looked guilty.

'Hi Desmond,' Harry began. 'What are you up to?' Dan thought that was a casual inquiry, but Desmond's face flushed in response.

'Nothing. I'm not up to anything,' he said, clutching the laptop case. Then he gave Harry a surprised look. 'The police let you go then?'

Harry nodded. 'Yes, I only had to answer some questions.'

'Actually,' Dan put in, 'they were also asking Harry about Leanne Nelson's disappearance.'

Desmond's eyebrows shot up. 'Leanne Nelson? What about her?'

'Some students have been alleging that Keith had something to do with it,' Dan said. He couldn't quite work out the expression that passed across Desmond's face, but if he had to name it he'd say guilt.

'I thought the police proved he wasn't involved?' Desmond said, looking at Harry.

'I thought so too but maybe we missed something,' Harry said.

'The students are still saying it now,' Dan added. 'The police may have reopened the investigation, but I suppose with Keith dead there's nothing much they can do.' He watched Desmond for a response and was not disappointed. The expression was something akin to relief.

Desmond looked Dan up and down, clearly trying to cover his own awkwardness. 'Who are you?' he asked.

Harry shook his head. 'Sorry, Desmond, where are my manners? This is Dan Sullivan. He's a reporter at the Allensbury Post, but he used to be—'

Before Harry could finish, Desmond paled, muttered something and scuttled away down the corridor. Harry looked after him with a puzzled expression on his face.

'What did I say?' he asked.

Dan smiled. 'I think we've found another suspect. No one reacts to a journalist like that unless he's got something to hide. Did you see his face when you asked what he was up to?'

Harry nodded and they continued along the corridor, arriving at his door. As he unlocked it, he looked towards Keith Williams' office.

'Is Desmond's office down there as well?' Dan asked.

'No. It's that way.' Harry pointed in the direction the head of department had gone.

'Are you thinking what I'm thinking?' Dan asked.

Harry stared at him. 'What?'

'That Desmond may have been in Keith's office?' 'Why would he be in there?' Harry pushed open his office door and went inside, Dan following.

'You think Desmond is involved?' Harry asked, sitting down behind his desk.

Dan sat in the visitor's chair and dumped his bag on the floor.

'I don't know,' he said, resting his elbows on the armrests. 'I mean, he led the investigation into the allegations against Keith last year, he's always allowed Keith to get away with causing havoc for you, students have raised complaints about him over the years and Desmond has just swept them under the carpet.'

Harry leaned forward, resting his forearms on his desk. 'You think he was covering something up? That Keith had something on him?'

Dan shrugged. 'It's an idea. Keith could have been blackmailing him and Desmond finally had enough. He follows Keith to the library, finds him alone, gets angry and, whack.' He slammed his hand onto his thigh.

Harry stared at him. 'But Desmond always seems so placid, so calm,' he said. 'I can't see him whacking someone on the head.'

'I can't see you whacking someone on the head, or drowning them in the lake, but the police seem to think it's possible,' Dan countered. 'Everyone has a limit as to how far they can be pushed.'

Harry exhaled heavily. 'I suppose you've got a point.' He sat back in his chair, which creaked slightly. 'So who else could have killed Keith?'

'Olly Murton for one,' Dan said. 'They were up to something and Olly went really weird when I tried to get it out of him. Listen.' He pulled out his phone, found the right recording and played the section where Olly talked about the project he was working on with Keith Williams. When Dan stopped the recording, he looked up at Harry who was still staring at the phone.

'They were working on something to do with the Cold War?' Harry asked, frowning. 'I wonder what that was.'

Dan watched him thinking. Clearly Harry didn't know what Keith's research was about, despite Olly's suspicions, so the student's theory that Harry killed Keith for it were definitely wrong. Or was Harry pretending? Did he have another reason? He couldn't rule that out. Dan cleared his throat, bringing Harry's attention back to him.

'If Olly and Keith were working on something and Keith decided to cut Olly out, that would give him a motive,' Dan said.

'He was in the library too, on the night Keith died,' Harry said.

'Had he actually been inside? I saw him in the crowd after everyone was evacuated and he implied he'd only just got there. But if he was inside, there's his opportunity, and we don't need to worry about means because the murder weapon was on hand.' Dan sat back. 'That could have been the something terrible that Olly was going to tell the police,' he said.

'But then who murdered Olly?' Harry asked.

Dan scratched at a bit of stubble he'd missed when shaving that morning. 'I hadn't got that far yet,' he admitted. He paused and then said, 'Going back to Keith, before we move on to Olly, who else have we got? Will Turner was pretty angry with Keith about Leanne Nelson. He was obviously still hoping that the investigation would restart and catch Keith out. Maybe that's why he was pushing Emma to do the appeal for information.'

'But would he kill Keith?' Harry asked, swinging his swivel chair slightly side to side.

Dan shrugged. 'Maybe if he confronted Keith and Keith denied everything again, he might have lost his temper.' Then he said, 'Hang on, when I asked Will if he knew Olly Murton he was really evasive. He said he only knew him by sight, but he was definitely hiding something.'

'Did you not find out what it was?'

Dan grinned. 'No, at that point his mate dashed in and said you'd been arrested, so I thought I'd better come to the rescue.'

Harry laughed. 'Good job you did. So, what's our next move?'

Dan scratched his chin again. 'Let's go back to the scene of the crime. I get the feeling we're missing something.'

Chapter forty-one

The walk to the library took Dan and Harry through the chemistry department car park, which was next door. Dan was chatting away about a job he had the following day – covering a charity cheque presentation – when he realised he was talking to fresh air. He turned and found Harry standing a few feet away staring at a green Vauxhall Mokka. 'What?' he asked, walking back.

'That's Keith's car,' Harry said, pointing. 'What's it doing here?'

'Maybe he couldn't find a space anywhere else?'

But Harry was shaking his head. 'He liked to get as little exercise as possible. He'd never park this far away from the department, plus it's always in exactly the same spot in the politics car park.' He walked to the car and peered in through the window. He wrinkled his nose. 'What a tip. There's sweet wrappers all over the place and an old sandwich packet.'

Dan frowned. 'How is Keith's car still here? Would the police not have tracked it down?' He pulled out his phone. 'I'll call Burton and let her know. Might score myself some brownie points along the way.' Then he stopped. 'Hang on a second, why haven't the police found it? Surely he'd have had his keys on him when he died, they should have them, and then they'd know what car they're looking for.'

'You've got a point,' Harry said. 'So if the police haven't got them because Keith didn't have them, where are they? In his office?'

Dan shook his head. 'I don't think so. The police will have searched it. If he's parked this far away, he must have had the keys with him. He must have parked here to go to the library.' He paused and then pointed towards the building. 'You don't think that he could have left them in there?'

'Why would he leave his keys in the library?'

'I don't know. Why would a creature of habit suddenly park his car in a completely different place on the day he gets murdered?'

Harry nodded. 'I see what you mean.'

Dan frowned. 'Right, to the crime scene and let's see what we can find.'

The sensible place to start was the lost and found box at reception, but when Dan asked if they had a set of Vauxhall car keys he was met with shaken heads.

Harry began to walk towards the stairs but Dan pulled him across to the lift.

'I always take the stairs,' Harry said.

'Maybe you do,' Dan said, 'but the lad I spoke to said he saw Keith in the lift, so let's try and retrace his steps.' They stepped out onto the second floor and looked around.

Harry frowned. 'There's a lot of ground to cover. Where do we start?' he asked.

'The politics section seems the obvious choice,' Dan said. He turned in that direction, but then stopped.

'What?' Harry asked.

'What if he only ended up in the politics section?' Dan said. 'That lad said Keith seemed to be looking around for someone. What if he was trying to get away, rather than find them?'

Harry stared at Dan. 'He was being followed, you mean?'

Dan nodded. 'What if Keith came here to hide from someone, or at least shake them off?'

'And he assumed they'd think he would go straight for politics, so he went a different way,' Harry suggested.

'Exactly.' Dan looked around and then pointed. 'These shelves here are the nearest, so I think he'd have gone this way.' He began to walk towards the shelves to the left, Harry following.

He began to make his way through the corridors created by the shelves, turning left and right until he arrived at a space where there were more tables. Heads popped up to see what they were doing. Again, Harry and Dan stepped into the relative privacy of a row of bookcases.

'He arrives here,' Dan said in a low voice. 'Then realises he's not lost the person following him. What does he do next?'

'He ended up over there,' Harry pointed. 'But which way did he go?'

Dan turned on the spot for a moment and said, 'If it were me, I'd want to get a bit further away without boxing myself into a corner. I'd go this way.' He followed a path through several more bookcases and stopped. 'Then I spot my man there.' He pointed again. 'I realise that the game's up, I might not escape and I need – for some reason – to hide my car keys. So, the keys must be down here somewhere.' He gestured down the row of bookshelves they were standing in.

Harry began to walk along, glancing from side to side at the shelves. Then he stopped and stared.

'Oh it couldn't be—' he began.

'What?' Dan followed.

Harry put out his hand and pulled a book from the shelf. 'Tremlett and Stour. It's his favourite text for teaching.' He reached his hand into the space left by the book and grinned. He pulled out a set of Vauxhall car keys. 'And we've got them,' he said.

Chapter forty-two

Shepherd sat at his desk staring down at the printed pages in front of him. His hands were clasped in fists in his lap and his shoulders were scrunched up almost to his ears. He wasn't sure whether it was an instinctive reaction to wanting to punch someone. He looked up as Burton appeared in front of him.

She nodded to the papers. 'What have you got?'

'I'm just having another look at that stuff Dan Sullivan gave us.'

'And your body language tells me that it's important.'

An ugly frown crossed Shepherd's usually open demeanour. 'It's made me angry,' he said. 'Williams has abused his position of trust at best, or at worst potentially caused this girl to go missing.'

'You think he's behind that?'

Shepherd shrugged. 'It just seems weird that she goes off to see a guy that Williams has told her to meet, texts her mate to say that she'll be home later and to wait up because she's forgotten her keys. Why would she then disappear of her own accord? It just doesn't make sense.'

Burton frowned. 'Whose case was it?'

'Alan Chandler.'

Burton sighed and rolled her eyes. 'Pull the file. I want to have a look at that before we tackle Chandler. Let's just hope he did a proper investigation.'

'He won't like us poking our noses in.'

'Well, he'll just have to wear it. I'll explain it to the boss first.' She paused. 'Once we've read that file, we'll track down Will Turner and his mates and see what they have to say about Keith Williams' murder.'

When Burton returned from seeing their boss, she found Shepherd staring at his computer screen, eyes flicking back and forth as he followed the text. She pulled up a chair from a nearby desk and sat down next to him.

'Got anything?' she said.

'The file's a bit basic but it seems to have covered all bases.'

Burton frowned. 'Seems?'

'There are a few questions that I'd like to ask Chandler,' Shepherd said. 'See this?' He pointed to the screen. Burton read silently and then sat back in her chair frowning.

'She bought a bus ticket on her bank card. Where did she go?' she asked.

'That's just it. There's no information to show that,' Shepherd said, shaking his head. 'I can't see any bus station CCTV or anything like that recorded in the file. She bought a weekly ticket at the bus station but there's no suggestion of where she went.'

'Going to a lecture or something?' Burton asked.

'That's what I thought at first, but no one saw her on campus that day, according to the file.'

Burton fiddled with the end of her blonde ponytail. 'It's a big campus though. She might have been there just that no one saw her.'

'Fair point,' Shepherd said. 'But she obviously wasn't planning to leave town, or she wouldn't have bought a weekly ticket.'

'And no one saw anything of her after she bought the bus ticket?'

'There's no witnesses after she was at the bus station, and no

CCTV either. We don't know if she got on a bus or whether she bought the ticket and wandered off.'

Burton frowned. 'There's no way of knowing if she used it?'

Shepherd shook his head. 'No. According to the file it's a paper ticket so you just show it to the driver. There's no electronic monitoring of it.'

Burton sighed. 'Well, I've got the boss to agree that he'll make Chandler talk to us, so I've asked him to come along. He should be here shortly.'

When Detective Inspector Alan Chandler arrived, he did not look impressed. He was a big man, fat rather than muscle, and stank of cigarettes. Although she didn't want to pollute her office air, Burton thought it was better to conduct the discussion in private. She invited him in and quickly opened the window as she walked around her desk to sit in her high-backed swivel chair. Chandler sat in the visitor's chair glowering, and Shepherd dragged in a chair from outside before closing the door. Initially he sat alongside Chandler, but Burton saw his nose twitch and noticed a discreet movement away.

'What do you want?' Chandler demanded, clearly deciding to go on the attack.

'I wanted to speak to you about Leanne Nelson,' Burton said.

'The student who went missing last year?' Chandler asked. 'What about her?'

'She's still not turned up,' Burton said. 'Any new leads?'

'Nope, I had one of her mates on the phone recently asking that and I told him the same thing.'

Burton looked at the printout of the file Shepherd had given her. 'I've read the file so I've got the basic details,' she said. 'What I wanted to ask is why there's no bus station CCTV?'

'Wait a minute–' Chandler's face was flushing red '–why are you raking this up now?'

'The file isn't closed,' Burton said, 'meaning it can be reviewed at any time.' She was speaking calmly and this seemed to be irritating Chandler more than if she was aggressive. 'But the reason we're asking is that one of the victims in our murder inquiry is Professor Keith Williams, who was initially implicated in Leanne's disappearance.'

Chandler sat up straight in his chair. 'He's dead?'

'Yes,' Shepherd said. 'Did you have any idea that he might have had anything to do with it?'

'At first we did, because her mates were so vocal about it, but as time went on there was no evidence of any contact between them. All we had was what her friends told us.'

Burton frowned. 'What about the bus ticket?' she asked.

'What about it?'

'She bought the ticket at the bus station. A weekly ticket, so she was obviously planning to stay in Allensbury. Did she get on a bus?'

'We don't know,' Chandler said, not quite meeting Burton's eye.

'Why didn't you get CCTV?' Shepherd asked, earning a glare from Chandler.

'We didn't need it. There were a lot of witnesses there at the time and no one saw her. There wouldn't have been anything on the CCTV.' But Chandler was beginning to squirm in his chair.

'You don't know that for certain though, do you?' Shepherd continued. 'Knowing which bus she got on would have been really helpful in establishing where she went that afternoon.'

'Look,' Chandler began to bluster, 'she was an adult. She was free to go off as she pleased.'

'But her friends were expecting her home,' Burton said, holding up Will Turner's statement. 'You did a thorough search around the campus; you don't do that if you think she's just wandered off.' Her voice was rising with tension. 'You didn't follow up the bus angle, you let the allegations against Keith Williams drop really easily and you didn't make any efforts to find out who she was supposed to be meeting that day.'

'Keith Williams had an alibi for the whole day,' Chandler said.

Burton looked at Shepherd and frowned back at the file in front of her. She rifled through a few pages. 'Where does it say that?'

Chandler looked down at his hands clasped in his lap. 'It's not in the file,' he said, refusing to look up at Burton. 'Someone told us he was with Williams all day, so he can't have been meeting her.'

'He didn't have to meet her,' Shepherd said. 'All he had to do was send her off to whoever this guy was. What did you do about finding him?'

'We didn't need to look for anyone. She'd made that up to give her an excuse to wander off.'

'She didn't take any clothes with her and her bank card wasn't used after she paid for the bus ticket.' Shepherd's voice was raised now and he jabbed a finger at the report in front of him. 'That's not the act of someone who is going off willingly. She even told her friends that she'd be home.' He rose to his feet but Burton waved a hand to indicate he should sit down again.

'Who gave you the alibi?' she asked quietly.

'It was off-the-record,' Chandler snapped. 'I didn't need to write it up.'

'Who was it?' Burton asked, the volume of her voice rising as well.

'Desmond Danby,' came the reply.

Chapter forty-three

Desmond Danby was dictating to his secretary when Burton and Shepherd arrived. He quickly asked her to go and she obeyed, promising the letters would be ready by the end of the day. He thanked her and indicated for the detectives to sit down.

'What can I do for you?' he asked, sipping from the mug that was placed near his elbow. 'Oh, I'm sorry, my manners. Would you like one?' He indicated the mug, but Burton and Shepherd declined.

'Not a social visit then?' asked Danby.

'No,' said Burton. 'I'm afraid not. We need to ask you some questions about Leanne Nelson.'

Danby looked genuinely puzzled for a moment and then the light of recognition came into his eyes. 'Oh, of course, poor Leanne. Yes. What can I tell you?'

'Was Leanne having problems with anyone?' Shepherd asked.

Danby shook his head. 'I honestly don't know. We don't really see much of the students outside the classroom. I certainly never heard anything.'

'You didn't hear anything about Keith Williams, for instance?' Shepherd asked.

Danby clasped his hands on the desk like a television newsreader and leaned forward. 'Like what?' he asked.

Burton eyed him. 'Like he may have been involved in Leanne's disappearance?'

'Really?' Danby sounded shocked but Burton recognised fake surprise when she saw it.

'You know there was an allegation that he'd offered to help Leanne when she was short of money, that he sent her to meet "a guy" and she subsequently went missing.' Danby opened his mouth to speak but Burton continued. 'You said you would investigate but Professor Williams was never punished. Why was that?'

'We didn't find any wrongdoing,' Danby said. 'There were claims from her friends but never any evidence of what she'd told them. So there was nothing we could do.' He spread his hands wide, palms upwards.

Shepherd decided to take a different tack. 'Where were you on the day she went missing?' he asked.

'I was here all day. I had some tutorials and then I was in here working,' Danby replied.

Shepherd looked at Burton and she nodded. 'Was Keith Williams with you?' Shepherd asked casually.

'Why no, why would he—' Danby broke off and his face flushed.

'That's funny because a colleague of ours told us that you'd given Professor Williams an alibi for the day that Leanne disappeared. Are you telling us now that you lied about that?'

Danby dropped his eyes to his desk and nodded.

'Why?' asked Shepherd. Danby said nothing. 'You know that perverting the course of justice is a serious crime, don't you? You can go to prison for it.'

'What? No, I—' Danby started to speak but Shepherd interrupted.

'You gave Professor Williams a false alibi and then fabricated an investigation to cover for him, didn't you? Why?'

Danby's mouth opened and closed a few times. Shepherd fell silent, knowing that it would encourage Danby to talk.

'I didn't really think he had anything to do with it,' Danby said miserably. 'At least, I wanted to believe he had nothing to do with it.'

'What did he tell you?'

'He said that there were people trying to spread lies about him and that if I was asked I should say that he was with me all day.'

'Would people not think that was odd?' Burton asked.

'No, I told them we were working on some research.'

Shepherd shook his head. 'That seems to be a catch-all excuse around here.' Danby didn't look up to meet his eye. 'Where was Professor Williams if he wasn't with you?'

'I don't know,' Danby said quietly. 'He never told me.'

'Why, Professor Danby?' asked Shepherd. 'Why did you lie for him?'

Danby was quiet for a moment and then said, 'I slept with a student.'

Burton and Shepherd looked at each other in surprise. It was the last thing they were expecting the meek man in front of them to say.

'It was a long time ago, the student has long since left so nothing ever came of it. But Keith knew about it. I don't know how he found out but he always made it abundantly clear that he would tell the university management if I didn't do what he wanted.'

'Hence the reason he's got away with not producing any new research for so long,' Burton said and Danby nodded.

'I didn't know what to do. I had to protect my reputation. I don't know whether he was involved with Leanne or not. I never asked where he really was and he never told me.'

Burton was silent, staring at Danby and he squirmed under her gaze.

'Where were you when Keith Williams was killed?' she asked.

Danby stared at her. 'I didn't kill him,' he said.

'Where were you?' Burton repeated.

'I was at home.'

'Can anyone verify that?' Shepherd asked.

'I don't know. My wife was out when I got home so she wouldn't be able to tell you. One of my neighbours might have seen me.'

'And what about the afternoon when Olly Murton was killed?' Burton asked.

Danby put his head in his hands and the detectives waited. 'I didn't kill Olly either,' Danby said dragging his hands down his face. 'I was in a meeting with human resources talking about recruiting to replace Keith.'

'Isn't that a bit soon?'

Danby shook his head. 'I have an idea who I want and I don't want to wait in case she goes somewhere else.'

Burton was thinking fast. Then she said, 'Do you know what this research project is that Professor Williams was working on?'

Danby shook his head. 'No. He's been going on about it for months, but wouldn't tell anyone what it is. Kept saying it was going to be the best thing he'd ever done.'

'But you didn't see any evidence of it?'

'No. But if it was anywhere it would be on his laptop.'

'Any idea where his laptop is?' Shepherd asked.

'Normally I'd say it would be in his office, but it wasn't there when you looked around before.'

'Would he have kept it anywhere else?' Burton asked.

Danby shrugged. 'It may be in his car, I suppose.'

Shepherd raised his eyebrows. 'What car does he drive?' he asked.

'A Vauxhall Mokka.' Danby turned his chair around and looked out of the window, which overlooked the car park. 'Actually I'm

A DEADLY TRUTH

surprised that it's not out there. Did you take it away?'

Burton looked at Shepherd. 'No, we didn't,' she said. 'Any idea what the registration number was?' Danby shook his head. Burton got to her feet. 'Thanks for your time, Doctor Danby. If you think of anything else, you know where we are. We may need to speak to you again later.'

She turned and left the room, Shepherd close behind. When they were in the corridor, she stopped, hands on her hips.

'Why didn't we know there was a car?'

'I don't remember seeing car keys on the inventory after the post-mortem,' Shepherd said.

'Right, get on to campus security, and see if it's anywhere around here. Get the registration out to traffic as well in case it's been spotted on ANPR.'

'I'll go and see if there's a list of car registrations in the reception office,' Shepherd said, pulling out his phone as he walked away down the corridor.

Burton followed him. If Williams had taken his car with him on the night that he died, where were his keys and how were they going to find them?

191

Chapter forty-four

Within minutes Dan and Harry were outside and hurrying back to Williams' car.

'What do you want to do now?' Dan asked. Harry looked at him.

'I thought we were going to look in the car.'

Dan stopped in the middle of the car park, keys swinging from his finger.

'You're sure you don't want to tell the police first?' Dan asked.

Harry looked down at the ground and Dan could tell he was fighting an internal battle. He knew which way he wanted Harry to go. 'You're the one they've been interviewing and questioning. It's your call.'

Harry glanced around them. There were very few people around. 'Let's just open it up and see what's in it.' They continued across the car park and arrived beside the Mokka.

'If it's something important we can just tell the police afterwards,' Dan said.

'Not sure how they'll feel about that, but I want to know what Keith was hiding.'

Dan looked at Harry. 'You're after his laptop, aren't you?'

'No,' Harry said, looking irritated. 'Why does everyone think I want to steal his laptop?'

Dan gave him a sideways look. 'That new research is probably on it,' he said. Harry glared at him. 'OK, OK,' Dan said holding his hands up in surrender. 'Just checking.' Dan bleeped the remote control on the keys, the indicators flashed and the door locks clunked open. He reached out a hand to open the door, then stopped and looked across the roof of the car at Harry who stood by the passenger door. 'It must be something important, right? I mean, Keith died protecting those keys.'

Harry nodded and pulled open the passenger door. Dan opened the driver's door, and peered inside, sniffed and wrinkled his nose.

'Ugh, stale smoke,' he said, pulling away in disgust.

'Hmm he was rather a fan of cigars, our Keith.'

Harry walked to the back of the car and pressed the button to open the boot. Nothing happened. He tried again. 'That's odd. I think it's broken.'

'Ooops, sorry.' Dan pressed the central locking button and there was a click. Harry popped the boot open. Then he stopped and stepped back in surprise. 'What is it?' Dan asked, seeing the expression on his face.

'Come and see.'

Dan joined Harry and stared into the boot. 'I wasn't expecting that,' he said.

The boot was neatly packed with a suitcase, several pairs of shoes, three coats of varying thickness and a laptop bag.

'I was right,' said Harry. 'The laptop is in here.'

'But why is his car packed up?' Dan asked. 'Term's only just started.'

Harry stepped forward to pick up the laptop bag when a voice rang out.

'Doctor Evans, stop right where you are.'

Harry turned and his heart sank as he saw Burton and Shepherd striding towards him across the car park.

Chapter forty-five

Burton marched across the tarmac and snatched the keys from Dan's hand.

'Where did you get these?' she demanded, dangling them from her finger.

'How did you know we were here?' Dan asked.

'We were speaking to the security team, looking for that,' Burton said, jabbing a finger towards the car, 'and there you were on the CCTV.'

Dan opened his mouth to say something but closed it again under the weight of Burton's glare.

She raised the keys. 'I'll ask again. Where did you get these?'

'We found them,' Dan said, looking at Harry who seemed to have been struck dumb in the face of Burton's anger.

'Found them where?' Burton demanded.

'In the library,' Dan said.

Burton stared. 'What?'

'In the library. Behind a book.'

Shepherd joined them and stared at Dan. 'Behind a book?' he repeated, looking puzzled.

'On a bookcase,' Harry said, suddenly coming back to life.

'And instead of reporting it to us, you decided to take the keys,

194

come here and possibly destroy evidence?' Burton asked.

'We wanted to see what he was trying to protect,' Dan said. 'We thought it might show us who killed him.'

Shepherd pulled out his notebook and pen. 'Why didn't you tell us that Professor Williams' car was here?' he asked.

'We didn't know until this morning. We thought you probably already knew about it,' Harry said, looking sideways at Dan, who nodded along.

'How did you find out it was here?'

'We were walking to the library and we just saw it in the car park,' Harry said. 'It hadn't even occurred to me that it wasn't in its usual space behind the politics department building until I saw it here. I thought that you must have taken it.'

'What made you think to go looking for the keys?' Burton asked.

'We figured that if you hadn't taken the car then you probably didn't have them,' Dan said. 'The last place he'd been was the library so we thought they might be in there. They weren't in the lost and found so we searched on the shelves.'

'They were hidden behind one of Keith's favourite books,' Harry put in, looking awkward.

'Were you looking for his laptop?' Shepherd asked, scribbling in his notebook.

Harry frowned. 'Why does everyone think I'm looking for his laptop?'

Shepherd looked up, his brown eyes boring into Harry. 'Were you?'

Harry sighed. 'I knew it was missing. Desmond told me. When we saw the car, I wondered if Keith had left it in there.'

'Olly Murton told us that Professor Williams' new research is all on that laptop,' Shepherd said. 'Is that why you were looking for it? For the research?'

'No.' Dan stepped forward. He didn't like where this was going. 'We were looking to see if the laptop was there, but we weren't going to take it.'

Shepherd looked at him and raised an eyebrow. Then Burton coughed and Shepherd turned to look at her. She was standing behind the car and looking into the boot. Shepherd joined her and looked equally surprised.

Dan braced himself. He wasn't sure which direction the detectives were going to go in next. Harry was looking at him as if he was desperate to think of something to say. Dan shrugged at him. Whatever way this went they were in trouble.

Shepherd stepped away and spoke into his phone. Dan strained his ears but Shepherd's words were lost in the open air.

Burton was striding towards them. 'I don't want you two going anywhere until we've had a good chat about this.' She waved a hand back towards the car. 'We're going to find a meeting room in there– ' she gestured towards the chemistry department '–and you're going to explain to me what's going on.' Dan opened his mouth to speak but she held up a hand. 'Just be glad you're not going back to the station for this conversation.'

'They've got a CSI team down here now.'

Dan stood at the window of the meeting room staring out through the horizontal blinds. He'd been there ever since Burton had shown them inside and told them to sit tight before heading back outside.

It was a swanky new seminar room, with chairs that were not designed for any shape or size of bottom. Dan looked across the room at Harry who was slumped awkwardly in one of those chairs.

'Why would Keith have packed up his car?' Dan asked.

Harry shook his head. 'I've no idea. It's only the start of term so

I've no idea where he could have been going. It looked like he was packed up for a long time.'

'Clearly he knew once he'd escaped he wouldn't be coming back again,' Dan said, turning back to the window and parting the blinds with his fingers so he could peer out.

Harry looked up at him. 'You think he was leaving for good?'

Dan shrugged. 'I reckon he was going on the run. He was up to something and got found out. He was scared so he decided it was time to get away and never come back.' He paused. 'That would explain why his laptop was in there when he was known for never taking it out of his office.'

'You think he was in trouble.'

Dan turned his back on the window and walked over to sit down at the table.

'I think it might be because of his research. Maybe he got himself into some trouble because of that. Someone was after him; we know that because he was probably being followed. He abandoned his car here and went into the library to hide. Maybe he thought he could get away from them in there, but it failed. He wanted to protect the research that was in his car so he hid the keys. Presumably he thought he could go back for the keys when he'd lost the person who was chasing him.'

Harry looked down at the table top sadly. 'But they caught up to him.'

Dan nodded. 'What was he into?' he asked, getting up again and walking to the window.

'Whatever it was, Olly Murton was into it too,' Harry said. 'And now he's dead as well.'

Dan turned from the window frowning. 'So, when Olly told me that he'd done something bad, it wasn't murdering Keith, it was something to do with the research.' He looked at Harry. 'We need to find out what this research was.' Then he slapped himself on the forehead. 'I'm so stupid.'

'What? Why?' Harry asked, sitting up straighter in his chair.

But just then the door opened and Burton came in.

'We'll talk later,' Dan muttered.

Burton sat down at the table and pulled out a notebook and pen.

'Why didn't you come to us when you found the car, never mind found the keys?'

'We'd only just found them,' Dan said, sitting down across the table from her.

'But you should have come straight to us,' she said. 'See, now I have to question how long you knew about the car and the keys. You'd better hope there's someone who can corroborate your story.'

'Ask the librarian on the desk,' Dan said, with a flash of inspiration. 'We asked her whether they were in the lost and found, which they weren't. She'll remember us.'

Burton frowned and made a note. 'You didn't know anything about Professor Williams planning a holiday?' she asked Harry.

He shook his head. 'No, I hadn't heard about it, but then he'd be unlikely to tell me.'

'Is there anyone he might have told if he was going away?' Burton asked.

Harry frowned. 'He'd have had to tell Desmond because he'd need a holiday request form authorised. Although I doubt he would have given permission for Keith to take time off given that we're in term time.'

The flicker of an expression crossed Burton's face but Dan couldn't quite decide what it was. She sat silently for so long that Dan began to fidget.

'Do you need anything else? It's just that I've got to get back to the office,' he lied.

Burton seemed to shake herself. 'Yes, fine. That's all we need for now. But don't go far,' she said. 'We'll need to speak again.'

She showed Harry and Dan out into the car park and walked away towards Keith Williams' car where Shepherd stood watching the forensic team.

'Why are you stupid?' Harry asked, turning to Dan.

Dan grinned. 'I think I've had a clue in my bag the whole bloody time and I didn't realise until just now. I'll show you. Come on.'

Chapter forty-six

Burton emerged from the building and, after pausing to watch Dan and Harry walk away with their heads together muttering, quickly crossed the tarmac to where the Vauxhall Mokka stood with all four doors and the boot wide open. White-suited CSIs combed the car's interior and one pointed a camera at the contents of the boot. White plastic sheets had been spread out on the ground around the car, ready to catch any trace evidence that might be dislodged as the CSI team carried out their duties.

Shepherd nodded towards the departing figures. 'They look like they're up to something,' he said.

Burton took a breath and puffed out her cheeks. 'I'm sure you're right. Let's just hope it doesn't get them anywhere.' She looked past the CSI photographer into the boot of the car. 'Neatly packed,' she said.

'It looks like he was planning on going away for a while, doesn't it? He's certainly packed enough jackets,' Shepherd said,

'Is that how you judge the length of someone's holiday?'

Shepherd gave her a patient look. 'I'm just saying that he's got coats for summer and winter weather. It's not cold enough for this one, just now–' he pointed to an anorak before being shooed away by a CSI '–but later in the year it might be.'

Burton was frowning. 'Desmond Danby told us that Williams didn't have any holiday booked, that he wouldn't have been allowed to go away anywhere this close to the start of term.'

Shepherd tapped the end of his pen against the notebook clutched between his fingers and thumb. 'But, we also know that Professor Williams had blackmail material on Danby that he clearly used to get what he wanted.'

Burton shrugged. 'I still say that wherever he was going, it was probably without permission,' she said, hands on hips.

Shepherd thought for a moment and then said, 'I think he was doing a bunk.'

Burton raised her eyebrows. 'But why?'

'That's where I'm a bit stuck. Something must have happened in the last couple of days that freaked him out,' Shepherd said. 'It's going to take some digging though because it doesn't sound like there was anyone that he told about it.'

'He seems very low on friends, doesn't he?'

'Right. He's got no one to turn to so what does he do? He packs up his car and then he—' Shepherd stopped talking and frowned.

'What?' Burton asked.

'It doesn't make sense. He must have known when he left the house that morning that he was going to do a runner or he wouldn't have packed up the car.'

Burton frowned. Then she smiled. 'What if something happened during the day,' she said 'that upset or frightened him so much that he went straight home and packed. He was going to leave immediately, but then realised he'd forgotten his laptop and had to come back for it.'

Shepherd nodded slowly. 'Whoever he was frightened of must have followed him to campus, or was already here, so Williams went and hid in the library. He was probably trying to lose them in there and head back to his car.'

'But he couldn't get away so he hid his car keys behind a book?' Burton asked, looking sceptical.

'Why not? He might have thought that if he told this person he didn't have what they were looking for, maybe told them it was somewhere else, they'd leave him alone. Then he could go back and get his keys later. Unfortunately for him, they killed him anyway without getting their hands on whatever it was.'

'They didn't get the keys in the library and he didn't tell them where his car was so they couldn't go and get it,' Burton added. 'You think he was protecting something in the car?'

Shepherd pointed to the luggage piled outside the car boot, bagged up and neatly labelled by the CSI team. 'The mystery of the missing laptop,' he said, pointing to a neat black leather shoulder bag, which was propped open to show a shiny silver computer.

Burton smoothed a hand over her hair and shook her ponytail. 'This laptop seems to be at the centre of everything.'

'Hmmm, the infamous research,' Shepherd said.

Burton nodded. 'Exactly.'

But before she could say anything further, a muffled voice that seemed to come from beneath them called, 'Come and look at this.'

They walked around to the side of the car to find one of the techs lying on the ground, as far under the car as he could get without jacking it up.

'What is it?' Burton asked.

'You have to get down here to see it,' the man replied.

Burton glanced at her skirt and tights and then pointed to Shepherd. 'Your turn,' she said.

He laughed and lay down on the ground beside the tech. 'What have you got?' he asked, peering under the car.

'Right here.' The man pointed to one of the pipes on the underside of the car. 'Do you see what I mean?'

Shepherd exhaled a long breath. 'Very interesting,' he said. 'Could that have happened gradually?'

The man shook his head. 'It's difficult to see from this angle, but that hole is too rounded to have happened through wear and tear. We'll need to recover the vehicle and put it up on a hydraulic lift to make sure.'

Burton impatiently nudged Shepherd with her shoe. 'Any chance of finding out what you're up to?'

The two men slid out from under the car and got up, Shepherd looking grim.

'There's a load of fluid on the ground under the car,' he said, brushing his hands together and then trying to dust the car park dirt off his suit.

'Water?' asked Burton.

'It doesn't smell like it. What do you reckon, Andy?' He looked at the technician standing beside him.

'I reckon it's brake fluid,' the man said, blushing slightly as Burton turned towards him.

'Brake fluid? Are you sure?' Burton asked.

'We'll have to lab test it but that's certainly what it feels like, sir,' said Andy, holding up the oily fingers of his latex gloves. 'Plus you can see where it's dripping from.'

'The brake pipes are damaged?' Burton asked.

'Only one,' Shepherd replied.

'Cracked?'

Andy shook his head. 'Looks like the damage is man-made, sir. I think someone deliberately damaged the brake pipe so the fluid would leak out.'

Burton frowned. 'Why not just cut it altogether?'

Andy almost put his hand up in his hurry to answer the question. 'When the driver pressed on the brakes the first time, they would work, although they'd feel a bit spongy. But the pressure will force out some of the fluid. Each time he'd pressed it, more fluid would leak out until it was all gone.'

'Finally the brakes wouldn't work at all,' Shepherd put in. 'Eventually he would have crashed into something.'

'But it would look like an accident,' said Andy. 'Any damage could be put down to wear and tear if you weren't looking at it closely.'

'Someone clearly had a backup plan in case they didn't manage to catch Williams in the library,' said Burton.

'I think bashing him on the head was Plan B,' Shepherd said. 'They were going to make it look like an accident.'

'What do you think happened?' Burton asked.

'That damage could have been done days ago, or even weeks ago, and it was just a matter of time before there was an accident.'

Shepherd frowned. 'The accident theory suggests that they just wanted to get rid of him. Plan B suggests they needed something from him before killing him so they followed him.' He scratched his chin. Then his face lit up. 'If they knew that he never took his laptop out of the office, they might have counted on being able to get in there and steal it. But for once he took it with him. They needed to follow him to find out where the laptop was. When he wouldn't tell them, they killed him.'

'We need to get that laptop analysed, and quickly,' Burton said, pointing to the bag. 'We need to find out what this research was and why it got both Professor Williams and Olly Murton killed.'

Burton and Shepherd had to follow the CSI team back to their lab in order to be able to look at Williams' belongings as soon as possible. Rather than being able to handle each item themselves, they had to watch as one of the technicians opened the suitcase found in the boot

of the car. They all stared at the unmitigated mess of clothes inside.

'He's not a very neat packer,' the technician commented.

Shepherd nodded. 'Wherever he was going, he wasn't going to look very good when he got there,' he said, as the woman pulled out a couple of very creased shirts.

'I don't think he cared,' Burton said. 'This has the feeling of someone who packed in a hurry, and wasn't even thinking about what or how he was packing.'

Shepherd was peering over the technician's shoulder as she continued to check through the contents of the suitcase.

He put out a hand to pick up the laptop bag. The technician slapped it away and handed him a pair of gloves.

'Sorry,' Shepherd mumbled, pulling them on. The woman made him wait until she'd snapped pictures of the laptop case from all angles and done fingerprint testing. Then she gave him the nod to continue. Unzipping the bag, Shepherd busied himself pulling out neatly tied cables and finally the laptop itself. The woman continued to snap photographs as Shepherd worked.

'Hmmm, he's a lot tidier in his computer cables than his clothes,' he said. He flipped open the lid of the laptop and pressed the power key. The home screen loaded up in seconds but demanded a password.

'We're going to need some help with this,' Burton said. 'Reckon your guys will be able to do this as a rush job?' she asked the technician.

The woman frowned. 'We do have a backlog at the moment.' She smiled at Shepherd. Burton recognised the longing in the woman's eyes and was pleased when Shepherd's returning smile seemed to do the trick.

'Leave it with me and I'll see what I can do,' the woman said.

'Thanks. Let's go,' Burton said to Shepherd.

As they left the building Burton's phone buzzed. She glanced down at the screen as they walked towards their car and frowned.

'Back to the station?' Shepherd asked.

Burton sighed. 'Nope, we've got another stop to make first. Olly Murton's house has been broken into and his room's been ransacked.' She shook her head. 'What on earth had he got himself into?'

Chapter forty-seven

Dan was struggling to get his key into the front door of his flat, impatient in his excitement.

'What's the hurry?' Harry asked.

'I told you. I know what the research is.' He flung open the door and kicked off his shoes in the hallway. Harry did the same and followed him into the living room.

'But how? I don't understand.'

Dan had dumped his bag on the sofa and was rummaging inside. 'I was sent this in the post a few days ago. I didn't think anything of it at the time, but look.' He pulled out the pages and shoved them into Harry's hand. 'There.'

Harry looked at the top page. 'When did you get this?'

'The day after I found Olly dead.'

'You think it came from him?' Harry asked, eyes widening.

Dan nodded. 'I thought I recognised the handwriting. He wrote his mobile number down for me.' He dug in his bag again and took out his note book. He found the right page and held it up against the envelope. 'See?'

Harry squinted at the page. 'I'm not sure.'

'Oh, come on, you're his teacher. You should know.' Dan's voice was rising excitedly.

'Essays and emails are mostly typed these days, but it does look a bit similar.' He turned his attention to the sheets of paper. Dan was almost bouncing on the balls of his feet.

'Is that—?' Harry asked.

'Chemistry,' Dan said.

Harry frowned. 'Chemistry?'

'Yes. I've no idea what it is, but it suddenly came to me while we were talking before. We've assumed that Keith and Olly were working on something politics related, but what if they weren't? What if it's something else?' He tapped on the edge of the pages. 'Why else would Olly send this to me if it's not connected?'

Harry sat down on the armchair staring at the pages. 'But I—' He looked up to find Dan rummaging in a pile of newspapers on the floor in the corner of the room. 'What are you doing?'

'Good job I always forget to do the recycling,' Dan muttered, emerging with a copy of the Allensbury Post and a smug grin on his face. He held up the front page to show Harry.

'Scientist found dead,' Harry read. 'You showed that to me a couple of days ago.'

'Yes, and remember what happened while we were looking at it?'

Harry looked up at Dan, realisation spreading over his face. 'Keith barged in and snatched it away.'

Dan was nodding. 'Yup. He looked like he'd seen a ghost. An odd reaction to seeing the news about a stranger, don't you think?'

'You think the research had something to do with this guy?' Harry asked.

'Don't you think it's odd that this guy, Keith and Olly died in such a short period of time?'

Harry frowned. 'What do you think this is?' He held up the sheets of paper.

'We passed any knowledge I have of chemistry a long time ago,' Dan said.

'We could ask someone in the chemistry department,' Harry suggested, and then saw the expression on Dan's face. 'What?'

'Three people are dead and it may have something to do with that.' He pointed to the pages in Harry's hand. 'I'm not sure I want to bring someone else into it.'

'We could do it quietly, and not tell them why we want to know about it?' Harry suggested.

Dan paced up and down the room once and then stopped in the middle of the floor.

'We need to keep it offline,' he said. 'I don't want anything written down.'

'We're going to have to if we want someone to look at it,' Harry said. 'I know someone in the chemistry department, I could email her and—'

'No, that's what I mean. We can't email it in case someone is watching.'

'You think they might be watching my emails?'

'Not really, but Harry, it's too much of a risk. We don't know who's behind this.' Dan took the pages and flicked through them again, frowning.

'What do you want to do?' Harry asked.

'Call your mate and ask if we can pop round to see her. I'll make a copy of these and then we can give them to her. I want this under the radar so we only use phones. No email.'

'No paper trail?' Harry asked.

'Exactly.'

Harry paused, with his phone in his hand.

'What?' asked Dan.

'Should we not give this to the police? If we think it's this dangerous?'

'We don't know what it is. It could be someone's chemistry homework, completely innocent. If we're going to hand it to the police, we need to make sure it's worthwhile.'

Harry nodded and began to dial a phone number.

Chapter forty-eight

The uniformed constable on duty at the gate of Olly Murton's house nodded to Burton and Shepherd as they passed him and made a note on the clipboard of the time of their arrival. A white-suited forensic technician was dusting the front door with fingerprint powder. He handed Burton and Shepherd some protective shoe covers and they pulled them on. Shepherd's booties only just fitted over his large shiny black leather shoes. The man then stood back and let the detectives past. In the carpeted hallway they could see Sergeant Sue Stevens talking to Ian. The student was shivering slightly and had his arms folded protectively across his chest. When Stevens saw Burton and Shepherd, she patted Ian on the arm and dispatched him and a female uniformed officer towards the kitchen.

'Hi Mark, hi sir,' she said, approaching them.

'Hey Sue,' Burton replied. 'What have we got?'

'Ian says all the lads left home this morning to go to campus or to work, two of the lads have part-time jobs.' Burton nodded and Sue continued, reading from her notebook. 'He got to the bus stop and realised he'd forgotten his mobile so he came back. He didn't see anyone around but the front door was ajar. He says he did a quick check around to see if anyone was inside.'

'Brave lad,' Shepherd said. 'The burglars could still have been here.'

'He hadn't thought of that at the time. He thought at first that one of the others had come back like he had. But as he went upstairs he realised something was wrong.'

'How did he know that?'

'Tom's bedroom door was open but Ian swears it was closed when they left the house. His room is on the floor above Tom's so he had to walk past on his way out. Olly Murton's door was also open and, well, you'd better come and see.'

She led the way upstairs and Burton frowned when she saw that files had been thrown around, their contents spilled across the floor and desk drawers dragged out.

'It wasn't like that when we left,' she said.

'And Ian swears they've not been in the room since you told them not to. Apparently one of the lads was traumatised by Mark in his latex gloves.' She grinned at Shepherd who laughed.

'Aren't we all?' Burton remarked with a pale smile. 'Am I OK to come in?' she asked one of the CSI team.

'If you stay on the paper we've put down,' the figure said.

Burton stepped carefully into the room and looked around. 'It's too much of a coincidence for this to have been a random burglary just after he's found murdered.'

'They obviously didn't care about making a mess. What were they looking for?' Shepherd asked. 'Were they after his computer? Not realising we got to it first?'

'It's possible. Maybe they think there's a copy of this research project on it. Did we get his mobile at the scene?' She looked at Shepherd.

He frowned. 'I don't think it was on the inventory. Why?'

'I know my phone and computer sync up so I can see documents on my phone that I've saved on the computer.'

'In the cloud, you mean?' Shepherd asked.

Burton folded her arms. 'Exactly. If they've got his phone, they must know that there's a copy on his laptop, or at least that it can be accessed from there.'

Shepherd frowned. 'Meaning they can delete stuff remotely as well?' he asked.

Burton nodded. 'Did tech say if they'd copied Olly's hard drive?' she asked.

Shepherd pulled out his phone and began to scroll through his emails. He selected one and held it out to Burton. 'They copy it as soon as they get it,' he said. Burton puffed out her cheeks in relief. 'At least we've got everything safe and we'll know if anything gets deleted,' Shepherd continued.

'Is anything else missing?' Burton asked Sue.

'Ian hadn't checked. He glanced into the room, saw the mess and called us. He was sitting on the doorstep when we arrived.'

'Is he OK?' Shepherd asked.

'A bit shocked, I think. Having your housemate murdered and then being broken into is a lot for anyone to take in. I've sent him to the kitchen and asked someone to make him a cup of sweet tea.'

'Could you ask Ian to come and have a look around?' Burton asked.

The sergeant nodded and turned away. They heard her footsteps on the stairs.

Burton exhaled heavily. 'Do you think he had a copy of this research project?'

Shepherd shrugged. 'I don't see why not. If he was working with Professor Williams on it, why would he not have a copy?'

'I don't understand what this research could be,' Burton said, stroking her chin. 'Why would someone kill two people for it?'

'Maybe it would make someone a lot of money?' Shepherd asked.

Before Burton could reply Sue Stevens appeared in the doorway with Ian peering over her shoulder.

'How are you?' Shepherd asked Ian.

'OK, I suppose.' Ian still had his arms wrapped protectively across his thin body.

'Can you have a quick look at Olly's room and tell us if anything is missing?' Shepherd said, stepping back to let Ian through the door.

Ian stepped inside onto the paper the CSI team had spread on the floor. He looked around the room, eyes wet with tears. Then he stared at a drawer that had been ripped out of the desk and dumped on the floor. He pointed to it.

'That's where Olly kept his safe,' he said.

Burton raised an eyebrow. 'A safe?' she asked. 'Why did he have a safe?'

Ian shrugged. 'I don't know. I mean it wasn't a very good one so I told him it was a waste of time.'

'What sort of safe?' Shepherd asked, scribbling in his notepad.

Ian held up his hands, drawing a rectangular shape about the size of an A4 piece of paper. 'It was fireproof but it didn't fasten to anything so it wasn't very secure. He only hid it behind the drawers.'

'Did he ever show you what was in it?' Burton asked.

Ian shook his head. 'I only knew he had it because I walked in and saw him hiding it. He made me swear that I wouldn't tell anyone.' His voice trembled. 'Is it not enough that Olly's been killed, but someone had to steal from him as well?'

'Why don't you head back down to the kitchen and let us finish up,' Sue said gently, guiding him back towards the stairs.

Burton looked around the room, hands on hips. 'Why would a student have a safe?' she asked.

'For personal paperwork?' Shepherd suggested. 'Birth certificate? Something like that? He might have been worried about identity theft.'

'But left his bank statements in a file on a shelf where anyone could find them?' Burton chewed the inside of her mouth. 'No, someone went to a lot of trouble to break into the house and wreck his room.'

'How did they know he had a safe?' Shepherd asked.

'Maybe they didn't,' Burton said. 'I think they wanted something from Olly but he wouldn't give it so they killed him and came here looking for it. They don't know what it looks like so they've taken the room apart and come across the safe.' Burton turned on the spot.

'They must think that whatever they're looking for is in there,' Shepherd said. 'They didn't take anything else.'

'They might have been disturbed so they just grabbed it and ran. What are they looking for?' Burton asked. Then she exhaled heavily. 'Right, there's nothing else we can do until forensics are finished. We need to find out what Olly Murton may have had in his safe that got him killed.'

When they got back to the police station, Burton and Shepherd had just entered their office when the latter's mobile started to ring. He stopped and spoke into it for a few minutes then said, 'Thanks, no problem,' and hung up. He sighed heavily.

'What's going on?' asked Burton, turning to look at him.

'You know how Olly was supposed to be going to meet a Detective Sergeant Adams on the day he died?'

'Yes.'

'Well, I've now exhausted every contact I have in every neighbouring force and no one has a DS Adams on their staff,' Shepherd said.

Burton frowned. 'No one?'

'Yup. No one.'

'So who was this DS Adams?' Burton was frowning. 'And did Olly actually meet him? Or her?'

Shepherd nodded. 'I'm guessing that he did and that's who killed him.' He consulted his notebook. 'Unfortunately, the whole lake area isn't covered by campus CCTV. They must have killed and dumped Olly in one of the black spots.'

Burton swore under her breath. She frowned for a moment and then said, 'Right, let's look at this another way. Get the CCTV from Olly Murton's street and the surrounding area. I want to know who broke into the house.'

'You think it might be the same person?'

'Yes, they must have tried to make Olly tell them what he knew. When he wouldn't, they killed him. His phone must have shown what files were on the computer so they're clearing up the mess.'

Shepherd was already seizing his phone. 'I'm on it.'

Burton frowned. 'With a bit of luck, we might get a picture of who did it and be able to get a name.'

Chapter forty-nine

Burton was in her office on the phone updating the DCI on progress in the case. As she hung up, she sighed. No matter how much progress they made, it was never good enough. She'd barely replaced the receiver when the phone rang again.

'Burton speaking.'

'It's the front desk. There's someone to see you.' When Burton heard the name, she was on her feet and dashing through the office, pausing only to grab Shepherd. He quickly delegated the hunt for CCTV to Garry Topping and followed.

In the reception they found two young men waiting for them.

'Will Turner?' Burton asked. One man nodded.

'Yes,' he answered, 'and this is Wesley Spencer. We were housemates of Leanne Nelson.'

'She went missing,' said Wesley in an accusatory tone.

'Yes, the investigation is still open,' said Shepherd. 'Let's go in here.' He gestured to the officer on the reception desk and the meeting room door was buzzed open. He led Will and Wesley into the interview room and Burton closed the door behind them.

'We've not come to speak to you about Leanne though,' said Will. 'Well, not really.'

'Right,' said Burton. 'You've come about the murder of Keith Williams?'

Will looked surprised. 'Yes, how did you know?'

'Dan Sullivan said he'd been talking to you. But you weren't on our list of people interviewed in the library that night.'

Will looked down at the table. 'I was there, but I didn't know what had happened. When we were told to leave I just went home. I didn't realise they meant leave the building and then wait for the police.'

Shepherd gave a small smile as he made notes in his book.

'In fact, we only heard about what happened to Keith the following day,' put in Wesley. 'I mean we knew he was in the library because we saw him, but that was while he was alive. Tell them, Will.' He nudged his friend's arm.

Will took a deep breath. 'I went to look for a book that I needed and I saw Keith wandering among the bookcases. I noticed because he looked a bit shifty and he never really looks like that. Usually he looks like he owns the place.'

'What do you mean, "shifty"?' Burton asked.

'He kept looking over his shoulder and he was peering into the spaces between the bookcases before he walked round the corner.'

'Did you see anyone else? Harry Evans, for instance?'

'I did see him,' Will said, 'but that was a bit later. Maybe twenty minutes. I sort of saw someone else as well. It was weird, it was more like I had the sense someone was there and a smell of perfume.'

Burton noticed a look pass across Shepherd's face but he didn't speak.

'Perfume? Like what?' she asked.

'It was kind of flowery.'

'Where was that?' Shepherd asked.

'I was between two bookcases. I saw someone move on the other side of the bookcase. The backs of the shelves are open so you can see through them. There was a flash of leather jacket and that scent and then nothing.'

Shepherd pulled the forum printouts from his inside jacket pocket and smoothed them down on the table in front of the students. Wesley's face fell when he saw them and he looked at Turner. His face was set and he looked back at Shepherd, hard faced.

'This is you, isn't it?' Shepherd pointed to the name 'WillT1998'.

Will Turner nodded. 'I was trying to warn other people to stay away from him.'

'What did you think he'd done to Leanne?'

'I don't know. All she told me was that she was short of money and needed to get some quickly. She said Keith was going to help her.'

'What did you think she meant by that?' Burton asked, as Shepherd's pen flew across the page.

'I don't know. When she left that morning, all she said was she was going to meet some guy. That Keith had put them in touch.'

'And she never came back?'

'No,' put in Wesley. 'She texted saying she was going to, but she never did.' He stopped suddenly, breathing heavily. 'And when we reported her missing your lot didn't care. They didn't do anything to help or—'

'Wes, that's not fair,' Will interrupted. He looked at Burton. 'Your guys did investigate but they didn't find anything.'

'They didn't do it properly, that's why,' Wesley said, cutting across Will. 'They just said she'd run off. But she didn't. She wouldn't. Leanne wasn't like that.' His last word came out almost as a sob.

Will patted his arm. 'Sorry,' he said to Burton and Shepherd. 'It's all still too fresh, you know.'

Burton nodded. 'I know this is really difficult.'

'It's just the not knowing,' Will said, as Wesley wiped his eyes on his sleeve. 'We don't know what happened to her. I'm sure Keith knows – knew – but he wouldn't tell us.'

'What about Olly Murton? Did you know him?'

Will snorted. 'Him? I never liked him. He was up to his neck in whatever Keith was doing.'

'What did you think that was?' Burton asked.

Will shook his head. 'I could never find out. I even tried asking Olly about it but he wouldn't tell me.'

Shepherd looked up, frowning. 'Did you email him about it? Asking if he knew where your friend was, and threatening to break his legs or worse?'

Will looked surprised. 'How do you know about that?'

'We have Olly's computer and his emails,' Shepherd replied.

'I'd never have done anything to him,' Will said. 'I was angry. He kept trying to avoid me. When I saw him on campus and shouted at him, he just brushed it off.'

'That's the argument, Tom, Olly's housemate, witnessed,' Shepherd whispered to Burton and she nodded.

'So you blamed Professor Williams and Olly Murton for Leanne's disappearance,' Burton said to Will and Wesley.

'Why not? They were obviously in on it,' said Wesley aggressively.

'But you have no proof,' Burton said.

'They weren't stupid enough to leave evidence,' Wesley said.

'You were trying to get the Allensbury Post involved again?' Burton said.

'Yes, the reporter was really nice to us at the time so we hoped she'd help us,' Will said. 'The police, that Chandler bloke, wouldn't do anything. We thought the paper might, but they couldn't,' said Will.

'Or wouldn't,' put in Wesley.

Burton thought for a moment. 'What subject was Leanne studying?' she asked.

'Chemistry,' was the reply. 'Why?'

'How did she come across Professor Williams? They weren't in the same department.'

'He'd advertised for help with a project he was working on. She contacted the email address and said she'd been selected to take part.'

'Selected?' Shepherd asked, leaning forward. 'She actually said selected?'

Will looked surprised. 'Yes, that's what she said.'

Shepherd looked at Burton. She shook her head, and he didn't say what he was clearly thinking.

'Did the advert say what it was about?' she asked.

'No. Just that they were looking for people to take part.'

'Did Leanne know what it entailed?'

'She didn't say.' Will was looking from Burton to Shepherd and back, like a tennis spectator.

Burton sat back, folded her arms and stared at the ceiling. Then she looked at Will and Wesley. 'Look, I can't promise that we'll find anything, but Leanne's disappearance will be re-examined as part of this current inquiry.' She raised a hand as both students started to speak at once. 'Like I said, we may not find anything, but it certainly merits extra scrutiny at this point. But–' she leaned forward '–I don't want you to tell everyone and I want you to stay in town where I can get hold of you if I need to.'

Both students nodded eagerly and, when Burton showed them out, they thanked her profusely.

When she returned to Shepherd, she perched on the table. 'What was that look for?' she asked. 'When Will mentioned the time?'

'The clock,' Shepherd said. 'The bloody clock in Harry Evans' office is set fifteen minutes fast.' Burton stared at him. 'So when he swiped into the library at five-twenty-five, he thought it was five-forty. That's why he's adamant that he went to the lake to meet Olly

Murton at three o clock when he couldn't possibly have been there.'

Burton sighed heavily. 'Why didn't we think of that sooner?'

'It only fell into place when that student said twenty minutes. It had been really bothering me that the times didn't tally.'

'Right, with Dr Evans off the list of suspects we need to crack on with the next lead.' She rustled the pages showing the forum comments.

'We're reopening her inquiry?' Shepherd asked, following her out of the door. 'Chandler's not going to like that.'

'I don't care what he likes or dislikes. The cases are connected in some way, and I think there's also another case we need to re-examine as well.'

Chapter fifty

Harry's friend in the chemistry department was in her office the next day when Dan and Harry went to see her with a photocopy of the formulae. She looked down at them and her eyes widened.

'You know what it is?' Dan could feel his stomach flickering again.

She shook her head. 'No, I've never seen anything like this before. You'll have to leave it with me. I can always ask someone else in the department if—'

'No, please don't tell anyone else,' Dan said, raising his palm towards her. She looked at Harry who shook his head.

'It's really important that no one finds out about this,' he said.

'Why?' The woman cocked her head to one side. 'What's this about, Harry?'

Harry paused and Dan could see that he was itching to explain what was going on so he jumped in.

'We just need to know what it is. It's for a—' he paused, not sure what excuse he was going to give.

'For a thing?' she asked, raising an eyebrow. Dan was puzzled and he knew it showed in his face. She laughed. 'That's what my students always say when they don't want to tell me why they're asking for help with something.'

'Please, if you can work it out that would be a great help,' Dan said, putting on his most appealing look. The woman laughed again.

'Leave it with me. I'll do some research into it and see what I can come up with. Give me a day or so.'

After thanking her, Dan and Harry walked out into the corridor and made their way outside. The sun was shining and the air felt quite warm. Dan stopped just outside the door, causing Harry to bump into him.

'What's the matter?' Harry asked.

Dan frowned. 'We need to find proof that Keith and Olly were working with George Peters.' He started to walk down the path at the side of the chemistry department building.

'How do you plan on doing that?' Harry asked, jogging to catch up with him.

'We can't go and search Olly's house because his mates will be there. So, we're going to search Keith's office. If there's anything, then it'll be in there.'

By charming the department secretary, Harry was able to get the key to Keith's office.

'Why do you want it?' she asked, eyes narrowed suspiciously.

'Keith borrowed a book,' Harry said. Dan almost sighed out loud. It was a lame excuse.

'The police have already searched in there so I don't see the harm,' she said.

As they walked up the stairs to the first floor, Harry looked down at the key in his hand.

'I hadn't thought of that,' he said.

'What?' Dan asked.

'If the police have already been through it, what are we likely to find?'

Dan paused at the top of the stairs. 'I don't know, but it's the only way I can think of to take the investigation forward.' He started to walk again and stopped outside the office. 'Let's see what we can find,' he said.

The door lock clicked as Harry turned the key and they stepped inside, closing the door quickly behind them.

Harry stood in the middle of the room looking around, hands on hips.

'What are we looking for?' he asked.

'Anything we can find about the research. Anything that proves they were working on that chemistry stuff. Anything that connects them to George Peters.'

Dan's stomach was flickering again. He was sure that there was something in here, but what? He stood staring at the bookshelves on the wall. Every single volume Keith had ever written was on one shelf. He could hear Harry moving around behind him, trying drawers and looking inside the ones that were unlocked. He was staring at the row of books when one title jumped out at him.

'The *Psychology of Truth*?' he said out loud.

'What?' Harry's voice was muffled as though he was speaking from under Keith's desk.

'There's a book here, The *Psychology of Truth*,' Dan said. He reached out a hand and pulled the hardback book down from the shelf. Harry joined him and they peered at the front cover of the book.

'Why would Keith have this?' Dan asked. 'Was he into psychology?'

Harry shrugged. 'I've no idea,' he said.

Dan frowned and ran his finger across the edges of the pages, fanning them out. The spine creaked a little bit as he opened it. 'I wonder if Keith has even read it,' he said. Then something fluorescent orange tucked between the pages caught his eye. He turned back to that page and held the book open.

'What's that?' Harry asked.

Dan picked up the note between his thumb and forefinger and one glance made his stomach flicker on double time.

'This is what we're looking for,' he said.

On the brightly coloured square of paper was a mobile number and the name 'George Peters'.

Chapter fifty-one

Dan and Harry didn't speak again until they were safely back in Harry's office. Dan laid the book down on Harry's desk and they both stared at it.

'Well, we got the proof you wanted,' Harry said, sitting down in his chair.

'I didn't think it would be that easy,' Dan said, without sitting down.

He picked the book up and looked at the note, which he'd stuck back on the page where they'd found it. The note marked the start of a chapter called 'Persuasion in truth'. Dan skim read the first page of the chapter and frowned at it.

'Why was Keith reading about truth and the effects of persuasion to make people tell the truth?' he asked. 'This is also asking about when persuasion becomes coercion.' He looked at Harry and knew that his bafflement was reflected in the other man's face. 'What on earth was Keith doing?'

Harry was frowning. 'I have no idea. I don't think he's ever written anything about psychology before, and he certainly wasn't known for telling the truth.'

Dan looked at him and nodded. He could see the irony, given what Keith had put Harry through with his lies. He held up the note.

'What do we do with that?' Harry asked.

Dan looked at him, puzzled. 'We ring it, of course.'

Harry raised his eyebrows. 'Ring the mobile number of a man we know is dead?'

Dan shrugged. 'Why not? You never know, there may be someone on the end of it.'

He handed the note to Harry who dialled it on his desk telephone. It rang and rang and eventually he got a message saying the voicemail box was full, and he hung up.

Dan frowned. 'What shall we—' he began, but the phone on Harry's desk interrupted him. They stared at each other. Dan pointed at the phone.

'Quick, answer before they hang up.'

Harry pressed the speakerphone button and said, 'Hello?'

A woman's voice spoke on the other end. 'I'm sorry. I just missed a call from this number. Who's speaking please?'

Harry looked dumbstruck and so Dan stepped in.

'Hi, my name is Harry Evans, I work at Allensbury University,' he said. Harry stared at him and Dan waved a hand to stop him speaking.

'Oh, hello,' the woman said, sounding a little confused.

'I'm trying to reach George Peters,' Dan said. Harry was looking at him like he'd lost his senses.

'Sorry?' the woman asked.

'I work with Professor Keith Williams at the university. He died recently and I've been helping to clear out his office. I think he and George Peters must have known each other because I found a book belonging to him and I wanted to return it.'

There was a pause on the other end of the phone. Then the woman said, 'I see. Well, the problem is that my brother is dead.'

Dan stepped back slightly, acting surprised even though the

woman couldn't see him. 'I'm terribly sorry,' he said.

'That's OK.' There was a pause again. Dan held on, knowing that she was going to say something else. 'I suppose I should collect the book. I don't want to leave George's possessions lying around.'

'I could bring it to you if that's easier?' Dan said.

'Yes, that's probably for the best.'

Dan grinned at Harry. 'Where should I meet you?' he asked.

'Do you know the Turpin Hotel in Allensbury,' the woman asked.

'Yes I do. Why don't I head over now and then I can be out of your hair?' Dan asked. 'I'm sure you have a lot to do.'

'Yes.' The woman sighed. 'I hadn't realised how much.'

Harry was holding up a piece of paper saying, 'What's her name?' Dan flapped a hand to say that was what he was about to ask.

'Who should I ask for at the hotel?'

'My name's Anna, Anna Peters. Why don't we meet in the lounge for a coffee?'

'That sounds great.' Dan glanced at his watch. 'In about half an hour?'

'That works for me.'

Dan said goodbye and hung up the phone. He looked at Harry and Harry looked back at him.

'Well,' Dan said, 'we've got a date with George Peters' sister. Let's go and find out if she knows what her brother was up to with Keith and Olly.'

Chapter fifty-two

Burton spread the pages of George Peters' investigation file on the table in the corner of her office. A copy had already been sent to the coroner's officer, once it had been established that the cause of death was heart failure, but something was niggling at her.

When Shepherd arrived balancing a tray of coffees in one hand and a bag of sticky buns in the other, she was standing looking down at the table, hands on hips, and scowling as if the file was refusing to give her what she wanted.

'What are you doing?' Shepherd asked, holding out the coffee tray. But Burton's hand grabbed at the bag of buns first. She plucked one out and took a big bite, sighing with pleasure.

'Hi baby,' she said to the bun, before placing it and the bag on the desk behind her. Shepherd laughed as she took the coffee cup from him.

'Hi yourself,' he said, earning himself a half-glare. Burton quickly put down the cup realising that the contents were too hot. Then she sat on the corner of her desk and picked up her bun again. She demolished it in a few bites.

'I need the sugar,' she said. 'It gets my brain firing.' She wiped her fingers on a tissue she'd had tucked up her sleeve.

Shepherd sat on one of the chairs by the table and sipped at his coffee. 'What's made you come back to this one?' he asked.

Burton was still cleaning the sugar off her fingers, a frown on her face. 'I don't know. Three people have died in a very short space of time. I want to make sure that we're not missing a connection.'

Shepherd put his coffee down on the table. 'But this guy died of a heart attack, according to the medical report,' he said.

'So did Olly Murton,' Burton said, picking up her paper cup of coffee.

Shepherd frowned and then pulled the file towards him and read the page at the top. 'The victim is found dead in his front room, having had a heart attack while sitting in an armchair. Doors and windows locked, no sign of a break-in. No one seen near the house around the time he died,' he said, with a shrug. 'That happens to people every day.'

Burton exhaled heavily. 'I know it's possible but something just feels wrong.' She rubbed a hand across her chin. 'If we didn't have a report that he'd been abducted I'd be happy to accept heart failure, but—'

Shepherd nodded. He moved the pieces of paper around until he found the timeline. Peering at it, he said, 'So, George Peters is snatched as he's leaving work—'

'Running away from work,' Burton said, pointing at him with her coffee cup. 'Dan Sullivan said he was running and was then dragged into a van and driven away at high speed.'

Shepherd nodded. 'And the next time he's seen he's dead in his armchair,' he said. He sat back in his chair and looked up at Burton.

She was fiddling with the end of her ponytail. 'Another angle is that we have a missing student from the university and another who's been murdered. To say nothing of the lecturer who's been murdered.' She put down her coffee and rubbed her face with both hands, exhaling heavily. She looked at Shepherd. 'Who kidnapped him?' she demanded. 'Why was he kidnapped? What was he running away from?' She paused. 'Was Leanne Nelson abducted?'

Shepherd exhaled heavily. 'I know it's sometimes a relief to leave work,' he said. 'But I've never literally run out of the door.'

Burton frowned. 'He worked for GITech Pharmaceuticals, didn't he?' she asked. When Shepherd nodded, she said 'What do they do?'

Shepherd leaned his elbow on the table. 'They were a bit technical when they were explaining, but I think the simple version is that they create drugs. They're quite experimental apparently,' he said.

'What does that mean?' Burton asked, pulling a face.

Shepherd laughed. 'I think that was a way to tell us that they don't just manufacture paracetamol,' he said. 'They said their work is very confidential.'

Burton was chewing the edge of the plastic lid of her cup. 'Did they say what he was working on?' she asked.

Shepherd shook his head. 'Not in so many words. Some sort of anti-psychotic drug I think.'

Burton bit her lip for a moment. 'That's not something that would get you kidnapped, is it?' she asked. She sighed. 'I just wish we had evidence of him being abducted. If we could trace that van—' She walked to the window and stared out, hands on hips.

Then she turned back. 'I'm all out of ideas at the moment,' she said. 'I've got Brody going over the Peters post-mortem report to see if she spots something. She didn't do the initial examination so maybe a fresh set of eyes will help.'

'Anything else?'

Burton nodded. 'Just a thought. Ask Suzy Press Office if she can have a look back at any media coverage from the time that we might not have seen, and anything online about George Peters, what his job was, local connections, that kind of thing.'

'Will do.' Shepherd started towards the door and then turned back. 'You've called Suzy that for so long, do you even remember what her actual surname is?'

Burton smiled and took another sip from her cup. 'I'm not sure I do.' Then she became serious. 'We're missing something, I know we are. Let's just hope we can track it down soon, for the sake of his family.'

Chapter fifty-three

When Dan and Harry entered the lounge area of the Turpin Hotel, a woman with long dark hair in a ponytail looked up expectantly from one of the deep leather sofas.

'That must be her,' Dan said, setting off towards the sofa that she was rising from. But Harry grabbed his arm.

'Go gentle,' he said. 'We need to get as much out of her as possible.'

Dan frowned. 'I can be gentle.'

They reached the sofa and the woman was already on her feet. She was tall and dark and gave off the air of great energy, as if being still was an anathema to her. But her face looked guarded.

'I was only expecting Harry Evans,' she said.

Harry offered his hand. 'That's me.'

The woman shook the offered hand and her eyes flickered towards Dan. 'And you are?'

'This is my friend Dan Sullivan,' Harry said.

Dan held out a hand and the woman gave him the most cursory handshake she could manage.

Anna sat back on the sofa and indicated for them to sit. Harry sat alongside her on the sofa while Dan sat opposite on an armchair. She was still looking doubtfully at Dan.

'This isn't about a book you found in someone's office, is it?' she asked.

'No, I'm a reporter on the local paper,' Dan said. 'But Harry does genuinely work at the university.'

Anna's face had entirely shut down and she looked very uncomfortable. 'Why is a news reporter getting involved in this? I've nothing to say.' Her hand moved towards her handbag as if she was preparing to leave.

'I'm not looking for a comment for a story,' Dan said, but Anna interrupted.

'You mentioned clearing out someone's office? Was that just a lie to get me here?'

'No, not entirely,' said Harry.

Dan could see that Harry's words were not helping to break down Anna's defences and her hand moved slightly towards her handbag again. He needed to stop her leaving.

'Keith Williams was killed last week, murdered in the university library,' he said. 'That's why we were in his office.' Anna's hand froze. 'He was working on a new research project, and when we found your brother's mobile number in his office, we thought they must have been working together.'

Anna was staring at him. 'What research project?'

'That's the thing, we don't know,' Dan explained. 'We were hoping you might be able to tell us that.'

There was an awkward silence as the waitress arrived at the table. Anna ordered a second pot of tea, while Harry and Dan opted for coffees. When neither Harry nor Anna said anything, Dan decided on his line of questioning.

'What have the police told you about your brother's death?'

Anna sighed. 'Surprisingly little. All they've said so far is that he had a heart attack. But—' she paused.

'But you don't believe them?' Dan asked, his stomach flickering again.

'I don't understand. George had just had a medical and got a clean bill of health. Why would he have a heart attack?'

'You think there's more to it?' Dan asked.

Anna looked mystified. 'Why would there be? But if you say he was involved with someone who's been murdered maybe there is.'

She paused as the waitress returned with their drinks. Coffees in large heavy cups and saucers were slid in front of Harry and Dan, followed by a teapot for Anna, milk in jugs and sugar cubes. Then the waitress almost curtsied and left them alone.

Dan poured milk into his coffee and stirred. Then he looked at Anna, hoping that if he kept quiet she would continue speaking.

'Have the police said anything to you?' she asked Dan, looking at him from under long, dark eyelashes.

'Not really. When it originally happened I took it at face value so there didn't seem to be much to tell.' He paused. 'Can I ask how they found him?'

'He didn't turn up for work one morning and his colleagues were worried about him. They tried to phone him but his mobile was off and his home number was just ringing out.'

Dan frowned. 'Did he often turn off his phone?'

'Only when he was in the lab. But it had actually run out of battery. I'd been trying to get in touch because I'd not heard from him for a couple of days. I left a few messages and they're still on there.' She pulled a smart, black, touch-screen mobile phone from her handbag and put it on the table.

'How long had he been dead when they found him?'

'They thought it might have been forty-eight hours at the most.'

'What did his workmates do?' Harry asked.

'Three of them came round and knocked and rang the bell. The woman next door heard them and went to speak to them. She said she'd heard George come home two days previously but hadn't heard anything since then.'

'Had she seen anything?' Dan asked.

'Like what?'

'Like people hanging around?'

Anna looked at him with a frown. 'Why would you ask that?'

'I spoke to another of his neighbours when I attended the scene,' he said. 'She said she'd seen some guys going into George's house two nights before he was found. They seemed to have a key.'

'Was George with them?' Anna asked.

'She didn't say. Maybe he was, or maybe he was already inside.' Dan paused then asked, 'What did George's friends do after they'd spoken to the neighbour?'

'They broke in. Smashed a pane of glass in the front door with a stone from the garden. They said he was just sitting in the chair. They thought he was asleep, but when they tried to wake him and checked his pulse, he was dead.' Her eyes filled with tears and she dragged a tattered tissue from her pocket.

'I'm sorry that we're making you go through it all again,' Harry said.

'That's OK. Maybe it's good to talk about it.' She gave a wry smile.

'Did George's friends notice anything different in the house? Anything that seemed out of place?' Harry asked.

'One of them said it was really hot. The heating had been turned right up to maximum and George would never have done that.'

'Anything else?'

'He said the place looked untidy,' Anna said. 'George was always really particular and made sure everything was in its place, but the flat looked dishevelled. That was the word he used.'

'Was there anything else?' Harry asked.

'His laptop is missing.'

Dan looked at Harry, who was looking back at him wide eyes. Dan's stomach was flickering.

Dan leaned forward, putting his elbows on his knees. 'Where would it normally have been?' he asked.

'It was usually in his study.'

'Could he have taken it to work with him?' Dan asked.

Anna shook his head. 'No, this was his personal laptop. He had a separate one for work. That one is in his office at GITech.'

'And the laptop isn't anywhere in the house?'

'I've been over the place with a fine-tooth comb and I can't find it anywhere.'

Dan rubbed his chin. 'Did you tell the police about that?' he asked.

'The police already knew. They'd checked the house over when they were first called out and they couldn't find the laptop either. They said there were no hairs or fibres that weren't George's. Not even fingerprints.'

There was another silence at the table as they all took a sip of their drinks. Dan's brain was rattling with information. Where was George's laptop? Had he hidden it in the same way Keith Williams had or had it been taken? Why would either of them think they needed to hide their computer?

Anna was now looking at them both. 'What's your interest in this?'

Harry answered first. 'We think that Keith was involved in some research that may have gone bad. Like I said, he was killed last week and when we found your brother's number, we wondered how they were connected.'

'Now we know that they've been working together,' Dan put in, 'it's too much of a coincidence that they would both die within a matter of days.'

'Do you know what they were working on?' Anna asked.

'No,' Dan said quickly, hoping Harry wouldn't mention the formulae that he'd been sent. 'We were looking for evidence in Keith's office but we didn't find anything.'

Anna leaned forward. 'Did Keith Williams have a laptop? Could there be evidence about the research on there?'

'The police have got that,' Dan said. 'We didn't even get a chance to look at it.'

'Where was it?' Anna asked.

'Where was what?' Dan asked, puzzled.

'The laptop.'

'It was in his car,' Dan said. He was about to say more but stopped when an expression he couldn't quite identify flitted across Anna's face.

'A student was also killed,' Harry told her. 'He was drowned in the lake on campus.'

Anna raised an eyebrow. 'A student? Why was he killed?'

Harry nodded. 'He was a friend of Keith's and we think he was involved in the research as well.'

Anna puffed out her cheeks. 'This is so weird. I came to clear out my brother's house after he died of a heart attack and now I find he might have been involved in something that got him killed.'

'Do you know what he was working on?' Dan asked. Out of the corner of his eye he saw Harry pause with his coffee cup halfway to his lips as he waited for Anna's answer.

'No,' Anna said, stirring her tea distractedly. 'He was always really secretive about his work. He did say something about finding out the truth, but I don't know what he was getting at.'

Dan caught Harry's eye just as Harry opened his mouth to speak and gave a slight shake of his head. This was the second time truth had been mentioned. He looked back at Anna but if she'd noticed Harry's aborted speech she didn't show it.

She sipped her tea. 'So do you know what they were working on?' she asked.

Dan shook his head. 'That's the missing piece of the puzzle. But if we can work out what it was, we might be able to work out why it got the three of them killed.'

Chapter fifty-four

Eleanor Brody sat in her office, a cup of tea at her elbow, flicking through the printed pages of the file she'd been emailed. She was leaning back in her chair with her feet on the desk, brow furrowing as she read. George Peters' post-mortem report was making her head hurt. She'd worked with the other Allensbury-based pathologist for a number of years and he was more than happy for her to take a look at the file. He was as frustrated as anyone by the lack of progress and he'd even sounded pleased when he found out why she was calling.

'I'm grateful for all the help I can get, to be honest,' he'd said. 'It's a bit of a puzzler this one. I just can't get to a cause of death. At first I thought it was a heart attack, but the medical history just won't stand it up.'

'Could it be sudden arrhythmic death syndrome?'

'I considered that, but usually there's some genetic links or heart problems in the family with that, and his family is completely clear. Also, there's often an exercise link to SADS and I just don't think he was exercising enough to bring that on.'

'And you don't mind if I look at the report?'

The man sighed. 'No, please do. As I said it's got me completely stumped. I've tried every type of toxicology screen I can think of and it's all come back negative. No alcohol, not even paracetamol.'

'Sounds interesting. Leave it with me and if I get any inspiration I'll let you know.'

Brody was now absorbed in the report, eyes scanning each word. She didn't want to miss a thing. She took a distracted sip from her cup of tea and grimaced. It had gone cold. She rubbed her forehead. So far everything about George Peters was normal, apart from the fact he was dead, seemingly for no reason. But there had to be some connection between the three bodies in her morgue. She'd never heard Burton be so adamant, but her hunches were often right so Brody would give her the benefit of the doubt. When she got to the page about the body's organs, she pulled her feet off the desk and sat up straight, staring at the page. A bell wasn't just ringing in her head; it was clanging loudly. Seizing the phone, she dialled her assistant's number.

'Sam, will you bring me the file on Olly Murton, please? Yes, now.'

'Well, I can tell by your face that you've got something,' Burton said, as she and Shepherd sat down in Brody's office. The pathologist was sitting behind her desk, beaming.

'I have, and it may surprise you.' She opened one file. 'Remember when we did the post-mortem on Olly Murton and I remarked on the size of his heart.'

'You said it was enlarged,' Shepherd put in.

Brody smiled. 'Correct,' she said.

Burton frowned. 'So, his heart was enlarged. What does that mean?'

'On its own, it may be nothing, but look what I spotted when I looked back at George Peters' post-mortem.' She spun the file around and pushed it towards Burton. She and Shepherd peered at the typewritten numbers.

'I don't understand,' Burton said.

'The weight of a healthy human heart in a man is about three hundred grams,' Brody said. George Peters and Olly Murton's hearts were both more than seven hundred grams.'

Burton raised an eyebrow. 'What would cause that?' she asked.

'Usually that would mean a diseased heart,' Brody said, 'but neither of our victims had any medical history to suggest heart problems and they were both relatively healthy. For them both to have enlarged hearts that led to random heart attacks is just too much of a coincidence.'

'You think they were both killed by the same thing,' Burton said.

'Yes. But as for what killed them, I'm still not sure.'

'What caused the enlarged hearts?' Burton asked.

Brody wrinkled her nose. 'That's where I'm stumped. Both tox screens came back clear and George Peters' samples have been through just about every test known to forensic science.'

'What happens next?' Burton asked.

'I'll get my colleague to look at Olly Murton's PM report and see if there's anything I've missed.'

'You? Miss something?' Burton asked with a grin. Brody mock-scowled at her.

'I'm only human,' she replied. Shepherd laughed but quickly turned it into a cough as Brody turned her glare on him. 'What are you going to be doing?' Brody asked.

'George Peters is clearly connected to Olly Murton through Keith Williams,' Shepherd said.

Burton nodded. 'It's all coming back to this research project, isn't it?'

'Did Williams have an enlarged heart too?' Shepherd asked Brody.

Brody shook her head. 'No, it wasn't a healthy heart, but it was normal for his age and size.'

'Slightly odd to have three deaths, but only two fit the pattern,' Shepherd mused.

'What are you thinking?' Burton asked.

'It would make more sense if they were all killed in the same way.'

'We don't know what killed these two,' Burton said, pointing to George Peters' file 'and the third was hit on the head.'

Shepherd was frowning. Burton and Brody were both watching him.

'Remember how Olly Murton had that puncture mark on his shoulder?' Shepherd asked.

Brody and Burton nodded.

'Did George Peters have one too?'

Burton sat up straight. 'You think they'd both been injected with something?'

'Exactly, something that could have caused an enlarged heart or brought on a heart attack. Could you check that?' Shepherd asked Brody.

She nodded. 'There's nothing in his report, but I'll ask my colleague if he noticed anything. We'll go back and look at the body if we have to.'

Burton was frowning. 'If we assume they were all killed by the same person, why were they planning to kill Williams with his car? Why not just inject him with whatever did for Olly Murton?'

'Maybe they couldn't get near Williams?' Shepherd suggested. 'Maybe he knew they were after him and was on the lookout.'

'Can you check back on Williams too? Just in case he had any puncture wounds?' Burton asked.

'Yup.' Brody scribbled it on her notepad.

'Right.' Burton stood up. Finally they at least had something of a breakthrough. At last they had some leads to chase up.

Chapter fifty-five

Sam was rolling the trolley containing the domed-stomached body of Keith Williams into the middle of the morgue's inspection room when Brody arrived.

'You're keen,' she remarked.

Sam grinned. 'I'm intrigued to see what we missed,' he said. 'And how we missed it.'

Brody frowned. 'Me too.'

Sam looked down at the body wrinkling his nose. 'I don't ever want to look like that,' he said.

'Stay away from excess alcohol and fatty foods and keep up your exercise regime.' She looked the young man up and down with a professional eye. 'But you've got the sort of build where you're unlikely to end up like Professor Williams.'

'Phew.' Sam laughed. Then he frowned down at the body. 'We're looking for an injection site?' he asked.

'Yes.' Brody consulted the clipboard she had placed on the work bench to the left of the room and turned back to him. 'Another of the three victims had an injection in this area.' She indicated the part where her neck met her shoulder. 'We're checking up on the third.'

'OK,' Sam said, taking a deep breath. 'Let's do it.'

They both snapped on surgical gloves and approached the table.

Shining torches onto the body, they worked systematically across the torso and neck.

'What was he wearing?' Sam asked.

'Collar and tie.'

'I thought academics were more relaxed than that.' Then Sam frowned. 'Then there's no point in looking below here.' He held a hand to Williams' neck where a shirt collar would rest. Brody nodded.

'Correct,' she said.

'In fact, if he had his collar fastened, then there'd be an even smaller area of skin for them to aim at,' Sam said, feeling excitement flaring in his stomach. 'They'd have almost had to inject him in the base of his skull.' He pointed to Williams' hairline. 'Maybe they weren't expecting him to be wearing a collar and tie.'

Brody frowned. 'You're right. But if they'd been watching him, why weren't they expecting that style?'

'Maybe the collar and tie were a one-off and they weren't ready for it. Maybe they were expecting a T-shirt or something.'

'That's a good point,' Brody said.

'And when they realised that they couldn't get access to his neck, they whacked him.'

Brody stared at him. 'That would explain the use of a book. They had to improvise.'

Sam watched her, his heart pounding. 'What do you think?' he asked.

'I think that's a very good theory,' Brody replied. Suddenly she frowned and walked to the computer. She tapped at the keys for a few moments.

'What is it?' Sam asked, moving to look over her shoulder.

'Remember when we were in the library and you found that glass on the floor?'

'Yes.' Sam stopped, his eyes wide. 'You think that was a syringe?'

'Very possibly.' Then she sighed heavily.

'What's the matter?' Sam asked.

Brody pointed to the screen. 'It's not in the inventory.'

'What? I swear I catalogued everything that came back.'

'I'm sure you did, which means it didn't come back to us.' She looked at Sam. 'We need to find that syringe and quickly.'

Sam looked up in surprise as Burton and Shepherd pushed through the door into the morgue. How on earth had they got there so quickly? Brody had only called them twenty minutes ago to say she thought they were onto something.

'Hi Sam,' said Shepherd, his voice slightly too cheerful for the setting. Burton was eyeing a jar containing a piece of tattooed skin floating in formaldehyde with distaste.

'What have you got?' she asked Sam.

'I'll let her tell you.' Sam grinned and reached for the phone. At that moment Brody came through the other door to the morgue. Sam stared at her, phone receiver still in hand.

'How did you know they were here?' he asked, hanging up the phone.

'She sensed our presence in the building,' said Shepherd with a grin. 'Two more live people must put the ambient temperature up.'

Brody gave him a patient look. 'Reception called me,' she said.

'No sixth sense then?'

'Nope, just modern technology.'

But Burton had had enough of the pleasantries. 'Well, we're here. You said you found something at the Williams crime scene.'

'Your boys had accidentally–' Brody put emphasis on the word '– packed up a load of stuff from the library crime scene and taken it to the station instead of giving it to me.'

Burton pulled a face. 'That's because you intimidate them and stop them thinking properly.'

Brody smiled. 'Flattery will get you nowhere,' she said, causing Shepherd to give a snort, which he attempted to turn into a cough. Burton glared at him, but Brody continued.

'Among the odds and ends in the box, we found several evidence bags, one of which contained this.' She placed the bag on the table in front of the detectives. They both stepped forward and peered at it.

'Some bits of glass?' Burton looked up at Brody.

'Not just any bits of glass, they come from a syringe.'

'A syringe? What would a syringe be doing in a library?' Burton asked.

'More importantly, what is a *broken* syringe doing in the library?' Brody asked.

'Could it have belonged to a diabetic or something like that?' Shepherd asked. 'Anyone could have dropped it; it is a public place after all.'

'I already considered that. The glass is mostly broken, but there was some substance clinging to the largest fragment. I tested it and it's not insulin.'

'What is it?'

Brody shrugged. 'I've sent it next door and pulled some strings to get it done. James said to give him about forty minutes and he'd report back.'

There was a silence and then Burton asked, 'When was that?'

Brody consulted her watch. 'About thirty-eight minutes ago.' Burton opened her mouth to speak, but as she did so a man in blue scrubs clutching a clipboard pushed open the door.

'James,' said Brody smiling. 'You're early.'

The man looked slightly grim. 'You're not going to like this.'

'What?' asked Brody, her voice suddenly sharp.

'I don't know what it is,' he said simply. Burton groaned aloud, but Brody looked thoughtful.

'How can you not know what it is?' Sam asked. 'Was the sample not big enough to test?'

'A small sample isn't ideal, but I managed to run some tests. The only problem is they came back negative. So we have no idea what it is.' James handed Brody the top sheet from his clipboard and turned to go.

'Thanks, James,' she said. She turned to Burton with a smile.

Burton looked irritated. 'Why are you smiling? There was nothing to tell us. We've come down here for nothing.'

'No, we haven't,' said Shepherd suddenly.

Brody looked at him and smiled. 'You've worked it out?' she asked.

'We were looking for a connection between George Peters, Olly Murton and Keith Williams – now we've got one,' Shepherd said. 'Two of them were killed by a mysterious injection, and now we've got a broken syringe in the library. They were going to inject Williams but the syringe got broken.'

'And they had to improvise,' Sam said.

Shepherd nodded. 'Yes.'

'If they'd succeeded with the plan, he'd have been found dead in the library of a suspected heart attack and no one would be any the wiser,' Brody said.

'They must have been desperate to kill him to risk getting caught like that,' Shepherd said.

Burton nodded. 'We need to go back through Williams' computer and see what he'd been up to for the last few days. Let's see where that takes us.'

Chapter fifty-six

Burton was in her office typing up a progress report for the boss when there was a tap on her office door. She looked up to see the press officer looking in at her.

'Hi Suzy, come on in,' she said. 'Actually, ask Mark to join us, will you?' She laughed as Suzy leaned around the door and flapped a hand to get Shepherd's attention. He looked at her in a baffled way and wandered over to join her in the doorway.

'Do you want something?' he asked, shoving her gently with his shoulder and smiling down at her.

'Burton asked me to get you. I thought that was more polite than yelling "Oi" across the room.' Shepherd laughed and followed her into the office. They took chairs opposite Burton's desk and both detectives looked expectantly at Suzy.

'What have you got?' Burton asked.

'Not a massive amount at the moment,' Suzy said. 'All the Allensbury coverage, you've seen already. The family isn't local and wouldn't speak to the Post to do a tribute piece. I contacted the local paper where the family live. They didn't get an interview either, despite the fact that George was in the paper for winning chess competitions and chemistry prizes when he was at school.'

'Is it unusual that they don't want to talk?' Burton asked.

Suzy shrugged. 'It depends – usually if someone is well-known locally and dies, the family speak to the paper to pay tribute to them, etcetera etcetera. In this case the family is the most insanely private group of people I've ever met. They barely wanted to speak to me.'

'Worried that they might give something away?'

'That's the only reason I can think of,' Suzy said. 'All they would say is that he was a hard worker, good at his job, often working on things that were classified. The mother seemed most proud of that.'

'Was there anything else about him?'

'The most I've been able to do so far is a few Internet searches, so all I've got is some journal articles he's written and a story about his company winning a big grant from a research council.' She glanced at her watch. 'Unfortunately I've got no more time today, so I'll have to pick things up in the morning. I just wanted to give you an update so far.'

'Thanks, Suzy, that's great work. Keep me posted.'

The press officer grinned and left the room with a cheery wave.

Shepherd looked at Burton. 'So nothing new there,' he said, shoving his hands into his trouser pockets.

Burton frowned. 'There's something in this, something we're missing and I just can't put my finger on it.'

'We spoke to Dr Anthony Bellswick, his boss, as part of the investigation into his death. We need to talk to him again and see if he can shed some light on the matter,' Shepherd said.

'But why?' Burton asked, pulling on the end of her ponytail. 'What else can we get out of him?'

'We can ask if he'll tell us more about what George was working on, and whether he'd outsourced anything to the university?' Shepherd suggested.

Burton chewed the inside of her mouth for a moment. 'You think the company had brought Keith Williams and Olly Murton in to work on a chemistry project?'

'When you put it like that it sounds stupid,' Shepherd said.

'It's like a bad joke, isn't it? A politics academic, a student and an experimental chemist walk into a bar,' Burton said, shaking her head.

Shepherd laughed. 'If we knew the next part of the joke we might get a bit further.'

Burton leaned forward, putting her elbows on the desk and steepling her fingers. 'I think you're right. We need to go back and speak to George Peters' boss again. If he was working on something classified that was dangerous enough to get him killed, I want to know what it was.'

'Reckon Dr Bellswick will tell us?'

'If I have to, I'll arrest him for obstructing a police investigation,' Burton said. 'Maybe a grilling in an interrogation room will get him talking.' She paused. 'We've got three bodies now; I want to make sure there isn't a fourth.'

Chapter fifty-seven

Dan was typing energetically at his keyboard on Monday morning when his mobile rang. The screen said it was Harry calling.

'Hi mate, what's up?' Dan asked, tucking his phone under his chin and continuing to type.

'Can you get to my office on campus now?'

Dan glanced around him. There were only a few reporters in the office. 'It might be tricky to come right now. Why? What's so urgent?'

'Anna Peters is coming over. She has something to show us. It's important.'

'How important?'

'Very,' Harry said. 'George's laptop has turned up.'

'Say no more.' Dan looked at his watch. 'I'll make some excuses and be there in half an hour. Wait for me.'

'We'll try.'

Harry was sitting at his desk tapping his fingers impatiently. His clock told him that it had only been twenty minutes since Anna had called and said she would be there in half an hour. Although he knew there was no way she could get across town from George's house in Castle Street, where she said she was staying, that quickly at this time of day, he was already on the edge of his seat. He jumped when the phone rang and reached for the receiver with a slightly shaking hand. It was the office secretary.

'There's a woman here to see you,' she said, sounding intrigued.

'Yes, I'm expecting her. Please send her up.' He could tell the secretary was desperate to ask questions but was far too well-mannered to pry.

Harry was already out of his seat and halfway across the room when Anna tapped at the door. He pulled it open and waved for her to come in.

'How are you?' he asked.

She placed the badly wrapped parcel on his desk and stepped away. 'I'm not too sure. Up and down by the hour, I think. I can't believe he's really gone.' Her eyes filled with tears and she tried to wipe them away with the back of her hand.

'Here.' Harry stepped forward, pulling out a clean cotton handkerchief and handing it to her. She smiled a thanks and buried her face in it, trying to dry the tears that continued to flow. Harry stepped towards her and rubbed her arm awkwardly, not really sure how to offer comfort. Before he could do anything, Anna had stepped forward and buried her face in his chest. He tried to sort of pat her on the back.

Anna stepped away and their eyes met. Harry was finding it hard to look away when there was a knock and the door flew open. This time it was Dan, looking slightly dishevelled.

'Sorry I've taken so long,' he said. Then he stopped, taking in the physical closeness of Harry and Anna, and sensing the mood in the room. 'Am I interrupting?' he asked, looking from one to the other.

'No, you're right on time,' said Harry, quickly stepping away behind his desk. He gestured to the laptop that Anna had placed on the desk in front of him.

'Where did this come from?' Dan asked, stepping forward eagerly and dumping his bag onto a chair. He leaned on the desk and peered down at the black laptop in front of him.

'I received this,' Anna said, pulling an envelope from her handbag and handing it to him. Dan pulled out a sheet of paper and opened it. It contained a sequence of letters, which made no sense to him. He handed it across to Harry who looked at it, equally puzzled.

'I don't understand,' Harry said, holding the note out to Anna.

'It's in code,' Anna said, taking it from him. 'It's from George.'

'From George? But how?' Dan asked.

'He's the only one who knows that code. He invented it. It's like an anagram. He taught me how to solve it. It's all about working out what order the letters go in.'

'When did it arrive?' Harry asked.

'This morning.'

Dan stared at her. 'Not meaning to be callous,' he said, 'but George has been dead for nearly a week. Did it get lost in the post or something?'

Anna shook her head. 'No, I think he left it with someone to be sent to me if something happened to him.'

'That's a bit cloak and dagger, isn't it?' Dan said, raising his eyebrows.

Anna shrugged. 'Maybe he knew he was in danger, so he'd hidden the laptop. The letter was addressed to me at his house. He must have known I'd be there.' She paused. 'It contained this.' She held up a small metal key. 'And gave me directions to a sorting office where this parcel was being held in a PO box.'

'And the laptop was in it?' Dan asked.

Anna nodded.

'Why go to such lengths to hide a laptop?' Harry asked.

'There must be something on it that George didn't want anyone to know about,' Anna said. 'He must have thought someone else wanted it.'

'Clearly he was right,' Harry said.

Anna looked puzzled for a moment and then her eyes widened as the implication of his words hit her. 'You mean someone went to his house looking for it and killed him when he wouldn't give it to them?'

Harry nodded. 'Exactly. He must have known what would happen so he made sure it wasn't in the house. That way he couldn't be persuaded to give it up.'

Anna got to her feet and paced the room. 'But why not just send it to me? I'd have kept it safe for him.'

'Maybe he didn't want to put you in danger, or he might have thought he could get away from them.' Harry looked at the laptop in silence for a few moments. 'What do we think is on it?'

Anna looked surprised. 'I don't know, but it must be important or he wouldn't have hidden it.'

'Why did you bring it here?' Dan asked, facing Anna and shoving his hands into his trouser pockets.

Anna looked worried. 'I think I was followed when I went to collect it this morning.'

Dan frowned. 'How do you know you were followed?' he asked.

'I kept seeing the same guy everywhere,' Anna said, wrapping her arms protectively around her torso. 'On the street, outside the sorting office.'

'What did he look like?' Dan asked.

'A dark jacket and a baseball cap was all I saw,' Anna said, pointing to her own head.

Dan looked doubtfully at her and then Harry. 'That sounds like a character from a bad spy film,' he said.

But Harry was nodding at Anna. 'It sounds like someone was

expecting you to go and pick up the laptop,' he said. 'Did he try to speak to you?'

Anna shook her head, eyes fixed on Harry. 'I made sure he didn't get close enough and then I jumped on the bus and came here. I didn't dare go back to the house because I'd be on my own. I couldn't think of anywhere else to go.'

Dan was still frowning. 'If you thought you were being followed, why not get a taxi?' he asked. 'That would have been—'

Suddenly the alarm clock on Harry's desk rang, making them all jump.

'Oh shit, is that the time already?' Harry grabbed his leather jacket. 'Look, I should only be an hour or so at this lecture. Stay here and we'll look at the computer together when I get back. Are you OK to hang on, Dan?' he asked.

Dan nodded. 'Yeah, sure. My boss thinks I'm out on a story.'

Harry grinned and disappeared with his backpack in his hand. The door banged shut behind him.

Dan turned back to Anna and found her looking at him suspiciously, her arms folded. 'Is my brother the story?' she asked, pointing at the laptop.

Dan decided to be honest. 'In a way. There's something weird going on here. Three murders that are connected to each other through a research project. The question is, what the hell were they researching that was important enough to get them killed?'

Chapter fifty-eight

No sooner had Dan spoken than his mobile began to ring. He looked at the screen and cringed.

'My boss. This should be interesting.' He hovered for a moment, looking at Anna, and then answered.

Daisy's voice was shrill. 'Dan? Dan, where the hell are you?'

Dan tried not to sigh out loud. That would be like waving a red flag in front of a bull. 'I told you,' he said. 'I'm out on a story.'

'Will this actually provide me with something to print in the paper?' When Dan said nothing, Daisy ran on. 'Honest to God, Dan, I need you here actually doing some work.'

'I am. I'm—' He looked over at Anna, who was studiously pretending not to listen. Dan moved into the corner of the room with his back turned. 'I am onto something but it's going to take a while to bottom it out,' he said in a low voice.

Daisy sighed heavily. 'But I need you here now. I've got pages to fill.'

Dan glanced at his watch. 'Give me an hour or so and I'll come back. I just need to—' but Daisy had already put the phone down after a terse goodbye.

He turned back to find Anna tapping away at the laptop's keyboard.

'How's it going?' he asked, pulling up a chair next to her.

'I've made a start,' she said, indicating the screen.

'What have you found?'

'Nothing so far. It was password protected but I broke that quite quickly.'

Dan raised an eyebrow. 'Good skill to have.'

She smiled. 'I work with computers so George would know I could crack it.'

'What is it you do?'

'I'm a systems analyst.' She grinned. 'I'm also a bit of a technology geek.'

Dan laughed. 'Then this really shouldn't be a problem for you.'

'It shouldn't be,' Anna said, frowning. 'But it is.'

Dan looked at her. 'Why?'

'It's encrypted,' she said.

'Encrypted?' Dan asked, peering over her shoulder at the screen. It was black apart from a message saying 'Locked'. This was getting weirder by the minute. 'Ah. What do we do?'

'I've tried a couple of things but nothing has worked. It's not an encryption I've seen before. I think George has had a special program designed. Clearly this information is important.'

'It's important enough for someone. They killed him for it.' Dan looked at her and could have kicked himself for his bluntness. But Anna's eyes, although still a little red, were dry and her fingers were still poised over the laptop keyboard. 'Sorry, I didn't mean to—'

She waved a hand. 'It's OK, it's just the idea that someone wanted to kill George. I don't understand. He wouldn't hurt a fly.'

'Maybe he hadn't done anything,' Dan said. 'It might have been something that he knew.'

'What do you mean?' Anna asked.

'He usually worked on sensitive stuff, didn't he? Maybe someone was trying to steal it and George tried to stop them?' He paused. What if George was leaking details of a project and he'd been killed to stop him talking? But where did Keith and Olly fit in?

He realised Anna was staring at him and frowning. He had the impression she'd just asked him a question.

'Sorry?' he asked.

'I said, George must have known they were coming for him. He hid the laptop and left me instructions how to find it. He must have known I could break the encryption.'

Dan nodded. 'And that you would understand what was on it.'

'Exactly.'

'Bit risky hiding the laptop and sending you a message to his home address. What if you weren't there?' Again something was nudging at the back of his brain and his stomach was flickering. He was missing a connection, but had no idea what it was. He needed some quiet time to think, but he knew he couldn't let Anna out of his sight until he'd seen what was on the laptop.

Anna shrugged. 'Maybe he assumed that I'd be there to sort out his stuff. He knew that I'd want to be the one to do that, I suppose.' She fell silent, looking sad, but Dan saw her sneak a look at him as if she was trying to work out what he was thinking.

Then she stood up, beginning the log-off process of the laptop.

'Where are you going?' Dan asked, getting to his feet.

'Back to George's place. There must be something there to help us get into this.' She held up the laptop and then tucked it into her bag.

'What about Harry?'

Anna checked her watch and shrugged. 'He'll just have to catch us up.'

Chapter fifty-nine

It took a while, but Dan eventually found a parking space a street away from George Peters' house and tucked the car safely away. As they walked back towards the house, Anna clutched the bag containing the laptop.

Dan looked at her. 'Are you guarding that with your life?' he asked, with a grin.

Anna nodded. 'After being followed when I collected it, I'm not taking any chances.'

Dan thought she was being a bit over the top, but decided it was better to act as if he agreed with her.

They walked in silence for a while and then Anna asked, 'How do you know Harry?'

'Oh, I did my bachelor's degree at Allensbury Uni,' Dan said. 'I was on a couple of Harry's courses.'

'And you stayed in touch?'

Dan shook his head. 'Not really. I moved away for a while for work, but since I came back and started at the Post, I've spoken to him for a couple of stories. Then more recently we bumped into each other in the university library. We got chatting and—' Dan stopped speaking, not sure that he wanted to tell Anna about Harry being suspected of Keith Williams' murder. She might assume that Harry was therefore involved in her brother's murder.

But he needn't have worried. Anna wasn't really listening to him. Instead she was constantly looking around the quiet street.

'What are you doing?' he asked.

'I feel like we're being watched.'

Dan laughed. 'We probably are. There are a lot of nosy neighbours in this street and they've been watching George's house ever since the police descended on it.'

But Anna didn't smile. 'What if that man is around?'

Dan frowned. 'The one that followed you this morning?'

'Yes.'

Dan said nothing. He wasn't sure Anna had seen anyone earlier. In fact, he was pretty sure she was imagining it. Even so, he glanced up and down the street as well as he followed Anna up the front path. As she unlocked the door, he tried to lighten the mood. 'It's a nice house. Nice area.'

'Yes,' Anna said as she turned the key in the lock. 'The house belonged to our gran, and when she died it passed to Mum. She let George live here because it was more convenient for work.'

'Generous.'

'Yes, she is, but George looked after it well.'

Anna pushed open the door, stepped into the hall and stopped suddenly. Dan walked into the back of her, almost knocking her over.

'What is it?' he asked, putting his hand against the wall to steady himself.

Anna bent down carefully to pick an envelope up from the floor without dropping the laptop. She straightened up and turned it over in her hands. Dan gently pushed her inside and closed the door. She walked into the living room without speaking and Dan followed.

'What is it?' he asked again, dropping his bag onto the sofa.

'See for yourself.' She held out an A5-sized white envelope. The name and address on the front was Keith Williams, Politics Department, University of Allensbury. But this had been crossed out and 'Return to sender' scrawled on the front. Dan turned over the envelope and on the back was written George Peters' name and address. Dan stared.

'Why would George post something to Keith?' he asked, frowning. 'Why not go and see him? Or send it by email?'

Anna shrugged. 'Maybe this was the most secure way of sending it,' she said. 'Maybe they didn't want to be seen together.' She took back the envelope and weighed it in her hands. It was heavier and lumpy at one end.

'What's in it, do you think?' Dan asked.

'Only one way to find out.' Anna hooked a finger under the seal of the envelope and tore it open. She tipped it upside down and a flash drive fell into the palm of her hand. She stared at it and Dan picked it up.

He held it out to Anna. 'Let's see what's on it.'

She looked at it for a moment. 'What would George be sending to Keith Williams?'

'Research notes?' Dan asked. 'Something he'd discovered for their project? We'll never know if we don't open it.' He nudged her arm.

Anna pulled George's laptop out of her bag and put it down on the table. Dan looked surprised. 'You're going to use George's laptop? I thought you couldn't get into it because of the encryption?'

'Call it a hunch,' Anna said as the computer whirred into life. The computer screen lit up, requesting a password, which Anna typed in carefully. A black screen appeared.

Dan frowned. 'That's what happened last time,' he said.

But Anna shook her head. 'I think it's waiting for this,' she said, pushing the USB stick into the slot on the computer. An egg timer appeared on the screen.

'Is it supposed to do that?' Dan asked.

Anna inhaled deeply. 'No idea. Let's wait and see.' The egg timer emptied and flipped over three times then faded away and the computer's desktop appeared.

'It was the encryption program,' Dan said, eyes wide.

'Why would George have sent that to Keith Williams?' Anna asked.

'God knows. Harry said he's really inept with technology.' He leaned on the back of Anna's chair, peering over her shoulder at the screen. She was opening and shutting the documents saved on the laptop's desktop.

When she opened the sixth document, Dan said, 'Stop,' and held out a hand over hers on the laptop's track pad. He stared at the image on the screen in front of him. 'That looks really familiar,' he muttered.

'What?' Anna asked, surprised and turning in her seat to look at him. 'You know what it is?' But Dan didn't answer. He turned away to the sofa and fished in his bag for some printed A4 sheets of paper. Keeping his back to Anna, he scanned them glancing once over his shoulder at the laptop screen.

'Dan? Dan, what is it?' she demanded, beginning to get up from her seat.

Dan shoved the pages back into his bag and made a big deal of looking at his watch. 'It's getting late. I'd better get back or my boss will kill me. Call me if you find anything else.'

He was out of the door and running back to his car before Anna knew what was happening.

Chapter sixty

Harry was frustrated when he returned to his office to find no sign of Anna or Dan. He was about to call the latter when his phone burst into life. A call from Anna.

'Hi, Harry, it's Anna Peters.'

'Thanks for ditching me.' Harry knew he sounded petulant and hated himself for it. He felt like a child who'd been left out of a birthday party.

'Sorry about that,' Anna said in what sounded like an attempt at a conciliatory tone, 'but we thought we were onto something. I wondered whether there was something at George's house to help us get into the laptop.'

'And was there?' Harry asked, feeling excitement bubble in his stomach. Anna explained about the envelope and the flash drive and what they'd seen on the screen. 'It's a bit strange though because Dan saw it, looked at some papers in his bag and then said he had to get back to work.'

'Really?' Harry was surprised that Dan had missed out on trying to solve a mystery. It didn't sound like him.

'Yes, he dashed off without saying anything else,' Anna said. 'I wanted to catch up with him, but I don't have his number. The only one I had was yours.'

Harry was silent for a moment. He could try and track Dan down or he could go and help Anna and get himself back into the investigation. Then Anna made the decision for him.

'I want to go and see George's boss. I've managed to get an appointment to see him today. Would you come with me?' she asked.

'Me? Why?'

'He was a bit cagey with me on the phone and I'd like to get a second opinion on whether he's telling me the truth,' Anna said. 'I want to know what George was working on and how it could have got him killed. If it was related to his job then they have to tell me what was going on.' She paused. 'It would make me feel better to not have to go alone.'

Harry nodded even though Anna couldn't see him. 'Of course. I'm happy to help.'

'It might also tell us what happened to your friend, Professor Williams,' Anna said.

'Yes, that's true,' Harry said, glossing over the fact that he and Keith had never been friends. He did, however, want to know what part Olly had played in it and why someone had killed him.

'OK, no problem.' He grabbed a pen and scrap of paper and jotted down the address Anna gave him.

The he glanced at his watch. 'I've got the car today so I'll swing by and pick you up in about twenty minutes?'

Anna thanked him and hung up.

As he almost ran to his car, he tried to call Dan at the office. Another reporter told him Dan wasn't there. Harry frowned. Dan had told Anna he was going back to work. He crossed the car park to his car, dialling Dan's mobile number. It rang for a long time and then Dan's voicemail kicked in, asking him to leave a message.

'Dan, it's Harry. Call me as soon as you get this.'

He had less luck than Dan in getting a parking space and instead had to pull up outside George Peters' house and beep his horn to get Anna to come out. She dashed out of the door, coat and bag in hand, and jumped into the passenger seat. Harry steered them through the streets out onto the ring road and then followed Anna's directions to Allensbury Science Park. Using the map at the entrance, they located the GITech Pharmaceuticals building and parked outside.

'Right,' said Harry, as they stepped out of the car and headed into the reception area. 'Let's see what they have to say for themselves.'

Although Dr Anthony Bellswick had agreed to see Anna, he didn't seem all that happy that she was keeping the appointment. From the moment she and Harry were escorted into his office, the man fidgeted and checked his watch.

'I'm sorry, I don't have long,' was his opening conversational gambit. 'It's one of those days, I'm afraid.' He gave a little laugh, but they didn't join in.

'I'm sorry, Dr Bellswick,' Anna replied, 'but I need some answers.'

The man sat back in his chair and clasped his hands across his rounded stomach. 'What answers?' he asked.

'About my brother and why he was killed.'

Dr Bellswick looked surprised. 'I thought he died of a heart attack.'

'He was too healthy for that,' Anna shot back at him. 'We–' she pointed at Harry and then back at herself '–think that George was working on something that got him killed.'

Bellswick raised an eyebrow. 'Really?'

'Yes. So what was my brother working on?'

Bellswick shook his head. 'I'm afraid anything your brother worked on was confidential. I can't tell you anything.'

'Was he working with Allensbury University at all?' Harry put in.

Bellswick cocked his head to one side. 'Sorry, I didn't catch that,' he said.

Harry had a feeling that the man was only pretending that he'd not heard.

'The university,' Harry prompted. 'Did George do anything with them? Was he working on anything with anyone from the university?'

'Like who?'

Harry looked at Anna and she nodded. 'We believe George was working on a project with Professor Keith Williams. He's a politics lecturer,' Harry said. 'Did you know anything about that?'

'No, no, I didn't.' Harry thought that Bellswick's face showed it was news to him, and not good news. 'By that, I mean I was aware of all the work George was doing and none of it involved politics. Or anyone from the university.'

Anna frowned. 'I'm surprised because we've found evidence on his laptop that he was involved in a project with Professor Williams,' she said. Harry tried to keep his face impassive. As far as he was aware, they knew no such thing.

'You've got his laptop?' Bellswick asked.

'Yes, and I suggest that you tell me the truth about what happened to my brother.' When the other man didn't speak, she said, 'Please, Dr Bellswick, please help me.' Her voice cracked a little. 'Please tell me what happened to my brother. I deserve to know that much.'

Bellswick sighed. 'I doubt I know any more than you. George didn't turn up for work one morning. He'd been feeling really tired recently, so at first I put it down to that. I decided that he either wasn't well or had slept in.'

'And you did nothing?'

'Your brother is a very good worker, Miss Peters. Or, should I say, was a good worker. I had a lot of time for George and I could allow him to slip away from our procedure of calling in sick, just this once.

But then when he didn't come in the following day, some of his friends decided to go to his flat. You'll have heard the rest from the police, I've no doubt.'

'That they went round, broke in and he was dead,' said Anna, flatly.

'Yes, just so. I'm sorry, Miss Peters, but there isn't any more to tell you.'

'You won't tell me about his work?' Anna asked, wiping a finger under her eye to remove a stray tear.

'It's not a case of won't, it's a case of can't,' Bellswick said, gesturing around his office. 'We have strict confidentiality clauses in work contracts here. Our work is a very closely guarded secret, for business reasons, and I can't tell you anything.' He glanced at his watch. 'Now, I'm sorry, but I have meetings to go to, so you'll have to excuse me.'

He got to his feet and Anna and Harry did the same.

At the door, Anna turned back. 'We've also got a journalist working on this,' she said. 'You might find that he's better at uncovering secrets than we are.' She turned and left the room with Harry following her.

As they crossed the reception area and headed out of the front door, Anna said, 'That was worse than useless.'

But Harry shook his head. 'No, we now know that George was working with Keith.'

Anna stopped. 'What? How do you know that? He didn't say anything.'

'His reaction when I asked if he knew about Keith,' Harry said. 'He said he didn't, but I don't believe him. He looked annoyed that we knew about it. That makes me think he does know exactly what they were up to.' They'd reached the car. 'Dan's been right all along,' he said. 'Something very strange is going on and it involves your

269

brother, Keith Williams, and probably Olly Murton as well, and they're now all dead.'

'But what could it be? I mean, what could possibly bring them together?' Anna asked.

They reached the car and Harry looked back at the GITech Pharmaceuticals building. 'Dr Bellswick is hiding something. I think he knows exactly what George was up to. That's why he couldn't wait to get rid of us.' Harry unlocked the car and they got inside.

'Where to now?' Anna asked.

'I'd like to speak to Dr Bellswick again, but I doubt he'd give us the time of day,' Harry said. 'We need to go and find Dan and tell him what we've found out. He may have something for us too.'

But they were out of luck. Dan couldn't be found anywhere. Calls and texts to his mobile were still unanswered. Even stopping by his office didn't help.

'I'm sorry,' said the receptionist, after Dan's extension was answered by another reporter. 'He seems to be out. Can anyone else help at all?'

'No, thanks,' said Harry.

When they were outside the Post's office on the street, Anna said, 'What do we do now?'

'Let's go back to George's house and regroup,' Harry said. 'Then we can decide what we need to do next.'

Chapter sixty-one

Dan was sitting at the dining table in his flat with his laptop in front of him when there was a knock at the door. He was puzzled as no one had rung the doorbell from outside the building. He paused as he walked from the lounge into the hall. Should he be worried about someone sneaking in? Then he shook himself. He was being stupid.

When he pulled open the front door, there was a flash of red hair as someone flung themselves into his arms.

'What are you doing here?' he asked, grinning and hugging back tightly.

'I was worried,' Emma said, untangling herself from the hug. 'I kept turning all the stuff you told me over in my mind and it made me really anxious.'

Dan laughed. 'So you dashed back to the rescue? I bet your mum wasn't happy about that.'

Emma shook her head as she pulled off her coat and hung it on a peg by the door. 'That was because she thought I was trying to come back for work, but she understood when I said it was about you. You know how much she loves you.'

Dan grinned. 'Can I get you a cup of tea?' he asked, leading the way into the lounge.

'God, yes.' Emma followed him and flopped on the sofa. 'I've been driving for five hours straight to get here.'

Dan filled the kettle and flicked the switch before coming back to stand in the doorway between the kitchen and lounge.

'So,' Emma said, 'what have I missed?' She peered at Dan who was staring into space. 'Dan, what are you not telling me?'

'Something very strange is going on. You remember I was telling you about the murders at the university?' Dan asked.

Emma sat forward on the sofa. 'The professor and the student, yes,' she said.

'Well, it looks like they might be connected to another murder.'

'Really?' Emma sat further forward on the sofa and almost slid off onto the floor. She regained her balance and asked, 'Who?'

'That chemist guy?' Dan said, trying not to laugh at her.

'The one you saw get abducted?' Emma sat back into the sofa, head tilted to one side.

Dan leaned against the door frame, his hands in his trouser pockets, and nodded.

Emma frowned. 'How are they connected?'

Dan scratched the back of his head. 'I got sent some chemical formulae through the post, anonymously, but I've just seen them again on the scientist's computer.'

Emma looked surprised. 'How did you get his computer?' she asked.

'Harry and I met his sister,' Dan said. 'She told us the laptop was missing at first, but then it got sent to her. In a kind of a roundabout sort of way.'

'How do you mean by a "roundabout" sort of way?' Emma asked slowly.

Dan frowned. 'She got a letter through the post telling her where to look for it. It was in a PO box.'

'Why was it in a PO box?' Emma sat forward onto the front of the sofa cushion again.

Dan shrugged. 'God knows.' He went back into the kitchen, made tea and returned, putting the mugs down on the table on coasters and walking away down the room. 'But there's definitely something weird going on. She managed to decrypt the laptop and—'

'His work laptop?' Emma asked.

Dan turned back to face her, rubbing his nose. 'I could understand if it was his work laptop—'

'It's his personal one?' Emma interrupted.

Dan nodded.

Emma was silent again. Then she said, 'God, Dan, what the hell is going on? Why would a personal laptop need encrypting?'

Dan picked up his mug and took a sip of tea. He winced as it burned his mouth and stared down at the floor.

Interpreting his silence, Emma said, 'I'm sensing it's not the only thing that's weird here.'

Dan shook his head. 'I did an Internet search for George Peters and all I found was stuff connected to the company he works for, GITech Pharmaceuticals. But when I searched for them it opened up a whole lot more questions.'

'How do you mean?' Emma asked, picking up her own mug.

'I'll show you.' Dan got to his feet and Emma followed him to the dining table, mug in hand. Dan sat down on the chair while Emma leaned on the back, looking over his shoulder. Dan moved the mouse to wake up the screen. 'The search threw up this blog,' he said, pointing at it. Emma moved to his side and leaned down to read the text in front of her. As she did so, Dan slid an arm around her waist and held onto her.

She grinned. 'You must be worried if you're being all affectionate.'

Dan pouted. 'I'm always affectionate,' he said.

Emma laughed and put an arm around his shoulders.

'Only kidding.' She scrutinised the screen again. 'This is really strange. This blog alleges that GITech is creating some dodgy chemicals using the funding they secured from the government.'

'But it doesn't say what those chemicals are,' Dan pointed out.

Emma frowned and stood up straight.

'There's a whole series of posts,' Dan continued, 'building up all kinds of accusations, and the writer says he's going to reveal all in the next post – but then the blog just stops.'

Emma folded her arms and walked across the living room to stand beside the sofa. Dan turned sideways in his chair to look at her. He waited, recognising that she was thinking. Then she turned to him.

'Why?' she asked.

'Why what?'

'Why did the blogger just stop? It sounds like it's working up to a good exposé. Would you stop just as you were about to publish the big reveal?'

'I see what you mean.' Dan rubbed his face with both his palms. 'So, what if the company found out and stopped the blogger from publishing?'

Emma pointed at the laptop. 'Exactly. And who do we know that works for the company who has recently been stopped from doing everything?'

Dan sat up straight and looked at her. 'You think George Peters wrote the blog?'

Emma shrugged. 'Why not?' she asked. 'It sounds like he's found out that something has been going on and he's going to blow the whistle.'

'And the company found out and killed him?' Dan stared at her, brow furrowed. 'I don't know, Em. Does that not sound a bit extreme?'

Emma shrugged. 'I'm just saying. It's a bit too convenient that the blog stops right around the time he got killed.'

Dan nodded. 'Well, if we take that as a starting point, George must have found out something was going on at the company, and that they were making some dodgy stuff. Maybe he didn't like what they were doing? Maybe he was jealous of the project because he wasn't working on it?'

Emma shook her head. 'I doubt that he planned to reveal all because he was jealous,' she said. 'I reckon that he got wind of something bad going on and decided to put a stop to it.'

They were both silent for a moment and then Emma said, 'Seems harsh that he was trying to do the right thing and got killed for it.'

Dan stared at the wall, then he said, 'That makes sense of George Peters' death if he'd upset someone at his work, but what about Keith Williams and Olly Murton?'

'You said they were working on a project with George Peters. Maybe it was this?' Emma pointed to the computer screen.

Dan wrinkled his nose. 'They were helping him to blow the whistle?'

'Why not?'

Dan frowned. 'From what Harry's told me, Keith wasn't in the business of helping people, but—' He stopped and stared at Emma.

'What?' she asked.

'What if Keith and Olly were involved in whatever George had discovered?'

'And they killed him to protect themselves?' Emma asked doubtfully.

Dan shook his head. 'No, you're right. That's a daft idea. I can't see either Keith or Olly as killers. Well, definitely not Olly.'

Emma looked at Dan silently for a moment and then said, 'What about Harry?'

Dan looked at her sharply. 'What about him?'

'Could he have killed them?'

'What, all three?'

Emma shrugged. 'You said it yourself that the three deaths are connected. Are they connected by Harry?'

'Harry doesn't know George Peters.'

'How do you know?' Emma sat down on the sofa and looked at Dan across the room. 'How do you know he doesn't?'

'He would have told me if he did.' But Dan could hear himself how lame the statement sounded. He got to his feet and walked to the other end of the room. Emma was still watching him.

'I don't want you to turn against him,' she said. 'I just think he's in a unique position where he had access to two of the victims. There's a third victim so he might be connected to him too.'

'But he didn't get on with Keith and Olly so he wouldn't—' Again Dan stopped speaking and looked down at his feet, noticing that he was wearing odd socks. 'Has he been playing me all this time?' he asked. 'Have I just been helping him to cover his tracks?'

Emma stood up and crossed the room to hug him. 'Probably not, but it's best to make sure. Is there a way you can find out if Harry knew George Peters?'

Dan shook his head. 'I don't think so. He only has George's mobile number because we found it in Keith's office. We called it and George's sister answered.'

Emma took a deep breath and exhaled heavily. 'So, what do you want to do now?'

Dan began to count on his fingers. 'We need to find Harry, find out if he knew George and whether he knows what this blog malarkey is all about.'

'Right,' said Emma. 'We'd better get started.'

Dan picked up his phone and opened the screen. 'Oh,' he said. 'Three missed calls and a couple of texts from Harry and a voicemail.'

He dialled his answering service and put the phone onto speaker so Emma could hear. Harry's voice was clear as a bell as he told Dan to call him straight away. Dan made an angry noise in his throat. 'That was ages ago,' he said. 'I must have put the phone on silent.'

They sat waiting as Harry's phone rang and rang and finally went to voicemail too.

'He's not answering,' said Emma.

'Thanks for stating the obvious,' Dan said.

Emma glared at him and he blew her a kiss. She pretended to catch it and throw it back at him. He laughed, dialling Harry's number again. When there was no response, he shook his head.

'We're going to have to go to campus and see if he's there,' Dan said, heading into the hallway for his coat.

'Let's go,' Emma replied, following him.

Chapter sixty-two

Shepherd looked up from his computer screen as Garry Topping burst through the door to the office.

'You've got something,' Shepherd said, taking in the triumphant expression on the detective constable's face. Topping waved a cardboard folder.

'I think you'll be interested to see this,' he said, handing it over.

Shepherd flicked open the file and looked at the numbers on the bank logo-headed pages.

'George Peters' financials,' he said, eyes skimming down the page.

'Yup. Look at this.' Topping pointed a slim finger at a cash deposit.

'He's not getting paid his salary in cash, surely?' asked Shepherd.

Topping laughed. 'No.' He pointed at another line labelled GITech. 'That's his salary.'

Shepherd looked at the figure. 'OK. I assume that there's something else coming?' he asked.

Topping was bouncing on the balls of his feet. 'There is more,' he said.

'Hang on,' Shepherd said. 'That cash payment—'

'Is almost as much as the salary payment,' Topping finished.

Shepherd stared at Topping. 'What on earth was he doing to earn that much extra cash?'

At that point Burton appeared from her office, drawn in by the voices and not wanting to miss anything.

'Struck gold?' she asked.

Topping turned towards her. 'George Peters certainly had.'

Burton raised an eyebrow. 'How so?'

Shepherd spun on his chair to face Burton and held up the file for her to look at. She took it and scanned down the columns.

'His salary stays the same, this is it here.' Shepherd indicated the GITech payment with a stubby finger. 'But then he starts making these separate cash payments. It's at roughly the same time each month.'

'That's a lot of extra cash,' Burton said. 'What was he doing to earn that?' She looked up at the blank faces of Shepherd and Topping. 'Well? I'm open to ideas.'

Topping raked his hand through his blond hair. 'It can't be extra hours at work,' he said. 'That would be in his salary.'

Shepherd was shaking his head. 'We didn't hear anything from his friends – such as they were – when we questioned them after he was killed. No one mentioned a second job or anything like that.'

Burton flicked to the next page and then stopped.

'What?' asked Shepherd.

'Look at this.' She turned the piece of paper towards Shepherd and Topping. Her finger pointed to a payment to another bank account.

'Twenty-two grand?' Shepherd asked, eyes wide. 'Clearly he's been getting those deposits for a while.'

'And look at that.' Topping pointed to another payment.

'Expedia?' Shepherd asked. 'So he was planning a holiday?'

'No,' said Burton slowly. 'I think he was going to make a run for it. He's cleared his bank account and he's bought a ticket out of here.'

'Was he going with Keith Williams?' Shepherd asked.

Burton shrugged. 'No idea, but they'd both clearly realised they needed to get away.'

'They weren't taking Olly Murton with them,' Shepherd said.

'I don't think either of them cared what happened to anyone but themselves.' Burton closed the folder and handed it to Topping. 'I want to know where he was going and whether it was a one-way ticket,' she told him. He nodded and turned away immediately. 'We–' she pointed at Shepherd '–are going to see George Peters' boss and see if he knows where the extra money was coming from, and whether he knows George was planning a holiday.'

Chapter sixty-three

George Peters' supervisor looked uncomfortable. Two visits from the police in almost as many weeks seemed to be putting Dr Anthony Bellswick on edge.

He invited Burton and Shepherd to sit, and then positioned himself with his wide wooden desk between them.

'I don't understand,' he said, crossing and uncrossing his legs at the knee. 'I've told you everything I know already.'

Overhead a fluorescent light fitting flickered and Shepherd squinted. 'Sorry,' Bellswick went on. 'I keep meaning to get that fixed.' He seemed flustered. 'I'm sorry but I don't know what use I can be to you.' He spread his hands and then clasped them together.

'Some new evidence has come to light,' Shepherd said.

'New evidence? What new evidence?'

'We now suspect that George didn't die of a heart attack, at least not a natural one.'

The man stared at them, his eyes wide. 'What? What makes you think that?'

'We have evidence that George was injected with something that more than likely caused the heart attack. We're waiting for confirmation on the substance used,' Burton said. 'Do you make anything like that here?'

Bellswick looked shocked. 'What? No, we don't. At least, not that I know of.' But he couldn't meet Burton's eye, instead focusing on a spot on the wall beside her left ear.

'There's no way George could have come into contact with it while at work?' Burton asked.

'No, of course not. We make medicines, but they're designed to help, not to kill.'

'It doesn't necessarily have to be something that's designed to kill,' Shepherd said, eyeing Bellswick. 'The medicines may have been misused.'

Bellswick said nothing; he tried to return Shepherd's stare, but it was he who broke the eye contact first.

'You told us last time we spoke to you that you couldn't think of anyone who'd want to harm George,' Burton said as Shepherd looked down to scribble in his notebook.

Bellswick nodded. 'I'm sure all the others said the same too.'

'They did,' Burton said. 'And that strikes me as a little odd.'

'Odd?' Bellswick was puzzled. 'Why is that odd? George was a very likeable person.'

Burton leaned forward. 'No one is that popular. There will always be someone with an axe to grind. Plus he was murdered,' she said shortly. 'So someone didn't like him.'

'It wasn't anyone in my team,' the man protested, sounding bewildered. 'We'd been working together for ages.'

'He didn't always socialise though, did he?'

'He usually got on with his work, and often a lot of other people's stuff too,' Bellswick said, shifting awkwardly in his seat.

Burton frowned. 'He was pushy? Ambitious?' she asked, thinking that this didn't sound like the description of George Peters they'd heard from others.

Bellswick shook his head. 'No, just very talented. He was very quick and clever; the others were usually pleased when he offered to help.'

'They used him?' Burton sounded faintly disgusted.

The man shrugged. 'Maybe a little. George could be a naïve, like all very clever people. They get caught up in what they're doing and they don't read people very well.'

'So all the team loved him because they could dump the crap on him?' Shepherd asked.

'No,' Bellswick shook his head impatiently. 'He was a genuinely nice guy. That's the reason everyone was so upset when he died. Because we'd lost such a good person, not because there'd be extra work.'

'Did you never think they were being unfair to him?' Burton's brow was furrowed.

'I monitored the situation and made sure he was OK,' Bellswick said, leaning forward with his forearms on his desk. 'I liked him as a person as much as I liked his work ethic. If I thought he was unhappy, I'd have stepped in. Although…' he trailed off, frowning.

'What?' Burton asked leaning forward.

Bellswick seemed to be pondering whether to continue with what he was about to say. He clearly came to a decision because he said, 'I was a bit concerned about George, particularly in the last few weeks. He seemed to be tired all the time and said he wasn't sleeping very well. When I tried to talk to him about it, he just clammed up and when I joked about it being a guilty conscience, he turned really pale.'

'You didn't tell us this before,' Shepherd said, pulling out his notebook and beginning to write down Bellswick's words.

'No, I'd forgotten all about it until you reminded me. It's funny how the mind plays tricks.' Bellswick gave a little laugh and then seemed to think a serious facial expression was more appropriate. 'I was so shocked about his death that I forgot,' he added.

Burton and Shepherd looked at each other.

'You mentioned previously that George had been noticed by upstairs because of his work,' Shepherd said. 'What did you mean by that?'

The man frowned. 'It was a bit odd. As I said, George was really shy and quiet, but his work on our latest project has been so key to its success that I made him write the report and give a presentation about it.'

'Was that usual?'

'The report and presentation were, but George giving it wasn't. That would normally be me, as team leader. He loved the report writing bit and designing the presentation but on the day he was really nervous. Then when I introduced him to the room, he really blossomed. It was extraordinary. The presentation was the best we'd ever given and our chief executive insisted on thanking George personally.'

'Was anyone else at this presentation?' Shepherd asked, his pen scratching across the surface of his notebook.

'All the project heads were there to give their own presentations. I think there was a bit of jealousy because my project had done so well.' The man looked smug. 'But it was all down to George's hard work and I made sure they knew it. Credit where it's due, and all that.'

'Were there any visitors there?' Burton asked. 'Anyone from outside the company?'

The man looked shocked. 'No, there would never be. All our work is kept very confidential at that stage.'

'There were no other people there apart from company staff?' Burton repeated.

Bellswick shook his head.

'Does the name Keith Williams mean anything to you?' Burton asked, head tilted to one side.

Bellswick frowned. 'No, should it?'

'He wouldn't have been at the presentation?'

'I don't know the name so I doubt it.'

'He works at Allensbury University,' Shepherd said, scribbling in his notebook. He looked up just in time to see a look flicker across Bellswick's face. But the man shook his head.

'No. I don't know him.'

'What happened after George's presentation?' Burton asked.

'He was riding high for a few days afterwards. People were coming by to congratulate him on a job well done and calling about the project. He was a bit of a celebrity.'

'How did George like that?'

'He was a bit uncomfortable with the attention but he loved sharing information and talking about his work.'

'When did "upstairs" get involved?' Shepherd asked.

'George went out for lunch one day, and when he came back he seemed a little awkward,' Bellswick replied.

'Awkward? In what way?'

'He kept knocking things over and making mistakes. Plus he couldn't look me in the eye. It just wasn't like him at all. Then I found out why. He'd been taken out for lunch by Tim Lynchman.'

Burton raised an eyebrow. 'Who's he? A competitor?'

Bellswick scowled. 'No, he's one of the other project managers,' he said.

'Is he a problem?' Burton asked.

'He's a bit of a shark really,' Bellswick said, a black expression twisting his face. 'Always seems to get the best projects to work on and cherry-picks the best staff.'

'You thought he was trying to poach George?' Shepherd asked, looking up from his notebook.

'Yes, I did. I was surprised when George told me about the

meeting,' Bellswick said. 'But I said to him, much as I'd like to keep him on my team, I'd understand if he wanted a change of scene.'

'Very charitable of you,' Burton remarked.

'It wasn't out of charity. It's not easy to refuse Tim Lynchman anything. I care about my people and their careers, and I didn't want to see George's get messed up.'

Shepherd frowned. 'In what way?'

'It was never proven, but the last person who crossed Tim Lynchman ended up getting fired for gross misconduct. I'm not wholly sure he's ever found another decent job since then.'

'Did George say he was going to leave your team?' Burton continued.

Bellswick got to his feet and walked to the other end of the room. Burton and Shepherd watched him in silence.

'He said the meeting hadn't been about a job,' Bellswick said, with his back to them. 'Lynchman had wanted his advice about something. That surprised me more than if he'd offered George a job.'

'Why?' Burton asked.

Bellswick turned to look at her. 'George was talented and could have advised anyone, but I've never known Tim Lynchman to want help,' he said.

'Bit arrogant, is he?' Shepherd asked.

Bellswick gave a little snort. 'That's an understatement. He's always looking down his nose at everyone else. He's not the only person here with a PhD.' The man's tone was petulant and made Shepherd shoot a glance at Burton to see how she was taking it. Burton's face was impassive, which was never a good sign. She was clearly beginning to lose patience.

'What did he want with George if not his advice or a job offer?' she asked.

'I assumed George was lying to try and protect my feelings,' Bellswick said. 'I assumed that Lynchman had made George an offer of a job and it was only a matter of time before George would have to accept it. But he must have turned it down because he never mentioned it again.'

Burton and Shepherd exchanged a look.

'We think he may have taken the job and was moonlighting,' Burton said.

Bellswick stared at her for a moment. 'What do you mean?' he asked, returning to sit at his desk.

'We've found that George was being paid large sums of cash on top of his salary,' Burton said.

'And you think Tim Lynchman has something to do with it?' Bellswick asked.

Burton shrugged her shoulders. 'It's a possibility. What other work could he be doing?'

Bellswick was silent for a moment and then reached into his desk drawer. 'Something now makes sense,' he said, pulling out some printed pages.

'What does?' Burton asked.

The man shuffled through the papers and handed two sheets to her. She looked down at them.

'Timesheets?' she asked.

'George's timesheets.'

Burton held up the top two sheets, one in each hand. 'These are for the same week, but they have different values,' she said.

'Yes.' Bellswick sat back in his chair, looking slightly smug.

'I don't understand.'

'The sheet in your left hand is the hours George said he spent in the lab working. The one in your right is what I calculated he's spent in the building. You have to swipe an ID card to get in and out of the building, and it records the time.'

'It's almost double,' Burton said.

'Exactly.'

'Would he have been paid for this?' Burton held up the estimated sheet.

'Nope, he'd be paid for the one he handed in. I thought it was a one-off but I monitored him over the next month and the same things happened. I was going to challenge him about it, but then he died.' The man stopped suddenly, looking downcast.

'Any idea where he was when he wasn't in the department?' Shepherd asked.

'All I could think was that he was doing some research of his own. He shouldn't have been doing that on company property. I'd diarised a meeting with him to discuss it quietly and ask him to stop, but that turned out to be the day he died.'

'No one ever reported to you that they'd seen George around at the times when he was swiped in but not in your lab?' Burton asked.

Bellswick shook his head. 'I asked a couple of people in a very discreet way. I didn't want anyone to think I was checking up on him.'

'I think that's all for now.' Burton got to her feet. Then she said, 'By the way, did his missing laptop ever turn up here?'

'No, but it's a personal laptop, so it's not really our business.'

Burton smiled. 'Thanks for your help. We'll be in touch if we need anything else.'

Bellswick's hands shook slightly as he closed the door behind them.

Chapter sixty-four

Burton and Shepherd got as far as the reception area when she stopped. Shepherd walked a few more steps and then turned back to look at her expectantly.

'While we're here,' she said, 'I want to try and see Dr Tim Lynchman.'

'You think he's involved?'

'I certainly think it's worth a look. See what he does when we tell him George Peters was murdered. He might also give something away about the money trail.'

They had their work cut out trying to get in to see Lynchman without a prior appointment. He was a busy man, Burton and Shepherd were told. The receptionist wasn't even sure if he was in the building, but she'd call his PA and see if he was available. They were left to take a seat on some uncomfortably hard sofas. Burton was beginning to fidget and Shepherd knew Dr Tim Lynchman was not making a good impression.

Eventually a woman in a smart suit appeared in front of them.

'Dr Lynchman doesn't have long but will see you now,' she said, indicating for them to follow her.

As they waited for the lift, Shepherd tried to engage her in some small talk but she gave one-word answers to his questions and he soon gave up. The lift arrived and as they rode to the fifth floor, Burton noticed Shepherd staring at the lift buttons.

'What is it?' she hissed at him when the lift doors opened but before he could answer the woman was ushering them into Lynchman's office. He was seated behind a wooden desk and when the detectives sat as instructed they found their chairs were deliberately set lower than his. It was a bit like being granted an audience with a deity.

'What can I do for you?' Lynchman asked, glancing at his watch. Burton bristled and Shepherd began the interview.

'We're investigating the murder of someone who worked here,' he said. 'A chemist called George Peters.'

'I heard about that, yes, but I thought it was a heart attack,' Lynchman said in a flat, disinterested tone.

'We've since established that Mr Peters was murdered,' Shepherd said, notebook in hand.

Lynchman looked uncomfortable when he saw the notebook and pen, but he didn't object. 'Murdered? How?' he asked.

'We think he was injected with a substance that brought on a heart attack,' Burton said.

Lynchman's eyebrows shot up towards his receding hairline but all he said was, 'I see.'

'You don't seem very bothered that a work colleague has been murdered, if I may say,' Shepherd said, looking up from his notebook in surprise.

Lynchman shrugged. 'I didn't know the man.'

'That's odd, because his line manager, Dr Bellswick, says that you recently took George out for lunch and you may have offered him a job,' Shepherd said.

Lynchman looked like he was going to disagree but then seemed to think better of it. 'Yes, I liked his work and I offered him a job,' he said, with something resembling a shrug. 'There's no law against that, is there?'

'He turned you down though, didn't he? Wanted to stay working for Dr Bellswick?' Shepherd asked.

Lynchman snorted. 'Yes, that was the top and bottom of it.'

'Did you take no for an answer?' Burton asked.

'Of course I did. Why would I not?'

'We've heard that you don't give in easily, that you once ruined someone who went against you,' Burton said, glancing down at her fingernails casually.

Lynchman made a growling noise in his throat. 'Bloody Bellswick,' he said, 'tells that story to anyone who'll listen.'

'Is it true?' Shepherd asked.

'No, it's not. Bellswick's always been jealous of me. He—'

'So you didn't ruin a man's professional life?' Burton asked, breaking in before Lynchman could launch into a rant.

Lynchman scowled. 'It wasn't ruined and I did the company a favour. The man was a menace. Didn't know what he was doing. No talent and almost ruined the project I was leading. I can't have that.'

'I have to ask,' Burton said, 'what did you say or do to George Peters after he refused to work for you?'

Lynchman glared at her. 'Nothing,' he said. 'George was good at what he did and I respected him for that.' He looked from Burton to Shepherd.

Burton was frowning. 'You see, after your lunch with George, when he'd supposedly turned down the job with you, he suddenly started to work more and more hours.'

Lynchman humphed. 'Probably needing to clear up after the messes Bellswick left.'

Shepherd shook his head. 'No, Dr Bellswick noticed that he was working in the building for a lot longer than he was actually in the lab, but his timesheets were the same as normal. We know from his bank records that he was getting paid for whatever he was doing though, in cash. Know anything about that?'

'No,' said Lynchman, looking like a man about to lose his temper. 'Once Dr Peters turned me down, I left him alone. I don't think I ever spoke to him again. It would have been a waste of my time.'

'What was the project you were working on? That George would have been working on?' Shepherd asked.

'I'm afraid that's confidential.'

'This is a murder inquiry, nothing is confidential,' Burton said sharply.

'Then let's just say it's business sensitive. It wouldn't do for our competitors to find out what we're working on. It certainly wouldn't kill anyone, though.' Lynchman was getting to his feet.

'You know that for definite, do you?' Shepherd asked, not moving.

Lynchman looked down at him from his standing position. 'Well, if that's all, I'm afraid I must get on. I have a lot of meetings today.'

Burton got to her feet as well but Shepherd remained seated.

'What's on the seventh floor?' he asked.

Lynchman looked puzzled. 'Seventh floor? There are only six floors in this building,' he said, frowning.

'Oh, my mistake.' Shepherd smiled sweetly and clicked his pen to put away the nib. Then he very deliberately flipped his notebook shut and put it in his pocket. Lynchman was beginning to sigh irritably by the time Shepherd had got to his feet. Burton was watching, wondering what he was up to.

Lynchman pressed the intercom and his secretary appeared to escort the detectives out of the building.

When the door had closed behind them, Lynchman seized his mobile phone and dialled a stored number. When it was answered he spoke urgently.

'The police were here. They know about the seventh floor.' He listened briefly. 'Yes, I know. That means it will have to happen sooner. We must act.'

'What was that all about? The number of floors in the building?' Burton asked as they walked across the car park towards their vehicle.

Standing by the driver's door, Shepherd pointed over Burton's shoulder.

'There were six floor buttons in the lift, yes?' he said.

Burton nodded.

'Right. Count the number of floors from out here.'

As she stared at the building, Burton was silent and then turned slowly to stare at Shepherd, who nodded grimly.

'If there are six floors in the lift,' Shepherd said, 'how come there are seven floors from out here?'

Chapter sixty-five

'Is it much like you remember?' Emma asked Dan as he pulled the car into a parking space behind the politics department building on the university campus.

Dan shrugged. 'Bits of it. The department's the same.' He pointed to the building. 'The accommodation is all new though, and that section there.' He pointed to a series of new buildings huddled around a central quadrangle.

Emma got out of the car and stared at the buildings. 'Very fancy for a university,' she said.

Dan looked at her across the roof of the car as he pressed the remote to lock the doors and set the alarm. 'It's one of the science blocks,' he said. 'They need all the state-of-the-art facilities.' He pulled a face.

'Whereas you poor little humanities students get the draughty old library,' Emma said, slipping her hand into his and grinning.

'They didn't even buy us comfortable chairs,' Dan said, pushing out his bottom lip. 'When you're sitting studying for hours—'

'Ha, like you ever did that,' Emma cut in, laughing.

'I did sometimes,' Dan said defensively. 'Usually around essay deadlines and exams.'

Emma laughed again as they approached the politics department.

She pushed open the door and went through, holding it open for Dan to follow.

'So what are we doing?' she asked.

'We need to talk to Harry. I want to see what he and George's sister are up to.' He frowned. 'They looked a bit cosy earlier.'

'Cosy?' Emma asked.

'Yeah, they were standing a bit close together when I arrived in his office the other day. They looked shifty and there was definite tension in the air.'

'Sexual tension?' Emma asked. When Dan nodded, she said, 'But didn't you say he's married?'

'That's what he told me, but Anna's quite pretty and—' He stopped, seeing the look on Emma's face. 'I mean some might say she's pretty but—'

Emma laughed. 'Quit while you're ahead,' she said, punching him on the arm. As they climbed the stairs she continued, 'You don't think he'd cheat, do you?'

Dan shrugged. 'I don't know that side of him, but I know he and his wife have been having problems recently.' Dan's sentence was left hanging as they reached the landing and headed down the corridor in silence. They arrived at Harry's door and Dan knocked.

'He must be out,' Emma said when there was no response. 'Could be at a lecture or something.'

Dan put his ear to the door. 'He must be. I can't hear any movement inside.' He turned the door handle and it opened. Dan stepped back in surprise. 'I expected it to be locked,' he said.

'Maybe he's not gone far,' Emma said. 'Shall we wait inside?'

Dan pushed open the door and they entered the room.

Emma shuddered violently. 'Urgh, it's so dirty in here.'

Dan laughed. 'Resist the urge to clean.' He looked around. 'It's not really dirty, just messy.' He ran a finger along a shelf and held it up. 'Hmmm, a bit dusty though.'

Emma closed the door but didn't move away from it. Dan walked round the desk and sat in Harry's chair.

'I suddenly feel like I'm getting cleverer just by sitting here,' he said.

Emma laughed. 'Let's hope your brain doesn't expand so far that you can't get back out of the door,' she said. She was looking around the room and then glanced at her watch. 'How long do you think he'll be?'

Dan poked at some of the papers on the desk. 'I can't see a schedule.' He hooked a finger under one stack of papers and levered them up, trying not to dislodge everything. 'Hmmm, his laptop's still here.' He frowned. 'He can't have gone far if he's left his door unlocked.'

Emma spotted a book sitting on Harry's visitor's chair. She walked over and picked it up.

'*The Psychology of Truth*?' she asked. 'Doesn't sound very political.'

Dan swung back and forth on Harry's desk chair. 'We found it in Keith Williams' office,' he said.

Emma looked at the cover and turned the book over to read the text on the back. 'Looks quite complicated,' she said. 'Not something you'd expect a non-psychologist to read. Was he into that sort of thing?'

Dan shrugged. 'I've no idea. I'd guess not because Harry was surprised he had it, but then they weren't exactly friends.' Dan walked across the room and took the book out of her hand. He pretended to be surprised by the weight and mimed dropping the book. Emma gave him a patient look. He flicked through the pages to the section marked by the Post-it note and held it out to her. She took it.

'He'd bookmarked this chapter,' Dan said, returning to the desk chair and spinning in a full circle.

Emma read through the first few paragraphs and frowned. 'It's interesting,' she remarked.

Dan tapped his fingers on top of Harry's desk. 'Do you know what, I'm going to call Harry again and find out where he is. There's no point sitting around here.'

Emma nodded distractedly as her eyes continued to skim down the page. She wandered to the visitor's chair and sat down, holding the book in both hands.

Dan scrolled through the contacts on his phone and retrieved Harry's mobile number. 'With any luck he won't be too far away and we can go and meet him.'

But Harry's phone went unanswered, going through to voicemail and asking Dan to please leave a message.

'What now?' he asked.

Emma looked up from the book. 'He might be in a lecture or something with his phone on silent. We could wait here a bit longer?'

'You just want to read that book, don't you?' Dan asked in a teasing tone. 'It's always the same.'

'You never know, it might come in useful,' she replied, not lifting her eyes from the page.

Dan got to his feet. 'We could go to George Peters' house on Castle Street. His sister is staying there. Harry might be with her.' He jingled the car keys.

'OK,' Emma said, getting to her feet and walking towards the door, book in hand.

'You're taking that with you?' Dan asked.

Emma turned back and held up the book. 'We know Keith was working with George Peters, but what has chemistry got to do with psychology?' she asked, tapping a finger against the cover.

Dan frowned. 'Carry on,' he said.

'They're both clever guys, so I'm guessing they'd have no problem reading this, but the connection is missing. The police have Keith's laptop, which presumably has all his research notes on it. In the absence of access to those, I thought this might be the next best thing,' she said, holding up the book in one hand. 'There's no guarantee that it'll tell us anything, but it's worth a try, isn't it?'

Dan frowned. 'It can't hurt, I suppose.'

'I'll bring it back when we're finished with it.'

Dan shrugged. 'Fair enough,' he said.

Emma turned and pulled open the door. Dan followed her out into the corridor and closed the door quietly behind them.

They didn't see Desmond Danby down the corridor, watching them walk away.

Chapter sixty-six

When Dan and Emma parked and walked down Castle Street, all was quiet. There was no longer any police tape marking out the house as a crime scene and Dan didn't notice any twitching curtains. Clearly the residents had returned to their normal lives after all the excitement.

'Hard to imagine anything as dramatic as a murder happening here,' Emma said in a low voice.

'I think it gave the residents a bit of a shock,' Dan replied.

They arrived at the gate of George Peters' house and Dan pushed it open. He walked up the path and knocked on the door. They waited but no one came.

'They might be in the kitchen or something,' Dan said, knocking again harder. 'It's at the back of the house.'

But after another couple of minutes on the doorstep, there was no response.

'I'm going to try Harry again,' Dan said, pulling out his mobile. He dialled and waited for the call to connect. 'Where on earth—' Dan started but Emma grabbed his arm.

'Shhhh, can you hear that?' she whispered.

'What?'

'Keep ringing his number.'

Dan stared at her but did as he was told, hitting the redial button. Then he heard the muffled ringing coming from inside the house. Emma was treading through a dried-out flower bed to peer through the window.

'Shit,' she gasped. 'Dan, there's a guy lying on the floor halfway behind the sofa. He's not moving.'

Dan almost elbowed Emma out of the way as he clambered across to join her.

'Double shit,' he said. Then he grabbed a rock out of the flower bed and climbed back to the front door.

'What are you doing?' Emma asked, following him.

'I'll apologise later,' Dan said, smashing through one of the stained glass panes in the door. He cleared away the glass from the window space and then reached inside, carefully pulling his sleeve down to cover his hand, to open the lock. He shoved the door open and dashed down the hall into the sitting room, Emma in hot pursuit. She was already on the phone asking for an ambulance when Dan dragged the sofa away from the man lying on the carpet. He dropped to his knees and turned the man over. Then he sagged in relief.

'It's not Harry,' he said. Then he looked up at Emma who stood with the phone to her ear. 'But we're going to need the police as well.' He pressed his fingers to the man's throat and shook his head. Then he pointed to the red stain on the man's shirt. 'He's dead and it looks like he's been stabbed.'

Chapter sixty-seven

When Burton and Shepherd arrived in Castle Street, they found the road blocked by police cars and George Peters' house once again cordoned off by crime scene tape. They nodded to the police officer keeping guard at the end of the street and walked towards the house. They found Dan leaning against the pavement side of the garden wall and Emma perched on top, one hand on his shoulder to steady herself. She jumped down when Burton and Shepherd approached.

Burton shook her head. 'Why is it always you two?' she asked. 'I thought you were on holiday,' she said to Emma.

'I was, but—'

'You heard about the excitement and had to come back?' Shepherd asked smiling at her.

Emma laughed. 'Something like that.'

'Did you touch anything?' Burton asked, indicating the house with a jerk of her chin.

Dan nodded. 'We had to break in because we could see the man on the floor. We didn't realise he was dead until we got inside. I turned him over to check for a pulse,' he said.

Burton was frowning. 'Why were you here anyway?' she asked.

'We were looking for Harry,' Dan said, as if that made perfect sense.

LM MILFORD

Shepherd looked surprised. 'Why would Dr Evans be here?'

'He's been working with Anna to find out what happened to George. He wasn't answering his phone so we went to the campus. He wasn't there either so we came here.'

Burton was puzzled. 'Anna?' she asked. 'Who's Anna?'

'Anna Peters, George's sister,' Dan said.

Burton looked at Shepherd and raised her eyebrows. He stared back at her. 'How did you meet up with her?' she asked Dan.

Dan looked shamefaced for a moment. 'We found a note in a book in Keith Williams' office. It had George's number on it so we called it and Anna answered.'

Shepherd leaned close to Burton and, turning his head slightly away from Dan and Emma, whispered, 'How did the sister get the phone? It wasn't in the house when we searched it after he died.' Burton nodded and then returned her attention to Dan and Emma.

'When you couldn't find Dr Evans you came here. Why?'

'Anna's been staying here.' Dan frowned. 'Don't you guys already know this?'

Burton didn't answer. 'What did you do when you got here?' she asked.

'We knocked on the door a few times, but there was no answer. So I rang Harry's mobile.'

'And we could hear it ringing inside,' Emma put in. 'I looked through the window and we could see the man lying behind the sofa. He wasn't moving.'

'We broke in to see if we could help,' Dan finished the story. He looked down at the ground. 'I thought it was Harry,' he said quietly, raising his eyes to look at the detectives.

Shepherd looked at Burton. She sighed.

'Right, I need you both to go to the station and give full statements. I'll get someone to drive you there.' She turned looking for a uniformed officer.

But Dan interrupted. 'If it's OK, we can drive ourselves. The car is just over there.' He pointed towards the end of Castle Street.

'OK, off you go,' Burton said. 'I'll have someone there to meet you.'

Dan and Emma began to walk away but then Dan stopped and pointed. 'Speaking of cars, there's Harry's.' He pointed to the red Fiesta parked in a space opposite the house. He looked at Emma and back at Burton and Shepherd who were both staring at the car.

Burton came out of a reverie and said, 'Right, off to the station you two. I'll have someone take your statements.'

Dan and Emma looked as if they were going to argue, but then turned and walked away, Dan looking back at Harry's car.

Burton looked at Shepherd. 'His phone is here and so is his car,' she said. 'Am I wrong to have a bad feeling about this?'

Shepherd shook his head. 'No, you're not.'

'Right, let's find out what's going on inside,' Burton said, turning towards the house.

Chapter sixty-eight

'What have we got?' Burton asked as an opener.

'A man who's been stabbed in the chest,' said Eleanor Brody, without looking up from where she knelt on the floor. She held up a hand to stem the question she knew would be coming next. 'And don't ask me for any more at the moment.'

Burton laughed. Then she looked around the room. 'It's not been searched or anything like that, has it?' she said.

Shepherd shook his head. Topping appeared at his shoulder.

'Anyone else here?' Burton asked.

'No, but there's fresh milk in the fridge so there's definitely been someone staying here. There's women's clothes and things in the bedroom and bathroom. Apart from the stuff that was George's, which was here when we looked round before.'

Burton was scowling. 'Dan Sullivan said that it's George's sister, Anna,' she said looking around the room. 'I want the whole house carefully searched and full forensics.' Shepherd opened his mouth to speak, but Burton held up a hand to stop him. 'Yes,' she said, reading his mind. 'That's why we're doing it.' Shepherd nodded.

'Any idea who this is?' Burton asked Brody, pointing to the body. The pathologist held up a plastic bag containing a wallet and mobile phone. Burton took it in her gloved hands and opened the bag. She pulled out the wallet, flipped it open and scrutinised the driving licence inside. 'Stephen Curtain,' she said, comparing the picture to the face before her.

Topping was already nodding. 'I recognised him,' he said.

Burton and Shepherd turned to look at him. 'Really? Why?' Shepherd asked.

'He's a mate of George Peters,' Topping said. 'I interviewed him after Peters died. He said Peters was acting a bit weird recently.'

'Weird how?' asked Shepherd.

'Well, he said he saw Peters a couple of days before he died. They met up for a drink and when they went their separate ways at the end of the night Peters hugged him and the goodbye felt very final,' Topping said.

Shepherd raised his eyebrows. 'That fits in with our theory that he was going away somewhere.'

Topping tapped his pen on his notebook. 'Mexico,' he said.

'What?' Burton asked, turning to look at him.

Topping nodded. 'I found a printed confirmation from a travel website and he was off to Mexico.' He held up a forefinger. 'One way.'

Burton looked from Topping to Shepherd and back again. 'He was doing a bunk,' she said, slowly putting her hands on her hips.

'Looks like it. But he hadn't told any of his friends he was going,' Topping said.

'Frightened he was going to leave a trail perhaps,' Shepherd said.

'But he didn't do it quickly enough,' Topping said. All three police officers were silent for a moment thinking about how scared George Peters must have been to plan a getaway.

Burton spoke first. 'Harry Evans' mobile phone was found here,' she said, back to business. 'Where is it?'

Topping turned to the nearest CSI to ask the question and was handed the mobile in a plastic evidence bag. He, in turn, handed it to Burton.

She looked down at the phone and weighed it in her hand. 'Where has he gone without his phone?' she asked.

'Something tells me he didn't go willingly,' Shepherd replied. 'I mean, I take my phone virtually everywhere because it's in my pocket. The only time I don't have it is when I play rugby.'

'If we assume that wherever Evans went, he didn't want to go and someone took him by force. So, did he accidentally drop the phone, or did he know we'd come here and find it?'

'Leaving a trail, in other words?' Topping asked.

'But it doesn't help us know where to look for him,' said Shepherd. 'It means that we can't track him, either by phone or by his car because that's outside.'

'Any sign of keys?' Burton asked.

'Not that we've found so far,' Topping said.

'Right,' said Burton. 'Let's allow these people to get on with their job.' She gestured around the room. 'We'll get back to the station. We need to speak to Dan Sullivan and Emma Fletcher.'

But as they walked out of the garden gate onto the pavement a voice called to them.

'Excuse me.'

They turned to see a short, dumpy woman with a Yorkshire terrier under her arm standing a short distance away. She looked nervous as all three approached her.

'Has something awful happened?' she asked, looking towards the house.

'A man's been found dead,' Burton informed her.

'Oh goodness, not again.' The woman squeezed the Yorkshire terrier in her anxiety and it yelped.

'There's been a woman staying here,' Burton said. 'Do you know her?'

The woman shook her head. 'No. I tried to speak to her but she just ignored me. She's much noisier than George was.'

'How do you mean?'

'George used to come and go twice a day, morning to go to work, evening to come home, although he did seem to be coming home later and later,' she said. 'But this girl is in and out at all times of the day, slamming doors. And the number of men who have been in and out of there is a disgrace.'

'Lots of men? Did you see any of them?' Shepherd asked.

'No.' The woman shook her head. 'I only really heard voices.'

Shepherd paused for a moment and then said, 'Did you see any activity this morning?'

'Why yes, I saw her come in with a man with short dark hair. They seemed quite friendly with each other. Then later another two men arrived. They were a bit odd.'

'Why?' Shepherd asked.

'Well, one seemed to be pushing the other. They certainly didn't like each other at all. They rang the bell, the door opened, I heard a little shout and then the door slammed and nothing.' She looked at each of the detectives in turn. 'Does that help you?'

Shepherd smiled. 'Yes, Mrs...?'

'Middlehurst.'

'Mrs Middlehurst, you've been very helpful.'

But the woman wasn't finished. 'It was strange though because they went off later,' she said. 'But just three of them.'

The three detectives stared at her.

'What?' asked Burton.

'The woman and two of the men, they went off in a car about forty-five minutes ago,' she said. 'I don't know what had happened to one of the men but they were practically carrying him.'

'Which man, Mrs Middlehurst?' Shepherd asked.

'It was the one who arrived with the woman. He looked very unwell. They put him into a car and the woman drove it away. I assumed she was taking him to hospital.'

Shepherd smiled at the woman and took down her contact details in case they needed further information. She sensed a dismissal as he snapped his notebook shut and reluctantly walked away down the road. Shepherd waited until they were at a safe distance, before he turned to Burton and Topping and said, 'Thank the Lord for nosy neighbours.'

Burton and Topping were staring at him.

'It sounds like Stephen Curtain didn't come here willingly,' Shepherd said.

'He must have been killed not long after they arrived and then Harry Evans was carried out to a car,' Burton said.

'Mostly likely he was drugged before he was taken away,' Shepherd replied. 'Now we just need to find that car.'

Chapter sixty-nine

Emma sat in the police station reception area, distractedly flicking the hardback front cover of *The Psychology of Truth* back and forth between her hands. She was waiting for Dan to finish being interviewed by Burton and Shepherd. She'd had her turn but hadn't really been able to add much. She hadn't mentioned anything about the psychology book as she wasn't really sure why she thought it would be useful.

Dan had shown her the chemical formulae he'd been sent and she hadn't been able to make head nor tail of that either. She stared down at the cover of the book again. Then she flipped through the book to the chapter that Keith Williams had bookmarked. She scanned down the first two pages again. It still didn't make any sense. If the book was about the chemistry of truth, it would make more sense with the George Peters connection but, again, how would that work?

She put the book down on the chair beside her and pulled her phone out of her coat pocket. She activated the screen and clicked onto her browser app. Then she stared at the cursor blinking in the search box. What was she even looking for? She was almost certain she was barking up the wrong tree with the psychology angle. But what if she needed to look at the complete opposite? Typing the 'chemistry of lying' into the search engine she mentally crossed her fingers. A page of results appeared before her. There were any number of articles about lying. She began scanning through the list of search results. Halfway down the second page she found what she was looking for. She frowned. This made more sense to her and suggested the link to George Peters.

Before she could do anything else, the police station door opened and Dan appeared, flanked by Burton and Shepherd.

'Was that useful?' Dan was asking.

Burton was nodding. 'Thanks. It was. If you think of anything else, you know where to find us.'

They said goodbye to Burton and Shepherd and walked round to the car park.

'Are you OK?' Dan asked. 'You look a bit distracted.'

Emma held up the book and her phone. 'I've been reading and I've got something interesting for you.'

'I've got something interesting for you too,' Dan said. 'I've just been told that George Peters doesn't have a sister.'

Emma stopped dead and stared at him. 'So who have you and Harry been hanging out with?'

Dan nodded grimly. 'That's exactly what I want to find out. Harry could be in big trouble.'

Chapter seventy

Dan and Emma pulled into the parking space outside Emma's cottage in silence. The silence continued until they got inside the house and the kettle was on to make tea. Dan leaned against the kitchen worktop as Emma bustled around fetching mugs, teabags and Penguin biscuits. She turned and caught the look on Dan's face as he stared at the floor.

'Penny for them,' she said.

'I'm worried. Really worried,' Dan said. 'Harry's alone with God knows who, unaware of how much danger he's in.'

'We may be wrong,' Emma said, but she looked as if she didn't even believe the words as she spoke them. Dan looked at her and smiled weakly. 'Sorry,' she said. 'Blind optimism, I think.' She poured water into mugs and then turned back to Dan. 'What do we do now?'

'We've got to find Harry,' Dan said, hands on his hips. He took two steps, reaching the opposite side of the kitchen and turned back. Two more steps and he was back to where he'd started.

'Burton and Shepherd will be all over that,' Emma said, using a spoon to remove the tea bags from the mugs. 'They'll be able to find him.'

'We've got to do something,' Dan said. 'We can't just sit here.'

As he spoke, his mobile began to ring in his pocket. He pulled it out and looked at the screen.

'Hmmm, withheld number,' he said. He touched the phone's screen and answered the call.

'Hi, is that Dan?' came a cheerful voice.

'Yes?'

'Hi, it's Jamie. I'm a friend of Harry Evans. You gave me some formulae to look at.'

'Oh yes, hi.' Dan turned and walked into the living room. It was crowded with chunky sofas, a coffee table and bookcases but he managed to circumnavigate it with practised ease.

'I've been trying to call Harry but I couldn't get an answer so I thought I'd try you,' said Jamie.

Dan wasn't sure what to say. He knew Harry didn't have his phone – it had been at George Peters' house – but he didn't know how to explain that to Jamie.

'I've not heard from him either,' he said awkwardly. 'What did you want to tell him?'

'I might have some answers for you, although I wouldn't get too excited.' Dan turned and found Emma was watching from the kitchen doorway. He beckoned to her and they sat side by side on the sofa. 'Jamie, my friend Emma's here too. I'm going to put you on speakerphone.'

'OK, hi Emma,' said Jamie, her voice sounding a little tinny coming out of Dan's phone.

'Hi Jamie,' Emma said, advancing into the room and sitting down on the sofa. Dan sat next to her, holding up the phone.

'What have you found out?' he asked.

Jamie sighed. 'It's way above my skill level to create this stuff, but I think they're trying to design something that will mask the effects of epinephrine and dopamine.'

Dan and Emma frowned at each other. 'What?' they both said together.

'They're creating synthetic hormones,' Jamie said. 'Or at least they're trying to. I've no idea how they're doing it. As I said this is way above my level of knowledge.'

'What would they want with that?' Dan asked.

'I don't know,' said Jamie. 'I think what they're creating so far would make you a bit woolly headed, for want of a better phrase. You'd be really relaxed and not really able to think straight.'

'So you'd be susceptible to the power of suggestion?' Dan asked, looking at Emma.

'Yes, but it isn't that straightforward,' Jamie said. 'They're also trying to add something else into it. I'm not a hundred per cent sure exactly what, but I think the effect they're trying to create is to make memories disappear.'

'Disappear?' said Dan and Emma at the same time.

'Yes. You remember the film *The Eternal Sunshine of the Spotless Mind* where Jim Carrey and Kate Winslet tried to erase memories of each other after a bad relationship?'

'Yes,' Dan said and Emma nodded.

'I think they're trying to do that,' Jamie said.

Dan and Emma stared at each other. 'That's a bit science fiction, isn't it?' Dan asked.

'What would you even use it for?' Emma asked.

'Search me,' Jamie said, and they could almost hear her shrugging her shoulders.

'Thanks, Jamie,' Dan said. 'You've done great work.'

Jamie laughed. 'Just tell Harry he owes me the biggest Toblerone he can find.'

Dan was frowning. 'I'll do that,' he said distractedly. Then he paused. 'Jamie, have you told anyone else this?'

'Yes, I left a message on Harry's mobile phone earlier to tell him what I just told you. When I didn't hear back from him I called you.'

Dan leapt to his feet. 'Where are you?'

'I'm in my lab. Why?'

Dan threw Emma the car keys and grabbed his coat. 'Lock the door and stay inside. We're coming to get you. Don't answer the door to anyone but me.'

He hung up as Jamie protested.

'Why are we going to find Jamie?' Emma asked as she followed Dan out of the house. He was running to the car as she locked the door and rattled it four times.

'Come on, hurry up. We don't have time for that,' Dan yelled.

Emma jogged to the car and climbed inside. 'What's the hurry?' she asked, firing up the engine.

'Don't you see? Jamie left a message for Harry telling him all that. No doubt Harry would have shared the information with that Anna woman, so they now know what Jamie knows. We've got to get to her before they do.'

Emma nodded and drove her car like it was stolen towards the university.

Chapter seventy-one

Emma almost skidded as she turned sharply into the chemistry department car park. The car looked like it had been abandoned as she parked almost in a space on the end of a row and they both leapt out.

'Where's her lab?' Emma panted as Dan began to run across the car park.

'This way,' he called, pointing towards the main entrance. But he hadn't gone ten steps when he came to a halt, trainers slipping on the tarmac road surface. Emma collided with him and grabbed his arm.

'What?' she panted.

Dan pointed to a big black Audi parked directly across the entrance to the department. 'Am I wrong to be suspicious of that parking?' he asked.

They watched as two burly men climbed out of the car and looked up at the building. They walked inside.

'Shit,' said Dan. 'They're here already.' He looked around frantically.

'Is her lab on the ground floor?' Emma asked.

'Yes. Why?'

'Where is it?'

Dan pointed.

'Quick, this way.' Emma grabbed Dan's arm and began to drag him along a path down the side of the building. There were small bushes between the gravel path and the building, and Emma was peering through them. 'Which window?' she asked.

'Just there,' Dan pointed.

Emma pushed her way through the bushes and arrived at the window. A woman inside in a white coat was sitting at a work bench on a high stool writing in a notebook. When Emma banged on the window, she looked up. She walked over to the window and pushed it open.

'What are you doing?'

'I'm Emma, Dan's friend. We were on the phone just now. It's Jamie, isn't it?'

Jamie stared at her. 'Yes, but—'

'You have to leave now,' Emma said. 'Some men are coming to get you.'

Jamie stared at her. 'What?'

Dan pushed through the bushes to join Emma and said, 'It's true; they're in the corridor. Grab your stuff and get out of there.'

As he spoke, Jamie looked back towards the door. 'There's footsteps outside,' she whispered. Then there was a heavy knock on the door. Jamie didn't need telling twice. She quickly grabbed her handbag and the notebook she's been writing in and climbed onto the windowsill. Emma shoved the car keys into Dan's hand.

'Get it started and be ready for a quick get-away.'

Dan didn't wait a second but pushed his way back onto the path. They could hear his running footsteps as Emma pulled the window open as wide as she could to help the chemist climb out. Jamie landed clumsily beside her and they began to run towards the car park just as the men barged through the door to the lab.

They'd reached the end of the path when Dan screeched up in

Emma's car. Emma yanked open the rear door and almost threw Jamie into the back seat. Then she pulled open the passenger door and jumped in.

'Go!' she yelled at Dan and he obeyed, slamming down on the accelerator and swerving across to the exit.

Looking through the back window she saw the men running to their car and climbing in.

'What the hell's going on? Who are those men?' Jamie whimpered, cowering on the back seat.

'You don't want to know,' Dan said. 'Shall I try to lose them?'

Emma looked at him patiently. 'You're not Jason Bourne, you know?' she said. 'We can't go home and we can't allow them to force us to stop. Go to the police station.' She pulled on her seat belt. 'We need to get Jamie somewhere safe.'

Chapter seventy-two

Harry opened his eyes gingerly. For some reason he was expecting bright lights to dazzle him and hurt his eyes. It was a reasonable assumption since every other part of his body hurt. But the room was entirely dark. He tried to move but found he couldn't. He was lying on his side on a lino floor, his arms pinioned tightly behind his back with what felt like cable ties. He tried to move his legs but they were tightly tied together too. He tried to wriggle his toes and the agony of pins and needles ripped through both his feet, making him wince and moan in agony.

'Anna?' he said quietly. There was no reply. 'Anna?' he said again, a little bit louder. Nothing. They must be keeping her somewhere else.

He tried to remember what had happened. The last thing he did remember was talking to Anna at the house on Castle Street. They were sitting at the table with George's computer, drinking tea. He had felt really tired. The next thing he remembered – well, he wasn't sure if it had really happened – was being in a car. He'd been too sleepy to know what was happening.

And finally he'd woken up to find himself in this room, in the dark. In fact it was so dark he couldn't have sworn to the size of the room.

Where was he? What had happened to Anna? He hadn't been able to speak to Dan, so would anyone know he'd gone?

He tried to struggle against his bindings but all that did was make his shoulders hurt more. All he could do was lie there and wait for what would happen next.

Chapter seventy-three

Shepherd sat beside the CCTV controller staring at the TV screen in front of them. Footage from earlier in the day was playing as they watched. There was one camera that showed the end of Castle Street in the extreme right corner of its picture.

'Don't you have a better angle than that?' Shepherd asked, squinting at the screen.

The man shook his head. 'Sorry, Sergeant Shepherd,' he said, shaking his head. 'That camera was installed to cover this parade of shops here.' He pointed to the middle of the screen. 'They were having trouble with teenagers hanging around and causing a nuisance.' He frowned. 'It's not really supposed to look anywhere else, but you never know, we might get lucky.'

Shepherd shrugged. 'It's worth a try,' he said, sitting back in his chair.

'What time did you say it was?' the man asked, using the rolling ball on his control panel to scroll through the pictures.'

'They would have left Castle Street at about two-thirty,' Shepherd said, glancing down at the notebook in his hand.

The man nodded and scrolled to roughly two twenty-five. 'Give ourselves a margin for error,' he said, eyes glued to the screen. 'Have you got a reg number? Make and model?' he asked.

Shepherd shook his head. 'Sadly the witness is an elderly woman and couldn't give us any details.'

The man nodded. 'Hard to see it if the car is driving away from you,' he said. Eyes glued to the screen, he paused the recording and pointed to the corner. 'Is that it?' he asked.

Shepherd leaned forward. 'It could be,' he said. 'Are you able to zoom in? There should be a woman driving and a man in the back.'

The man clicked a few buttons and the car suddenly became very big on the screen. He frowned. 'OK,' he said. 'That looks like a woman in the driver's seat to me.'

Shepherd nodded. 'I agree. Any chance we can see anything else?'

The man rolled the footage forward. 'If we're lucky,' he said slowly, 'the car will turn towards us.' The car did and the man froze the image and zoomed in so that the registration plate could be seen. Shepherd grinned and pulled out his notebook and pen.

'Good work,' he said, as he squinted at the screen and scribbled down the registration. 'Can you see where it went next?'

The man shook his head. 'The next two cameras are out for maintenance,' he said.

Shepherd swore under his breath. 'Is there any other way to find out which way it went?'

The man swung around in his chair. 'Without knowing the direction of travel,' he said, almost to himself, 'it's difficult to know which camera they'll appear on next.' He got to his feet. 'We'll just have to do it the old-fashioned way,' he said, walking to a large map on the wall. He scanned it for a moment and then put his finger on a particular point.

'Right, Castle Street is here,' he said. Shepherd turned around on his chair to watch the man at work. The man was muttering and drawing his finger in various directions. The door opened and a woman entered carrying two mugs of tea.

'Oh sorry, I didn't realise we had company,' she said, spotting Shepherd. He grinned. 'Did you want one?' she asked indicating the mugs.

'No, it's OK. I'm all tea-d out for the day, I think.'

'And you don't want one of these either?' The woman pulled two slightly squashed Mars bars out of her trouser pocket.

'He's not having mine,' said the man at the map without turning round. 'I've been looking forward to that all day.'

Shepherd laughed. 'I'm not one for nicking other people's chocolate,' he said.

The woman was looking at her colleague. 'This must be a tough one if you're getting into the map,' she said, sipping at her mug.

'We've got a car leaving Castle Street at two-thirty and we've got no idea which way it went or where it's going,' he said.

The woman raised her eyebrows. 'We'd better get started,' she said, and sat down in front of the monitor. Then she looked over at her colleague. 'Any thoughts?'

'Without knowing a destination it's tricky, but try this way.' The man traced his finger along a couple of streets running perpendicular to each other, reading out the names.

The woman picked a camera from a screen of different street angles and ran the recording back to two-thirty. 'Make, model and reg number of the car?' she asked. Shepherd held up his notebook so she could see the registration number.

'No make and model,' he said. 'Although it looked to me like a Ford Focus.'

The woman nodded. 'That's enough to be going on with,' she said. Her eyes returned to the screen but after a few minutes she said, 'Nope, nothing there. Throw a six and try again.'

Her colleague drew another set of lines on the map, read out some directions and she repeated her process. Again, nothing. They tried

A DEADLY TRUTH

again. There were three further efforts and then Shepherd saw the woman stiffen in her seat.

'I think we've got something,' she said. Shepherd wheeled over to her on his chair and the other CCTV operative came to stand behind her. 'I don't think these guys know where they're going,' she said. 'They're not going by a logical route at all. They're cutting across the streets rather than taking a straight route.' She pointed to the screen and then scrolled in. Shepherd squinted at the screen. He could just pick out the car they were looking for waiting at some traffic lights.

'That's the one,' he said, noting down the location. 'Where does it go after that?'

The woman chose another camera and they watched the car drive along the street out of view. The next camera picked it up again and they followed its progress. Then the car did a random left turn. The white car behind followed it. At the end of the street the same thing happened again.

'Is that white car following them?' the male CCTV operative asked.

'I think you're right,' Shepherd said. 'Can you get make, model and reg for that car?'

The female operative squinted at the screen. 'I can't do make and model but I can do you a reg number and this.' She pointed to the screen as the white car turned right.

'A taxi logo,' Shepherd said.

'That should make it a bit easier to track down,' the woman replied.

'Thanks, guys.' Shepherd was already digging into his pocket for his phone as he left the room.

Chapter seventy-four

Burton and Shepherd converged on the Echo Cars office from opposite directions, both arriving on foot.

'OK, what have you got?' she asked.

Shepherd held out his phone. On it was a still image from the CCTV camera, which showed a taxi waiting beside the car they were tracking at the traffic lights.

'Right,' she said. 'Let's see what they've got to say for themselves.'

They pushed into the reception area and the dispatcher looked up with a smile. 'Where are you off to?' he asked, seizing a pen and notepad.

'Nowhere,' said Shepherd, as they held out warrant cards. The man's face fell a little. 'You might be able to help us with something.' He held out his phone with the picture on it. The man took the phone and peered at it.

'That's one of ours,' he said in surprise. 'What you want with him?'

'He might be a witness in a potential abduction,' Burton said. 'Do you know where he is?'

The man's eyebrows shot up. 'I know where all my drivers are,' he said, sounding offended. He reached for the microphone attached to his dispatch system.

'Dave T, Dave T, report please,' he said into the microphone. There was a moment of crackling and then a voice spoke.

'I'm outside, mate. Can't you see the car?' There was the thud of a car door closing and a short, wiry man appeared, stuffing his car keys in his pocket and grinning. Then he saw Burton and Shepherd and pulled out his keys again. 'Where will it be, folks?' he asked.

'They're police, Dave,' the dispatcher said, before Burton or Shepherd could speak. They held out warrant cards again and Dave studied them.

'What can I do for you?' he asked, sitting down in the reception area and indicating for Burton and Shepherd to sit as well. Shepherd pulled out his notebook. Burton offered Shepherd's phone to the man.

'This is you,' she said.

The man nodded. 'Yeah, that's right. What's this about?'

'You're following this car,' Burton continued, pointing to the car carrying Harry Evans, which was waiting alongside at the traffic lights.

The man shook his head. 'I wasn't following it then.'

'So when were you following it?' asked Shepherd, mystified.

'When it pulled away from the lights. I wasn't on a job or nuffink,' Dave said, looking up at the dispatcher who was listening in, 'but there was something weird about that car.'

'Weird in what way?' Burton asked.

'Well, as I pulled up alongside, I could see there was a woman driving. She was quite pretty as it happens and that's why I noticed. But then I saw the bloke.'

'Bloke?'

'He was in the back seat. I could see him when I looked over my shoulder at her car. He looked well out of it. Slumped forward with his head against the side window. But what really spooked me was the fact he was trying to knock on the window,' the taxi driver said.

'Knock on the window?' Shepherd asked, scribbling furiously.

'Yeah. It was really weird. It seemed like he was too tired to knock properly. The woman must have heard him cos she turned around and spoke really nasty to him. Then the lights changed and, I dunno, something made me turn that way as well. I followed her for a little while but she must have seen me because she started making all sorts of weird turns. I lost her but it seemed a bit obvious where she was eventually headed.'

'How do you mean?' Burton asked.

'That route would take you up towards the bypass. So I assumed that's where she was headed. She would have come out up by Allensbury Science Park.'

Chapter seventy-five

'All roads lead to the science park,' Shepherd said as they strode along the road towards the police station. Burton nodded grimly. Her mobile began to ring and she pulled it from her pocket.

'Topper? What is it?'

Shepherd could hear the muffled voice of Garry Topping.

'Guv, something weird has happened.'

Burton stopped walking and stepped into the doorway of an empty charity shop. Shepherd stepped in beside her and pressed his ear to the back of her phone to listen.

'What's happened?' Burton asked.

'This woman just walked into reception,' Topping replied. 'She said that some men are chasing her.'

'Really?' Burton wrinkled her nose. 'What men?'

'She didn't know. She said Dan Sullivan and Emma Fletcher turned up at her lab at the university and told her some men were after her. She climbed out of the window just as the men burst in. Dan and Emma dropped her off here and told her to report this to you.'

'Right, we're on our way back. Keep hold of her.'

'But get this, guv.' Topping sounded excited. 'She's a chemist.'

Burton and Shepherd looked at each other. 'Chemistry,' said Shepherd. 'It's all about chemistry.'

Chapter seventy-six

Harry had about two seconds warning – the beeping of a security lock keypad – before the door of his prison was wrenched open. A beam of light shone across him where he lay on the floor, blinding him.

'Who are you? What's going on?' he cried, screwing up his eyes against the glare. He couldn't see the men with the light in his eyes but two pairs of hands grabbed him roughly by the clothes. The ties on his feet were cut away, he was yanked to his feet and pushed towards the door. Harry almost fell as the blood began to return to his legs.

'Boss wants to see you,' said one, shoving Harry out of the door. Once they were in the corridor, Harry's eyes adjusted to the light and he began to look around him. He was being escorted by two stocky men in leather jackets, one blond and one with a shaved head.

Harry looked around him, searching for any hint as to where he might be but the corridor was nondescript. Its plain white walls seemed to stretch on forever and when they turned a corner, it was into an identical corridor. Then, without any warning, the two men abruptly turned right and pushed Harry through a door that stood ajar. The room was as blindingly white as the corridors and a mirror stretched across one wall. Before he could say anything, he was thrust into a black leather chair with arms, much like a chair in a dentist's consulting room. But Harry felt more apprehensive about this than he'd ever felt about a trip to the dentist. The two men stood over him, hands clasped behind their backs like sentries on duty. Harry fidgeted, trying to get comfortable, which was almost impossible with his hands still fastened behind his back, and was rewarded with a glare from one of the men. Footsteps echoed in the corridor outside and a grey-haired man entered, a clipboard tucked under his arm. He was wearing a white lab coat over a smart three-piece suit. He closed the door behind him smartly and the quiet click told Harry it was locked.

'Doctor Evans,' the man said, observing Harry as if he were a specimen in a glass case. 'Or may I call you Harry?'

'Call me what you like.' Harry tried to sound nonchalant. He wanted to shrug, to look like he wasn't scared, but he couldn't with his hands still handcuffed behind his back.

'Where are my manners? At least make the doctor comfortable.' The man indicated for Harry's arms to be released. 'I don't think he'll try anything, will you, Harry?'

Harry shook his head. Once his wrists were freed of the cable ties binding them, he stretched his shoulders and flexed his hands.

'What do I call you?' he asked, trying to sound more confident than he felt.

'That's not important right now. I'm sorry we have to conduct business like this–' the man gestured around the room '–but it's best this is kept confidential.'

'What needs to be kept confidential?'

'You've seen something of ours.' The man looked up from his clipboard and met Harry's eyes steadily. 'Something you shouldn't have seen.'

Harry raised his eyebrows. 'Really? What might that have been?'

he asked, struggling to keep his voice level.

'Don't be coy, Harry; it doesn't suit you,' the man said sharply. 'We have the laptop and we know you've seen the contents. Now who else have you told?'

'No one. I haven't seen anything on any laptop,' Harry said, now feeling confused.

'But you know what was on it?' When Harry didn't speak, the man smiled. 'Yes, I thought you might know.'

'Not really. Like I said, I didn't see anything.' Harry was desperately trying to keep his voice steady, but he could hear a shrill note in it. He cleared his throat.

'You don't know what it is then?'

'All Anna said was—' Harry stopped, worried that he'd given too much away.

'Ah, yes. Anna,' the man said with a smile.

'Where is she?' Harry demanded. 'Have you hurt her?'

The man smiled. 'She's here. I'll be having a conversation with her shortly.'

Harry tried to pull himself upright into a more dignified position but it was impossible on the slippery leather surface and the angle it was tilted at. 'What do you want from me? I've told you, I don't know anything.'

'You know enough,' the man said looking back at the notes on his clipboard. 'You know what's on the laptop.'

Harry realised there was no point in lying. 'There's some chemical formulas on it,' he said, 'but I've never seen them before and I don't know what they mean.'

The man leaned forward and wagged his pen at Harry. 'It's bad enough that you know they exist, but you told a friend as well,' he said.

Harry stared at him blankly for a moment. 'What friend? I don't know what you're talking about.' But he soon realised who the man meant.

'We know you've told her because she left a voicemail message on your phone,' the man said. 'She seems to know quite a lot about what we're doing.'

'What phone message? What are you talking about?'

The man shook his head. 'You shouldn't leave your phone lying around, Dr Evans,' he said. 'There is a young woman who is helping you find out what we're doing. Don't worry; it was easy to track her down in her lab.'

Harry felt cold dread spread into his stomach as he realised who the man meant. 'Jamie,' he said, under his breath. Suddenly an idea flashed into his brain. 'How did you know about the message? Who has my phone?'

But the man ignored him. 'You really shouldn't have brought your friend into this.'

'What have you done to her?' Harry demanded.

'We went to her lab to apprehend her, but unfortunately she escaped.' When Harry raised his eyebrows, the man said, 'A man and a woman helped her to climb out of a window. But don't worry, they won't get far.'

Harry held his breath. He hoped the man was Dan. If it was, then Jamie was in safe hands. Dan wouldn't give up without a fight.

'We'll speak again soon,' the man was saying. 'And if you don't tell me what I want to know, we have ways to loosen your tongue.'

'You're going to torture me?' Harry hoped he was putting on a good performance of being confident. Inside his stomach was clenching.

'I'll use whatever methods I need to get what I want from people, but you'll find we are a little more sophisticated than physical torture,' the man said. 'You'll tell us everything you know and then you won't even remember the conversation.'

The man smiled and gestured towards the door. The two men in leather jackets seized Harry by the arms and cable ties were once again tightly fastened around his hands. They marched him back along the corridor. Harry struggled, desperate to do something. No one knew where he was. In actual fact, he didn't know himself.

All he could do was wait for whatever was going to happen next, and hope that someone would find him before it was too late.

Chapter seventy-seven

'I think we lost those guys at the police station,' Dan said, looking in the rear-view mirror for what felt like the hundredth time. 'At least we managed to get Jamie inside before they turned up.'

'I'm guessing the sight of the police station was enough to make them pull back,' Emma said. 'They'll never get her now she's in there.' She held up a hand. 'I've still not stopped shaking.'

Dan took one hand off the steering wheel and squeezed her fingers. 'That was a great idea, getting her out through the window.'

'I couldn't think of any other way to do it,' Emma said. 'We'd never have got past them in the corridor. Thank goodness her lab was on the ground floor or we'd have been in real trouble.'

'We got to her just in time,' Dan said soberly. 'I bet Harry played the message for Anna, not realising she's involved in this.'

'And now she's got Harry,' Emma said. She looked around. 'Look, we can't just drive around blindly. We need to stop somewhere and think.' She paused and said, 'Turn left here.'

Dan obeyed. 'Where are we going?'

'There's a little parade of shops here with a café in the middle. We can take a breather in there.'

Dan was shaking his head as he negotiated the turns into the street Emma pointed out. 'We need to find Harry.'

'We're not going to find him if we just keep driving in circles,' Emma said. 'We have no idea where they've taken him.'

Dan parked up outside the café.

'How did you know this was here?' he asked, as they climbed out of the car.

'I hid in here once before when I was trying to speak to someone about a court case they were involved in,' she said. 'Nice scones, from what I remember.'

'Good. I'm starving,' said Dan.

'So the stress hasn't dampened your appetite?' Emma asked, grinning, as she pushed open the café door. It was empty apart from one table with two rotund ladies sipping coffees and munching doughnuts.

They took a table as far away from the women as they could and gave their orders of coffee and scones to the waitress.

'So,' Dan took a deep breath, 'we've got three murders—'

'Four,' Emma said.

'Four?'

Emma nodded. 'Including the guy in Castle Street. The one we found today.'

'Oh right, sorry. We've got four people dead, three of whom are connected and the fourth we have no idea about.'

'We know that Keith Williams and Olly Murton were working with George Peters on something, which may be a chemistry project, but we're not sure about that,' Emma said.

'And whatever it is, someone killed all three to make sure they won't spill the beans about whatever is going on,' Dan said.

'We also know that someone is trying to make, if Jamie is right, some synthetic hormones, which may relax you so much that you can't think straight and become susceptible to suggestion. They're also trying to add something else to it to make you forget stuff.' She paused. 'Do you think they're actually making it?'

Dan nodded. He paused while the waitress put down their food and drinks in front of them. Once she'd departed he said, 'I think that's exactly what George Peters was trying to do.'

'Work out a formula and make it?'

'Yes.' Then Dan frowned. 'But why would Keith and Olly have got involved with that? It doesn't make sense.' He buttered his scone and took a big bite.

Emma stirred her coffee slowly. Dan looked up at her. He knew her well enough to understand the tilt of her head. Something was percolating in her brain.

Suddenly she sat up straight, causing Dan to pause with his scone halfway to his mouth.

'That blog,' she said, dropping her spoon into her saucer with a clatter. 'We decided, didn't we, that George Peters wrote that blog?'

Dan nodded.

'What if he was using that to blow the whistle on the project?' Emma asked.

'That doesn't make sense,' Dan said. 'Why sabotage your own project? Surely you would want to get a result for the work you'd put in.'

Emma frowned. 'What if he realised that it was never going to work? So he tried to stop the project?'

'And they killed him?'

'Yes.' Emma sighed. 'The more I think about this the crazier it sounds.'

'It all sounds crazy.'

Emma took a bite of her scone, chewed, and wiped her fingers on a napkin. 'I didn't get a chance to tell you what I found out,' she said when she had finished. She pulled out her smartphone and activated it. A few taps on the screen and she brought up the article she'd been reading. Dan took the phone when she held it out to him. He started to read the article and then looked up at Emma, frowning.

'If what Jamie says is right, and we've no reason to think it's not, then they're trying to create a hormone that will block you from lying but also make you forget what you've done,' Emma said.

Dan stared at her and put down the piece of scone he'd been about to bite into. 'You mean they're making a truth drug?' he asked slowly.

Emma nodded. 'I think so.' Then she frowned again.

'What?' Dan asked.

'Jamie said they were *trying* to add something. That suggests they haven't made it work yet.' Then a look of horror spread over her face. 'They're experimenting.'

Dan picked up the piece of scone. 'What?' he asked, catching the look on Emma's face.

Her eyes were wide and scared. 'They'd have to test it to see if it works,' she said staring at Dan.

The penny dropped and the half-eaten scone fell from Dan's fingers onto his plate scattering crumbs onto the table.

'Leanne Nelson,' he said.

Emma frowned. 'That student? The one who went missing? What's she got to do with it?'

'Her housemate said she was involved with Keith Williams and he was going to help her to get some money,' Dan said, rubbing his fingers hard with a napkin to get rid of the butter residue.

Emma nodded as the pieces of the puzzle started to drop into place. 'And all she had to do was go and meet a man,' she said. 'You think she's involved in this?'

'Well, she was never seen again after going off to do this thing for Keith Williams,' Dan said.

Emma frowned. 'What are you thinking?'

'I think they're testing whatever this is on people,' Dan said, balling up the napkin and dropping it on the half-eaten scone on his plate.

Emma's hand flew to her mouth. 'They're live testing without permission, aren't they?' she gasped.

Dan was on his feet, throwing money down onto the table to pay for their food. 'Yes, and it's not having the effect it's supposed to have. That's why George Peters decided to blow the whistle.' He yanked open the café door and ran out to the car, Emma following. 'And if I'm right, they've got Harry and they think he knows something. He could be about to join the medical trial.'

'What do we do?' Emma was pulling open the passenger door to the car at the same time as Dan flung open the driver's.

'We've got to go back to where this all started,' Dan said, stepping into the car. Allensbury Science Park. We'll find the answers there.'

Chapter seventy-eight

Burton and Shepherd had just arrived back at the station and were walking into the reception area when their mobiles rang at exactly the same time. Both answered and had short conversations.

Turning back, Burton said, 'We need to get to Allensbury Science Park. Now.'

Shepherd was already pulling out keys as they dashed across to their car, Burton's heels clicking against the tarmac. He beeped the remote control, opened the driver's door roughly and swung inside quickly. Burton landed in the passenger seat next to him and he was reversing out of the space almost before she shut the car door. Firing up the lights and siren on the unmarked car, he pulled out of the car park into the traffic and put his foot down.

'What was your call?' Burton asked, clinging to the door handle with one hand as she made a call for back up with the other. Shepherd made a neat change of lanes and then skipped the next set of traffic lights.

'Someone else knows about the science park and is headed over there. We need to get there first,' he said grimly.

Chapter seventy-nine

Harry was beginning to think his captors had forgotten about him altogether. He had no idea how long he'd been imprisoned in that room because there were no windows and he couldn't see his watch. Thankfully the men had fastened his hands in front of him this time but no amount of fidgeting could get his watch to turn to a position where he could see the face. He just sat there with his back against the wall in the dark, trying to piece together the bits of information he had.

Whatever Keith Williams, Olly Murton and George Peters were working on it was enough to get them killed. George had hidden his laptop, and Keith had hidden his car keys in the moments before his death. Clearly they were both aware that the knowledge they had was dangerous. But what were they working on? What could an experimental chemist have in common with a politics professor?

There were too many unanswered questions. Anna had said that the laptop had chemical formulae on it and Dan had been sent formulae through the post. Where had they come from? George Peters and Keith were both dead by then. Was it Olly, as Dan suspected?

The phone message from Jamie had got the man spooked, but Harry hadn't really understood what her message meant. He'd missed the call when he and Anna were in the kitchen making tea.

After they listened to the message, he'd suggested to Anna that they called Jamie back so she could explain it. Then there'd been a knock at the door and two men had arrived. One had looked terrified and tried to run. He'd been silenced by a knife to the ribs, but Harry couldn't really remember what happened after that.

Before he could get any further, a series of beeps on the security keypad told him his captors were unlocking the door. He tried to stand before the door was opened but hadn't got further than his knees before they'd entered, hauled him roughly to his feet. He was marched along the identical corridors again, turning left and right, all the time feeling as though they were walking in a big circle. The men stopped at what looked like the same door as before and Harry was shoved inside.

Harry could see his pale, scared face reflected in the mirrored window on the wall and wondered whether the outside world was beyond it. Harry was once again secured in the dentist's chair and his arm was strapped to an armrest, palm turned to face the ceiling. The men nodded to a woman standing in the corner and left the room, the door hissing as it closed behind them.

'Anna,' Harry cried as she turned to face him. 'Are you OK?'

'I'm fine.'

Harry stared at her, wondering at her unconcerned tone. 'What's going on?' he demanded. 'We need to get out of here.' He pulled against the bindings on his arm.

'You're not going anywhere,' Anna said quietly.

Harry stopped struggling and stared at her. 'What do you mean? Look, see if you can get these things off my wrists.'

But Anna didn't move. 'How well did you know George?' she asked.

Harry stopped tugging at the cable ties around his wrists and frowned at her. 'What? I didn't know George. I never met him, never spoke to him. I told you that.'

'But you were involved with Keith Williams and George was feeding you both information about what he was doing. How did you find him?'

Harry was gazing at Anna wondering if she were crazy. 'What are you talking about? Find who?'

'George,' she said, folding her arms across her chest. 'How did you find him?'

Harry was staring at her, completely baffled. 'I don't know what you mean. I'd never heard of him until I found his name in Keith's office.' He took a deep breath. 'Look, Anna, I don't—'

Anna interrupted, her voice harsh. 'You need to stop lying, Harry. We don't have patience with liars.'

'We?' Then Harry felt his stomach drop like a broken lift. 'You're in on it, aren't you?'

Anna gave him a slow round of applause. 'Very clever, Dr Evans. I'm surprised it took you this long.'

'But why would you do all this? Why would you do this to your own brother?' When he saw the look on Anna's face, he could have kicked himself. 'You're not George Peters' sister, are you?'

The woman shook her head. 'Nope. Sorry.' She didn't sound at all apologetic.

'What's going on?' Harry asked. 'I don't understand. Who are you?'

'I'm a person who can make life very easy for you or very hard. You don't want me to be the latter, so you're going to tell me what I want to know.'

But Harry shook his head. 'I don't know anything,' he said.

She gave him a disdainful look. 'Of course you do. You've seen the laptop and what's on it.'

Harry was silent.

'You've seen the formulae and now you know what they do, thanks to your little chemistry friend.'

Harry shrugged. 'I heard what she said, but I didn't understand any of it,' he insisted.

Anna was looking at Harry in a way that made him feel like a bug under a microscope. Then she crossed the room and leaned down with her hands on the arms of Harry's chair, her face only inches from his. It was difficult to keep staring into her eyes, but Harry was determined not to blink.

'Where are the research notes?' she asked in a quiet, threatening tone.

'What research notes?'

'Stop playing dumb,' she said, suddenly grabbing Harry's little finger and bending it in a direction it was not supposed to go. He yelped in pain and she held it for another ten seconds before she let go. 'That's only a very small part of what I can do to make you talk.' She hadn't moved away from him and Harry was only just managing to stop himself shrinking back in the chair.

'Where is your copy of the research notes? We're still looking for Olly Murton's and we have George's. I want yours too.'

'I don't have any. I was never part of any project with Keith, Olly and George.' Harry could feel his heart rate rising as he began to panic. Anna grabbed his finger again. He yelled out in pain, but this time she didn't let go.

'You were going to publish a paper about our project and we couldn't allow that to happen.' She wrenched his finger again and Harry thought he heard a snap in the joint. She released his hand and stepped away. Harry whimpered as he tried to flex his fingers, but the finger was already swelling and too painful to move.

Without warning the door opened and the grey-haired man entered. He wore a lab coat over his suit and an open-necked shirt and carried a tray. On it was a syringe and a small medicine bottle without a label. He moved and stood beside Anna.

'Anything?' he asked.

She folded her arms and shook her head. 'Still insisting he knows nothing.'

'Let's see if we can't loosen his tongue.' The man put the tray down on a ledge on the side of Harry's chair. Harry tried to push it away with his tied hands but couldn't move far enough.

'What are you doing?' Anna asked the man, suddenly sounding worried. 'Is that a new batch?'

The man nodded, picking up a syringe and filling it from the little bottle. 'We've made some alterations.'

'But there's still no proof it will work,' Anna said urgently.

The man shrugged. 'Maybe, maybe not.'

Anna inhaled sharply. 'You can't use it. If he has a heart attack like George Peters, you'll never know—'

But the grey-haired man waved a hand to silence her. 'George's death opened us up to better experimentation. This batch will be better and if it isn't, then…' He trailed off as he turned his attention back to the syringe.

Harry was looking from one to the other, feeling the panic rising. 'Who are you people?'

The grey-haired man stepped back and thought for a moment. 'We're scientists,' he said, looking at Harry in surprise. 'We're making a very important breakthrough that could change the world of criminal investigation.'

Harry stared at him. 'That sounds like so much pretentious bollocks,' he said, speaking without thinking. The man looked up from his syringe. 'You haven't made any breakthrough,' Harry continued. 'All you've done is killed two people who had nothing to do with whatever it is you're working on.'

'Keith Williams and Olly Murton had got into something they should have left alone. George had told them everything. They were going to expose our work. George was worried about "what it had become",' the grey-haired man said. 'The other two had seen all the materials George had access to, all his records and journals. If fact, the young man was the one who had found George. The fool had been posting on the Internet about our work.'

Harry stared at him. 'How do you know Olly did it?'

'He told me,' Anna said. 'People tend to get very talkative when they have a gun to their ribs.'

Harry shook his head, thinking about how scared the student must have been. 'I can't believe it. But why bring me into this? I know nothing about it,' he insisted.

'Olly was convinced that you were trying to muscle in once Keith and George were dead. He wanted to publish the research himself before you got to it,' Anna said.

Harry frowned. 'Why would he tell you all that?'

'He thought he was talking to DS Adams. I make a convincing police officer and he came to me willingly.'

'But I don't understand,' Harry said, shaking his head. 'George Peters died of a heart attack?'

'He did, brought on by this.' Anna pointed to the bottle on the tray. 'That's not what it's supposed to do, but…' She shrugged.

Harry stared at her in horror. 'But you didn't use that on Keith?' he said.

Anna shook her head. 'He struggled and the syringe got broken. I had to improvise.'

Harry was staring at her. 'I just don't believe it. What is that stuff?'

The grey-haired man had raised the syringe to eye level and was pressing out the air from inside. 'A little something to get you talking,' he said, smiling at Harry.

Harry struggled violently but the man advanced.

Suddenly the door burst open and a team of uniformed police officers filled the room. Shepherd reached the man first. He seized the syringe-wielding wrist and wrenched the hand away from Harry.

'That's quite enough, Dr Bellswick,' he said.

A light flickered behind the mirror on the wall and Harry saw that it was in fact a two-way mirror. Behind it stood a stony-faced Burton and a man wearing glasses. Burton pressed the button and spoke over the PA system.

'We heard every word. We'll get you out in no time, Dr Evans.'

Chapter eighty

The next few moments were a blur. Shepherd neatly released
Bellswick's fingers from the syringe without releasing his tight hold
on the man. He handed it to another officer who put it into a plastic
evidence bag he had pulled from his utility belt. A tough-looking
female officer was grappling with Anna but quickly managed to pin
her face-first against the wall. Anna kicked and tried to throw the
officer off-balance but to no avail. She was quickly handcuffed.
Shepherd grinned at the officer.

'Good work, Megan.'

The officer grinned back and pulled Anna away from the wall by
her arms. 'Let's go,' she said. But as she turned, Anna spat in
Shepherd's face. Both officers stared at her in disgust, and Shepherd
wiped his cheek on his sleeve.

'Get her out of here,' he said.

Another female officer was kneeling beside Harry, gently pulling
the ties away from his wrists, allowing her to use a pair of scissors to
remove them.

'Sorry,' she said. 'I'll have you out of there in a second.'

Burton stood over Harry, watching. 'Sorry we cut it so fine,' she
said. 'But we had to let them seem like they were going to go through
with it.'

'I don't understand,' Harry said, pointing to Bellswick, who was also being cuffed none too gently. 'That's not Anthony Bellswick. I've met George's boss and that's not him.'

Burton smiled grimly. 'The man you met earlier wasn't the real Dr Bellswick. It was a scam to stop you making connections.' She pointed to the man who was struggling fruitlessly against Shepherd. 'He's the real Bellswick, who we met.'

When his hands were released, Harry flexed his arms and hands, but when he tried to stand he found his legs had turned to jelly. He stumbled, and Burton and the woman officer caught him between them.

'Here,' the officer said, looping Harry's arm over her shoulder. 'Let me help.'

As they made their way out of the door, Harry turned back towards Burton. 'How did you know where I was?'

Burton indicated the man with the glasses who stood watching the police with interest. 'Meet Dr Tim Lynchman,' she said. Harry shook the hand that was held out to him. 'He realised that Bellswick was using the seventh floor for some experiments and that they mustn't be honest. He called us to say Bellswick was up here now and that we should get over here.' She smiled. 'Good job we did, eh?'

Harry smiled back. 'Certainly,' he replied. Then he said, 'How did you know what he was up to?'

Burton checked the screen of her phone. 'There's a nosy journalist outside who has it all figured out.' She gestured towards the door. 'Let's get you downstairs so you can hear all about it.'

Chapter eighty-one

Dan and Emma were leaning against their car when Harry and the police officer got outside. Dan pushed himself away from the car and strode over to seize Harry's other arm.

'Let's get him across to the ambulance,' the officer said.

'Burton says you've got it all figured out,' Harry said with a grin.

'Well, Emma helped,' Dan said, nodding towards her. 'This is Emma,' he said to Harry, realising they'd never met.

Harry smiled. 'Nice to meet you. Thanks for helping to save me.'

Emma laughed and assumed a superhero stance, hands on her hips. 'All in a day's work for the *Allensbury Post*,' she said.

They arrived at the back of the ambulance and Dan helped the police officer to sit Harry on the back step.

'Can I leave him with you?' she asked the paramedic, who smiled and nodded. He approached Harry and began to examine him, checking his eyes with a pen torch and then moving on to examine his right hand. Harry whimpered as the man touched his swollen finger.

'How did you find me?' Harry asked, looking up at Dan and Emma.

'It was a combination of things,' Dan said. 'When Jamie told us about what the formulae might mean, we worked out that what they were trying to make was a truth drug.'

'A truth drug?' Harry asked, frowning.

'Yeah, it's some sort of hormonal thing that make you relaxed and susceptible to questioning with another hormone that makes you forget. Well, that's the simple explanation,' Emma said shrugging.

'That's the message she left for me,' Harry said, nodding.

'You played it to Anna, didn't you?' Dan asked. The paramedic was trying to push him out of the way but Dan barely moved more than a few inches.

'Yes. She didn't seem overly interested in it at the time, which on reflection was a bit odd,' Harry said. 'I was all excited and all she wanted to do was make the tea.'

'She's not his sister, y'know,' Emma said, leaning against the ambulance door.

Harry nodded. 'I know that now,' he said. 'She told me, right before she decided to try and kill me.'

Dan and Emma stared. 'They were going to use the truth drug on you?' Emma asked.

'Yup. They thought I knew more than I did and were two steps away from testing whether this batch of the serum was any better than the previous one.' Harry whimpered as the paramedic started to examine his damaged finger. 'Fortunately the police arrived in the nick of time. Did you bring them here?'

Dan smiled. 'We all had the same idea at the same time,' he said. 'We'd decided to look for you here—'

'And for once Dan decided to be sensible and call for back up on the way,' Emma interrupted. 'When we called Shepherd, he and Burton had just been told the same thing by someone else.'

'A guy called Tim Lynchman,' Dan said. 'He works here and found out that someone was using the seventh floor, which had been closed off as it wasn't needed by the company.'

Harry was wincing as the paramedic flexed his finger. 'Sorry,' the paramedic said. 'I don't think it's broken or dislocated, but I'll splint it just to be on the safe side.' He pulled out a roll of tape and began to gently bind Harry's finger to its neighbour.

'They were using the seventh floor for testing the truth drug?' Harry asked.

Dan nodded soberly. 'For the live tests,' he said.

Before Harry could respond, the doors of the GITech Pharmaceuticals building opened and Shepherd appeared, frogmarching Anthony Bellswick to a police van. He shoved the man inside and slammed the door behind him. Anna Peters, or whatever her name was, was being put into another van. When the doors closed, both vans pulled away, heading back to the police station.

Burton approached and said, 'Come on. Back to the station. We've got to take some statements.' She led Harry over to her car where she was joined by Shepherd.

'We'll follow you,' Dan said. Once he and Emma were inside their car, they joined the convoy of vehicles heading back into town.

Chapter eighty-two

Once statements had been given, Dan, Emma and Harry were shown into a second interview room and given cups of tea. Harry's included many sugars as prescribed by Shepherd.

'Good for shock,' he'd said, dumping eight sachets beside Harry's paper cup.

He and Burton came back into the room and sat down at the table with them.

'Are they lawyering up?' Dan asked.

Burton shook her head. 'You're not in an American crime drama, y'know.'

Dan grinned. 'Anything you can tell us?'

'Don't you dare get that notebook out,' Burton warned as Dan's hand crept towards his bag.

'What are they saying?' Harry asked, trying to take a sip of his scalding tea and then thinking better of it.

'So far, nothing,' Burton said, tapping her fingers against the table surface.

'What I don't get,' Harry said, 'is how Keith ever met George Peters in the first place? It's not like they have anything in common apart from this project.'

'It was through a forum that George had been posting on,' Burton said.

'About the truth serum project?' Harry asked frowning.

'Yes. The forum posts started just over a year ago. We think that's when Keith made contact with George,' Burton said. 'Then, about two months ago, George started a blog.'

Harry stared at her. 'He'd been publishing stuff from the project?' he asked.

Burton nodded. 'It wasn't full details, just that something was being developed. At least that's how it began. He started to get more technical as time went on.'

'We saw that,' Dan interrupted.

'How did Keith find it? He wasn't the most technologically savvy person,' Harry said.

'I'm speculating a bit,' Burton said, 'but we think it was Olly that found it for him. George had been posting on some conspiracy theorists' websites as well, answering questions people were asking about the potential for this type of drug.'

'But what was Keith Williams looking for to find George Peters?' asked Emma.

'I think he was desperate for something to write about,' Harry said. 'He knew he was on borrowed time if he didn't come up with an article or book idea soon. He must have been looking everywhere for something.'

'He must have been desperate if he was turning to students for help,' Shepherd said, taking a sip of his tea.

'I don't know whether he asked Olly to find it, or whether Olly found it first and then gave it to him,' Dan said.

'Maybe that was part of their deal,' Harry said, cradling the hot paper cup of tea in both hands, wincing as it came into contact with his bruised finger.

Dan and Emma both nodded.

Then Emma said 'Where does the guy in George's house fit in?

The one who got stabbed.'

'I can answer that,' Shepherd said. 'His name was Stephen Curtain and he was a friend of George.'

Harry frowned. 'Why did they need to kill him?' he asked. 'Was he involved in the project as well?'

Shepherd shook his head. 'No, we think he went round to the house and one of the neighbours told him that George's sister was staying there.'

Dan's eyes widened. 'Of course,' he said slowly. 'He would know that George didn't have a sister.'

Shepherd nodded. 'He tried to come and report it to us, but their bully boys got to him first.'

'The same ones that tried to get to Jamie presumably,' Dan said.

Then Emma spoke, looking at Harry. 'We also worked out why Keith was so touchy about you finding out about the research,' she said. She pulled out her mobile, tapped the screen a couple of times and held it out to Harry. He took the phone and read the article on the screen. Shepherd leaned over his shoulder and read too. His brow furrowed.

'I don't understand,' he said.

'Harry does, don't you?' Emma said grinning smugly.

'The Cold War,' Harry said with a frustrated sigh and a shake of his head.

'What about it?' Shepherd asked.

Harry pointed to the screen. 'This article is talking about a truth drug the Soviets developed during the Cold War. I've heard about it before, but there's never been any evidence. Lots of papers and records were destroyed during or after that period, so there was never any proof of this type of truth drug. I thought it was just urban myth.'

'Clearly Anthony Bellswick saw this article too and decided to try and make it,' Burton said.

Dan nodded. 'But without any records they didn't know how to do it, so George Peters was experimenting to see if they could develop it,' he said.

'And it would make you tell the truth and then forget you'd said anything?' Shepherd asked. 'That seems a bit crazy.'

Harry shrugged. 'It may be crazy or it may be possible, we'll never know.' He passed Emma's phone back across the table.

'We think we know what happened to Leanne Nelson,' Dan told Burton and Shepherd. 'We think they'd started live testing, but rather than doing it officially—'

'They must have known they'd never get permission for something like that,' Emma put in.

Dan nodded. 'We think they were getting people from anywhere they could. Leanne Nelson went to Keith needing money and he got Olly to put her in touch with George. I don't think Keith and Olly realised what would happen to her; they were just trying to make the project work so Keith could write about it. That's why Olly told me he'd done something awful. He'd just realised what had happened to Leanne, and probably any other people he'd referred to George Peters.'

Burton and Shepherd looked at each other, their faces showing horror as the implication of Dan's words hit home.

'They were murdering people for this project?' Burton asked, looking rather sick.

'That makes sense of something Anna said,' Harry said, also looking pale. 'When Bellswick was going to inject me, she asked if it was a different batch and said it wouldn't do what he wanted it to do. She said that it had brought on George Peters' heart attack.'

'You were lucky these guys got there when they did,' Emma said, indicating Burton and Shepherd.

'I'm guessing that if you look at George Peters' notebooks or his laptop you'll find records of it,' Dan said. 'He seems like the kind of guy who liked notes.'

'Keith Williams liked notes too,' Burton said. When everyone gave her a puzzled look, she continued. 'That's what was on the flash drive that we took from Olly Murton. Our technicians managed to decrypt it and we found that Keith had sent him a copy of everything he'd written and all the raw materials he'd been using. He asked Olly to look after it for him.' She nodded to Shepherd. 'That's why the research wasn't on his laptop. He'd copied it and then deleted it.'

Harry sighed heavily. 'I feel responsible for all this,' he said.

Burton, who had just stood up, looked at him surprised.

'Why would it be your fault?' she asked.

'If the Cold War wasn't my specialism, Keith would never have gone after this project to get one over on me.'

'Look,' Burton said, 'this started long before Keith Williams ever found out about this project. They'd been working on it for months before he got involved. At least now we've found out about it and we've put a stop to it before anyone else gets hurt.'

She glanced at her watch. 'Right, they've had time to get lawyers by now. Let's get this started.'

Shepherd waved Dan, Emma and Harry into reception and then turned to head back to the custody suite.

They walked out through the automatic doors and stood on the pavement outside the police station looking at each other.

'What now?' asked Dan.

'Don't you have a story to write?' Harry asked.

Dan shrugged sadly. 'Unfortunately we can't write the full story until after the trial. We don't want to prejudice the case and risk them getting off.'

'At least we can tell Daisy that your being out of the office so much recently has paid off though,' Emma said.

'That's true,' Dan replied. 'I suppose I'd better go back now.'

Emma laughed and took his hand. 'I'd better come with you as evidence.'

They both looked at Harry.

'What are you planning to do?' Emma asked him.

Harry puffed out his cheeks. 'I suppose I'd better head back to campus and explain to Desmond what's been going on. Then I'm sure I've got some research to do or something.'

He grinned, and Dan and Emma laughed.

'Or I could just go to the pub,' he said. 'I feel in need of a drink. See you later,' he added and walked away towards the nearby bus stop.

'Definitely a drink at some point,' Dan called after him and Harry waved and nodded.

Dan turned back to Emma. 'Right, back to the office to tell Daisy the truth about what's been going on. I only hope she'll believe me.'

Chapter eighty-three

SCIENTIST JAILED FOR DEADLY MEDICAL TESTING

By Ed Walker, Crown Court Reporter

A scientist was today jailed at Her Majesty's Pleasure for the deaths of an undisclosed number of people during the illegal live testing of a new drug.

Dr Anthony Bellswick, 45, of Allensbury, was carrying out tests on what he believed was a truth serum developed during the Cold War.

Bellswick, who worked for GITech Pharmaceuticals, was also convicted, alongside a woman known only as Jane Doe, of the murder of Dr George Peters, who also worked for GITech. Dr Peters worked alongside Bellswick on the truth serum project, but was murdered when he tried to blow the whistle. Bellswick and Doe also killed Professor Keith Williams, who worked at the University of Allensbury, and one of his students, Olly Murton.

Tildon Crown Court heard how Professor Williams and Mr Murton were targeted after agreeing to help Dr Peters expose the live testing.

Bellswick's solicitor told the court that he believed he was doing the world a favour by experimenting with a drug, which could have been useful in the Government's war on terror.

However, Judge Ivan Temple told Bellswick and Doe, who masqueraded as Dr Peters' sister, 'You showed a callous disregard and disrespect for the lives of others. It would not be safe for the world at large if you were ever allowed your freedom again. The safest option for everyone is that you remain in prison for the rest of your lives.'

The sentence also covered the abduction and attempted murder of Dr Harry Evans, another lecturer from University of Allensbury.

The families of Dr George Peters and Olly Murton were in court for the sentencing but declined to speak to the media, other than to say they felt justice had been served.

THE TRUTH BEHIND THE SCIENCE FACT
By Dan Sullivan, Acting Crime Reporter

Doctor Anthony Bellswick was convicted and detained at Her Majesty's Pleasure for his part in a live medical testing programme that led to the deaths of an undisclosed number of people. Tildon Crown Court heard that although he kept detailed notes of how the chemical tests were carried out, there was no information about the number of people who had died as a result.

The court heard that whistle-blower Dr George Peters had been working on the project for some months, keeping notes of his experiments. It is believed that he decided to try to end the project after realising the drug, which did not react in the way it should, was killing the live human subjects, rather than making them tell the truth.

Dr Peters' notes have meant that police can trace Bellswick's project from beginning to end.

Detective Inspector Jude Burton, who led the police investigation, said: 'We believe that Bellswick's work began last year when he read an article in a journal about a truth serum used during the Cold War. There is no proof that this serum ever existed, but it is believed that it would make the victim tell the truth and then forget what they had said.

'Bellswick claims that he wanted to help the Government fight the war on terror, but in reality we believe he was motivated by the monetary value it might have on the open market.'

The journal article also said that the truth serum had been used by the KGB many times and allowed them to return victims to their normal life with no idea that they had informed on their family or friends.

The police investigation showed that Professor Keith Williams had discovered the same article in the course of his research and made contact with Dr Peters through an online forum for conspiracy theorists. They, supported by Mr Murton, intended to publish an article, detailing Bellswick's project so far. Progress on this article was not proceeding quickly enough for Dr Peters who knew about the live testing. Instead he published a blog aimed at bringing the project into the light, with a view to getting it shut down before more people were killed.

In a final post, which was not published, he wrote, 'I've always loved science and the positive work it can do, with medical cures for all sorts of ailments. That's the work I want to do. This project is the complete opposite of that.'

But before he could publish the final piece of the puzzle, he was murdered.

Detective Inspector Burton said: 'Dr Peters knew that he bore some responsibility for the deaths caused by the serum and we believe that's why he decided to blow the whistle.

'However, this sadly led to the deaths of Professor Williams and Olly Murton, who would not have been killed if they had not become aware of the project. From reading Professor Williams' research notes, it's unclear whether he knew about the live testing.

'We are pleased to have put a very dangerous man behind bars and prevent any further deaths.'

Tildon Crown Court also heard how Bellswick employed 'Jane Doe' to kill Dr Peters, Professor Williams and Olly Murton. Doe, whose true identity is not yet known, inserted herself into the investigation carried out by the *Allensbury Post* and Dr Harry Evans, by pretending to be Dr Peters' sister.

Dr Evans said: 'I had no idea that George Peters didn't have a sister. I only wanted to find out why my colleague and a student had been killed. Neither deserved to die and, if they'd never come across Dr Peters, they would probably still be alive.

'But at least their deaths are not in vain because their work has brought Bellswick's activities to light and halted the project.'

GITech Pharmaceuticals declined to comment.

Thank you so much for reading *A Deadly Truth*.

If you enjoyed it, please tell your friends,
or leave a review where you bought it.

You can follow me on Twitter @lmmilford or Facebook
www.facebook.com/lmmilford or keep up-to-date with
what's next by going to my website www.lmmilford.com and
signing up for my email newsletter.

9 781913 778064